D1051803

The
Last Wife
of
Henry VIII

Also by Carolly Erickson

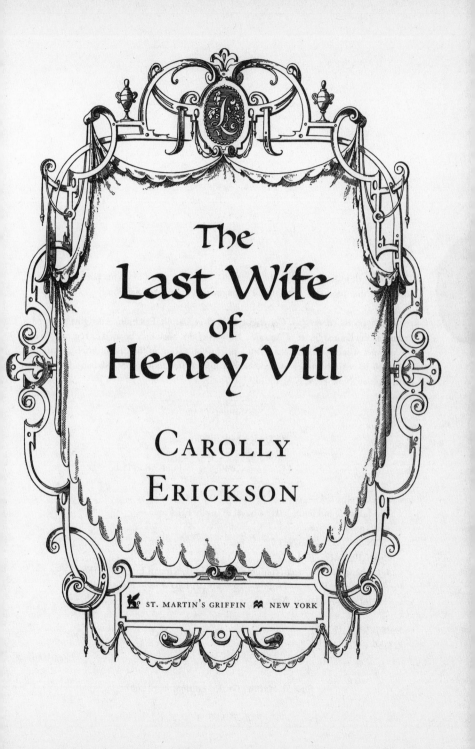

The
Last Wife
of
Henry VIII

CAROLLY
ERICKSON

ST. MARTIN'S GRIFFIN ☙ NEW YORK

www.stmartins.com

Design by Phil Mazzone

Library of Congress Cataloging-in-Publication Data

Erickson, Carolly, 1943–
    The last wife of Henry VIII : a novel / Carolly Erickson.
        p. cm.
    ISBN-13: 978-0-312-37461-7
    ISBN-10: 0-312-37461-5
    1. Catherine Parr, Queen, consort of Henry VIII, King of England, 1512–1548—Fiction. 2. Great Britain—History—Henry VIII, 1509–1547—Fiction. 3. Queens—Great Britain—Fiction. I. Title.

PS3605.R53 L37 2006
813'.6—dc22

                                                                          2006046404

First St. Martin's Griffin Edition: April 2007

10 9 8 7 6 5 4 3 2 1

The
Last Wife
of
Henry VIII

1

MY EARLIEST MEMORY IS OF A WINDSWEPT PLAIN IN FLANDERS called the Golden Valley. I was seven years old, a blue-eyed, fair-haired child in the retinue of Queen Catherine, and I rode into the valley on the back of a small cart filled with trunks and baskets and cages of squawking chickens and ducks. A light rain was falling, I remember, and I put up the hood of my cloak to cover my head.

As we trundled and rattled down through the hills the rain suddenly ceased and the sun came out. I could see the entire plain spread out before me, with the little town of Ardres beside the river on one side of the valley and the smaller settlement of Guines on the other side. Rows and rows of tents had been erected near each of the towns and a huge tent of gold cloth with a shiny statue atop it loomed over them like a broody mother hen over her chicks.

It was near sunset and the late afternoon sun struck the golden tent and turned it to fire, its red-gold glow spilling out over the nearby rooftops and gilding the river water. As I watched, all the windows in a nearby stone pavilion began to glow red, reflecting the setting sun, and I thought to myself, this must be the most beautiful sight I have ever seen.

I thought the grand display in the Golden Valley quite wondrous, but to my mother, who was a thrifty woman, it was an excuse for waste.

"I'm glad your father didn't live to see this," she remarked to me the following day, after we were settled into our lodging in Guines. "These two kings, Francis and Henry, are spending a fortune to impress each other. So much silk and brocade, so many feathered plumes and perfumed gloves and jeweled buckles. Why, our King Henry alone bought five hundred ells of fine Italian cloth of gold just to line his tent. There is so much of the stuff in view that the townspeople are calling this the Field of Cloth of Gold."

"Father, if he were here, would be wearing his best velvet doublet and his gold chain of office." My father had been controller of King Henry's household until his death three years earlier, and had been responsible for paying out all the expenses and wages. I remembered him as a vigorous, forceful man who loved his finery and took any excuse to wear it.

"Yes but he would have grumbled about the king's excesses at the same time. Now that he is gone, there is no one but Cardinal Wolsey to check the royal extravagance. And everyone knows how prudent the cardinal himself is with money."

I smiled. Even I, at seven years old, knew that the cardinal threw gold coins to beggars when copper would have been lavish and wore ermine-lined cloaks that were finer than the king's own. We all were in awe of Cardinal Wolsey.

"Now, Cat, I want you to remember what I told you. I will present you to Queen Catherine, you will kneel and be silent. She will bless you and smile, as she always does with children. She loves children. If you must speak, say only 'May God keep your royal highness.' Have you got that?"

"Yes, mother. 'May God keep your royal highness.'"

"Now, remember. No matter what others are here for, I have brought you with me to this place for one purpose only: to find a husband for you, and to arrange for your betrothal. When the queen requires my presence, I will serve her. The rest of my time I will devote to you."

She looked at me critically, smoothing down my hair and centering the pendant cross that hung from my gold necklace over my breastbone.

"Turn around."

I turned slowly.

"You'll do." She allowed her face to relax and smiled at me and kissed my cheek. "We'll make a fine match for you. One your father would have been proud of. You were his favorite, you know."

She took me by the hand and led me to where a groom was waiting with horses. A strong wind whipped at our cheeks as we rode to the newly built tilting ground where under a bright red awning trimmed in gold Queen Catherine sat with her ladies, doing her best to look content and interested in the spectacle before her though the weather was very cold and we all wished we were indoors by a warm fire. Coals burned in open braziers but the fires did nothing to alleviate the chill. As we approached the queen I could see that she kept her hands under a fur lap-robe and when she lifted one hand and delicately wiped her mouth her finger-ends were blue.

I had often seen Queen Catherine before, but had never been formally presented to her. My mother had been one of the queen's ladies-in-waiting for as long as I could remember. I thought she was the most beautiful of them, with her rich red hair and white skin and wide mouth, though I had to admit that Maria de Salinas, a striking brunette, was at least equally lovely. Queen Catherine was a small woman whose reddish-blond hair had begun to go gray and whose fair skin was wrinkled around the eyes and mouth. Her expression in repose was severe—I had often seen that, when I accompanied my mother to mass with the queen or when I entered a room where the ladies-in-waiting were and the queen was among them, reading. Yet when she smiled that severity melted and she looked quite joyful. I watched that transformation now as she saw my mother approach, with me in tow.

"So this is your little girl," she said, quite informally, holding out both hands to me and smiling.

"Yes, your majesty."

I knelt before her and bowed as my mother had told me to do and the queen placed her hands on my shoulders.

"Bless you, child. What is your name?"

"Cat. Catherine. I was named for you, your majesty."

"Well then, little namesake, stand up and let me take a look at you."

She regarded me gravely, and I felt kindness in her regard, not the harsh scrutiny I often felt from other adults. I was used to being stared at and judged. I knew very well that my worth, as a girl, lay in my appearance. And I knew that I was thought to be a pretty little girl.

"Has she any dowry?" Queen Catherine asked my mother.

"Only a modest one. Four hundred pounds."

"She has her looks, and her mother's royal blood, and the sponsorship of the queen—"

My mother curtseyed deeply. "Thank you, your majesty."

It was true, I was of royal descent. My mother's mother's family, the Fitzhughs, claimed as an ancestor John of Gaunt, a son of King Edward III. Though as I knelt before Queen Catherine, I felt very sharply aware of the difference between us. Her mother had been the great Queen Isabella of Castile, conqueror of the Moors and, with her husband Ferdinand of Aragon, uniter of all Spain. It had been Queen Isabella who sponsored the voyages of the Italian Cristobal Colon, the man who claimed the new lands of the Americas for Spain. Catherine was indeed a highborn queen, and she was honoring me with her recommendation.

"Ah, I see that my lord is ready to begin the joust." Catherine stood, her attention on the tiltyard, where a crowd had been gathering to watch the competition. A wide expanse of barren ground had been fenced off, the fencing decorated with bright red and blue banners and the heraldic shields of England and France. Pennons flew in the wind atop tall poles. Down the middle of the fenced-in area ran a long wooden barrier. Riders approached each other from opposite ends of the field, on opposite sides of the barrier. Using long wooden lances with blunt ends, each attempted to knock the other off his horse. It all took much strength and skill, and the champion of the tiltyard was always the hero of the court.

A loud blast of trumpets and even louder noise from the crowd of onlookers announced the start of the tilting.

With a thunderous pounding of hoofs an immense dun-colored stallion, mane and tail flying, galloped down the length of the wooden barrier as the onlookers shouted and cheered. The rider, his face hidden behind the lowered visor of his gilded and plumed helmet, was an outsize man with a broad, strong frame and powerful legs. He dipped his lance to the cheering spectators, then rode back to the starting point.

"It is the king! It is the king!"

I was so caught up in the excitement that I almost forgot where I was, and began jumping up and down. I felt a restraining hand on my shoulder and heard my mother whisper loudly, "Look at the princess! See how well behaved she is!"

I glanced over to where the blond, delicate four-year-old Princess Mary rested in the arms of Maria de Salinas, her eyes bright and intent on watching her magnificent father but her body obediently still. She was well trained to keep her composure and her quietness put me to shame.

But then, Princess Mary was the heir to the throne. If Queen Catherine had no son—and I had heard my mother and the other ladies-in-waiting say quietly to one another that she would not—then Mary would be the next ruler of England. No wonder she was so well behaved and dignified. She would one day be queen.

A second rider had now made his appearance and was introducing himself to the crowd. He was the great French champion the Sieur de Chatelherault, and I heard his name murmured through the mass of spectators as he rode up and down along the barrier as the king had, making his splendid warhorse sidestep and toss his head proudly.

In a moment the herald stepped forward and announced the first test of arms. Now the onlookers fell silent, watching the two riders take their places at opposite ends of the lists, adjust their visors and lower their wooden lances. At a signal they spurred their mounts forward and, amid much spewing of mud clumps and churning of earth, the horses flew toward one another and the riders took aim with their long lances.

There was a tremendous crash as the lances splintered with the impact of the two hurtling combatants—and then it was over, the French champion in his black and silver armor lay struggling on the ground, his mount shying and snorting.

The crowd roared "King Henry! King Henry!" again and again, and the king, who appeared unshaken by his clash with the Frenchman, raised his visor and waved, smiling to the entire assembly before resuming his place at the end of the field.

Another challenger was brought against him, and then another. Each time my heart beat quickly and I feared for King Henry's safety. Yet each time he thundered along the barrier, lance held securely, and unhorsed his opponent while evading being unhorsed himself.

His strength was prodigious, and his stamina even more so. I cannot now remember how long I stood watching, open-mouthed and in awe, but it seemed like a very long afternoon. Finally the herald announced the winner, in a voice that trembled with emotion: "King Harry the Eighth of That Name, champion!"

Yet another deafening cheer rose from hundreds of throats, and the champion made his tired mount trot up and down the tiltyard one last time while flowers were thrown in his path and tributes called out. Diverging from his path down the center of the jousting field, he turned his horse in the direction of a richly dressed young woman who stood in one of the royal pavilions adjacent to Queen Catherine's. As we watched, the woman held out a square of shimmering blue silk and he reached up and took it from her, kissing it and attaching it to his armor where it fluttered conspicuously against the gleaming silver metal.

I saw that the queen had been holding out a square of red silk, no doubt expecting the king to take it and wear it. When she saw him take the other woman's token she quickly withdrew her outstretched arm and handed the red silk square to my mother, who tucked it discreetly into the pocket of her gown.

"Why didn't the king wear the queen's token?" I asked my mother, who put her finger to her lips to silence me. Later, at the lavish banquet the king held to celebrate his victory, I had my answer.

In the torchlit banqueting hall of his newly built palace, King Henry gave a feast that night for the French king Francis that surpassed any feast I had ever attended. Long dining tables were heaped with platters of roast beef and pork, swan and pheasant, succulent puddings and towering miniature castles made from spun sugar and filled with marzipan and sweet comfits. The wine flowed freely and many toasts were offered to the jousters and their ladies.

I observed that Queen Catherine sat with the French Queen Claude and her ladies, not with King Henry. He sat at a table apart from all the others, the French king in the place of honor on his right hand but on his left, the young woman who had given him the square of blue silk.

She was very beautiful in her gown of deep red velvet, her abundant hair held back by a headdress that sparkled with gems. As if she did not have enough finery already, I saw the king slip an emerald ring on her finger, and her smile, when she looked over at him, was one of gratitude combined with deep pleasure and satisfaction. It was the smile of a woman who has achieved what she wants, and is well pleased with it.

I saw that several of the French ladies were looking over at Henry and his attractive companion and talking to one another about her. I had been instructed in French since I began my studies at the age of four, and I understood quite a bit of what they said. The woman's name was Bessie Blount, and she had been King Henry's mistress for several years. Evidently the king preferred her company to that of his wife.

One of the French ladies seemed to be staring at Bessie with fascination. She interested me because she spoke both French and English, and because I enjoyed watching her dance. She was graceful, she dipped and swayed to the music as if dancing rather than walking was her natural form of movement.

"That is Lady Elizabeth Boleyn's daughter, Anne," my mother told me. "She lives at the French court. She is one of Queen Claude's maids of honor. I suppose she will marry a Frenchman."

"She doesn't look like the others."

"No. She has a wild, gypsy look about her. Such dark skin and those black eyes. Unfortunate really. Still, I suppose some Frenchman will have her—if her dowry is high enough."

Later that evening my mother discussed my dowry with a tall, spare old man who leaned on his cane and looked at me carefully as they conversed, as if examining a painting. I looked back. After a time he smiled.

"She has heart, your daughter. Not one girl in twenty would look back at an old man like me in that unflinching way."

"She is her father's daughter, Lord Scrope. My late husband, Thomas Parr, as you may remember, was a valiant fighter. He fought at the king's side against the French here in Flanders some years ago. And he was a fearless rider and hunter."

"So he was. Can she ride?"

"I am told I ride well for my age," I said. "And I am learning to shoot. And to dance."

I could see that Lord Scrope was amused at my very forthcoming response. His eyes twinkled.

"We will have to talk further," he said to my mother. "Perhaps something can be arranged. It is a possibility." And he took himself off, limping on one leg and leaning heavily on his cane.

I have many memories of the Golden Valley. How the wind blew so hard that the horses lost their way, blinded by the dust in their eyes. How King Francis was injured while competing in the tiltyard and had to wear an eyepatch over his bloodshot right eye. I remember Queen

Catherine, when she thought no one could see her, crying quietly into her handkerchief and then drying her eyes and crossing herself. But most of all I remember King Henry, splendid in his suit of dazzling cloth of gold, a gold cloth cap on his head with a white feather plume, laughing and joking with Bessie Blount and his friends.

One night the French king gave a reception for the English courtiers in his huge silken tent and King Henry arrived late, making a great noise as he burst into the midst of the gathering. In his arms he carried a sturdy baby boy, dressed exactly as he himself was dressed in a small suit of cloth of gold with a feathered cap. The king went from one guest to another, showing off the baby to each of them in turn and asking, "Isn't he a fine boy, this son of mine? Truly England never had a more handsome prince." The baby, bounced up and down too often by his energetic father, or frightened by the sight of so many strangers, turned down the corners of his mouth and began to cry.

I looked at my mother questioningly. "But I thought Queen Catherine only had a daughter, Princess Mary."

"Yes," my mother answered through clenched teeth. "She does."

"Then who is this boy?"

"He's the son of Bessie Blount. Now, bow to King Henry and say nothing."

I obeyed. We bowed low to the king as he passed, smiling and chortling over his boy. He moved on, and I watched his retreating figure, thrilled to have been so near to him, honored that he should glance in my direction, and above all puzzled that with such a lovely wife and well-behaved daughter he should show such a marked preference for a mistress and a bastard son.

2

IN THE END MY MOTHER'S EFFORTS TO ARRANGE A MARRIAGE FOR ME WITH Lord Scrope's grandson came to nothing. The aging lord was a shrewd negotiator, and my mother had little to bargain with beyond the queen's sponsorship, my bit of royal blood and my good looks. I had no lands or wealthy titled relations, and I was not an heiress.

Mother kept on trying. There were other meetings with men—and a few women—who looked me over and considered me as a future bride for their sons or grandsons. I did my best to be agreeable. But I got older and older and no betrothal was agreed upon. My lack of a large dowry always got in the way. By the time I was fourteen mother was nearly frantic with worry. But by then, of course, she had found another way to secure my future, indeed to secure the future of the entire Parr family.

There were three of us children. I am the eldest, my brother Will is a year younger than I am and my sister Anne two and a half years younger. My brother, who at thirteen was already tall and broad-shouldered and who made friends easily, had the rare gift of being able to make everyone laugh. When mother took him to court he was a great success. He learned jokes and tricks from Queen Catherine's Spanish dwarf jesters Diego and Leon and from Jane the Fool, the king's principal entertainer, he learned how to sharpen his witty jests and barbs so as to amuse the courtiers without making them angry.

Everyone wanted Will to sit near them at dinner, and to entertain them with his mimicry and funny stories. Of course, he often went too far, catching frogs in the moat and putting them in the queen's chamber pot, unhinging the king's jousting armor so that the carcinet fell off as soon as he tried to put it on, putting soap on the privy closet stairs to make people fall down when they tried to climb them and dropping pig bladders full of water on dancers at royal banquets. We were used to these tiresome pranks within the family, and accepted them with resigned good humor because Will always made us laugh when he talked and his silliness redeemed him in our eyes so that we forgave his excesses.

What surprised us all was how Will's lighthearted nature and constant store of good humor won over one of the great heiresses of King Henry's court, Anne Bourchier.

I first met Anne one afternoon in the garden of the king's palace at Hampton Court—the one that used to belong to Cardinal Wolsey until the king asked him for it—and she was demanding that Old Squibb, one of the palace gardeners, pick some roses for her.

"I'll have some of those red ones," she said, pointing vaguely in the direction of some bushes bearing masses of blooms. Old Squibb, white-haired and slow-moving, the pain of his swollen joints evident on his grimacing features, bent to do her bidding.

"Not those, you imbecile, those over there." Her voice was querulous, petulant, and curiously high. The voice of a spoiled child, not a smooth-skinned, fair-haired, shapely young woman whose costly silken gown trimmed in gold spoke of wealth and breeding.

The old gardener, puzzled, began cutting roses from a different bush only to trigger Anne's impatience when he handed her a fistful of red blossoms.

She cried out and threw them on the ground.

"These have thorns! Remove them at once!" She thrust a bleeding finger in her mouth.

Old Squibb shrugged. "Roses have thorns, milady. That's the way they grow." He bent down to retrieve the rejected flowers.

She looked at him coldly. "I'll tell my father you said that. He'll have you dismissed."

"Or you could pick your own roses, forget what happened here and let Old Squibb know how beautiful his garden is," I said, walking up to the startled Anne and handing her the pruning knife I had been using to cut some lavender.

The gardener nodded to me, and I returned his greeting with a smile. "He was growing roses here before you or I were born. Isn't that right, Squibb?"

"Indeed it is, milady. When I was a boy I served the old king, the good one. King Edward. He loved his flowers, King Edward. Why, I remember—"

"Enough! Get on with your work and be silent!"

Anne turned to me and looked at me scornfully. I was suddenly aware that my old sarsnet day gown of a dull mulberry color, made over from one of Grandmother Fitzhugh's, was shabby compared to her finery of peach-colored silk.

"You're Cat Parr, aren't you. The one they can't seem to find a husband for. How old are you now, fourteen? Fifteen? Pity. Still, I daresay there must be some convent somewhere that would have you as a nun."

"I don't see a betrothal ring on your hand, and I believe you are several years older than I am."

She laughed, a laugh with a bitter edge.

"Oh, that's our choice. Mine and my father's." I was well aware of who Anne's father was, the very wealthy and influential Earl of Essex, one of the luminaries of the court.

Anne sighed. "Everybody wants to marry me. Or rather, to marry my fortune."

"You mean your father's fortune."

She gave a dismissive shrug. "What does it matter? My father is rich and I'll be rich one day soon, because he is old."

The callousness of Anne's remark took me aback. Didn't she love her father at all? I thought of my own father, who at the time of my conversation with Anne had been dead for many years. How I wished he were still alive to talk to and go to for advice!

I saw out of the corner of my eye that Old Squibb was approaching me, holding out a bunch of sweet william. "These have no thorns," he said, and walked slowly away again, ignoring Anne. I called out my thanks to his retreating back.

"When I marry," I said to Anne, "I hope it will be for love."

She snorted. "Love! Like the king and Mistress Anne?"

"Hush! We must not speak of such things. They concern only the king and queen."

"What a little prig you are! Everyone is talking about the king and his mistress—and wondering whether he's going to divorce the queen, and why Mistress Anne Boleyn isn't pregnant!"

It was the scandal of the court, in that year of 1527. Our King Henry, our warrior king and great champion, had become enamored of the Duke of Norfolk's niece Anne Boleyn, the black-eyed gypsylike girl I had once thought so striking when I saw her in Flanders in the Golden Valley. Then she had been a maid of honor to the French queen; now she was a maid of honor to Queen Catherine, and King Henry's favorite. She had displaced Bessie Blount and all the king's other sweethearts, even her own sister, who, it was said, had borne the king a halfwit son.

"She isn't pregnant," I said, keeping my voice low, "because she is a virtuous girl. Not like her sister."

"She's no more virtuous than I am. She's only doing what she's told, by all her relations. Don't give in to the king, they are telling her. Wait until he puts the queen aside. Then let him crown you. That's what they're saying. But then, you're too young to understand.

"Now, when I marry," Anne went on, "it will be for diversion. For amusement. Someone to keep the awful boredom of life at bay."

I thought to myself, how could anyone find life boring? When there was so much to see and do, so many interesting books to read and people to converse with. Walks to take and sights to see. To Anne I said, "I expect to love my husband and find him amusing. And handsome, and intelligent, and kind, and affectionate—"

"And rich, and famous, and saintly—"

We both began laughing. For the first time I saw something other than hauteur and hostility in Anne's eyes. I saw, for a moment, liveliness and even a hint of friendliness. Then the moment passed.

"Well, may all your romantic dreams come true." She swept up her skirts and left the garden, ignoring Old Squibb who looked up from his weeding as she passed, and shook his head.

It was only a few weeks later that mother told me, a look of immense relief and satisfaction on her face, that my brother Will was betrothed— to Anne Bourchier!

So she has got what she wanted, I thought to myself. She has found her diversion and amusement—my very amusing brother!

I told mother about my encounter with Anne and how self-centered and vain I thought she was.

"That's true enough. But don't forget, dear, she's an earl's daughter. Everyone caters to her. She's never known anything different. I moved heaven and earth to arrange this betrothal. I had to borrow from Uncle William, and even from your grandmother Fitzhugh. All your dowry funds went into obtaining Anne for William, and your sister's dowry too of course. Don't worry, once we have an earl's daughter in the family you two girls will have all the offers you can handle."

My grandmother Fitzhugh, whose lineage was as high as Anne Bourchier's, disapproved of the match for William and came up from the country to London, to our house at Blackfriars, to tell my mother so.

"I don't like it, Maud," she said bluntly. "I know the girl. She's flighty. Irreverent. No sense of family. No dignity. Only snobbishness. Probably a heretic."

I had to smile. Grandmother called everyone she was suspicious of a heretic. For several years we had been hearing about heretics, rebellious and dangerous followers of the German renegade monk Martin Luther. They were said to spread harmful ideas and to refuse obedience to the Holy Father in Rome. Grandmother blamed them for all the evils in the world.

As soon as Will's betrothal was announced our lives began to change. Tradesmen sought our business. Italian bankers came to see mother and offered to lend her money, which enabled her to repay grandmother and Uncle William and to buy luxuries we had never had before. All this newfound abundance came from Anne's future inheritance. Knowing that she would one day be very wealthy, merchants and bankers were more than willing to lend money now—at high rates of interest of course.

Will's wedding was very grand. My sister Nan and I held our new sister-in-law's long silk train and there were masses of lilies and gillyflowers, roses and flowering vines decorating the royal chapel. A bishop in gold vestments conducted the wedding mass, and the queen and many court dignitaries were present.

The Parrs were rising in the world. We moved to a finer mansion not far from our old house near Blackfriars. Uncle William, who had always been ambitious for our family and who had at one time been a gentleman of the chamber to the old king Henry VII, was rapidly becoming a wealthy landowner. He was borrowing a great deal, my mother told me, from the Italian bankers and buying estates in the North Country.

One day he came into the room where mother and I were sitting, rubbing his large hands together in satisfied anticipation.

"Well, Maud, it is all but done," he said. "They are coming this afternoon to look her over, but it is all but done."

"What is done?" I asked, feeling uneasy. Mother laid aside her embroidery and picked up her little tawny lapdog, holding him and stroking him as she did when she was nervous. She watched Uncle William's face intently.

"Why, Catherine's betrothal of course. It's high time she married."

"But you know I have been negotiating with Lord Abergavenny for her to marry his son. I have hopes that this time my efforts will be successful."

Uncle William waved one hand dismissively.

"That scrawny boy? I've seen him on the tiltyard and he can barely couch a lance, much less unhorse an opponent. He's a weakling, a sickly weakling. I doubt he'll last five summers. Besides, Lord Abergavenny doesn't have much money."

"You can't go judging every potential husband for Catherine by his skill in the tiltyard. Just because you were a champion at sixteen, or was it eighteen, doesn't mean that any man she marries has to be an athlete."

I thought I saw Uncle William smile ever so slightly at this remark as he murmured "True enough."

I had met Lord Abergavenny's son, and had no special liking for him, as he was shy and clumsy and had a constant silly half-smile on his face. Yet I knew that mother wanted me to marry him, and had been working hard to bring about our betrothal. Now Uncle William was shattering all mother's efforts—and my hopes.

"No, we will do much better for you, Catherine, than the puny son of Lord Abergavenny. It was Lord Burgh himself who approached me, as we were doing business together, inquiring whether you were free to marry into his family."

"Ah, the Burghs," my mother said, relaxing a little. "There are three of them, always together at court. Only the old man bears the title, of course, but in the queen's chamber we call them Old Burgh, Middle Burgh and Young Burgh." She laughed. "The old one drools, the middle one pinches and the young one is still wet behind the ears."

All three of the Burghs called on us that afternoon, and as I was introduced to them I saw the fitness of my mother's description. Old Burgh, the holder of the title Lord Burgh, who leaned on his son's arm, was stooped and bent and his gray hair hung in untidy wisps around his long, lined face. His eyes were bright as he looked at me, however, and though his thin lips were wet and parted, I saw no drool escape them. Middle Burgh, a spry and dapper man dressed in fine velvet whose intense face was almost womanish in its beauty, paid little attention to me but was effusive in greeting my uncle, whom he appeared to know well, and looked lingeringly and appreciatively at my mother, who as I have said before, was very pretty and very charming.

Young Burgh, who I liked immensely the moment I saw him, was a boy of about my own age who grinned at me as if to say, you and I have nothing to do with these old people! The boy had wavy brown hair and soft brown eyes and such smooth cheeks that I wondered if he had begun to be shaven yet. I wanted to sit beside him but knew I must not appear too eager. I sat beside my mother, yet when I looked over at Young Burgh I saw that he was looking at me, and we smiled at each other again.

Middle Burgh took charge of our little gathering, saying how happy he was to meet me and what pleasure it gave him that I was willing to become part of his family.

"Are you fond of Lincolnshire?" It was the loud, shrill voice of Old Burgh, interrupting his son. "The fens? The wolds?"

"I have never been there," I was forced to admit, "but I believe it is a very beautiful place. Very—remote."

"People are often drowned in The Wash while trying to get there," Young Burgh put in, making me laugh. I was sure he had done it deliberately. Middle Burgh glared at him.

I remembered being told by my tutor that once long ago King John crossed The Wash and lost the crown jewels when the tide came in too quickly for him to escape with all his possessions.

"Gainesborough Hall is an exceptional property—er, house," Middle Burgh went on.

"With many farms and tenants, I believe," said my uncle.

"Seventeen farms, all fully tenanted. Turnips, winter corn, meadowland for grazing. Abundant stock, of course."

I exchanged glances with Young Burgh.

"We have abundant stock on our farms in the North," my mother remarked, trying to keep up her end of the conversation. The men ignored her.

"How about swans?" Old Burgh piped up, looking at me. "Do you like swans?"

"I like them roasted, of course. Or baked, with sweetmeats and truffles."

A look of horror crossed the old man's wrinkled features.

"He raises swans as pets," Young Burgh explained to me. "He can't bear to eat them."

"I'm sorry," I told Old Burgh. "Yes, I enjoy watching our swans, in the river." Our house was just by the riverbank. At high tide the wherries, the swans and the floating garbage from downriver all drifted past our windows. "And I don't eat them very often. Only on feast days."

Young Burgh stood up. "Shall we see if there are any in the river now? I'd like to see your gardens."

"Yes, dear. You two young people go on. We can talk business in here without you." It was my mother's encouraging voice.

"But I—" Old Burgh said, attempting to rise to his feet.

"Stay where you are, father. If you try to get up you'll fall over."

Young Burgh held out his hand to me and I took it, eagerly, and we left the room.

As we stepped out into the sunshine and began to stroll together by the riverside I was aware of two things. First, the feel of Young Burgh's warm large hand holding mine. A feeling that made me smile and go limp with pleasure. And second, the heat of the sun on my upturned face.

"I'm Ned," Young Burgh said.

"I'm Cat."

"You're Will's sister. I beat Will at wrestling."

"He's not much of a wrestler. Besides, you're older."

"True. But even if we were the same age, I would beat him. I try harder. I want to win."

I saw no reason to disagree. We paused to look out across the river, still hand in hand. Church bells chimed the hour, and a wherryman called out "Bridge ho!" as he prepared to guide his craft through the fast-moving waters under a stone arch.

I looked up at Ned, thinking to myself, this is the man I am going to marry. The man who will be the father of my children. I was excited and happy. It could have been so much worse. He could have been someone ugly, or ill-tempered, or unmanly, or hideously marked with the pox. Instead he was Ned: tall, sturdily made, with pleasing looks, brown hair that curled at his ears and friendly brown eyes. How could I have done better?

I felt grateful to Uncle William and it was with that strong feeling of gratitude that, half an hour later, I reentered the room where we had left the others, Will's hand still in mine.

At once I was aware that something had changed.

My mother looked troubled, and Uncle William, when I looked in his direction, avoided my eyes.

"What is it?" I cried, dropping Ned's hand.

My mother rose and came over to me. "Cat," she said evenly, "your uncle and Lord Thomas"—she meant Middle Burgh—"have come to an agreement. You are to be the wife of John, Lord Burgh, the head of the family, who admires you and wishes to share his life with you."

It took me a moment to realize that she meant the old man, who was smiling broadly and wetly and reaching out toward me from where he sat.

Startled, I looked at Ned, who was dumbfounded.

"But I thought—"

Mother was swift to hush my words.

"No!" I cried out, appealing to Uncle William. "It can't be!"

"Excuse us," mother said to the others and hustled me, protesting, to a curtained alcove where she spoke to me very seriously.

"Cat, listen to me. You must accept what has been arranged for you without argument. This is an excellent match. Lord Burgh is a gentleman in his final years. He wants nothing more than a young wife of gentle blood to warm his bed. You will be well treated—and of course, the marriage will not be a long one. You will soon be free—and well-to-do. Now, we are going back to join the others, and I expect you to be sensible. And obedient."

Frowning in dismay, I followed mother back into the room. I looked at Ned. His face was dark.

"Catherine," Uncle William said, "if your father were here today he would be very pleased. You are to be Lady Burgh, the lady of Gainesborough Hall."

Boldly I walked to Ned's side and grasped his hand.

"The young lord has asked for my hand in marriage, and I have accepted him."

The others drew in their breath sharply.

Uncle William walked up to us, took hold of our joined hands and firmly separated them.

"Since you are not yet of age, Catherine, and your wardship belongs to your mother, the decision is hers. She has already made it."

Ned knelt before my mother, as respectful children always do before their parents when asking a special favor or a blessing.

"Milady," he said, "I would be greatly honored if you will allow me to wed your lovely and courageous daughter. Our fate is in your hands."

I knelt beside Ned. "Please, mother. Listen to Ned. I know young girls are often given in marriage to older men. But not men that are practically dropping dead!"

"Who's dropping dead?" Old Burgh shouted. "Anyone I know?"

There were tears in mother's eyes. Ignoring Lord Burgh's agitated query, she rose.

"Catherine, my decision is made. I must defer to your uncle's judgment. You will be the wife of Lord Burgh. The wedding will be held at Shrovetide." Her eyes grew soft as they rested on the man kneeling beside me.

"Young Ned, I thank you for your loyalty. I am very glad our two families are to be joined in marriage."

"Yes," Uncle William said, ignoring our act of rebellion. "We will all profit from this union." He went to the elderly Lord Burgh and congratulated him.

I was aware of murmurous sounds in the room, and of a relaxation of the tension that had been so oppressive a moment earlier. My heart was pounding and my cheeks felt hot.

Our guests were leaving. I got to my feet and managed to say a curt and civil goodbye to Lord Thomas and to the aged Lord Burgh, who grasped my hand eagerly and kissed it.

Ned looked at me sorrowfully, thoughtfully.

"Thank you for showing me the garden, Cat," he said. "It should be lovely tomorrow, even if it rains."

It seemed an odd thing to say—until I realized that he was giving me a message, telling me to meet him in the garden the next day.

"Yes, it should be." Ned's message gave me a flicker of hope. We would meet. We would try to find a way to change the betrothal arrangements. Ned wanted it as much as I did.

After the three men had gone I heard Uncle William talking to my mother.

"She must be made to obey, Maud."

"I understand that. She is a good girl. She will see reason."

"She had better. I won't have a rebellious foolish girl upset all my plans. If she does not obey, by all that's holy I'll smash her head against the wall until it's as soft as a boiled apple."

3

I THOUGHT OF RUNNING AWAY.

I thought of joining a convent, only I knew that no convent would admit me as an oblate unless my mother took me there in person and presented me to the sisters—along with a large dowry.

And then I thought of going to the king.

King Henry, who knew what it meant to be married to a woman he no longer loved, and kept from marrying his beloved. Surely King Henry would help me.

I found him in the tiltyard the following morning, riding up and down in the lists against an opponent. I recognized the king by his size—he was always taller and more muscular than his jousting partners—and by the fact that he won every encounter, shattering the other man's wooden lance and laughing with pleasure afterward each time.

I stood off to one side, under the eave of the stables, waiting for the exercise to end. Grooms came and went, attending to the horses, carrying buckets of water and bags of oats and lengths of harness leather. No one questioned my presence, though some of the grooms looked at me admiringly before continuing on with their work.

After an hour or more the sound of heavy hoofbeats ceased and in a few moments two burly men approached the stables, their armor having been removed and their splendid physiques covered only by thin linen shirts and trousers of rough brown cloth. Their boot heels crunched the small stones underfoot as they walked.

"I've sent Knyvet to Lille for tilting horses," the king was saying to his companion, who I now recognized as his black-haired, roguishly handsome brother-in-law Charles Brandon, the Duke of Suffolk. "There are none to be had in this country."

"Ireland, that's the place for horses," Brandon was replying as the two men caught sight of me, and the king stopped short.

"You're the Parr girl," the king said, looking at me keenly. "What are you doing here?"

"Waiting for you, your majesty," I said with a deep curtsey.

"For me?"

"Please help me. You're the only one who can." I spoke up, but my voice cracked and I felt my upper lip beginning to quiver.

"Brandon, this appears to be a private matter," King Henry told his friend with a wink. The duke grinned and went off, calling loudly for a cup of ale which sent the stable boys running to do his bidding.

The king showed me into a tack room filled with the rich aroma of saddle leather. Logs were stacked in the hearth but there was no fire, as it was summertime and the air outside was warm. The one small window let in only a little light, and the king shut the door firmly.

"No one will bother us here," he said, looking over at me with a glimmer of something—was it humor?—in his eyes.

"Now, my girl, what is it you ask of me?"

He took a step toward me and, preoccupied though I was with my plight, I could not help but feel the magnetism of his presence. He towered over me, broad-shouldered and blond and hearty, exuding health and vigor. His smooth skin, showing through the sweat-stained linen of his shirt, gave off a ruddy glow.

"Don't be afraid. Many of my subjects make free to ask a boon of their king."

"Sire, I am to be married."

"Yes?"

"But to the wrong man!" The words burst from my mouth. I could not stop them. "My uncle William has betrothed me to Lord Burgh, who is terribly old and can't even stand up by himself. I want to marry his grandson, Ned, who is young and strong and would make a fine husband."

"And who has no title and no income."

"But he will have, in time."

"Ah, the old dilemma! The old man can afford a wife but lacks the strength to enjoy her, while the young man can take pleasure with a wife but lacks the means to afford her. In a just world, the old man would graciously step aside, cede his title and all his goods to his grandson, and wander off into the wilderness to die. However, the world is unjust, and old men do cling to their titles and their possessions."

He began pacing up and down, lost in thought. I heard him mutter to himself, something about wardship, then a moment later, he said, "The Calais Spears, the Calais Spears, I wonder—"

He stopped pacing and came over to stand in front of me.

"Your uncle William, he was a soldier in my father's time, was he not?"

"He boasts of his service."

"Good. I shall offer him the post of Lieutenant of the Calais Spears, in return for his agreeing to reconsider your betrothal. He will agree, because the post brings fifty pounds a year. I will suggest a match between you and young Ned. He will say Ned is without lands or income. So I will have to find an estate and a post for Ned as well. Now, seeing all the trouble you put me to, what am I to have in return?"

His tone changed as he spoke these last words. I felt a subtle threat, and at the same time an unfamiliar excitement as his eyes traveled downward from my modest white peaked cap to my lips to my bare throat and the low neckline of my new green damask gown.

"You will have my deepest gratitude, sire," I said, my voice husky. I did feel gratitude, and great relief. I believed that the king would do as he said, and that all would be well. Then came the shock of his next words.

"You are a virgin," he murmured. "Virgins excite me."

I stepped back in alarm, remembering the firmly locked door, the solitude in which we found ourselves. I had told no one where I was going when I left home earlier that morning. Not even mother knew where I was.

The king took hold of me and, slowly and deliberately, traced the line of my cheek with one pink finger, all the while looking into my eyes. His eyes, I noticed, were a clear light blue flecked with gold.

"So you are to be a bride. No doubt you are familiar with the droit de seigneur."

It was an old term from feudal days. When a man married, his feudal overlord had the right to deflower his bride.

"As king, I am Ned's feudal lord. If I desire it, his bride shall be mine first, then his."

I suddenly felt cold.

"I have been to many weddings, sire. I have never seen that old outworn custom observed."

"Perhaps I shall revive it—in your case."

I was trembling now. He was so much stronger than I was, and his will ruled all. He was no ordinary man. He was the king.

I looked into his face and perceived, to my unspeakable relief, that he was toying with me, enjoying my fear. He was savoring his power over me, though the underlying threat of erotic possession was real enough. I was in his power. I was trapped. That, it seemed, was enough for him.

After a long moment, during which I mentally said every prayer I knew, he opened the door and sent me out into the bright sunlight. I blinked, and stumbled out into the stable yard, filled with activity and the warm, rich scent of horses and hay. I was free.

"Don't forget, girl," he called out as I left, "that you are in my debt."

4

How can I write of the happiest year of my life?

Of my married life with Ned, in the great mansion called Gainesborough Hall that his grandfather deeded to him at the request of the king?

Of the immense chestnut tree in the park where we used to go to picnic when the weather was warm, and the deer came down to take apples out of our hands?

If I say that no woman was ever happier, the words will sound empty—except that in my case, they were true.

I was just seventeen when Ned and I married, and he was only two years older. King Henry appointed him Deputy Warden of the Marches and gave him several lucrative wardships so we had enough to live on, plus the crops and animals on the estate which provided all our food and which our estate manager sold at a profit.

Our first Christmas together we gave a feast for all the tenants on the estate. Long trestle tables were laid out in the great hall which was green with ivy and holly branches. Our cooks roasted six oxen and untold numbers of pigs and chickens, and there was plum pudding and cider and sweet Christmas cakes. Our tenants came in their best clothes, stamping their feet and blowing on their mittened fingers as the night was very cold. They brought live rabbits and ducks and baskets of eggs and fresh cheese wrapped in cloth. Ned explained to me that the exchanging of gifts was a custom in rural Lincolnshire and I distributed caps and petticoats to the women while Ned gave out hoes and bags of seed to the men. For the children there were sugared almonds and comfits and wooden toys that clacked in the strong December wind.

"Joys of the season to you, young master sir," the tenants said as they came up to greet us, the men removing their hats respectfully and the women bobbing curtseys, "and to your lady."

I made an effort to learn their names but there were far too many of them and in the end the most I managed to do was to join in their country dancing while the fiddlers played and the snow whirled against the long windows and drifted in underneath the doors.

Ned's father and grandfather came too, as guests of honor, and sat with us at a special table. Lord Burgh was so frail he had to be carried in a chair, but he waved his soup spoon in the air with abandon in time to the fiddle music and appeared to be enjoying himself to the full. Ned's father Thomas, unconcerned with Christmas, spent his time querying the farmers about the size of their fall harvests and the yields on neighboring estates, while eyeing the plump young peasant girls and now and then reaching a searching hand under a full petticoat.

To judge from his behavior toward us, Thomas appeared to bear no grudge against Ned or me, even though we now occupied the mansion that would have been his on his father's death had the king not intervened to change things within the family. Thomas was buying up the neighboring properties and already owned a dozen large farms that bordered the Gainesborough estate.

In fact from the time of my marriage my father-in-law Thomas looked at me with newfound respect. He knew that I had a special influence with the king, though how I acquired it he could not fathom. I was not a royal mistress, as Mary Boleyn and Bessie Blount and others before them had been. I was a loyal, faithful wife to Ned. Yet the king's favor appeared to be mine to command.

It did not escape Thomas's notice that after our splendid Christmas celebrations at Gainesborough, we went to the royal court for New Year's. There Ned and I were granted a very special royal privilege: we were invited to take part in a masque, performed before the entire court.

It was called "The Fountain of Youth" and the king himself took part. I played the part of Innocence and rode on a horse trapped all in gold. Ned was a gargoyle holding up the fountain as it spewed water high in the air. The king, wearing a disguise, was the Fountain Master who dispensed the youth-giving waters to the onlookers.

My brother Will and his wife Anne were at the New Year's celebrations, Will enlivening the feasting and making the diners laugh. I noticed, however, that Anne, who at one time had laughed almost harder than anyone at Will's joking, now seemed indifferent to him. She turned away from him at the banqueting table and gave her attention to others—especially the king's lecherous friend Charles Brandon.

I had seen little of Anne since my own wedding, having spent all my time with Ned at Gainesborough while Anne and Will were with the king in the capital or nearby. Anne looked different to me, harder in her manner and more wanton in her dress. She had ordered her dressmaker to cut her gowns in the style then current in France, with necklines that were daringly low and skirts that rose coquettishly to reveal layers of frothy underskirts. She whitened her skin and rouged her lips and cheeks, and when she danced, it was not with grace and elegance like Anne Boleyn but with wanton abandon.

One day during the New Year's festivities when I was on my way to visit my mother in the queen's apartments I passed along a seldom-used corridor. A door was slightly ajar. Behind it I could hear sounds, indistinct sounds, suppressed laughter and muffled gasps.

Curious, I tentatively moved closer to the door and peered in, ignoring the sound of my mother's remembered voice in my ear that repeated, never spy on others! Spying went on in the palace constantly, I reminded myself. Servants eavesdropped on their masters, and on each other. Husbands spied on wives, brothers on brothers, even children on parents. It was a way of life.

What I saw through the slight crack in the door made me turn away in dismay.

My sister-in-law, her bodice lowered to her waist and her skirt raised to her thighs, stood pressed against the wall by a burly, bearded Charles Brandon!

I ran down the corridor, eager to reach the queen's rooms where a sense of calm and order was always to be found. Mother was there, in attendance on the queen, and when she saw me it was plain to her that

I was upset. I took comfort from her but did not tell her the reason for my distress. I was concerned, above all, for Will and wanted to protect him from scandal. Did he know about Anne's infidelity? Had he guessed? And was Charles Brandon Anne's only adulterous lover, or were there others?

Adultery was the great unspoken preoccupation at court that year and the king was the chief adulterer and was leading us all astray. King Henry was treating Anne Boleyn as his wife, and forcing us all to pay honor to her. Yet in the eyes of the church he was still legally married to Queen Catherine, and no matter how hard he tried, he could not manage to get his marriage to the queen annulled. It was embarrassing—and many of us felt very sorry for the poor queen, who was a good woman and blameless. Some of the Londoners hated Anne Boleyn so much that one afternoon they gathered at the riverbank and pursued her and tried to kill her.

It was no wonder I was upset by seeing my sister-in-law and Charles Brandon together. Yet when Anne herself confronted me about it, I tried not to let her see how much it bothered me.

"I saw you peeping through the door at us the other day, Cat," Anne said when she found me alone. "I suppose you ran right to your little brother and told him what you had seen."

"What you do is between you and your conscience, Anne. I am no talebearer."

"Still the well behaved girl, even though you are a wife."

"A faithful wife."

"No doubt you are more happily married than I am."

"I wish every woman were as happy as I am."

"Oh, don't be so pure and lofty, Cat! I'm sure your handsome husband has flaws. They all do."

I thought for a moment. As a husband, Ned was unfailingly kind and loving. But in handling the estate, I did see something in him that troubled me a bit. I called it his "hurry sickness." He tended to become too caught up in the tasks he undertook, and to feel that they were not being done quickly enough. Instead of letting the tenants on our estate weed the crops or build the fences or milk the cows and goats according to their own time-honored ways he would plunge in and work alongside them, urging them to work harder and faster until he all but collapsed from exhaustion. That winter he had shoveled snow until his hands bled, and I had to put a healing salve on his wounds and wrap them in bandages.

"Ned does get very caught up in what he is doing. Sometimes he can't seem to stop."

Anne's eyes widened. "Your brother, on the other hand, can't seem to start." She looked at me for a long minute while I digested this information. "Yes, you know what I mean. Frankly I don't think he likes women very much."

She paused, letting the meaning of her words sink in.

It couldn't be. Surely Will was not among those, accursed in the Bible, who practiced the abomination of sodomy? It was unthinkable: I did not let myself think it.

"Have you never wondered why we have no children? Come now, admit it."

"I have been expecting to hear good news from you for some time."

She shook her head. "There will be none."

"I'm sorry Anne. Perhaps things will change?"

"No."

"So," I said, after a time, "you take your pleasure where you can find it."

She smiled, a seductive smile.

"It finds me."

"I have not known illicit pleasure," I responded at length, knowing that my words made me sound more priggish than I actually felt, "but I believe it is said to be keener than the other kind."

Anne nodded knowingly.

"But then, little Cat, there is an illicit pleasure you do take, you and your husband."

"What is that?"

"You read forbidden books—or rather, one forbidden book."

I realized at once what she meant. Ned possessed a copy of the New Testament in English, as translated by William Tyndale who was burned at the stake for heresy a hundred years ago. Even though it was against the law, he had read it—indeed we read it together sometimes. We saw no harm in it—in fact it seemed to us, speaking only between ourselves of course, that to read the word of God in our own tongue brought us closer to the mysteries of faith. Yet we knew that such attitudes were condemned as "reformist" and we kept the precious Bible hidden in a storeroom. I was particularly careful not to let Grandmother Fitzhugh know that I had read the gospels in English. Had she known she would have called me a heretic.

But it seemed our secret was discovered.

"How did you find out?"

"You are not the only one that spies on people. I have known for some time."

"And you would use your knowledge against me."

"Only if I must—to prevent you from spreading stories about me."

She was threatening me, yet I felt no enmity from her, I was aware only of her skill at self-protection.

"We are not enemies, Anne," I said, meeting her level gaze.

"Let us hope we do not become enemies then," she said and left me.

When spring came, and the great chestnut tree bloomed and spread its leafy branches wide over the lawns and gardens around the manor house, I took long walks through the damp grass and rejoiced that warm weather had come again. I set the servants to taking down the hangings and airing out the featherbeds, wiping the patches of mold off the walls and applying new whitewash. The floors were washed and the cupboards cleaned and fresh sprigs of lavender and rosemary were hung in the wardrobes to make the clothes smell sweet.

I knew what to do, for I had observed my mother overseeing the spring cleaning at our old country house and at our London residence in Blackfriars many times and she was a good and thrifty housewife as well as being a fine and highborn lady.

Only one thing marred my happiness that spring: I was not yet carrying Ned's child.

And then in May my sister-in-law's wayward behavior became a family scandal. Anne announced that she would henceforth live on her own, as a free woman. She left Will and went away—no one knew where. Anne's father the earl was furious and sent out men to find her, but they returned without success. My mother and Uncle William were ashamed and embarrassed, though Grandmother Fitzhugh was full of "I told you sos" and was almost gleeful in her vindication.

Will was sad. I think he had loved Anne in his way, and missed her. What the truth was between them I didn't know, I had only Anne's word that theirs had not been a marriage in the physical sense, and that Will had not felt the love of a husband for a wife.

I kept Anne's secret, and wondered whether, after a time, she would either return to Will or seek an annulment. For though the church did not allow divorce, it was possible to have a marriage annulled, if it had not been consummated. Anne did neither. For the time being, she had simply dropped out of our lives.

Ned threw himself energetically into spring ploughing and planting, overseeing the preparation of the fields and joining in, as he usually did, to work beside the tenants and day-laborers. When he came home in the evening his shirt was sweat-stained and his boots muddy, and his fingernails were always so black with earth that he could not scrub them clean.

Some days I went out to join him in the fields, enjoying the scent of the freshly-turned soil and the anticipation of seeing the first green shoots rising from the muddy ground. I helped carry the midday meal to the laborers and joined them in their meal of soup and coarse black bread and slabs of cheese. I brought Ned his midday flagon of ale, which he drank heartily before lying down with me for an hour's nap.

Replete and happy, we lay in each other's arms, drowsing in the shade, while the afternoon drifted by. Then Ned was up and working again, his face full of purpose, a sheen of sweat on his brow, urging the others to ever greater efforts.

Sometimes the hurry sickness would overtake him and he would work on, alone, by torchlight, the others having given up from exhaustion, until nearly midnight. Then he would stumble across the threshold, bleary-eyed and weary, and sleep until noon the next day. I tried my best to reason with him, to make him see that a slow and steady pace was best and accomplished most. But he was stubborn. All my reasoning was wasted on him when the hurry sickness came over him and held him in its unhealthy grip.

Late one afternoon I heard the servants talking agitatedly to one another.

"It's a messenger!"

"No, soldiers!"

"Hundreds of them, milady, come and see!"

I went out onto the lawn and looked out along the road that led to Gainesborough from Netherhampton, our nearest town. Sure enough, there were hundreds of riders advancing along the road toward us. Each rider wore crimson, and each horse had crimson trappings.

I remembered where I had seen just such an array of red-clad horsemen before: in the Golden Valley, when I was a little girl. These were the attendants of the mighty Cardinal Wolsey, the king's chief minister.

Just as I thought, the cardinal himself soon appeared in the midst of his grand entourage, his large bulky figure draped in a scarlet cloak and a round red cardinal's hat on his head.

While we watched he was helped down from his mule and, escorted by two attendants, made his way to where I stood flanked by my chief household servants and a small crowd of kitchenmaids, gardeners and grooms.

He was very old and very fat. His ugly face with its small, close-set watery eyes and fleshy lips was gray and he was evidently weary, his gait was so slow.

I knelt as he approached and he held out his hand to me. I kissed his ring.

"Milady Burgh, I am sent by his majesty the king to give you the joyful news that he will soon be with you. He is on progress to the North, and will be at Gainesborough in six weeks' time."

Six weeks! At once I thought, how can we possibly prepare to receive the king here in six weeks?

"He brings but a small retinue. Seventy servants for himself and fifty for Mistress Anne Boleyn, who will accompany him."

But we have no room for so many people, I wanted to say. Gainesborough Hall is not a palace, merely a large country house. Where will we put them all? How will we feed them all? Because of my mother's long service to the queen I knew that each royal servant had servants of his or her own, not to mention horses and grooms and stable-boys.

"Milord Cardinal, may I ask how long his majesty will remain with us?"

"Perhaps a day or two, perhaps a week. It will depend on the hunting. I have drawn up a list of requirements," the cardinal said, reaching toward an attendant who handed him a roll of parchment. He unrolled it, looking it over briefly, and then handed it to me.

"Will you take some refreshment, your grace?"

"Thank you, no. We are expected at Ettinghall tonight."

Relieved, I knelt once again as the cardinal took his leave and the procession of riders resumed its course along the dusty road.

Ned, who had been out inspecting the fields with our estate manager when the cardinal arrived, received the news of the king's intention to visit us with an eagerness that surprised me.

"Don't you see, Cat, this is a great honor. It will be talked about in the neighborhood for years to come." His eyes were bright as he talked on, putting his arm around my shoulders and walking with me along the stream that bordered our front garden.

"I remember when I was very small, my grandfather told me about the time old King Henry, the present king's father, came to stay at a hunting lodge not far from here. There were hundreds of tents, he said, with servants preparing food, washing clothes, caring for horses and dogs. It was a bedlam!"

"Where did they all sleep at night? The hunting lodge couldn't have been very large."

"He said they slept on the ground. Underneath the carts, beneath the trees, wherever they could. Servants get used to sleeping rough."

"Not the women, surely."

"The turnspits and laundresses and maids, yes. They are tough. The camp followers bunk down with the men. No doubt the ladies required beds and a roof."

Ned talked on, and as I listened to him I lost some of my worries. We had six weeks to prepare for the king's arrival. We would do our best. The royal visit to Gainesborough Hall would be everything the king and his many retainers could desire.

5

IT SEEMED A TRULY MONUMENTAL TASK.

The more we thought about it, the more Ned and I realized that preparing for the royal visit was going to demand far more of us than we could ever provide.

It would not be like the visit of the late King Henry to the local hunting lodge that Ned had heard his grandfather describe. Then the king's own servants had done all the work and none in the royal party had expected much comfort. The day's sport had provided food. And the king's entourage had not been very large, perhaps a hundred people all told.

The royal visit we were expecting would be at least three times that size, with all the food to be provided from our own larders and pantries and cooked in our own kitchens. Our cellar would have to provide the wine and ale, our cupboards and chests all the linens.

Cardinal Wolsey had given me a list of things the king and Mistress Anne Boleyn would require. "My lord the king is fond of mugget," he wrote on the list, "and also of sturgeon's liver."

"The mugget we can manage," I said to Ned as we sat with our cook Mrs. Molsey and the steward Daniel Frith looking over the cardinal's list. "We have plenty of veal. But sturgeon's liver? In Lincolnshire?"

"I've never seen a sturgeon," Mrs. Molsey put in. "Let alone a sturgeon's liver."

"Rhenish wine, sponge cake, larks—the king is partial to baked lark's tongue—"

"Of course we will have to build another brewhouse," Daniel remarked. "Think of the barrels of beer all those southerners will want. We'll need another cooper, and more trenches dug to store the barrels against the heat. It would never do to serve the king sour beer."

"Mistress Boleyn requires seventeen buckets of warm fresh milk daily," I read aloud, my scorn no doubt apparent from my tone.

Ned laughed in astonishment. "Seventeen buckets! But we only have two dozen milk cows, and half of those are still suckling calves!"

"I've read about Roman emperors' wives who used to take baths in milk. Maybe the high and mighty Mistress Boleyn imagines herself an empress."

"I don't know how you can allow a woman like that under your roof," said Mrs. Molsey. "It's an insult to the good queen."

I kept my peace and said nothing, yet I agreed with her.

"We do as the king requires," said Ned gently but with finality. "We do not question his ways."

"I saw Mistress Boleyn once," I said at length. "I was only a little girl. She was very dark, like a gypsy. But she was a beautiful dancer."

"She's a witch, they say."

"Hush! If the king heard you say that he'd hang us all!" It was the steward, cautious and circumspect.

Mrs. Molsey lowered her voice to a whisper. "Well, what are we to think when she has six fingers! It's monstrous! She must be a witch!"

Ned cleared his throat loudly. "While she is under our roof, Mistress Boleyn is our guest—nothing more and nothing less. And I have been giving much thought to her comfort. I have decided to remodel the east wing of Gainesborough Hall, to accommodate her and her ladies."

It was the oldest part of the old house, built several hundred years earlier and not lived in for generations. Colonies of bats roosted there, the old high, narrow windows gaped open to the elements and the roof sagged and leaked. No one had tested the soundness of the old oaken floors in many years. But if it was renovated, the east wing could house the royal favorite and her ladies and servants, for it was spacious and had its own kitchens, laundry and great hall. The king and his retinue would occupy the main wing of the house, the one we lived in—and would have to move out of when the royal guest arrived.

I plunged into the work that lay before me with as much enthusiasm as I could rouse, trying not to think about how much there was to do but just to accomplish each task as it arose. I hired dozens of additional servants from among the villages of Netherhampton and Ettinghall, and a cooper and two bakers from Lincoln. Laborers from the local hiring fair were brought in to build the new brewhouse and cut rushes for the floors and drive cattle and sheep into pens for slaughter. The expense was great, and I wrote to my brother Will to ask for a loan. Will had always been generous, especially with me; now that he had control of his wife Anne's properties (though he no longer had Anne herself) he was wealthy as well. He sent me what we needed, and even promised to try to come and help with the preparations if he could.

One morning I was in the hen house where a hundred newly bought hens were sitting on their eggs. The smell of the place revolted me, and I felt my gorge rise. In a moment I was retching into the fresh straw. I returned to the house to lie down, and did not get sick again, but for the rest of the morning I felt queasy and was not able to finish all that I had hoped to accomplish.

The next morning the same sudden nausea came over me, this time in the pantry where I was overseeing the unloading of some barrels of flour and honey. I hurriedly excused myself and was sick in one of the storerooms. Afterwards I went outside into the fresh air and made my way to one of the duck ponds where I could be alone. I had to think; was all the worry over the king's visit to Gainesborough making me ill?

I was very concerned about Ned, who was working alongside the carpenters and masons to repair the rooms of the east wing. They were tearing out old walls and hauling off rotted timbers and ancient stone work from daybreak until sunset, and even after sunset they worked on by torchlight, driven to do their uttermost by Ned's tireless urging. Night after weary night Ned stumbled back to our bedroom, caked in grime and choking from the dust thrown up into the air from the crumbling walls. He had a bad cough, but worked on despite it; when he developed a fever he shrugged it off even though I saw him shivering with chills in the heat of midday.

I was concerned about Ned, yes—but as I sat beside the duck pond I realized that my worry was not the cause of my nausea.

With a thrill the truth came to me: I was carrying Ned's child.

I had not had my monthly flow since long before Cardinal Wolsey came to announce the king's approaching visit. My breasts were tender and sore and I was almost irresistibly sleepy in the afternoon. I had often heard women say that all these things, plus nausea, were signs that a child was coming.

I wished with all my heart that I could talk to my mother about this but she was far away, in attendance on the queen at Whitehall. Ned's mother I had never known, she had been dead for many years. There were midwives in the nearby villages, of course, but I had never had any reason to consult them. Somehow the idea of talking to a stranger, any stranger, about my condition made me hesitant. Yet I longed for a woman to confide in. Having none, I kept my joyful discovery to myself, vowing to tell Ned as soon as he was rested and well again, and the work of renovation was behind him.

It occurred to me that, in all our concern about food and lodging we had neglected to give any thought to King Henry's pastimes. We were at work adding stabling for his horses, but what if he brought hawks with him when he came, and caged ferrets? How many hounds would he have with him? Then there were his entertainments. He liked surprises, impromptu picnics, revels and pageants. Would he expect us to put on such entertainments for him? I didn't see how it would be possible.

One morning when I was lying down, feeling very ill, Mrs. Molsey came in, bustling and angry, with two of the kitchenmaids trailing behind her looking shamefaced.

"These girls will be the death of me, mistress! I'm trying to train them, but they will wander off and neglect their duties. What do you think happened to the load of trussed turkeys that just came from Netherhampton? The dogs came and carried them away, every last one, while the girls weren't looking!"

I almost burst into tears, but stopped myself. I had been taught never to show emotion in front of the servants—except anger, of course, when they failed to perform as they should. I sent the cook and the kitchenmaids out of the room with an impatient wave of my hand.

"Buy more turkeys!" I said. "And pen up the dogs!"

As soon as the women had gone, I gave way to my real feelings and sobbed. I was ill, I felt overwhelmed, I was worried about my husband and I had no one to confide in. I felt wretched—and I did not realize, at the time, what I know now: that a woman who is carrying a child can be overly emotional.

The king would be on our doorstep in only a few weeks and yet, try as we might to make everything ready for him, we were being blocked on every hand. A disease broke out among our milk cows and half of them died. We could not afford to replace them. Mistress Boleyn would have to forego her milk baths. Dogs were stealing our provisions. Poachers were at work in our park, shooting our deer—the very deer the king was coming to hunt. And most recently, we had quarreled with Ned's father.

Sir Thomas Burgh, my father-in-law, had taken no part in all the activity leading up to the king's visit. After all, King Henry was going to be our guest, and ours alone; though he now owned all the farms surrounding our estate, Sir Thomas had his own country house three days' ride from Gainesborough. He was not a part of our everyday lives.

Ned wrote to his father asking to borrow some silver plate and goblets and some lengths of fine damask for the king's table. He received a curt reply. "Alas, all our plate and goblets are in use, and our linens as well, for we are entertaining our kinsman Cuthbert Tunstall, the Bishop of Durham."

Ned became angry when his father's letter arrived. "It's a lie," he said, curling his lips in disgust. "I happen to know that Tunstall is in Rome, on a mission for King Henry. My father is just jealous, and unwilling to help us."

Ned could have left the matter as it stood, but he was too forthright. He wrote to his father and told him, in a respectful but firm tone, that he knew the story about the bishop was a lie and that he would have liked to count on his father's help. I urged Ned not to send the letter but he said it would be dishonest not to, and dispatched a swift rider to carry it to Sir Thomas's estate.

When the reply came back to Ned it was harsh and brusque. No good son dares call his father a liar, Sir Thomas wrote. No dutiful son questions his father's decisions about what to do with his silver plate and goblets or anything else. There was more—about my winning over the king's favor by underhanded means and achieving my own ends at the expense of the Burgh family. Ned was an ungrateful son, but I was the true villainess, according to Sir Thomas, I was the viper being nourished at the family's bosom. I was to blame for everything.

The venomed words and ill feeling could hardly have come at a worse time. Sir Thomas did not know it, nor did Ned, but I was carrying the next heir to Gainesborough. Ned was Sir Thomas's only child. My son would be his first grandchild. It was a season for family unity, not divisiveness.

But we hardly had time to ponder any of this, let alone try to set things straight, for a great storm swept down out of the north and for two days Gainesborough was all but drowned in drenching rain.

Hail and the ceaseless heavy downpour destroyed all our crops and we could not get all the animals to shelter. Streams rose and overflowed their banks, flooding the low-lying outbuildings. Our barns and storage sheds were knee-deep in muddy water. Animal fodder was ruined. We still had what food was stored in the cellars and larders of the main house, for it was built on a hill and the storm waters did not rise above its outer walls. But much else was lost, as day after day the black clouds hung low above us and high winds and lashing rain drove down in ceaseless fury.

Ned, refusing to be deterred in his determination to prepare Gainesborough Hall to receive the king, insisted upon continuing the work of renovating the east wing for Mistress Boleyn and her ladies. Though the lumber was damp and the plaster sodden he urged the laborers on to complete the spacious rooms with their high ceilings and tall windows. Only the decorative stonework for the wide hearths remained to be set in place.

"The stones are still at Netherhampton," Ned told me as he threw his thick felt cloak over his shoulders. "The masons haven't delivered them. I must go and fetch them."

"But how? The roads will be nothing but mud, after all this rain. You'll drown."

"Not if I'm careful."

There was no deterring him. I recognized the look of fierce determination in his eyes, the set of his jaw. I was frightened for him, but I knew it was no use trying to hold him back. I kissed him and saw him off, then watched from our bedchamber window as he rode down the hill and along the muddy road toward Netherhampton, his horse's hooves splashing through deep puddles as he went.

He left in the morning, a dull gray morning dark with the promise of more rain. When he had not returned by early evening I made my way to the stables and ordered one of the grooms to saddle me a horse. The hard rain had stopped, only a sullen drizzle remained. But my clogs sank into the marshy ground in the stable yard, and water dripped from the eaves in a steady trickle.

"Pardon milady, but you cannot mean to ride out on a night like this." It was our steward Daniel, a look of concern on his round face.

"My husband has not come back from Netherhampton. He should have been home hours ago. I must look for him."

"Then I'll go with you." He saddled his own mount and together we started out along the Netherhampton road, Daniel holding a lantern as our horses picked their way carefully past deep ruts and mudholes. We went slowly. Often we stumbled, or rather the horses did, and we held on tightly so as to avoid being thrown off into the quagmire.

After half an hour the sky cleared and the moon rose, a bright moon nearly at the full. It shone down on the wet road, turning it into a pathway of silver.

"No doubt the master stopped the night in the village," Daniel said. "He'll start out for home in the morning."

"I wish that were true. But I know he was in a great hurry to get back with more stones for the new hearths."

Daniel was silent as we went on, the twilight deepening around us. There was no one else on the road, and the only sound we heard was the plodding and plashing of our horses' hooves. After a time I began to think Daniel might be right after all.

We were on a long straight stretch of road when we heard hoofbeats and the clanking and rattling of a cart, its frame and wheels straining as if under a heavy load. We stopped to listen. The hoofbeats grew louder, approaching rapidly. Then, in the distance, we saw a cart pulled by two straining horses, the driver lashing at them with a whip. It was coming directly toward us, far too quickly for safety given the dangerous condition of the narrow road.

I knew at once that it was Ned—and I knew, in the same instant, that something terrible was about to happen. The cart was lurching crazily from side to side, and the horses whinnied with fear when they caught sight of us, standing still in their path.

"Quick, get off the road!" Daniel called out to me and we both kicked our mounts and tried to turn them toward the rock-strewn shoulder. But we were not fast enough. Our horses moved, but not before the cart, having swerved to avoid us, sank into a deep rut, broke a wheel and axle and turned over, crushing the driver under its full weight.

The horses were screaming, the cart wheels spinning in the empty air. I heard a dreadful cry and realized that it came from my own throat.

"Ned! Ned!" I got down off my horse, swearing at her when she would not stand still, and ran to the cart.

All I could see was wreckage. From beneath a mound of whitish stones an arm and hand protruded. Ned's arm and hand. I knelt and grasped the warm hand—and felt a faint pressure against my own fingers. He was alive.

Daniel had cut the terrified cart horses loose from their harness and they were struggling to their feet.

"Daniel! Help me! He's alive!"

With a strength far beyond any strength I knew I possessed I began, with the steward's aid, to free Ned from the weight under which he lay. We pushed away the broken axle and managed, grunting and straining, to throw aside the splintered wreckage of the cart which had shattered into many pieces. There remained the heap of stones. Fortunately they were not immense slabs but brick-sized chunks of rock, which we lifted and tossed onto the road as rapidly as we could. We could hear Ned coughing and struggling for air as gradually his arm and shoulder were exposed to the moonlight, then his sunken chest and finally his dear bleeding face, which was covered with a fine white dust.

"There now, master, we'll have you free in no time," Daniel was saying. "We'll get you home and call Dr. Swetnam over to see to you, and he'll soon have you well again!"

My own face was wet with tears. I bent to kiss Ned again and again, all the while lifting stone after stone and casting them aside. All I could think of as I worked was, let him live, let him live.

I do not know how long Daniel and I worked side by side, or how we managed to lift the groaning Ned, who was by this time unconscious, onto Daniel's horse and tie him there for the journey back to Gainesborough. The moon had nearly set when we finally reached the stable yard, Daniel shouting for the grooms and servants from the house running with lanterns to help us. I must have fainted, for I have no memory of being lifted down off my horse and carried into the house. All I know is that my sleep that night was troubled, broken by dreams of screaming horses and a huge and terrifying mound of stones falling on me and a shining silver path of road, lit by bright moonlight, that led downward and downward into a dark abyss.

6

NED WAS ALIVE—BUT ONLY JUST. HE LAY IN OUR BIG CANOPIED BED, his swollen eyes closed, his face a mass of purple bruises and angry red cuts. As gently as I could, I washed him and spread an ointment over the worst of his wounds. I hardly left his side. I rested on a pallet bed next to the larger one in which Ned slept, and I had my meals brought up to the bedchamber so that there would be no need for me to be away from him for even an hour.

Dr. Swetnam, a burly physician from York with deft hands and an empathetic manner, came to examine Ned daily. He did what he could, which was little enough.

"The broken bones I can bind so that they will heal," the doctor told me. "But what is broken deep inside of him I cannot reach. And without food—well, I think you know what the outcome must be."

Ned was unable to eat, the most he could do was to swallow a little of the wine Dr. Swetnam prepared for him, red wine into which he sprinkled a powder to make Ned sleep.

The doctor patted my hand. "We must ease his pain as much as we can. Meanwhile you need looking after."

He treated my raw, sore hands, full of splinters and cuts from handling the timber and rough-edged stones on the night we found Ned. A heavy stone had fallen on my left foot and the pain made me limp when I walked.

"You need food and rest. You must think of your child."

I looked up at Dr. Swetnam in alarm. No one knew about the child I was carrying. Not even Ned.

"Yes, my dear. Your condition is evident to me, if to no one else. Before long you will not be able to keep your secret."

I was very tired, and longed for sleep, but I continued to watch Ned hour by hour, sitting on the bed, looking down at him while he slept, wiping his poor face with a cool cloth when he sweated with fever and tossed restlessly.

Once, when I had dozed off, I was awakened by the sound of Ned's voice. I was startled. He hadn't spoken since the night his cart overturned.

"My Cat," he was saying, very softly, his voice hoarse. "My sweet Cat." His eyes were open and he seemed to look at me, just for a moment. Then his eyes glazed over and began to close.

"Ned, dear, don't go to sleep yet. I have some good news to tell you."

His eyelids fluttered. I hoped he could hear me.

"God has answered our prayers. Our child is living inside me. Our son."

"Our son." He repeated the words, very faintly. I thought for an instant that he smiled. Then he slept, his breathing ragged.

I wept, I couldn't help weeping. I knew that Ned would never see the baby I would bear. I would have to tell our boy what his father had been like. I would have to try to take Ned's place, to be both mother and father to my fatherless child.

All that night I stayed awake, lying beside Ned in the candlelit room, watching over him. Though I knew he could not hear me I tried my best to tell him how much I loved him. At dawn, when there was nothing more to say, I told a servant to bring in Father Ambrose, a monk from the nearby abbey of St. Mary's who had been waiting patiently to give Ned the last rites. The prayers were said and the ritual concluded. The pungent scent of incense filled the room. I took Ned's limp body in my arms and held him, there on the bed, until the breath no longer came and went in his chest and Father Ambrose told me gently that Ned's soul had flown.

"The Lord giveth and the Lord taketh away," he said as he made the sign of the cross over my poor dear husband. "Blessed be the name of the Lord." The familiar words brought me no comfort. I have no words to describe the pain I felt. I have known no other pain like it, then or since.

I slept then, the deep sleep of exhaustion, and when I woke I did what was necessary to arrange for Ned's funeral mass and burial in Gainesborough church. Father Ambrose and Daniel helped me. I had sent my brother Will a letter telling him what had happened. I hoped he would come to be with me and offer me support. But instead I got a letter in reply. Will was with our mother in Richmond, far to the south, and could not come to Gainesborough. Mother was ill and needed him.

Will had done one thing for me, however. He had taken it upon himself to tell Cardinal Wolsey of Ned's death in hopes that the royal visit to Gainesborough would be canceled or at least postponed. But the cardinal was adamant: nothing could alter the king's plans.

Exhausted as I was, grieving for my beloved husband and lonely and sad without him, I tried to rouse myself to return to the great task that had taken Ned's life: the task of making Gainesborough Hall ready to receive King Henry and his traveling court.

I tried—but my strength was not equal to the task. I had no appetite. I felt ill. I brooded about my fatherless child. And I cried, a dozen times a day, two dozen. I could not stop the tears. They seemed to flow from some deep well of inconsolable sorrow.

Even now, in the terrible isolation of my bereavement, I did not tell anyone that I was pregnant. It was easy enough to hide my condition. Dr. Swetnam had guessed the truth, but no one else suspected it. My belly did not yet bulge very much and my gowns and the shapeless aprons I wore over them concealed all. I hoarded my secret, as a miser hoards a treasure. The baby was all I had. All I had that was mine alone. All I had left of Ned.

The days were dwindling until the king was due to arrive. One afternoon I heard a commotion in the courtyard and Daniel's voice came drifting up to me, through my window, shouting to the grooms. I threw on a shawl over my plain gown and made my way downstairs.

Through the open doorway came my father-in-law Sir Thomas Burgh, in a doublet of fine dark blue brocade and silken hose, a gleaming gold-embossed sword hanging from his belt. Behind him came my uncle William, tall and imposing, a frown of displeasure on his broad manly features. Behind them came half a dozen men I did not recognize. They wore the uniform of the Calais Spears.

Neither Lord Thomas nor my uncle acknowledged me, but pushing past me, strode into the salon and began giving orders to the servants.

"Remove the wench," Sir Thomas said to two of the men he had brought with him when I protested.

"I am no wench. I am the lady of this manor."

No one leaped to my defense. I was taken by my arms and led roughly to my bedchamber and locked in.

I realized, in that moment, that it had been Ned who ruled Gainesborough Hall and not me, and that I had no real authority there—at least not while Sir Thomas was present and in command. Nearly all the servants on our staff had been Sir Thomas's servants before Ned became master; some had served Ned's grandfather Lord John Burgh before Ned was born. Their obedience belonged more naturally to Sir Thomas than to me. Besides, Sir Thomas's soldiers frightened the Gainesborough servants into obedience.

Hours later I heard a key turn in the lock and my father-in-law came in. I stood and confronted him.

"How dare you invade my house and make me a prisoner!"

He made a dismissive gesture with one hand.

"I am here at the command of Cardinal Wolsey, and by his authority. The house must be made ready for his majesty. You and my son were inadequate."

"Your late son."

Sir Thomas ignored my interruption.

"You and my son have done a poor job. I shall do what you could not."

His eyes were cold. Looking at him, I thought, not for the first time, how little Ned had resembled him. Ned's handsome face was frank and boyishly eager, his brown eyes warm and lively and capable of deep tenderness. Sir Thomas's face was feline, wary, shrewd and forbidding. Ned looked like his mother, whose miniature portrait he had kept in our bedroom.

"You will remain here in your room until the king has come and gone. I will say that you are indisposed. I do not know what influence you have with the king, or how you tricked him into giving his blessing to your marriage to my son and making Ned master of Gainesborough. Your means of bewitching the king is a mystery to me. You are clever, anyone can see that. You are lovely to look at. Yet there are many clever, good-looking women in and around the court. What gives you more of his favor than any other woman?"

He paused. He had allowed his resentment to make him vehement—and voluble, which was unlike him. He needed to regain his composure. When he spoke again it was in a calm, dispassionate tone.

"At any rate, I cannot take the risk of allowing you to be in the king's presence, or near it. You will stay in your room."

"But King Henry is coming to Gainesborough Hall chiefly because of me."

"I thought he was coming for the hunting."

"He can hunt anywhere. He chose Gainesborough as a compliment to me—and to Ned of course."

I saw Sir Thomas wince slightly at the mention of Ned's name. He turned to go, then, as he reached the door, he looked back at me.

"Don't think for a moment that I am unaware of what happened to my son. You drove him to do more than he could. You wore him out. You sent him to Netherhampton on the day he died. You caused his accident." He paused. In a low voice he added, "You killed him."

"No, no. You're wrong! He drove himself. He didn't know when to stop. I urged him to rest. I begged him not to go to Netherhampton that day, but he wouldn't listen." I broke down. For a moment my sobbing was the only sound in the bedchamber. My father-in-law stared at me stonily.

"I loved Ned. I would never have done anything to hurt him. You must believe me."

"I believe this. You, Catherine Parr, have brought grave misfortune on us all."

"My name is Milady Burgh. Kindly address me properly."

Sir Thomas cursed at me and left, slamming the door and locking it.

I felt shaky and unsteady on my feet. My heart was pounding and my head was beginning to ache. I lay down on the bed and tried to sleep, but restless thoughts kept me awake. What was I to do? I was at the mercy of Ned's merciless father, who hated me so much that he had convinced himself that I was responsible for Ned's death. The thought was so monstrous, so terribly wrong. Would Sir Thomas have treated me any differently had he known about the baby?

A new and very worrisome thought came to me. What future was I to have? How was I to provide for my child, now that Ned was gone? Surely my son would be the heir to Gainesborough Hall and all its lands and rents. But what if my child was a girl? She would inherit the property, but it would come under the control of her nearest male relative. Would that be my brother Will, or, more likely, her grandfather Sir Thomas?

I began to be frightened. I was shivering, and I drew the warm wool blankets over myself. I tried to sleep but my doubts and anxieties kept me awake. For what seemed like hours I lay in an unsettled state, distressed and uneasy.

I was roused from my dark musings by a pounding on my bedchamber door.

"A message from the king. For the Lady Catherine."

I sat up and, throwing the blanket aside, reached into my trunk for my morning gown. Hurriedly I fastened it around my waist and pulled on the sleeves, not bothering to attach them to the bodice. I tucked my hair under a French hood as best I could and stepped to the door.

"I am ready," I called out. "I cannot open the door from the inside." I heard the key turning in the lock. The door opened.

Before me stood a man in the king's livery. He held out a document to me. I could see that it bore the mark of an official seal.

"I was sent to deliver this to you, milady. And to you alone."

There was no sign of Sir Thomas or my uncle William in the corridor. Where were they?

I took the document, broke the seal and read the few words written on the page.

"The king having been informed that recent rains have spoiled the hunting in the neighborhood of Gainesborough Hall, has decided to hunt elsewhere for the present."

That was all. Those few words. The king was not coming after all. All our efforts and expense. All Ned's days and nights of labor. His accident. His suffering. His death.

I felt my knees give way under me and reached out to clutch the nearest object—which happened to be the carved oak bedpost—for support.

"Where is—my steward?" I managed to ask. "Send me my steward."

With a bow the royal messenger left and in a few moments Daniel Frith appeared in the doorway.

"Daniel, the king is not coming." My voice was very low. I could barely speak the words.

"I know, mistress. I have ordered all the preparations for his visit to cease. The messenger informed us."

"Where is Sir Thomas?"

"He has gone to his estate, and your uncle went with him."

"Oh Daniel, it was all for nothing! Everything we tried to do. Poor Ned's death. It was all for nothing!"

"Surely not, milady. The king is no doubt most grateful—"

"The king cares nothing for any of us! We are pawns on his chessboard, flies in his soup! We matter not at all to the king!"

I felt my face growing hot and saw that Daniel was looking at me in alarm.

"Don't distress yourself so, mistress! I urge you to try to be calm."

But calmness was the farthest thing from the feelings churning within me at that moment. I was aware of a great rage building within me. Rage against the waste of all our efforts—and above all, the waste of Ned's precious life.

I stood, and swore a great oath.

"Damn King Henry to hell, and all his court!" I shouted at the top of my lungs.

Then I collapsed.

When I awoke it was night. I was in bed, in my candlelit bedchamber, and Dr. Swetnam was sitting quietly by my bedside. Two of my maids were also in the room, murmuring to one another and fussing with some linens.

I was aware of pain in my belly.

The doctor was looking at me. He reached over and put his hand on my forehead.

"You must sleep," he said. "And you must drink this for the pain."

He put a goblet to my lips and I drank from it obediently.

"Is this what you gave Ned to drink?"

"Yes."

"Am I going to die?"

"No. You are going to live. But you have lost the child. I'm sorry."

The maids had ceased their chatter. They were not looking at me. Only the crackling of the fire in the hearth broke the silence in the dim room. That and the sound of my broken sobbing, my tears falling for the baby that would never live, for the last of Ned that had died with it, and for myself, alone and bereft, and wishing that I too were dead.

7

I WAS SHOCKED BY THE SIGHT OF MY MOTHER WHEN WILL BROUGHT HER to Gainesborough Hall to see me three months after Ned's death.

Illness had aged her. Her beautiful red hair was lusterless and graying, her fine white skin veined and lined, and her lips were cracked by the harsh dry October wind that blew in ceaseless gusts up and down our valley. Though she wore a fur-lined gown as she was carried into the house I could see that she was shivering, and I gave orders for more logs to be laid on the fire and mugs of hot cider to be brought for mother and Will and their servants.

Will embraced me and handed me a bouquet of flowers—though where he had found flowers at this time of year I couldn't imagine. He looked well-fed and prosperous in his thick felt cloak and blood-red doublet of fine cut velvet and his hat with a gleaming garnet and white feathered plume. He had been of the greatest help to me since Ned's death, for my hostile father-in-law had seized all the rents from Gainesborough Hall leaving me with no income and Will had been sending me much needed purses of coins each month to pay my servants and buy what I needed.

I smiled at my brother and bent down to smell the flowers he had given me. I felt a tickle in my nose, then an irresistible urge to sneeze. I sneezed—again and again, making Will laugh.

"Oh no, not that sneezing powder again," my mother said. "He's used it on me and everyone else I know."

I threw down the flowers and blew my nose into my silk handkerchief. While I recovered Will settled mother and himself into a long bench with cushions in front of the fire, chuckling to himself as he did so. I noticed that he had to lift mother out of her carrying chair and set her down on the bench. No one had told me that she was having trouble walking. With a final wipe of my nose I went over to mother and hugged her and kissed her dry cheek.

"From what I hear," mother said when I had sat down, "you haven't been taking very good care of yourself. Now I see it for myself. Look at you! Have you no better gown? I remember that one from three years ago."

"I am in mourning, mother."

"To show respect is necessary, yes. And your husband was a good man, by all accounts. I liked him—even though I always thought you ought to marry his grandfather."

"Yes mother, I know."

"And as to the child—well, we women all have our private sorrows. Best not to dwell on a loss like that. Heaven knows I have been through many such losses with our dear queen." I had written to mother to tell her about the child I had lost. But I had sworn her to secrecy. Apart from Dr. Swetnam and two or three of my chambermaids, who were discreet, only she and Will knew about the baby.

"Are you still able to serve the queen?" I asked, wondering how mother would perform the duties of a lady-in-waiting when she was unable to walk.

"Queen Catherine has given mother a long leave of absence from her post," Will told me, and I could tell from his tone that it was likely to be a permanent leave. "With her usual stipend. Mother has come to live with me for the time being."

I nodded, thinking how kind Queen Catherine was and how glad I was that Will was such a good son to our mother. Of our sister Nan we said nothing. She had married Sir William Herbert, an ambitious young soldier, and was keeping a cordial distance from us. Why, I didn't know for certain, although I had my suspicions. The scandal over our sister-in-law

Anne Bourchier, and my own early widowhood and conflict with my father-in-law made Will and me both objects of gossip. Nan was a deeply conventional girl. Respectability mattered far more to her than family loyalty. She did not want to be closely associated with us.

Our mugs of cider arrived and we drank the hot cinnamon-scented brew, mother wrapping her chilled fingers around her mug and holding it up to her face so that the steam bathed her cheeks and forehead.

"What of you, Will?" I asked after a pause. "Have you heard anything at all from Anne?"

"Best leave that subject alone," my mother said sharply.

"No, mother. Cat has a right to know what has become of her sister-in-law. Of course I have seen nothing of her for nearly two years. The last I heard she was living with a renegade priest and having his children."

I shook my head in wonderment. "Whatever would Grandmother Fitzhugh say?"

"That she was a heretic." We all laughed.

"Anne's departure has made Will a wealthy man, as I think you realize," mother remarked. "He has inherited her property, just as if she had died."

"I hope she has something to live on, at least," I said, remembering my own uncomfortable situation and trusting that Anne would not be left in want.

"I believe she has a small allowance. I would send her something myself, if I knew where she was."

Will spoke without bitterness. Apparently he was reconciled to his situation, as a married man but without a wife. But then, if what Anne had told me was true, he was probably happier without her.

After supper that evening, when mother had gone to bed and Will and I were lingering by the fire, I asked him about mother's condition.

"As you can see, her legs have given out. She can walk a little, if she has someone on either side of her to steady her and catch her when she falls. Her mind is clear though her tongue is more and more tart. We humor her, I do my best to make her laugh and forget her fainting spells and the soreness in her back, which sometimes keeps her up all night."

"The sneezing powder."

"The sneezing powder, yes. And the mechanical mole I bought to amuse her when I was in Saxony—they make the most remarkable things there—and the candles that you can't blow out and the drippy yellow stuff that looks just like egg yolk that I manage to spill all over her gowns now and then."

I smiled, remembering what it was like to live with Will.

"How can she be so ill, when she's not yet forty?"

Will shook his head. "We've called in the king's own physicians, and the queen's. They all say different things. No one has a name for her disease."

"I've heard that the best physicians come from Italy."

"We had an Italian one, a monk from Salerno. He said she had a wasting disease caused by too much bilious humor. He said she would die in three months. But it has been a year, and she still lives."

"Her mind is always active. She has been thinking a lot about you, as you will find out tomorrow. She has good news for you."

"Tell me."

"I'll let her have that pleasure."

I did not press him, but was very curious. Was I going to be liberated from my uncomfortable situation at Gainesborough Hall?

Everything about the house and grounds reminded me of Ned, and of the future I had hoped for with him. My father-in-law was doing all he could to force me to leave. He had threatened to evict me, and was suing for ownership of the manor, though he had taken no direct action against me as yet. I had no doubt that the day would come when I would have to fight for my right to stay in the house. I dreaded that day.

The following morning I was relieved to see that mother looked brighter and more rested as we sat down to our morning meal of white bread and kid stew. She ate heartily, and drank her flagon of small ale with relish.

"Now, Cat, it is time to speak of your future," she said when she had finished, her manner brisk. "It's no good your moping here. I advise you to come to an arrangement with Middle Burgh—I mean Sir Thomas— and let him buy the house and estate from you. I think he would prefer that to going to court. Once all that is settled there is a post waiting for you. I have arranged for you to join the court of young Henry Fitzroy, Duke of Richmond, the king's son."

The king's son, I thought. And Bessie Blount's. The boy I saw in King Henry's arms when I was a child in the Golden Valley. How old would he be now? Ten or twelve?

"Lord Fitzroy will soon be married," mother was saying. "You will be lady-in-waiting to his bride. There are great changes at court, you know. Queen Catherine, bless her, will be divorced. I have no doubt of it. Princess Mary will be disinherited. The king will marry Mistress Boleyn. If she has a child it will inherit the throne. But if she does not, then young Henry Fitzroy will become the next king. And you, my dear, will be lady-in-waiting to the future Queen of England."

8

I REMEMBERED MY MOTHER'S WORDS AS I RODE TOWARD THE MANOR OF Sheriff Hutton a week later, escorted by my faithful Daniel Frith and some half-dozen of my familiar servants from Gainesborough Hall. I was to serve the king's son Henry Fitzroy, Duke of Richmond, and his future wife. One day they might be king and queen.

But as soon as my traveling party rode into the courtyard of the large manor house I was reminded that the change of reigns, when it came, was likely to occur far in the future.

For there in the courtyard, bending back a thick ashwood longbow, was the tall, golden-haired King Henry, looking as strong and fit and youthful as any man I had ever seen. And beside him was a thin stripling, doing his best to bend back his own small bow but failing again and again to launch his arrow.

Man and boy were dressed alike, in the green jerkin and brown cloth trousers of foresters. Seeing them I was reminded of the long-ago day at the Field of Cloth of Gold when King Henry had carried his baby son in his arms to show him off to his court. Then the king and the boy had been dressed alike in suits of cloth of gold; now they were alike in being disguised in forest green.

They were greatly unalike, however, in their abilities. Young Henry Fitzroy was small for his eleven years, with narrow shoulders and spindly legs. When he attempted to draw the bow he clenched his teeth and drew his lips back into a grimace of ferocity, giving evidence of a considerable strength of will. Yet determination was not enough; his muscles were too weak to draw the heavy bow. Time after time he made a heroic effort. Time after time he failed.

I saw the king look over at the boy with an expression of resignation. He said little, he preferred to encourage and teach by example.

"Here, boy." He adjusted young Fitzroy's slender fingers into a tighter grip. He touched his narrow back, at a point between the shoulder blades. "Pull from here."

Without waiting to watch the boy's effort he strode a few feet away, took up his own bow, and drew back the hempen string with practiced ease. The arrow flew to the target, and struck its center, setting off a round of polite applause from the onlookers. Fitzroy looked at the ground. The king, not unkindly, patted him on the shoulder as he walked past him.

"Never mind, boy. We'll try you at tennis," I heard King Henry say as he walked nonchalantly off toward the stables, his figure magnificent even from the rear.

I was met at the door of the manor house by the head usher who led me to a small but well furnished sitting room and bedchamber. I settled in.

Officially I was to be a lady-in-waiting to Henry Fitzroy's wife-to-be, but since he was still unmarried I was given the very light duty of watching over the stillroom, that aromatic place where crushed flowers and spices were made into toilet water and perfume and cakes of incense. I had observed the operation of the queen's stillroom at Windsor and was familiar with how the sweet-scented liquids were blended. The stillroom servants, experts at their craft, would do the mixing and boiling and cooking in the perfuming-pan, I would merely oversee their labors and approve the finished products.

I began my duties conscientiously, but the king's presence at the manor disturbed and distracted me. I felt nothing but hatred toward King Henry. I blamed him for Ned's death and for the loss of my child. All our troubles had come upon us because of him. Because of him, and his vast and greedy household. The hundreds of royal servants in his entourage were not staying at Sheriff Hutton of course, they were housed in a nearby monastery with wide lands and many outbuildings. Henry and Mistress Boleyn and various members of their household made the journey to Henry Fitzroy's miniature establishment each morning and returned each evening after supper.

I had been told that the king intended to keep Christmas in the North with his son and then return to Greenwich for New Year's Day. I did my best to stay out of King Henry's presence, thinking I could avoid him until his visit was at an end. But when Lord Perpoynte, appointed Lord of Misrule for the holiday merrymaking, came to see me in the stillroom I knew that my intentions were about to be thwarted.

"Milady Burgh," he said, inclining his head to me out of politeness though his rank was considerably higher than mine, "our lord the king desires you to take part in the pageant of the Castle of True Hearts on Christmas Eve. You will play the part of one of the maidens dwelling in the castle."

"But I am not a maiden, as the king well knows. I am a widow. And I am still in mourning."

"The pageant is only make believe. If I can play the part of a swan (which I am being asked to do) then you can be a maiden—for one evening."

I could not go against the king's wishes and so I found myself in the grand salon taking instruction from a lithe, energetic French dancing-master along with the five other maidens in the pageant. I felt a slight tremor of distaste when I realized that one of the maidens was Mistress Anne Boleyn.

I had never spoken to her or had any direct contact with her, yet my hatred of the king, and my long-held loyalty to Queen Catherine (whose namesake I always remembered myself to be) made me dislike her.

Anne had been made a part of the royal circle, yet she did not belong there. She was usurping the place of the queen. She was part of all that was awry with the court. I could not help feeling disdainful toward her, while at the same time sensing the undeniable allure of her dark looks and natural grace. Mistress Boleyn was at that time a mature woman of thirty or thirty-one, while I was barely nineteen. Yet I had been a wife— and very nearly a mother. Anne was still waiting to achieve those goals nearly every woman shared.

She was staring at my feet in their dark green velvet slippers as the six of us repeated the dance steps we were being taught.

"This girl must keep up," Anne said to the dancing-master. "She is lame."

She was right. I was doing my best to execute the steps in time to the music of the drummer and piper but my injury from the falling stone on the night of Ned's accident hindered me. My foot dragged and I limped when I took a step onto my left leg. It was only a slight limp, but to a precise and light-footed dancer like Anne it must have seemed a major handicap.

The Frenchman stared at my foot.

"Turn," he said to me.

I turned.

"Walk."

I took a few steps.

He shrugged.

"It is nothing. No one will notice. Besides, she looks well. No one will look at her feet."

Anne's expression hardened. "I want her out."

"I fear the king will disapprove. He asked especially for her."

This surprised me. And worried me. Why should King Henry care whether I danced in his Christmas Eve pageant or not?

Anne did not challenge my presence further, but she criticized me unmercifully. One of the other dancers, a heavy, clumsy girl with a sweet face named Avice Odell, was much slower than I was to learn the steps of the dance and was close to tears by the end of our two-hour practice. Yet Anne ignored Avice and took out all her exasperation on me.

"That girl is still slow," she snapped after the dancing-master dismissed us to visit the dressmaker to be measured for our costumes. "If you can't replace her, at least give her extra practice."

My foot was hurting badly after all the dancing and the last thing I wanted was extra practice.

"Not today, thank you," I said to the dancing-master, loudly enough for Anne to hear.

"You'll do as I order you."

I faced Anne squarely. "You are not queen yet," was all I said—and all I had to say. Furious, Anne reached out as if to slap me but with surprising quickness for such a clumsy dancer Avice stepped between us and grasped Anne's beringed hand. Avice was not only heavy but muscular and strong. With an oath Anne managed to wrench her hand away and leave the room quickly.

Avice was not present at our next practice, and when on Christmas Eve the pageant of the Castle of True Hearts was held, there were only five maidens in the castle and not six. I learned from Daniel Frith, who kept himself well informed about what went on, that Anne had removed Avice from the pageant and had tried to remove me as well but the king forbade it.

"You're a favorite with him," Daniel said.

"Nonsense. It's only that I've taken part in these disguisings before. I know something of how they are performed." Daniel merely grinned and said nothing.

I was nervous as I dressed for the pageant on Christmas Eve in my gown of crimson cloth of silver embroidered with small jangling bells and pearls. I would see the king. And he would see me dance, something he very much wanted. The French dancing-master had cautioned us that King Henry, who loved to surprise people, might suddenly decide to take part in the pageant along with us, perhaps playing one of the knights who defended the Castle of True Hearts against its attackers.

"If he decides to put on a costume at the last minute, and if you recognize him, say nothing," we were cautioned. "Do not betray him. Just let him do as he likes."

The pageant was to be performed after supper, in the great hall of the manor house. The king and his son sat at an elevated table, the hundreds of guests ranged along the length of trestle tables below him. With the supper at an end, all watched eagerly for the entertainment to begin. At a signal from the Lord of Misrule the immense, thirty-foot-high castle in which we maidens were concealed rolled slowly into the hall on wheels. In the candlelight the walls and turrets of painted wood looked like stone, the moat of blue silk shimmered like real water. Imagination took hold, and the make-believe castle became, in the minds of the spectators, a miniature world.

"Behold the Castle of True Hearts, wherein the maidens Purity, Constancy, Chastity, Virginity and Fidelity are kept safe from danger." The Lord of Misrule spoke solemnly as the mechanical drawbridge was lowered and we descended onto the dance floor. The musicians began to play, and we went through the first of our stately dances, a slow pavane.

We must have looked well, for I heard several people catch their breath as we twirled and bowed and when we finished there was loud applause.

I looked out toward the raised table where the king and Henry Fitzroy had been sitting, but saw only the boy. The king had vanished.

"The Castle of True Hearts," the Lord of Misrule was saying, "often comes under assault. Wild Men of the forest pursue the maidens, who must be defended by the Knights Loyal."

Right on cue the Wild Men appeared, fearsome figures, their bodies and faces painted green, their hair matted and tangled, wearing nothing but loincloths. Capering and shouting in their own fantastic language, they came toward us menacingly, and even though I knew full well that the pageant was only make-believe I could not help feeling frightened.

Barbaric, near-naked, alien with their long green limbs and tossing snarled hair, their eyes bright in their green faces, the Wild Men were creatures out of a nightmare. The tallest and most muscular of them ran up to me and, with a yell, lifted me up in his arms and carried me away from the castle and into a dim corridor where torches burning in wall sconces gave the only light.

So swiftly did it happen that I barely had time to cry out. I was dizzy, I felt my stomach drop and lurch as the Wild Man seized me. I was aware of the scent of his warm green flesh—the scent of verdigris with which his body was painted. His arms were strong, his muscles hard and round.

"So ho, Lady Cat," the Wild Man murmured, his mouth close to my ear.

It was the king. I knew his voice, that soft and caressing tone he could adopt when he chose to. I had failed to recognize him, despite his height and well-muscled flesh. I was at once on edge, on guard. This was the man I hated—yet my body sought to yield to the strong arms that held me, the handsome, savage face that bent toward me.

I stiffened.

"Put me down. We are not in the pageant now."

"Are we not? Come now, you know there is a drama playing itself out between us."

He tightened his grip on me, still holding me in his arms. Though my body felt pleasure in the embrace I gathered my strength and, using my arms, pushed with all my might against his broad chest.

"Let me go!"

He set me down then, but almost before I could find my footing he kissed me.

I had never known such a kiss, hard and insistent. He kissed me as if he owned me, which in a sense he did. He was my sovereign, I his subject. I was his to command. I could not help but respond. I had loved kissing Ned, Ned who was all melting sweetness. But this Henry, this Wild Man, was all savage fire!

When at last the kiss ended the king looked down at me. "I told you once, virgins excite me."

I was no virgin, to be sure. Yet I had the feeling, in that moment, that the king had touched a part of me that no man had ever reached before. The Wild Man had taken the castle, and all its defenses were down.

It was such a disturbing feeling that I didn't let myself feel it for long. When a group of masked dancers hurried past us along the corridor, about to begin the next pageant, I took advantage of the commotion to leave the king and run back to the anteroom where we maidens had dressed in our finery. I felt ashamed because my gown was soiled, smeared with verdigris from the king's body. When I entered the anteroom I saw that Mistress Boleyn was there. A servant was unlacing the tight bodice of her gown. She glanced at me, saw the smears of green on my gown and sleeves and turned away.

Had she spied King Henry among the Wild Men and did she realize that he had carried me away from the others? What would she say if she knew the king had kissed me?

I confess I stole a glance at Mistress Boleyn while I changed my gown. I wanted to see whether what was said about her was true: that she had an enormous mole on her neck and that she had six fingers. I caught sight of a dark round spot on her neck that could have been a mole, but it was small. Her hands moved too rapidly for me to catch sight of the rumored sixth finger.

When I had changed my gown and returned the soiled one to the Mistress of the Robes (who gave me a very sour look) I went back into the great hall where another pageant was just concluding. The performers were acknowledging their applause when the Lord of Misrule came up to me.

"I should like you to join a few of the king's party for cards. We will be in the duke's apartments."

Ill at ease, I made my way to the suite of rooms occupied by Henry

Fitzroy and took my place at the gaming table. The king, no longer a Wild Man but his usual self, a blithe, handsome monarch in a doublet of light blue taffeta with silver trim, sat with his son and Mistress Boleyn and a dozen others at the long table.

"Now, boy," King Henry was saying to his son, "you've lost to me at the butts, and at bowls, and in the tiltyard. You can't seem to shoot a stag and you have no ear for the lute. Can you at least beat me at hazard?"

We often played hazard, I had learned the game as a young girl, watching my mother and Queen Catherine's other ladies-in-waiting play. I imagined that I was a good player.

"Give me the dice, father, and you'll soon see," said Henry Fitzroy.

The king took from his pocket a gleaming pair of silver dice, indented with black onyx to indicate the numbers on each face.

"These dice go to the winner," he said, "as a prize. Let the play begin!"

Despite the formality of the occasion, with no less an opponent than the king at the head of the table, we were soon drawn into the game and forgot ourselves in the heat of play.

"Double aces!"

"Six and five!"

"Ten shillings on a deuce!"

One after another we cast the dice and laid our wagers. King Henry played with more zest than skill, I noticed. Mistress Boleyn played with a grim focus, determined to win at all costs and wagering heavily—from a purse of coins the king handed her. When she lost, she swore, making the king laugh.

"There there, Brownie, you sound like a ferryman on the Thames or one of my gunners, not like a lady!" He called her Brownie, which my mother had told me was a version of her nickname at the French court. The French king Francis had called her Brunet, and the name stuck.

"By all that's holy I'll make you take back that insult! Four and four!" she called out, and cast the dice boldly.

She won. No one cheered, as they did when the king or his son won their toss. The silence was uncomfortable. Mistress Boleyn collected her winnings and tossed the dice to me with such careless roughness that they nearly fell off the table.

What possessed me then was something I'll never understand. I challenged her. I looked straight at her, wagered every coin I had, and called out, "Four and four again!"

It was an impossibly bold and risky bet, and of course when I cast the dice they came up two and six, and I lost. My face felt hot. I murmured, "With your majesty's permission, I will withdraw," and got up to leave the table.

"Wait! Stay a little, Milady Burgh. I'll stake you to another play or two."

He tossed me a purse of coins. It fell heavily on the table in front of me. I thought, there is enough in that purse for me to live on for a year.

"Take it," the king said. "I admire a courageous player. I'm something of a wild man myself."

He winked at me, and I blushed, though my face was already red.

"My mother," Henry Fitzroy remarked to his father, "is a skillful player. But she knows better than to overplay her hand. Or risk too much on a single throw."

He meant to nettle both me and Mistress Boleyn with this remark, and everyone at the table knew it. His mother Bessie Blount had never aspired to becoming queen, as Mistress Boleyn clearly did.

"Your mother was a whore."

"There there, Brownie, don't go too far."

I passed the dice to Henry Fitzroy, who with remarkable self-possession in one so young, kept silence as he took the dice and shook them.

"Double aces!" he called out, his eyes on Mistress Boleyn. He lost. He had wagered heavily, and now had nothing left. To everyone's embarrassment, he began to cry.

The king put his hand on his son's shaking shoulder.

"There there, boy. Hold on."

He reached for the dice and shook them, still holding onto Fitzroy's shoulder.

"I wager for the honor of Bessie Blount, fifty gold pieces."

Murmurs of approval greeted this announcement, and all around the table bets were laid. I put down a gold crown from the king's purse of coins as my bet. Mistress Boleyn was the only one who staked no wager. Her face was stony.

"Double aces!" the king called out. He cast the dice, watched them roll, and then let out a bellow of joy. There was loud applause, and everyone took up their winnings. Henry Fitzroy smiled through his tears.

The king rose, to indicate that the play was at an end. We all stood with him.

"Now, who has won the prize of these silver dice?"

"You, your highness!" came the response from half a dozen of those at the table.

"The Duke of Richmond!" shouted a few voices loyal to the young Henry Fitzroy.

"I think tonight the prize goes to the lady with the courage to risk all. Milady Burgh."

He handed me the gleaming dice and I curtseyed deeply.

"Your highness honors me."

I looked up into his eyes as I rose. He was smiling. The party began to disperse.

"Watch out for those dice," he said in an undertone before he moved away from me toward the waiting Mistress Boleyn. "They're rigged."

9

THE FIRST TIME I MET JOHN NEVILLE, LORD LATIMER HE CAME TO SHERIFF Hutton with my distant kinsman Cuthbert Tunstall, Bishop of Durham, to tell me that my dear mother had died.

Though I had been expecting this news for some time, as Will wrote me that mother had grown progressively weaker and weaker, still I was very sad to learn that she was finally gone and in my earliest memories of John I see him through a veil of tears.

My relative the bishop was not solicitous of my grief. I had barely begun to take in the lamentable news when Lord Tunstall unrolled a document and proceeded to read me a list of mother's possessions which I had inherited.

"She has left you her pearls, her pendant miniature of King Henry and Queen Catherine, her rosary beads adorned with gold that were a gift from the queen and her bed of purple satin paneled in cloth of gold, to be presented to you on your wedding day."

"But my wedding day is long past," I managed to say.

"Her intent was that you be given the bed on your next wedding day. Until then I shall retain it as executor of her estate."

"I have some documents for you to sign," the bishop went on, drawing out more papers from a leather pouch.

"Not now, Bertie," John said. "Can't you see the girl is upset?"

"Girls are always upset over something. These documents have to be signed, and signed now. I assume you can sign your name?" he asked me.

His condescension piqued my pride. I replied in flawless Latin, "Not only can I sign my name, I can translate Vergil, and quote Saint Augustine, and no doubt correct your grammar!"

"The girl's a wonder!" said John Neville, with a surprised pleasure in his small blue eyes—eyes that, I now noticed, were surrounded with a fretwork of wrinkles and had red pouches beneath them.

"She's wonderfully ill-mannered," the bishop remarked, unsmiling. "I had no idea Maud's older girl was so badly reared. The younger one seems acceptable enough." His light, dismissive tone irked me, but I was too wretched, thinking of mother, to challenge him. He placed the documents in front of me and called for a servant to bring writing materials.

"Just sign your name on these, no need to add any quotation from Saint Augustine or make grammatical corrections. I'll leave you to do it, meanwhile I'm going to greet the young Duke of Richmond."

He left me alone with John Neville, who was scratching his bald head.

"My dear girl," he was saying, "I'm truly sorry for the dreadful news we bring. Bertie and I were on our way to a meeting of the Council of the North and we received a message for you in the pouch of letters from court. Since Sheriff Hutton was on our way, and since Bertie is your mother's executor and kinsman, we thought we would stop and see you."

He paused, looking over at me kindly. "I hate bringing anyone bad news. Especially when it concerns family. I've had my own share. My first wife died bringing my daughter Margaret into the world. My second wife—may she rot in hell!—ran off and left me and then died soon thereafter. My own dear mother died of grief at the news."

I watched him as he spoke, his agitation a distraction from my sorrow. I supposed he was about my father's age—or rather, the age my father would have been had he lived. He was dressed more soberly than most noblemen, who tended to imitate the king and wear costly and showy embroidered doublets in rich reds and blues and greens with flashing jeweled buttons and thick gold rings and chains. His doublet was gray, his hat and hose black and his only ornament, a gold wedding band, held no jewel.

A servant brought in a tray with ink, quills and a knife.

"Perhaps you'd better sign these now, so Bertie will not bother you about them later."

I managed to read through the papers, which were copies of my mother's will and acknowledgments of receipt for my inherited goods. John sharpened a quill for me, and I signed my name to each. Though he was a stranger to me, I felt comforted to have him at my side as I wrote, and I told him so.

"I knew your father, you know. In the old days, when he was at court. I always admired his energy. I haven't got it, myself. Never did have. I always seem to be behind with everything." He smiled wanly, then got to his feet.

"Now then, I expect you'll want to be by yourself. I'll just take these papers to Bertie for you, shall I?"

"Thank you. That would be very kind."

He patted my hand. "Look after yourself, my dear." He gathered up the documents and left.

For several months after my mother's death I got into the habit of retreating each day to the quiet of the pear orchard in search of comfort. I wore around my neck the rosary mother had left me, and read the Psalms of David with their words of healing and strength. I even began composing some meditations on the psalms, imagining that I had arrived at insights that might be of use to others.

But I was careful to tell no one of my reading of the psalms in a forbidden English translation or of my written meditations. Religion had become dangerously controversial, with many people, especially in the North of England, cleaving to the traditional beliefs of the church of Rome and others eager to espouse the reforming views of Martin Luther, who had been excommunicated by the pope and who taught his followers to read the Bible in their own tongue and to put their faith in its teachings rather than in the corrupt church of Rome.

It was a confusing time, for King Henry, always in the past a faithful son of the church, was challenging the pope while claiming to be true to the faith. He condemned Martin Luther and his followers yet at the same time he refused to accept what the pope said about his marriage to Queen Catherine. The church was telling the king he must keep his wife and honor his marriage but the king had parted from his queen and forced her to live apart from him. And I knew from my own encounters with him how free he was with his desires. And was I not serving at the court of his bastard son, a son who, everyone assumed, would one day be king?

I spent my mornings in the stillroom, amid the pungent fragrances of roses and gillyflowers, marjoram and musk. In the afternoons, when the weather was not too raw, I walked to the pear orchard, my books and writing papers under my arm, and read and wrote and pondered.

Daniel found me there one day and greeted me.

"Come now, milady, you spend too much time alone. Come and watch the young duke compete. There's a tournament to be held this afternoon. Boys from all over the North are coming."

I went with Daniel to the tilting ground that had been built for Henry Fitzroy's use. It was a faithful copy of the king's own great tiltyards, of which he had several, but in miniature, built to a boy's scale. The distances were smaller, the barrier between the combatants lower. Young Henry tilted with a short lance and rode a small horse.

I had seen him go through his exercises before, and knew that he lacked both strength and agility. Because he was the king's son he was praised extravagantly (though never by his father) and thought more highly of himself than his abilities deserved. I wondered how he would fare in this feat of skill.

Among the boys who tilted against young Henry Fitzroy that afternoon was one who stood out for his outstanding ability and grace. He easily unhorsed all his opponents and the tournament master, foreseeing an embarrassing defeat for Henry Fitzroy, did not permit him to joust against this exceptionally able opponent. When the tournament ended I asked Daniel who the boy was.

"That's young master Neville. A likely boy, but a bit unruly. He'll make a good soldier." Without his jousting armor Johnny Neville was a lithe good-looking boy, blond and sharp-featured, quite unlike his jowly, balding father in looks. I saw him turn his level, unsmiling gaze on Henry Fitzroy, as if taking his measure. Of the two, I thought Master Neville much the more princely.

Whatever his shortcomings in the tiltyard, Henry Fitzroy was clearly being prepared for rulership. He was certainly as haughty as any princeling, legitimate or otherwise; he strode through the halls of Sheriff Hutton giving commands in his high voice, and barking out shrill reprimands to the servants when they displeased him.

He was thirteen years old in the year that I turned twenty, yet he was still a boy, slight and small and without any hair on his upper lip. He had no air of command. Looking at him, I could not help wondering, could this boy grow up to be king?

And in that year, for the first time, it was being whispered that he had a rival. Not his longtime rival, Queen Catherine's daughter Mary, but a new one. For Mistress Boleyn was pregnant with King Henry's child.

It was the thing most talked about, the change most feared. King Henry wanted to make Mistress Boleyn his queen, and now that she was carrying his child he was determined to force his will upon events, no matter what the cost.

"What do you think, Cat?" Avice said as she came into my bedchamber one morning. "We are summoned to London. The young duke is to be betrothed to Mary Howard, the Duke of Norfolk's daughter. We're to have new gowns to wear to the ceremony."

Avice, who had intervened to protect me from Mistress Boleyn's wrath during the previous Christmas season, was back in the household after having been dismissed following her contretemps with the royal favorite. I was glad for her return. Even though she was an earl's daughter she had no hauteur. Her manner was that of a practical, forthright countrywoman and I enjoyed her company.

With her broad, stout figure and outsize body, her lank dark hair and unappealing features Avice Odell was not likely to attract a husband, for her dowry was not large, and besides, she was nearing thirty; her parents had intended to make her a nun but she refused to enter the religious life. She shocked her family by agreeing with the reformers that the church of Rome was corrupt and like many others she secretly read the English Bible; when she discovered that I too read the Scriptures in translation it made us close friends.

"I'll be glad to go to London again. I haven't been there since my own wedding. And I can see my brother Will."

"You know who else is going," Avice was saying, her eyes twinkling.

"No. Who?"

"John Neville."

She teased me about John, who I had gotten to know fairly well in the past few months. He came to Sheriff Hutton often, as his own estate of Snape Hall was not far away and he was among those the king trusted to oversee Henry Fitzroy's household and make sure the boy was well tutored and well taken care of. I saw him at dinners and on saint's days, and he sought me out. I knew that he admired me, but thought little of it. He was kind and I liked his self-effacing manner, a manner rare in an important nobleman, which he clearly was. But he was old, and bald, and ill-favored. He aroused no feeling in me other than friendship. And I believed with all my heart that I would never again feel for any man the tender love I had felt for Ned.

"Avice, John Neville is old enough to be my grandfather."

"Not quite. He certainly doesn't look at you like a grandfather would."

"He takes a grandfatherly interest in me."

She laughed.

We were supervising the packing of our things for the trip south when we heard raised voices in the corridor outside. My maidservants grew pale and retreated to an anteroom.

"Here! Put him in here!"

"No! Find another bed. A big one."

The door of my bedchamber opened and five men came in, carrying a litter on which lay an injured man.

"This lord has a broken leg. He needs a bed."

"Why not put him in his own bedchamber?" Avice asked.

"He has none, milady. He was going to stay at the hunting lodge tonight, but it's twelve miles from here."

"Of course he can have this bed. Put him here."

I quickly moved off the bed some piles of clothing which my servants had been sorting. The injured man was laid on the bed. I saw then that it was John Neville, one bloody leg thrown out at an awkward angle. His eyes were closed.

"The doctor's been sent for, milady."

"Thank you. You can go now."

As the men left, a little girl came in. She was fair and pale, and her light blue eyes were troubled. Yet she showed much poise as she curtseyed to me and to Avice and then went up to the bed, which was so high that she had difficulty seeing the man who lay there.

"It's my father, isn't it. I'm Margaret Latimer."

"Yes, dear. The doctor is coming." I went to the girl and lifted her up onto the bed.

Watching her father as she spoke, she told us what had happened.

"We were on our way to London. The duke and some other men saw deer in the forest and went off after them. My father went too. Then they brought him back like this." Her voice trembled, but only slightly. I put my arm around her shoulders and she looked up at me, with a look I will never forget. Her entire face was a plea—for sympathy, for understanding—above all, for love.

"Don't worry, Margaret. Here comes the doctor now."

Avice lifted the little girl off the bed and, patting her head, drew her back to give the physician room.

Over the next several days, as we completed our preparations for the journey to London, John Neville had his broken leg set and bound in splints. The chambermaids brought him broth and cider and changed his linen and the grooms and pages heaped logs on the fire to keep him warm. Avice and I sat with him and helped to keep him in good cheer, while all around us the servants packed for our coming journey and took our trunks and satchels out to the carts and wagons that would take us to London.

I kept Margaret with me, ordering a trundle bed brought in so that she could sleep near her father and talking to her encouragingly about his gradual improvement.

And he did appear to improve. A ruddy color came back into his cheeks—his face had been gray and pale when he was first injured—and he ate well and was in good spirits.

"If only I could go south with you all," he said to me with a sigh on the evening before our departure. "I would dearly love to spend a few weeks at court. All that feasting and merriment!" His eyes shone briefly. "And there are things I must discuss with the king. The Council of the North is embattled. The king's authority is waning, and must be strengthened or we will face rebellion."

"Don't think about all that now," I told him. "Wait until you are stronger."

He lay back against his pillows and closed his eyes. I thought he might sleep, but after a few moments he opened his eyes again.

"Read to me, Cat, will you?"

"Of course."

"One of the old romances."

I knew he liked stories of olden times, tales of knights and ladies, dragons and sorcerers. He carried books with him wherever he went, unlike many noblemen and noblewomen, who had not been taught to read and who looked on reading as something for priests to do, a lowly activity and not a worthwhile one.

"Which one shall it be?"

"Read me the Tale of Gwennidor."

I found the book among his things, opened it and began to read.

It was an old familiar tale, of an evil beast who imprisoned a king in his castle and a maiden, Gwennidor, who assaulted the castle and freed the king and then married him.

I read on, the candles burning low and my voice as it rose and fell the only sound in the warm room.

"Read me the part about Gwennidor marrying the king again," John asked.

"And when she had freed him," I read, "and the rude beast had been slain, then the king said, Fair Gwennidor, all I have is yours, and my heart as well. And she gave him her hand with a right good will, and so they were wed."

"Yes, that's right. Fair Catherine, all I have is yours, and my heart as well. Will you agree to be my wife?"

I looked at him in surprise. I felt no particular pleasure at his words, but no revulsion either. Avice was right, I thought. She was right all along, about John's feelings for me.

"Milord, I am still in mourning for my late husband, and for my mother. I cannot think of marriage."

"I am content to wait until you are out of mourning. Bertie will give us his blessing and marry us. Will you agree?"

I shook my head. "I cannot ponder it, milord. Perhaps when I return from London—"

His face fell.

"Of course, yes. I understand. I should have known. It was only a thought. I am fond of you, and I could offer you a home, comfort, position. And Margaret has grown fond of you."

"Margaret is a dear child, and needs a mother. Only—"

"Only you want daughters and sons of your own. That is quite natural. We can have them, you and I. I am not too old."

A silence fell. Logs crackled in the hearth. I stood up. "I'll give you my answer when we return from London, John. And I thank you for honoring me with your proposal."

I turned to go, then on an impulse turned back and bent over John's recumbent form. I kissed him on the cheek, and he smiled.

"Goodbye, dear Gwennidor," he murmured, taking my hand in his and gripping it with a strength that surprised me. "Goodbye, my little bride."

10

THE JOURNEY SOUTH WAS COLD AND WET.

Each day we huddled under fur blankets and warmed ourselves by drinking mulled cider. Each night we stayed close to the fire in the manor houses that offered us hospitality, and dined at the table of the local lord. Henry Fitzroy was shown respect and courtesy but there were no banquets or special entertainments. Word of Mistress Boleyn's pregnancy had spread quickly, everyone expected her son, and not Fitzroy, to become the next king.

Once we arrived in London many in Henry Fitzroy's household sought employment in that of Mistress Boleyn, which was growing rapidly in anticipation of her becoming the next queen.

"I've heard she requires twenty new grooms," I overheard one of Henry Fitzroy's pages say to another. "And they'll be paid well. Far better than we are now."

"But she'd be the devil's own bitch to work for," came the reply.

"She is the devil's own bitch now."

"I'd rather serve the devil himself. King Henry doesn't throw things, or swear at his servants. Last Christmas he had a snowball fight with his grooms. When it was over he gave them five gold pieces to share."

I knew that the court ran on gossip, yet it seemed to me, in my first few days at Whitehall, that the level of gossip was at an all-time high. Whispers, titters and muffled laughter filled the long broad corridors of the magnificent palace, which I remembered well from my childhood though then it was called York Place. The palace was festive with green boughs and twining ivy, bright wall hangings and paintings done by visiting Italian and German artists.

All had been made ready for Henry Fitzroy's betrothal ceremony. Yet even at that ceremony, as Avice and I and four others stood in our finery beside Henry Fitzroy's pathetically young, blond bride-to-be Mary Howard, there were murmurs of sympathy and outbursts of giggling.

My brother Will was a font of jokes about Mistress Boleyn and her bulging stomach.

"Why is Mistress Boleyn like a whale?" he asked a group of us one night after supper. "Because her belly is bigger than her tail—and that's no fluke."

"What rises like dough, shakes like jelly and holds the next king of England? Mistress Boleyn's belly!"

On it went, jest after silly jest, each one repeated again and again as it made the rounds of the court. No one seemed to give a thought to poor Queen Catherine, far away in her neglected manor in the country, or to Princess Mary, who was also being kept away. Remembering them, I could not help thinking of my mother, who had loved the queen, and missing her terribly. It didn't seem possible that the vibrant life of the royal palace could go on without her.

I said as much to Will when we were alone.

"Of course, if mother were alive, she wouldn't be here. She'd be with Queen Catherine."

"Perhaps. But then, she was always very practical."

"If she were here I could ask her advice. John Neville has asked me to marry him."

Will laughed. "That old bumbler?"

"He is an old bumbler. But he's endearing."

"And important. His lands stand athwart the main roads into the North. He holds that region for the king."

Will looked thoughtful. "Of course he's much too old for you. But not as old as Old Burgh. And you nearly married him."

"I did not."

"I think if mother were here, she would say, 'You must be practical, dear. You must use your common sense.'"

"And what would common sense tell me, now that Mistress Boleyn and all her Howard relatives are so much in favor? Half of Henry Fitzroy's servants have deserted him, and are looking for posts in Mistress Boleyn's household."

"Very wise too."

Will looked at me. "I was offered a position myself, but I didn't choose to take it. I'm a rich man, thanks to my wife, and the intrigues of the court are not for me. I just make fun of them. You, on the other hand—"

He did not finish his sentence but I knew what he meant. I was young, I had an appetite for life. I had known sorrow but might still find joy.

"I am expected to serve Mary Howard when she marries Henry Fitzroy."

"A dismal prospect, I'd say. Poor Fitzroy will probably end up guarding some remote castle somewhere, an obscure nobody, while Mistress Boleyn's son becomes heir to the throne. Mary Howard will pine away in her husband's obscurity, and you will pine away with her."

"Don't say that. It's bad luck."

"All right. Nothing but cheer from now on." Will assumed the puckish face he wore when telling jokes.

"Why is Mistress Boleyn like a boil on the butt?"

"Tell me."

"Because both swell up and both are a pain in the ass."

He threw back his head and roared with laughter at his own joke, and went away to tell it somewhere else.

One Sunday after mass Avice and I were coming out of the royal chapel, following Henry Fitzroy and his betrothed as they walked along a colonnade toward the tiltyard. (She would not take his hand as they walked, I noticed, clearly she disliked him.) We heard Mistress Boleyn's shrill voice behind us and moved aside to let her pass. She wore a loose-fitting gown with a white lace apron over it, garments which emphasized rather than disguised her pregnancy. I thought it brazen of her to flaunt her condition, and said so to Avice, who looked frightened, pretended not to hear me and dropped back amid the crowd exiting the chapel.

"What's that you said?" Mistress Boleyn asked, turning as she passed to look at me, imperious and challenging. Beside her stood Sir Thomas, my vengeful father-in-law, who when he saw me, said to his companion, "Pay no attention. She's a mean, spiteful wench."

"She's the one with the limp. The one who defied me at the Christmas revels at Sheriff Hutton last winter. The one who bested me at hazard. I'll have her sent to Guernsey or somewhere. She'll never be heard from again. The king will see to it."

I was worried—until, a few days later, I was summoned into the presence of the king.

Servants were dressing him, as he stood, in his silken hose and smallclothes, arms outstretched, in the center of the room. I watched as each luxurious garment was removed from a trunk, then handed reverently to a second servant and then a third, who fastened it onto the royal person.

All the while, the room was filled with the sound of Master Cromwell's loud, insistent voice, reading to King Henry from a document he held. When I was ushered in through the massive oak doors Master Cromwell glanced at me briefly, his small porcine eyes dispassionte but observant, then went on with what he was reading. As he read, he paced agitatedly up and down, the folds of his long black gown entwining around his short legs. I thought him an uncommonly unattractive man, though a highly intelligent one. I knew that following the death of Cardinal Wolsey Master Cromwell had become the king's principal secretary, the most powerful commoner at court.

"All causes testamentary, all matrimonial cases shall be heard within the king's realm and not elsewhere," he read. "The See of Rome is to have no jurisdiction whatsoever over English cases or disputes."

"Ha! I like that. No jurisdiction whatsoever! Take that, Poop Clement—I mean Pope Clement. More like Pope Inclement. The Rainy Pope. Well then, let him thunder and rain all he likes, he'll have no more power over me!"

While the king spoke he waved his arms and stamped his foot for emphasis. His dressers, nonplussed, stopped what they were doing and waited until he had calmed himself before resuming his toilette.

"The wording of this act must be precise. We've already revised it seven or eight times. I've had it read by a dozen clerics and lawyers. Of course there's no precedent for any law like this. No one has ever tried to limit the legal rights of the pope before."

"Except by assassination," Henry put in. "That is very effective."

I saw Master Cromwell give the king a disparaging look.

"All we seek to do, in this instance, is to prevent Queen Catherine from appealing her case to the pope in Rome when you legally divorce her by act of Parliament. There is no need for violence or lawbreaking."

"And what does a pisspot clerk like you know of the business of kings? If I want Poop Clement killed, I'll order it done." He paused and stroked his red-gold beard. As he did so, he appeared to notice me for the first time. "The only trouble is," he went on, "there would be some other poop elected, and he'd say the same thing—that I can't divorce my wife."

Master Cromwell took his document to a desk, picked up a quill, and scratched out some words, adding others. The king continued to look at me, a half-smile on his face.

"Sometimes, Crum, I think the Mahommedans have the right idea. Four wives at a time. Four women in each man's bed. That would be about right, eh? What do you say?"

"They'd fight."

"Yes, I fear they would. And while a cat fight can be diverting, it isn't very erotic, would you say?"

Cromwell permitted a grin to cross his piggy face.

"I'll hear the rest of your act later, Crum. Leave me."

"But your majesty, the lawyers are waiting for your permission to proceed. We must draft this as rapidly as possible."

The king reached for the nearest solid object, which happened to be a silver bowl full of water for shaving, and flung it at Cromwell's head. He missed, but clipped the secretary's ear. Cromwell gave a startled cry.

"I said, leave me."

Holding a handkerchief to his ear, Cromwell quickly gathered up his papers and left. The king's dressers were fastening his doublet and attaching a cream-colored feather to his scarlet cap.

"Now, Milady Burgh, what's this I hear of some quarrel between you and my future queen? She tells me she wants you sent to Guernsey, of all places. Whatever have you done to offend her?"

"I know of no offense given, sire. Not on my part."

"Then on hers?"

"Surely the king's favorite can do no wrong, sire."

"I dislike evasive answers."

"Then perhaps you would prefer silence."

The king waited, but I said no more.

"We need your brother Will here. He always makes me laugh. Have you heard his latest joke? Why is Mistress Boleyn like a boil on the butt?"

"Yes, sire. I've heard that one."

"Oh."

"Well then. I can't very well send you to Guernsey, to disappear forever on that lonely shore, but I can attempt to mend your quarrel. My future queen is to be elevated to the peerage soon, as Marchioness of Pembroke. You will attend her at that ceremony. Try to be agreeable."

While we were conversing Charles Brandon had come in, and the king now turned his attention to him, dismissing me before I had a chance to object to taking part in Mistress Boleyn's ceremony. With many misgivings, I curtseyed and left.

On the day Mistress Boleyn was to become a marchioness, the two countesses who were appointed to help her dress had difficulty with their task. The crimson velvet surcoat she was to wear was too small. Dressmakers rushed in to open a seam and stitch in a placket, working amid a storm of abuse from the marchioness-to-be. Lady Mary Howard, Henry Fitzroy's fiancée, stood by holding Mistress Boleyn's velvet mantle and trying not to burst into tears during her cousin's tirade. I held a satin pillow on which rested the jeweled coronet the new marchioness would wear. I had nothing else to do, and so I stood quietly, looking at the carvings on the wall, the firedogs in the hearth, the pigeons fluttering outside the windows. Anywhere but into the eyes of the irate woman who expected to become the king's wife.

For a tense half-hour, while the surcoat was altered, she waited—and waited. Presently the Duke of Norfolk burst into the robing chamber.

"By all that's holy, what's keeping you, madame?" he fairly shouted at his niece, who glared at him.

"As you see, it's these hamfisted whores of dressmakers. They aren't finished with my gown."

"Madame has—has—put on weight—" one of the countesses began, hesitantly. "The surcoat has had to be enlarged."

Anne turned on the trembling countess and shouted in her face. "Nonsense! I've had two fittings on that gown."

"Several months ago," murmured one of the dressmakers. Suppressed laughter followed this remark. The duke slammed his fist against the wall and the laughter ceased. I was so startled I jumped.

"Come at once to the throne room," the duke said, his voice soft yet menacing, a snarl behind every word. "At once."

Mistress Boleyn's face had gone white. In that moment I saw stark fear in her eyes, and I realized that what the more astute observers at court said was true: that she was in fact nothing more nor less than the tool of her ruthless, ambitious family, and especially of her fearsome craggy-faced uncle Norfolk. Her hauteur, her rude and imperious manner were only a disguise, to hide her fear from others and deny it to herself.

I saw that she was trembling, her knees shaking. Everyone stood as if frozen. The duke had left the room. The dressmakers cowered.

Handing the coronet I was holding on its satin pillow to one of Mistress Boleyn's attendants I quickly helped her into her surcoat, which was not fully sewn together but covered her adequately and modestly. Her long black hair spilled down the back of the simple garment, making her look girlish and vulnerable. For the first time I felt empathetic toward her. I led her to the door and the others fell into place behind us. She said nothing, but let me guide her, her trembling gradually lessening, along the corridor to where the officers of arms were waiting to escort her into the throne room.

The great doors opened and I could see, from where I stood, the king in his glittering golden robes, seated on his throne, the Duke of Norfolk on one side of him and Charles Brandon, Duke of Suffolk, on the other. Flanking them were officials and noblemen wearing thick gold chains of office and twinkling gems that dazzled the eye. Toward this formidable phalanx walked Mistress Boleyn in her simple robe and unadorned hair.

A lamb to the slaughter, I thought as I watched her. No matter how she puts on airs and tries to force others to do her bidding, no matter how domineering she tries to be, Mistress Boleyn is just a sacrificial lamb.

I too felt a bit like a sacrificial lamb when I learned, a few days later, that I would not be returning to Sheriff Hutton with Henry Fitzroy and his household.

It was Daniel who brought me the news.

"I've just heard," he told me. "The royal controller has cut the Duke of Richmond's household budget. He will be moved into smaller lodgings, with a much smaller staff to serve him. You are among those whose position is being eliminated, milady."

I sat down, too surprised, for the moment, to reply.

"It was only to be expected, after all. Mistress Boleyn's child will be born before long, and Henry Fitzroy's name won't even be mentioned any more. When she has two sons the new succession will be certain. Young Fitzroy will probably be a scullion in the royal kitchens—if he's lucky.

"So that's why everyone has been trying to join Mistress Boleyn's household. It wasn't only that they wanted to serve a more important person. It was because they sensed that their old place would soon be eliminated."

I reproached myself for not having foreseen this turn of events. I had never been very astute in forecasting the shifting tides of the court. I was slow to realize that poor Henry Fitzroy, who had been the king's cherished hope and favorite ever since his birth, and whose betrothal had even now been celebrated with such pomp, would fall so far out of favor that most of his servants would be dismissed.

But where did this leave me? I was once again adrift, without a home of my own, without an income except for what Will gave me, without a future. I was still very young, and when I looked at myself in the glass I saw—when I was not too critical—a pretty young woman with creamy skin and auburn hair and a lively smile. I knew that my figure was very good and that my slight limp would not be considered a major flaw in my physical attractions.

I thought with a chill of the place I had heard about, the place they called the Maiden's Chamber at Shooter's Hill in Greenwich. It was the king's private brothel, an old lodge tucked away within the thick greenery of the wood, where a group of young women waited to serve the royal pleasure. Were it not for Will's generosity, would I have been forced to join the ranks of these unfortunate women?

But no—my uncle William would never have allowed that to happen. Much as he resented me, he would never have allowed me to disgrace the Parr family name by serving in the Maiden's Chamber.

There was no other choice. I would have to live with Will. Perhaps it would only be temporary. I hoped so.

Yet as my servants were packing my things I heard a brisk knock at my bedchamber door. It was Sir Thomas.

"I cannot pretend, madame, that I am pleased to see you," said my former father-in-law when he had been shown in. "I am here strictly in my capacity as chamberlain to the Marchioness of Pembroke. I have just been appointed to that office."

The Marchioness of Pembroke, I thought. The name by which we must now call Mistress Boleyn.

"I can hardly pretend to be pleased to see you, either. The last time you came to my bedchamber it was to lock me in."

"You appear to be none the worse for the experience." His tone was cold and contemptuous. I thought, how I wish I never had to see him again.

"It is the marchioness's wish that you join her household, as lady-in-waiting. I need hardly tell you that very soon the marchioness will be queen."

"I am honored but must decline," I heard myself say.

"I cannot take that message back to the marchioness."

"Why not?"

"No one has ever refused an appointment to her household before. She would not countenance it."

"Nevertheless it must be my answer."

He did not know what to say or do. He no longer had any power over me, to shout at me or lock me in my bedchamber. It was a small victory, to be sure, yet I felt like gloating.

"I must consult the king."

I gulped. The king. Of course, he would have the final say as to who served his future queen—assuming she became his queen—as lady-in-waiting.

"I remind you," Sir Thomas was saying, "that an invitation to serve the Marchioness of Pembroke carries the force of a royal command. Unless, of course, some binding obligation makes such service impossible."

At his words a series of images flashed through my mind. Of little Margaret Neville's upturned face, full of yearning. Of the level gaze and unsmiling eyes of handsome Johnny Neville in the tiltyard of Sheriff Hutton. Of kind John Neville lying in my bed, calling me Gwennidor and saying "All I have is yours, and my heart as well."

"But I am bound by an obligation," I told Sir Thomas, suddenly happy that what I said was true. "I am betrothed, to Sir John Neville, Lord Latimer, and we are to be married within the month."

11

MY MOTHER'S CARVED OAK BED WITH ITS CANOPY AND COUNTERPANE of purple velvet was brought to Snape Hall and moved into my elegant new bedchamber, the bedchamber I was to share with John Neville, Lord Latimer.

I had been born in that bed, and so had Will and Nan. I hoped that the next generation of our family would be born in it as well.

Not that I expected my marriage to John to be anything like my marriage to Ned. Ned was everything to me, the center of my life. I would never love anyone as I had loved him. But I was older now, I told myself, and I was ready for new responsibilities and a mature marriage with an older man. I was no longer a romantic child, I was a woman grown.

Besides, I was genuinely fond of John, who had been kind to me and who evidently loved me, in his own way. When I told him that I would be glad to accept his proposal of marriage his homely face became radiant. He beamed, and laughed, and said he had never been so happy.

I too felt a glow, and a sense of contentment. Now my future is settled, I thought to myself. I'll never again have to worry about having no home, no comfortable place at court, nothing to live on except the charity of my relatives.

Our wedding took place in the old, high-roofed chapel at Snape Hall, with choirs singing and my kinsman Bishop Tunstall performing the ceremony. John sent to York for bolts of fine French silk to make my wedding gown, and I wore Grandmother Fitzhugh's lace veil and some of my mother's long ropes of pearls. My stepdaughter Margaret walked solemnly ahead of me down the aisle casting out lavender sprigs and dried flower petals from a basket she held. It seemed as though there were hundreds of people in the candlelit chapel, nobles and tenants, men of business from York and all the members of the Council of the North.

After the ceremony the spacious banqueting hall was filled with music and loud talk, wine flowed freely and great haunches of meat and platters of fish and fowl were brought in until the entire large and noisy party was replete and content. John and I sat in the seats of honor, my hand in his. We received the congratulations of the guests and their best wishes for long and healthy lives.

I did my best to turn away haunting memories of my wedding to Ned, that blissful day, the joy I felt as his wife. Those memories made tears spring to my eyes, and sadness was the last thing I wanted to feel or display there in the banqueting hall.

On our wedding night, however, I could not help giving way to my feelings. John lay beside me in the great purple bed, smelling of the musk he had applied very liberally to his jowly cheeks, and wearing a lace-trimmed nightshirt. But the musk could not disguise the stale odor that clung to him—the odor of age. And beneath the nightshirt was the paunchy, sunken-chested body of an old man, gray hairs sprinkled across his torso, buttocks low-slung and deflated, neck scrawny and wrinkled.

I had thought that I could look past these signs of age and focus on the affection I felt for John. But I was wrong. There was no heat of passion between us. I had sworn to myself that I would be generous with my body, that I would do whatever John asked. I submitted willingly, but without desire. Afterwards I wept.

"There there," my husband said, patting my head soothingly, "we won't try this again until you are ready. I have my own bedchamber. I'll visit you when I am invited."

John was the most considerate of husbands, and I told him so. I wanted children of my own, yet I began to wonder whether a child begotten by an old man might be feeble and weak. It worried me. Out of kindness I continued to invite John into my bedchamber, and he sometimes enjoyed his nights with me, but after a few months he visited me less and less often, and finally his visits ceased. I resigned myself, for the time being at least, to not having a child of my own.

Perhaps because of this change in my expectations, I devoted a great deal of time to my stepchildren, chiefly to my stepdaughter Margaret. Shy and bookish, Margaret needed a mother to praise and encourage her and give her confidence. She had no cousins living anywhere nearby; for playmates she had only the children of household servants and officers, and there were few of these. Most were either the wrong age to provide her with companionship or were not intelligent enough to share her interests. She had not been very well educated. Like most noblemen John saw no reason to train a daughter, even a bookish one, in the classics and believed that girls should be taught to sew, dance and sing, and play the virginals.

Margaret and I began lessons in French and Latin each afternoon and we also read the Bible together, the king having authorized the distribution of an English translation of the Bible by Miles Coverdale. In mild weather we went on long walks, taking the steep trails that led downward from the castle on its height through the hills to the lush valleys of the Swale and the Ure. I had never been a sturdy hiker but I grew more surefooted and Margaret too seemed to thrive on the outdoor exercise.

"You're getting to be a regular little mountain goat," Johnny said to Margaret as he passed us on a trail one afternoon, on his way to St. Mary's Abbey. "Oh and by the way, how do you say 'mountain goat' in Latin?"

"Ask your monks," Margaret said curtly, turning her head away and walking on. Johnny often taunted his younger sister. I found his tormenting of her hateful, but I left it to his father to discipline him.

"We look forward to seeing you at the tournament in York," I said, trying to sound as pleasant as I could to Johnny, who had never been welcoming to me.

He shrugged and passed on. His rudeness irked John, who spoke harshly to him and threatened to take away his tilting ponies and even to whip him unless he learned civility. I didn't take offense, though I well might have. I remembered how brusque and aggressive my brother Will had been when he was Johnny's age, nearly fifteen, though Will, even when on his worst behavior, had always been amusing.

Instead of attempting to intrude myself into Johnny's life or win him over I watched him, and talked to John about what I observed.

"You know he spends a great deal of time at St. Mary's," I remarked one afternoon after we had seen the boy practice his wrestling, and praised him for his strength and his skill. In his athletic pursuits he was not only skilled, but determined, bent on winning at all costs and often contemptuous of his opponents. It was almost alarming to watch him, his face set in a grim rictus, his jaw locked and his eyes narrowed. He was like a warrior going into battle, fearsome and invulnerable.

"Yes. He's always gone there a lot. I used to think he might become a monk." John laughed. "That was before he began seducing the stable girls."

St. Mary's Abbey, only four miles from Snape Hall, was the greatest religious house for many miles around, indeed one of the greatest in all Yorkshire. With its flocks of sheep, vast pasturelands and woodlots it was wealthy, and the monks ate well and lived in comfort. Like all such venerable religious houses, St. Mary's provided alms to the poor and hospitality to travelers. The monks took in the sick and often cured them; many of the cures were brought about, so it was said, by the wonderworking powers of Saint Agatha.

Saint Agatha's tomb to the right of the high altar in the abbey church drew many pilgrims from Yorkshire and beyond. Parents brought their sick children, farmers their diseased cattle to the holy tomb and often both the children and the cattle were healed. Saint Agatha had lived in the tenth century, a peasant girl greatly favored by God who gave her the gift of curing disease and alleviating pain. After she died, her body was brought to the abbey and enshrined in its tomb in the church. In a golden reliquary were kept locks of her hair and nail parings from her slender white fingers, and each year the reliquary, together with a waxen image of the saint, were carried reverently around the abbey buildings three times with a great crowd of the faithful forming a procession.

In the year after John and I were married, we learned that the traditional procession had been canceled.

"Blasphemy! Sacrilege! The Holy Father will never allow it!" Johnny's shouting could be heard throughout the lower floor of Snape Hall. He came into the sunlit room where John and I customarily sat in the morning after we had broken our fast.

"You can't allow this, father. The procession must be held. It's always been held. It always shall be held, from now until the end of time!"

John raised his eyebrows and looked quizzically at his blustering son.

"If there is to be no procession, I cannot change that. I am not a churchman."

"You can make your friend Bertie change it!"

"Bishop Tunstall is his own master."

"No he's not! He answers to the Bishop of Rome! As a loyal son of the church you must hold him accountable!" Johnny stood, feet apart, arms folded, his every muscle tensed, aquiver with passion. "Tomorrow is the feast day of Saint Agatha. Our tenants, and the peasants from the abbey lands, have all gathered in front of the church. I've just come from there. They don't understand why the relics aren't being brought out and the cart decorated for Saint Agatha's image to ride in. They are confused. Tomorrow they will be furious."

"Son, nothing you or I might try to do would make any difference. The church in this realm is now under the headship of King Henry, not the Holy Father in Rome. King Henry is not in favor of showing special veneration to saints."

"Then King Henry can go straight to hell!" And before his father or I could react, Johnny ran out into the corridor and down the stairs into the courtyard. In a moment we heard the clatter of his horse's hooves as he rode away.

John swore, red-faced, got to his feet and started out after his son, limping on his imperfectly healed leg.

"Wait!" I cried. "You'll never catch up with him. Besides, what would you do if you did catch him? He's stronger than you are now."

"He wouldn't dare defy me!"

"Did you never defy your father, when you were fifteen?"

"Often. But he punished me. He used to shut me in the dog kennels with the hounds, and make me eat the scraps that were thrown to them. Once I was in the kennels for a week before my brother let me out. And even then my father beat me until I bled."

We saw nothing more of Johnny. Then, a week after he left, word reached us from St. Mary's that an important event was about to occur. The body of Saint Agatha was to be disinterred from its tomb. After nearly six centuries, the earthly remains of the wonderworking saint were to be brought once again into the light.

Johnny was among those we saw in the large crowd when we arrived at the abbey to witness the historic opening of the saint's tomb. Along with the hundreds of others in the abbey church, he knelt in prayer, head bowed, as the abbot asked God's blessing on the ceremony.

Silence fell as the work began. The only sound in the vast echoing nave was the clank and crash of pick on stone, followed by the shoveling of earth and then, after nearly an hour, by the groaning and tearing of ancient wood. The tenth-century casket was being opened.

We heard a gasp, then a cry from the abbot, followed by similar sounds of surprise and amazement from the workmen and others close enough to see what the casket held.

"Look, milord!" the abbot said to John, who went over to the lip of the tomb and peered down into it.

"By all that's holy! She's as fresh as the day she died. And she smells of roses!"

The cry was carried throughout the church. "The body is fresh! It smells of roses! There is no decay! Surely Saint Agatha is greatly beloved by God, to lie in her tomb for six centuries and know no corruption."

Spontaneously, with no one leading it, the congregation began to sing a hymn. The melody hung in the air, a reverent paean to the miracle we were witnessing.

"It is a sign," I heard people whisper. "The Lord has given us a sign. We may be forbidden to carry the saint's relics in procession, but Saint Agatha is stronger than any prohibition. She has been preserved uncorrupted. The old ways of the church will also be preserved, without taint or change, and we will preserve them."

I made my way to the casket and looked down into it. There, lying on a bed of lilies, was a young girl, her white hands folded across her chest, her eyes closed as if in sleep. Her long dark hair fell in waves to her shoulders. Her face held none of the waxy pallor of death.

I was astounded. There should have been nothing in the tomb but bones, yellow and shrunken by time. A grinning skull should have met my gaze—not this lovely, sweet-smelling body, its odor as fragrant as if it had been set in a garden of flowers. With the others in the church I knelt in reverence, and joined in the singing of the hymn, feeling with each rise and fall of its beautiful old cadences the worshipful response of a believing heart.

12

JOHN AND I RODE SIDE BY SIDE, OUR HORSES GALLOPING WITH A NOISY clatter along the wide, straight highway known as the Great North Road.

We were on our way to Durham, where a rebel army was said to be gathering, and where the Council of the North was about to meet in urgent session. We hoped to arrive by nightfall the following day.

Much had happened in the past six months, since the unearthing of the miraculously preserved body of Saint Agatha. Word of the remarkable discovery had spread rapidly, setting off a spontaneous rising of the devout peasants of Yorkshire, who came to St. Mary's Abbey in their thousands and then began marching, under the saint's banner, all across the region.

Wearing gray woollen robes with a white cross emblazoned on the front they walked in resolute procession from town to town and village to village, Saint Agatha's banner held aloft, stopping in churchyards and cemeteries, at wayside shrines and in monastery courtyards to recruit others to their cause. Dozens, then hundreds joined. Men and women paused in their labor, leaving fields untended and animals untethered, to follow the holy banners and add their voices to the chants and songs of the pilgrims.

"Saint Agatha and the True Church!" they shouted. "Restore the saints! Restore the relics!"

"All commons unite together! Saint Agatha forever!"

As their pilgrim army grew, they became more bold.

"Down with the Mouldwarp! The Mouldwarp sins against God; let him die!"

It was treason, this rallying cry, for the Mouldwarp was the mythic name being attached to King Henry, and the pilgrims were calling for the death of the king.

The Mouldwarp prophecy was an old one, attributed to the wizard Merlin in the days of King Arthur. According to the prophecy, a king would arise in England, a king destined to bring strife and bloodshed to the land as a result of his sins. He was seen as much monster as monarch, outsize and bestial, and according to the prophecy, he would be beset by enemies, and his inevitable defeat would be bloody and terrible.

King Henry, outsize and in conflict with the pope, the French king and Queen Catherine's nephew Emperor Charles, fitted the part of the Mouldwarp to perfection, and the pilgrims looked forward to the day of his certain defeat.

We heard them singing about it when we passed through Warringham, where a hundred gray-clad pilgrims were encamped in a field.

> Mouldwarp alive
> Evil will thrive
> Mouldwarp is dead
> Evil has fled.

They chanted the doggerel verse endlessly, clapping to its rhythm. I felt a chill, hearing the king cursed in this way. Somehow the religious devotion of these northmen had curdled into savagery, and no one knew where that savagery might lead.

We stopped in Stainford and lodged with a landowner who was arming his servants and the most trusted of his tenants.

"They captured the king's tax collector two days ago," he told us. "Before that they assaulted the justices as they were on their way to Durham for the assizes. You had best take care, milord, you and your lady. I hear they have sworn to kill anyone who serves the king on the Council of the North."

"We will guard ourselves, I assure you. Our best defense is disguise."
We were dressed as prosperous country folk, and our mounts, though
sturdy and fast, were not the fine horses in John's stables but serviceable
horses bought in York by Daniel.

The next day, outside the village of Randsby, we came upon a
crowd, chanting and shouting. They blocked the road. We were unable
to pass, so we paused on the edge of the noisy gathering to see what was
happening.

"We've got him! We've got the spy!" came the response to John's
query about what was going on.

A man was being dragged to the center of a hastily dug pit, the sort
of circle made for staging dog-fights or cock-fights. His hands were tied
behind his back and he was bloody; clearly he had been beaten.

As we watched a bullskin was brought and wrapped around the
sufferer, whose pathetic cries were all but drowned out by the roaring
and clapping of the onlookers. When the bullskin had been secured,
hounds were loosed. With a furious snarling and growling they sank
their sharp teeth deep into the bullskin, tearing it and ripping open the
flesh of the man beneath.

For one horrible moment the victim raised his head and screamed, so
that his face, his features locked in a rictus of agony, could clearly be seen.

"My God," I heard John say. "I know that man. It's Bertie's cook.
I've eaten his dinners a hundred times." He urged his horse forward, as if
hoping to intervene, but there was no parting the densely packed,
cheering spectators, some of whom had locked arms in solidarity.
Besides, in a moment it was evident that the thing the dogs were
consuming was no longer a man but a bloody corpse.

I said a prayer for the soul of the dead man, and for the misguided
and cruel zealots who had murdered him, and for our safety as we rode
on, silent and shaken, toward Durham.

No sooner had we arrived, road-dusty and stinking of horse sweat, at
Cuthbert Tunstall's episcopal palace than we were ushered into a
chamber where several dozen grim-faced men were assembled. I was
immediately aware that the men saw me as an intruder.

"Lady Latimer is my kinswoman," the bishop said, indicating a
carved bench where I was to sit, somewhat uncomfortably, listening to
the men talk for the next several hours. "She has been brought here for
her protection." It was not strictly true. John had wanted me with him,

partly for my safety as he expected to be away from Snape Hall for some time, but mostly for his own sake. He relied on me and needed me.

Bishop Tunstall wasted no time in accomplishing the vital business of the Council.

"We all know why we are here. The revolt that is spreading through the North Country is the most dangerous rising I have seen in my long lifetime. Every lord and gentleman is expected to raise his men and arm them to be ready to march on the king's order. That order has not yet come, but may come any day. We need to appoint a local commander. Is there anyone here who would oppose the naming of John Neville to be that commander?"

Silence.

"Good. John, you are to lead our forces."

"But his son is among the rebels. He's one of them. How can he lead an army against his own son?" For a moment the question hung heavy in the room.

"I don't know that Johnny is part of this rebellion," John answered at length, "only that he has left home and has been seen at St. Mary's Abbey."

"Then let me enlighten you," came another voice from among the council members. "Young Johnny is at Cairncliffe, near my estate at Highfield, wearing the gray robe of a pilgrim of Saint Agatha. He's in charge of a band of three hundred men."

John's face went pale. The bishop spoke up.

"I have no doubt that John can discipline his own boy. How old is he now? Fifteen? Sixteen?" My kinsman was coming to John's defense.

"About that."

"A boy that age has no experience of war. He'll run when he hears the sound of cannon firing."

"But we have no cannon." The objection came from Viscount Moreton, one of the few men in the room I recognized. Like John, he was one of the most powerful of the northern lords, wealthy and with vast estates. He was often at court and the king, so John had told me, trusted him and relied on him.

"None of the guns north of the Trent is fit to be fired, I'm told. We're short of gunners, in any case. And short of powder. I wonder, have any of you ever shot a cannon? Or an old bombard? They explode, you know, if they haven't been properly cleaned and maintained."

He rose, and began pacing around the room as he spoke. His voice was strangely light, bitterly ironical, yet his dark eyes were shrewd as they surveyed the faces of his colleagues, missing nothing.

"But the guns are only part of the problem. Our fortresses cannot withstand a sustained assault. The walls of Pontefract Castle are leaning and crumbling. The ramparts have fallen in places. No one has thought of repairing them in years, there's been no need. Everywhere you look—everywhere the rebels look—there is weakness, defenselessness. A land ripe for the plucking!"

Now others joined in, adding what they knew or had heard. The rebels had thousands, even tens of thousands, in their ranks. Members of the king's forces were deserting their garrisons and joining the pilgrims. Great ladies of the North were donating their jewels to the cause.

Amid the mounting babble John stood, his stooped, balding figure more prepossessing than I had ever seen it before. He stretched out his arms to calm the commotion.

"If only the pilgrims of Saint Agatha could see us now!" he shouted. "They'd think we were cowards! Mice! Bedbugs! Vermin, to be frightened out of their nests and destroyed!"

The talk became subdued, then died away.

"If there are disloyal men or women among us, even in our own families, we will punish them and imprison them. If our cannon need repair we will hire armorers or gunmakers to repair them. Powder can be sent from the Tower armory. As for our castles, we will find means to defend them."

Some of the men were nodding and murmuring assent. John went on.

"When King Harry was crowned, many years ago, I knelt before him to swear my allegiance. I became his liegeman for life. My oath was clean, and I have never betrayed it. I fought with the king in France and against the Scots in the marches, and I intend to fight now, against these rebels who call themselves pilgrims, to defend the might and honor of the crown. Who will fight with me?"

Every man in the room shouted his affirmation.

Having restored the bellicose mood, John turned his attention to practical matters, laying out a map and assigning each local lord his district to defend. I sat quietly, listening to it all, proud of my husband yet knowing that despite his confident demeanor he was well aware of the danger posed by the rebels. And I knew, too, that he was tired. Lines of weariness scored his forehead. I saw him grimace and knew that his leg was hurting him. I imagined that what he had learned about Johnny, his having joined the rebels and now leading a rebel band, angered him and worried him.

We dined that night with Bishop Tunstall, and started out early the next morning for York. I was to return to Snape Hall, then leave with Margaret for Kent where we would stay with Will until it was safe to return. John would go to York and remain there to coordinate the defense of the city, muster all the local militias, and ensure that the Great North Road would remain open for the use of royal troops.

We left the episcopal palace under gray skies and by the time we parted next day, John taking the road for York and I the path that led to Snape Hall, it was raining heavily. I was drenched when I arrived home, and gratefully handed my horse to a groom.

Tired though I was, I took notice of the man's face. I knew all our grooms, or thought I did; this man was a stranger to me.

"You there," I called out to him as he was leading the limping horse away, "I do not know you. Are you newly come into my Lord Latimer's employ?"

He hesitated. He turned toward me and said, in a broad Yorkshire accent, "Yes, milady."

My senses were alert. Something was wrong. I looked more closely at the man's clothes and saw that they were the ragged trews and torn tunic of a laborer, not the brown uniform worn by all our stable hands.

I started to cry out, then felt rough hands seize me from behind. The cool metal of a knife blade touched my throat.

"The pilgrims of Saint Agatha are in charge here now, Lady Catherine," one of my captors said. "Let us go inside, where it is warm, and get out of the rain."

13

THE PILGRIMS OF SAINT AGATHA HAD TAKEN OVER SNAPE HALL, AND Margaret and I were their prisoners.

All our servants had fled—or joined the ranks of the pilgrims. Every room in the mansion had been ransacked, all the valuable furnishings dislodged. Paintings and tapestries, carpets and statues were heaped in untidy mounds in the corridors, to make room for dozens of makeshift beds where the pilgrims slept, dormitory-style. Margaret and I were shut in a tiny room in one of the castle towers, too high above the ground to climb out the windows and escape. The cold wind blew in through cracks in the old walls and we had very little wood for our fire. Margaret quickly developed a cough and we both shivered day and night.

I asked the girl who brought us our soup and bread if she could allow us to have more wood.

She was young, barely sixteen I guessed, and she looked at me unhappily, evidently uncomfortable. She wore the gray woollen gown of a pilgrim.

"I'll do my best, milady," she said, eyes downcast. "It isn't up to me, you know."

"I understand. You're only doing what you are told."

She wanted to say more, but bit her lip. After a moment's struggle she found her courage.

"I do what I'm told, indeed," she whispered. "But I don't like it. They say we are doing God's work. But how can it be God's work to take what isn't ours, and hurt people, and keep fine ladies locked up in the cold?

"I'll never forget you, milady," she went on. "How you came to Grundleford—that's my village, milady—when the snow was deep and brought us baskets of food and candles and a tun of cider. It helped us get through the winter, it did."

"It was little enough," I told her. "The Bible teaches us to share what we have. I'm sure you would have done the same, if you had plenty to share."

"I hope so, milady. Now I will see what I can do about getting you some wood."

By the fourth day of our captivity I was worried about Margaret, whose cough was getting worse, and about John. Was he still in York? Had he been captured? Were the royal forces really as weak as the critics in the Council of the North had said?

We had no word of what was happening outside our tiny tower room. From the windows I could see riders and carts on the road, groups of pilgrims arriving and leaving. I longed to see John, riding at the head of a hundred strong men, gallop into view and storm the castle, throwing down the banners of Saint Agatha and rescuing us and restoring our great house to what it had been before the devastation the invaders had caused.

How I longed to see him! But he did not come, and I continued to watch from the windows, and try to comfort Margaret—and to befriend the girl who served us.

Her name, I discovered, was Becca. She was seventeen years old, and with her fellow-villagers of Grundleford she had been swept up into the rebellion after witnessing the disinterring of Saint Agatha. Just when the pilgrims began marching and all the turmoil in the neighborhood started Becca had been on the point of getting married. Her betrothed, I learned, was also at Snape Hall and was a tenant of St. Mary's Abbey.

Becca was talkative. She admired and trusted me, and disliked the position in which she found herself, keeping watch over me and my stepdaughter—in effect, serving as our jailer—while providing for our needs. She told me, among other things, that there were two pilgrim guards outside our room, that there was plague in Grundleford and that royal troops had taken over St. Mary's Abbey.

This was startling news. Royal troops were in the abbey, only four miles away! If only I could get word to them, I thought. If only they would come for us.

"When the king's soldiers marched into the abbey, Saint Agatha was moved out," Becca said. "She was taken from her tomb and brought here, to Snape Hall."

Now I was truly surprised. Saint Agatha, the wonderworking, uncorrupt saint, in our house?

"It was necessary. The king's soldiers would not have shown her proper respect." Becca paused, then bent toward me and whispered in my ear. "Besides, she was starting to smell."

"But I thought her body was preserved, free of corruption."

"So they say. I believed it—until I was cleaning the floor of the abbey chapel one day three months ago and looked down into the tomb, and I could swear that Saint Agatha had changed. The face I saw in the tomb was longer and narrower than the face I had seen when her casket was first opened.

"I was very upset. I went to the prior, Brother Wulfstan, and told him what I noticed. I thought grave-robbers had stolen the saint's body and left another one in its place."

Becca looked at me. I was utterly focused on the story she was telling me. I did not move or speak.

"Do you know what he said to me?" she whispered. "He said they had to bring in a new body every few weeks. Otherwise the smell became very noticeable."

Stunned and bewildered by what I was hearing, I shook my head in disbelief—yet what this girl was telling me rang true. I saw no reason for her to lie, and there was nothing but candor in her eyes. Candor—and the sorrow of disillusionment.

"Do all the pilgrims know that a new Saint Agatha is put into the tomb every few weeks?" I asked.

"Oh no, milady. Hardly anyone knows. And Prior Wulfstan made me swear never to tell anyone about it. He said the saint would strike me dead if I told."

I could not help but smile, Becca was so serious, despite the evident fraud with which she was confronted. "Aren't you worried?" I asked her.

"No, milady. Not about Saint Agatha. The real saint is in heaven, isn't she, and not in some tomb or in the banqueting hall downstairs."

I thought of our banqueting hall, a long, narrow room with an immense hearth and tall windows and a magnificent hammer-beam ceiling. Apparently the current body of Saint Agatha was enshrined there. It was hard to imagine.

"Yes," I said to Becca. "You're right. It is the soul that truly matters, not the body. All the same, it would come as a shock for the pilgrims to discover that their miraculous ancient saint is really a dairymaid who died a day or so ago."

"Or a plague victim," said Becca in a low voice. "The new Saint Agatha is a girl from my village, Emma Hauser. She died of the plague. I know. I recognized her."

Margaret, who had been asleep, stirred and opened her eyes. Her face had an unhealthy flush. She needed medicine for her fever, and a poultice for her cough. I had to get help for her, and I had to get word to John.

I lay awake most of the night worrying over these things, and pondering all that Becca had told me, as I listened to Margaret's coughing and, at cock crow, heard the guards outside our door exchange brief greetings with their replacements.

I finally fell asleep, only to be awakened after far too short a time by noise outside our window.

A large company of pilgrims was arriving, most of the gray-gowned men and women on foot but some mounted. They carried aloft banners with Saint Agatha's image, the banners hanging limp and damp as a light rain was falling. At the head of the group, mounted on a black horse, was a fair young man who rode with the assurance of a leader. When the group reached the courtyard of Snape Hall others rushed to hold his horse while he dismounted, and listened attentively to the orders he gave.

Not long after the arrival of these newcomers a guard opened the door of our Tower room, and the fair young man came in.

"Johnny!" I could not help exclaiming when I saw him, and realized that it had been he who led the newly arrived pilgrim band. He looked so much older than he had the day he left Snape Hall so many months earlier. Then he had been an angry, grim boy, rebellious and truculent. Now he had become a man, imposing and vigorous and confident despite his youth. He looked at me for a moment, his gaze level, then called out to those in the corridor behind him. "Bring the prisoner in."

A hunched, thin figure was half-pushed, half-dragged into the small room and all but thrown onto the bed. His balding head was lowered, his hands tied behind his back with a piece of thick rope. With a shock I realized that it was John.

At once I moved to his side and took his weary drooping head in my arms. Margaret gasped. "Father!" she called out, and tried to raise herself, only to fall back with a spasm of coughing.

"What have you done to him! How dare you!"

"There, there, Gwennidor," I heard John say. "Have a care in what you say. I am not hurt, only tired and hungry."

Johnny regarded his father coolly, turning to glance at Margaret who continued to cough spasmodically, her every breath loud and effortful. Her face was white.

I heeded John's warning and kept silent, though I felt my own face grow hot and it was all I could do to keep myself from slapping Johnny and shouting at him in my anger. I sat down beside John on the bed and put my arm protectively around his shoulder. He was shaking.

"Father has been liberated from the evil army," Johnny was saying. "He was leading the king's men, defending St. Mary's Abbey. Now he will take his rightful place at the head of Saint Agatha's pilgrims, when we march into York and capture it."

"He will do this," Johnny went on, "because he is a good Catholic and because he would not want any harm to come to you, stepmother, or to Margaret."

So these were Johnny's cruel terms. His father would lead the pilgrims into battle against the forces of King Henry or else condemn us to continued imprisonment and possibly worse. John would be forced to compromise his honor, and his sworn loyalty to the king, his sovereign lord, for our sakes.

"He knows that you, stepmother, are not a good Catholic but a reformist, a follower of the apostate Luther and other blasphemers who read the Scriptures in English and presume to interpret them. If the faithful soldiers of Saint Agatha were to discover that you possess an English Bible, they would bring down the wrath of the saint on you without mercy."

I thought of the dreadful execution John and I had seen, the man torn to pieces by dogs, and of other assaults by the pilgrims that we had witnessed and heard about on our journey to Durham.

"I believe you have also taught Margaret to read the English Scriptures. This puts her in danger as well."

I could no longer restrain myself.

"Margaret, as you can see for yourself, has a tertian fever. She is very ill. We have not been allowed any medicine. She badly needs syrup of poppy, and a poultice for her chest."

"When father leads us into York, we will get her what she needs."

"She needs the medicines now. Do you want your sister to die?"

I thought I saw the merest shadow of an anxious look cross Johnny's impassive features, but it came and went in a heartbeat. He drew himself up to his full height and looked down at his wretched father, who met his glance.

"Well father, what say you? Are you ready to put on the gray gown of a pilgrim, and lead the army of Saint Agatha?"

With tears in his eyes, John nodded.

"Very well then." With a deft slice of the knife he wore at his belt Johnny cut the rope that bound his father's hands and, taking his arm, helped him to his feet.

"Come, father, we will find you bread and mutton, and a mug of cider to wash it down." Together they went out into the corridor, leaving the thick oaken door of the Tower room ajar. I went to the doorway and looked out. There were no guards in the corridor. Margaret and I were free.

14

W E WERE FREE—BUT STILL PRISONERS OF THE PILGRIM ARMY, AND OF
Johnny. Margaret and I were allowed to move back into what had been
my bedchamber, and I was not hampered in moving about the manor.
Yet I was aware of being watched, my movements noted. And Becca
continued to serve as our maid and guardian—with the one alteration in
our arrangements that at night, Becca went back to her village of
Grundleford and we were left in peace.

John was not allowed to stay in the same room with us. He was kept
under Johnny's care in another room far from ours. Together John and
Johnny were making plans and readying the pilgrims for the march to
York, which Becca said was to be in a few days. Word had come that
more royal troops were on their way northward to defend York, and this
news gave renewed urgency to the coming rebel campaign to seize York
and bring all the North Country under the dominion of the rebels, the
Pilgrims of Saint Agatha.

I walked through the corridors and rooms of Snape Hall almost as if
I were a stranger. Everywhere I turned I saw devastation.

"We mean no harm," Becca told me as we stood in one of the great
chambers, which before the rebellion had been hung with beautiful

tapestries in gleaming reds and blues and golds. Now the tapestries were heaped on tables and piled in an untidy mound at the center of the room. Chests, upholstered benches, overmantels and candelabra were stacked carelessly on top of one another; some had fallen and been broken. Carved paneling was scraped and marred, the result of the pilgrims' hasty moving in and making themselves at home. No one, it appeared, had done any cleaning; dust and dirt lay on everything, and a layer of soot darkened the hearth, the windows and even the floors.

"Truly, we never wanted to destroy anything, only to make room for ourselves. And to take inventory, of course."

"Take inventory?"

"Of the contents of the house. They will be sold to raise funds for the cause. We pilgrims must eat, after all."

"Yet you told me you were opposed to taking what isn't yours, in the name of God's work."

"I am, of course, but the prior said this house was to be consecrated to Saint Agatha, to be her temporary resting-place. Therefore it belonged to her, and not to those who lived in it."

"The prior of St. Mary's Abbey, Wulfstan?"

"Yes."

"The same man who secretly puts new Saint Agathas in the coffin when the old ones begin to smell?"

Becca's face fell. She followed my logic. When she answered me her voice was low. "Yes."

"Prior Wulfstan is a deceiver. I imagine he said the treasure of St. Mary's was to be consecrated to Saint Agatha too. Am I right?"

Becca nodded.

"I imagine that if you look in those abbey treasure-chests, you will find that Prior Wulfstan has emptied them of gold."

Becca said nothing more to me that day about the condition of Snape Hall or the machinations of Prior Wulfstan, but I could see that she was troubled by what I had said. Meanwhile I turned all my attention to Margaret, who was very weak, her small face flushed, lying restless in her sickbed.

At John's insistence an herb woman was sent to me with powders for Margaret. There was a stillness around her as she approached the bed where Margaret lay, put her wrinkled hand on the girl's sweat-beaded forehead and looked down at her wan little face. She took from around her own neck an amulet on a string, and, lifting Margaret's head, placed the amulet around Margaret's neck. Then she made the sign of the cross over her and murmured, "The Father is Uncreated, The Son is Uncreated, The Holy Spirit is Uncreated" three times.

She turned to Becca. "Find a spider, put it into a nut shell, and dip the nut shell in milk. Bring it here."

Becca went out at once to follow the old woman's instructions.

"Does she have a rash?" the old woman asked me. "Under her armpits, in her groin?"

"I did not see one when we bathed her yesterday."

"That is good." She drew a small cloth bag from the basket she carried. "This is powdered myrtle and rose leaves. Mix it in ale, and it will lower the fever. I will also leave you a comfrey posset to help her breathe. But if you see a rash"—she shuddered—"it will mean—"

"What?"

"The worst affliction of all. The one only God can cure."

I knew at once what she meant. It had come to afflict us twice, once when I was a very little girl and again near the time when Ned and I were married. It was deadlier than the plague. People called it the Sweating Sickness. It swept throughout England, and thousands of people died.

"I understand. I will watch for the rash."

"When the girl returns, tell her to put the spider charm under the bed." With this final injunction the old woman was gone.

That night I sat at Margaret's bedside, asking myself again and again what I could do for Margaret, for John, and for myself. It seemed to me that we were trapped, caught up in the destructive vortex of conflict swirling around us. The more I thought about all that had happened, the more I realized that forces larger than ourselves were compelling events: the deep Catholic faith of the pilgrims, and their veneration of Saint Agatha; the longstanding distrust of all northerners for the king in London; the hatred felt by traditionalists for the king's religious innovations.

We were caught up in a drama vaster than ourselves, yes. But the longer I turned everything over in my mind, the more I came to feel that we were not, after all, helpless. The revolt of the pilgrims had been set in motion by one man, Prior Wulfstan of St. Mary's, with one act—the unearthing of Saint Agatha. All else had resulted from that single action.

Why couldn't I, in the same way, reverse the momentum of the revolt and restore harmony?

At last, toward morning, I dropped off to sleep. I dreamed I was searching for something, but I could not remember what it was. I wandered through the rooms and along the corridors of Snape Hall, then through the royal palace of Whitehall, and finally through the grounds of St. Mary's Abbey. I mingled with a crowd of people coming to visit Saint Agatha's shrine, and walked up to the saint's tomb, as it had been in the past, before the saint's body was removed.

In my dream I heard a voice from the tomb. "Find my mother," it said. "Find my mother."

When I awoke I could still hear the voice, and the memory of the dream lingered. What did it mean? Who was Saint Agatha's mother? I didn't remember ever hearing any legends or stories about her. Was she too a holy woman, revered by the local people for her healing gifts?

Becca brought us a loaf and a wedge of cheese, though Margaret turned her head away when offered the food. She took a mouthful or two of broth, nothing more. After I had eaten, Becca went out and returned with a dark-haired young man, her fiancé Jacob, dressed, as she was, in a gray pilgrim robe. He had soft brown eyes in an open, trusting face. He reminded me a little of Ned, though he showed no sign of Ned's intensity or excessive tenacity.

"Becca has told me everything, milady," he said. "About the different bodies for Saint Agatha, and about Emma Hauser's body being in her tomb now. I knew Emma. Everyone in Grundleford did. She was a pious girl. She wouldn't want to be used like this, to deceive other good sons and daughters of the church."

"I told Jacob what you said about Prior Wulfstan, and the chests of treasures from the abbey," Becca told me. "He knows where the chests are kept. We can go and see them whenever you like."

At my urging Jacob led us to a storage room filled with tuns of cider and barrels of flour, bins of onions and turnips, empty sacks and baskets that had lately held greens, bits of the leaves still clinging to their insides.

"These are from the St. Mary's vault." He pointed out several large wooden chests, securely padlocked. "Should I break one of the locks?"

"In the name of the king, and under my husband's protection, yes."

Jacob lifted a heavy stone and dashed it against the padlock, which gave way after several blows. Eagerly we lifted the lid. The chest was full of rocks.

"Where is the abbey gold?" Greatly dismayed, even distraught by what we saw, Jacob went on to break another padlock. The second chest too was full of rocks.

Swearing, weeping, beside himself with fury, Jacob began ranting that he would find Prior Wulfstan and kill him.

"No, Jacob, no!" I caught hold of his tunic and held him back. "You would only be torn apart by the other pilgrims. There is a better way to expose the villainy. Come, let us go to Grundleford."

15

WITH THE OCCUPANTS OF SNAPE HALL ENGAGED IN PREPARING FOR the march to York, I found it less difficult than I had thought to leave the castle. Becca provided me with a pilgrim gown, and Jacob brought us horses for the half-hour ride to Grundleford, a small cluster of houses and cottages in the shadow of a hillock. An expanse of fields, bare now in early winter, spread out from the houses, with rock walls separating them one from another. There was a sheep-washing pool, frozen at its edges, and as we passed it a gritty wind blew in our faces, making our eyes water. In the distance, a curlew cried.

When we came to the first of the houses we heard the lively sound of a fiddle playing.

"It's market day," Becca told me with pride. "Everyone comes to Grundleford Market."

It was true—or at least it seemed true. Hundreds of people were wandering among the colorful booths and tents spread out along Grundleford's one street. They seemed to care little that the day was raw and the air cold. We left our mounts in the shed behind Becca's house and mingled with the fairgoers.

A second fiddler joined the first and soon young couples were dancing. Jacob, his fury tempered by the long ride and the festive atmosphere in the village, swept Becca up in his arms and they joined in the intricate steps of a country dance, stamping their feet and shouting, while around them people gathered to clap and hum the tune. I walked past tables where gooseberry tarts were spread out for sale, along with crisp late apples and bunches of dried blue graegles, cooking pots and lengths of homespun cloth and ribbon. A grizzled old man sat beneath a house porch selling small bags filled with toads' legs, which he said were certain to cure scrofula.

"Here, milady, feel this," he said, handing me one of the bags. I took it and, holding it, felt a twitching of the legs inside.

"If they twitch they work twice as well."

Country girls with round, plump faces passed me pushing carts, grinning boys pelted each other with acorns and clods of frozen earth. There were snakes in cages and pigeons and larks for sale, to be taken home and made into pies. I marveled at the freaks on display, especially the Grundleford Giant, a man seven feet tall who had served in the king's guard in his youth and still had his halberd painted with the royal arms.

While I walked along I listened to the buzz of talk around me, eager to know the thoughts of the villagers and how they could enjoy themselves and put themselves into a carefree mood while the region was in such an upheaval and so many in their village had died of plague.

I overheard a good deal of gossip. The wife of an elderly farmer was pregnant—and not (so it was whispered) by her feeble husband. One of Jacob's cousins had been caught poaching rabbits and was to be sentenced by the Justice of the Peace—only the justice had been kidnapped by the pilgrims of Saint Agatha and no one had seen him for months. Two farmers, brothers living in a cottage in the dale, had hanged themselves. No one knew why.

Much of the talk was about the weather.

"We knew a bad winter was coming. We knew by the shrew-mice. They dug their holes deep this year, and on the east side of the ditches and furrows instead of the west. As soon as we saw that, we said, it'll be a bad one this year."

"Frogs too. Stronger legs, bigger eyes."

"Rowan leaves off the trees earlier. Spindly rowans. Not like last year."

Amid the talk of immorality and crime, weather and crops, I detected an undercurrent of nervousness. The people of Grundleford were on edge. Beneath their surface gaiety they were apprehensive.

I went into a tent where cider was being served, and sat down at the far end of one of the long tables. The tent was crowded, warmed by a log fire, and the men and women sitting at the tables had lingered to enjoy the warmth and had drunk a good deal of the rich and potent cider. It made them talkative.

I sat drinking my cider, a woman alone in a gray pilgrim gown, and I drew attention.

"Are you off to kill the king then?" one of the rough farm laborers asked me, his rural accent thick. "That's what those pilgrims of Saint Agatha want, isn't it? They want the king dead, and no mistake."

Before I could answer another voice rose above the noise of the general conversation, a woman's voice. She was a hard-eyed, dirty-aproned matron of forty, her manner brazen and her face and neck lined and worn.

"He deserves to die, the old Mouldwarp! He's cruel and he's a sinner many times over. He brings bad luck on us all! Why do you think the plague came to Grundleford last summer? Because God was angry at the king, that's why! I say kill him, let the pilgrims kill him!"

Angry voices rose, some vehemently agreeing that the king should die, others defending him.

"God has put him on his throne as our anointed sovereign lord," came a man's voice. "God alone can punish a king, not the villagers of Grundleford, or the pilgrims of Saint Agatha!"

While the others were arguing another man came up to me and took off his cap.

"It's Lady Latimer," he said, and as he spoke the noise in the room began to abate. "Have you joined the pilgrim army then, milady?"

"I have always venerated Saint Agatha," I answered, aware of how keenly the others were listening, now that they had taken notice of me. "But this talk of killing the king, and all the beatings and murders that have gone on—I don't hold with that. It's un-Christian."

A chorus of aye, aye, it's un-Christian greeted my words.

"But milady, what of the miracle of Saint Agatha? Her pilgrims are being led by God, who has shown his favor in the preservation of her holy body. The pilgrims can do no wrong!"

"Yes! Saint Agatha cured many of the plague—before she was kept from us by the king's soldiers, when they captured St. Mary's Abbey!"

I stood. "I have come to Grundleford to bring you the good news that Saint Agatha is no longer being kept from you. She is at Snape Hall, where she sleeps within a new shrine. I urge you all to come and worship there, and bring those who are sick and dying. Surely by the saint's power many will be healed!"

My words sent a surge of energy and hope through those gathered in the tent. Several people rose.

"Will you lead us there?" someone asked.

"Of course. As soon as you are ready."

But one woman in the group was sobbing, and her anguished cries could not be ignored. I went to her side. Her shoulders shook, she seemed utterly broken in spirit.

"I can't bring my daughter," she managed to say, her tears still flowing. "She is dead. My Emma is dead. And I don't even know where she is. Her body has been spirited away."

It must be Emma Hauser's mother, I thought. The woman whose daughter lay in Saint Agatha's coffin.

I remembered the voice from my dream. Find my mother, the voice had said. Find my mother.

Now I had found her. Not the true Agatha's mother, but the mother of the girl who lay in Agatha's tomb. And if I could manage to bring mother and daughter together, Prior Wulfstan's fraud would be revealed.

"Come with us!" I said to the distraught woman beside me. "Saint Agatha will help you find your daughter's body. I'm certain of it."

Half an hour later a group of villagers left Grundleford and began making their way along the road toward Snape Hall. They came in twos and threes, some leading sick animals, some riding on carts carrying men or women afflicted with plague. Sick children were trundled in barrows or carried on broad backs.

The fair was all but deserted, everyone was going to the hall where the saint now lay enshrined, their gait slow but their faces hopeful, worshipful, as the sun sank low in the western sky and the chill wind rose around them.

With Becca and Jacob and Emma Hauser's mother at my side, I led the way, grateful for the warmth of my pilgrim robe, praying that I was doing the right thing, determined to confront the dark fraud that lay at the heart of the rebellion and bring it out into the light.

16

THROUGH THE TALL WINDOWS OF THE IMMENSE BANQUETING CHAMBER in Snape Hall came the dull gray light of late afternoon. The chamber had been transformed into a chapel, with a raised platform at one end where Prior Wulfstan in his clerical robes was preparing to serve mass. Behind him was a large carved marble statue of Saint Agatha, nearly lifesize, brought from the abbey, and beside him, lying deep in her flower-draped coffin, was the body which I knew to be that of Emma Hauser.

The pilgrims were gathering to attend the mass, and to pray for the success of the campaign against York. With our arrival the room became very crowded, as one by one the villagers from Grundleford brought their sick relatives and animals to lay before the makeshift altar, the beasts lowing and bleating restlessly and the invalids groaning weakly and crying out, some reaching out their hands toward the holy coffin in mute appeal.

I saw Johnny come in, and my heart sank, for behind him came two men carrying a pallet bed on which Margaret lay. Gently they placed the bed near the saint's coffin, but Margaret did not stir. She lay as if asleep, her features calm in repose, her skin as alabaster white as the statue of Saint Agatha that smiled benignly down upon the entire gathering.

In the few hours that I had been away in Grundleford, Margaret had weakened further. I went up to her bed and, looking down at her, saw the marks of the dreaded red rash on her arms. As the herb woman had feared, she had the Sweating Sickness. Clearly she lay near death.

I returned to stand with the others, Becca and Jacob and Emma's mother, and was soon joined by John, looking stronger and more fit though in evident sorrow over Margaret's decline. He put his arm around me and I leaned against his bony shoulder, glad to inhale his familiar musky stale scent and glad too to close my own eyes, for a moment, within the safety of his embrace.

Wulfstan began to chant the opening prayers and the celebration of the mass began. I looked over at Becca and Jacob, with whom I had shared my hope that, once Emma's mother saw her daughter and recognized her, the fraud surrounding Saint Agatha would be revealed and the plans of the pilgrims disrupted. Stay close to me, I had said. Whatever happens, let us stay close together. They had readily agreed.

Wulfstan chanted the Kyrie and Gloria and the lengthy Credo, the Latin statement of belief. Long accustomed to hearing the endless unintelligible words—unintelligible to all but a tiny few of those present—the congregation stood patiently, not distracted by the human and animal noises or by the discomfort of the overcrowded room. A hymn was sung, Wulfstan chanted more words and prepared to serve the congregants, lifting the chalice of wine high over his head.

One by one the worshipers came forward to receive their bit of blessed bread, following which they gazed down into Saint Agatha's coffin and asked for her blessing. I joined the line, with Emma's mother ahead of me and John following me. I glanced at Margaret, who lay unmoving on her pallet, her eyes closed. I could not tell whether she was still breathing, so motionless was her small form under the thick blanket.

Emma's mother came to Prior Wulfstan, opened her mouth to receive her morsel of bread, and moved on. I held my breath.

As I watched, she walked the few steps to the coffin and looked down—into her daughter's face.

She screamed.

A terrible, loud, wailing scream. An unearthly scream, like that of one waking from a hellish nightmare.

I froze, as did those around me. For an instant, time stopped. Then, with an angry roar Emma's mother rushed at Wulfstan and began to beat at his chest with her fists.

"This is not Saint Agatha!" she shouted, loudly enough for many in the room to hear. "This is my Emma! You have stolen my daughter! My Emma!"

Others rushed to look down into the coffin, some of them from Grundleford where Emma was well known.

"It is true! It is true! This is Emma!"

I was buffeted as people pushed past me, eager to confirm with their own eyes what they were hearing. There were more shouts, more screams. A woman fainted. Emma's mother, restrained by two pilgrims in gray robes, continued to denounce Prior Wulfstan at the top of her lungs, tears streaming down her face.

I felt John clutch my hand. Becca and Jacob had been pushed away by the crush of bodies, now clustering around the altar, but I could still see them.

All around me there were cries of alarm, murmurs of bewilderment and discontent. Who has done this terrible thing? I heard a voice say. Who has committed this sacrilege? It can't be, surely she is mistaken, came another voice.

Not Saint Agatha. Not Saint Agatha. Gradually the full realization spread throughout the room. Outraged, in fury, the disillusioned worshipers sought to vent their wrath. Some attempted to rush toward Prior Wulfstan, others uttered loud curses, some struck out blindly, convulsed by rage.

Johnny leaped up onto the platform and attempted to shout above the noise and chaos, the panicked mooing and bleating of the animals, the shouts and cries. But he was drowned out and shoved aside. Prior Wulfstan jumped down off the platform and tried to push his way out of the room, but was snatched at and held by dozens of angry worshipers, demanding to know how the body of a dead village girl came to be in the saint's coffin.

Shoved this way and that as those around me pushed and were pushed, I was nearly knocked off my feet. I thought, we will die here. We will all die here. We will be trampled. Into Thy hands, O Lord, Into Thy hands—

But then, just as I was feeling at my most powerless, and resigning myself to die, something very remarkable happened.

Whether it was the setting sun breaking through the dark clouds, or whether, as it seemed at the time, a light from beyond our earthly realm began to penetrate the room, there was a sudden illumination.

Bright light flooded in through the tall windows of the immense room, shafts of clear golden light, magnificently radiant, shining on the angry, shouting faces, the flailing arms and clenched fists, the tearstained cheeks and eyes filled with disillusionment and pain.

To us who were witness to this seeming marvel the light appeared to gather focus on the statue of Saint Agatha, bathing it in a golden glow. To our awed eyes it appeared that the statue, her face gracious and benign, began to smile. Such a smile it was! A smile of infinite and tender kindness, of forgiveness, of holiness.

As rapidly as the impulse of anger and violence had spread through the mass of worshipers, there now came a cessation of fury and struggle, a wave of peace.

"It is Saint Agatha! The true saint! It is a sign from Saint Agatha!"

In quiet reverence the pilgrims knelt and crossed themselves. Emma Hauser's mother knelt beside the coffin where her daughter lay. Prior Wulfstan, looking up in amazed wonder at the golden statue, fell on his face before it.

"Agatha, blessed Agatha, forgive me!"

The animals had fallen silent, the invalids too were hushed, the wonderful light illumining their faces so that they blinked in amazement, seeming to forget their suffering.

Margaret too opened her eyes, blinked and looked around her. As I watched, too overjoyed to speak, half afraid that I was only imagining what I thought I saw, she slowly sat up. Seeing John, she held out her bare arms to him—arms which, I saw clearly, no longer bore the red rash of the Sweating Sickness.

"Father!" John went up to her, the kneeling pilgrims parting to let him by, and lifted her in his arms.

This was our moment. I felt it. I looked at John, and he seemed to understand. Instead of coming toward me he made his way toward the outer door of the banqueting hall, Margaret in his arms. I followed him. Together we passed through the door and into the courtyard where Jacob, anticipating our departure, soon met us with horses.

Taking only what we had with us, and hoping we would not encounter any brigands or suspicious pilgrims on the road, we spurred our horses along the highroad toward the south and safety, surrounded by the glowing golden light of the setting sun.

17

WHEN I SAW KING HENRY RIDING IN FULL ARMOR AT THE HEAD OF his army I was quite overawed by the sight. Here, coming up over the brow of the hill, was a force of men—pikemen, bowmen, spearmen, strong and fit and girded for war—with a tall, resolute commander on a fine Barbary stallion in the forefront, banners with the Tudor coat of arms flying at his side.

Henry rode in his golden armor, which gleamed and shone and flashed in the sunlight. His feet were in golden spurs, the trappings of his mount were of red and white and gold and even the tail of his splendid horse was braided with gold.

We had known for several days that he was coming, determined to reclaim the rebellious North Country for his own and to punish those who had risen against him. But we were not prepared for the overwhelming impact of him, our sovereign king and lord, riding in his might and glory, with all the thunderous power of a thousand men-at-arms at his heels.

For two weeks we had been at Briarknoll, an estate near Gadbury, where we had taken refuge from the turmoil that followed the collapse of the pilgrim revolt. Margaret was recovering wonderfully (thanks be

to Saint Agatha!). Johnny, sobered and even contrite after his discovery
that he and the other pilgrims had been deceived and led astray by Prior
Wulfstan, was preparing to join the Calais Spears, my uncle William's
troop of fighting men who guarded the king. John, weakened by the
ordeal of his capture and looking pallid and frail, kept to his bed and
rested, while I read to him from his favorite books of romance.

But we all, even John, went up on the roof of the manor house
to watch the approach of the royal army, with King Henry in the
vanguard, and we all cheered and waved as the men passed by, on their
way to St. Mary's Abbey which was to become the king's headquarters,
and we were delighted when some of the men raised their hands to us
in acknowledgment, and shouted "Down with the rebels! Down with
the filthy pigs of rebels!" and other oaths and curses which I will not
record here.

I had not seen the king since he became a widower, since word
reached us that he had accused his queen, Anne Boleyn, of adultery and
ordered her executed.

We were not altogether surprised by this news, though it made me
shudder when I heard it and cross myself. Visitors from the south had
kept us informed of the king's marriage to Anne and the turbulent, often
bruising course it had taken. How the king had married Anne and had
paraded his new pregnant bride before the Londoners. How she had
borne his child, only to have that child turn out to be a princess, Princess
Elizabeth, instead of a prince. And how Queen Anne, as many said, lay
under a curse from that day forward and had been unable to give Henry
a son.

Then a messenger had come to John from the court with a letter
from the royal council, informing him that Queen Anne had been
charged with treason and would lose her life. Swift on the heels of the
first messenger came a second, bearing happier news: King Henry had
married one of the late queen's ladies, Jane Seymour.

He must be content with his new wife, I thought as I watched the
royal army pass with the king riding in all his magnificence in the
vanguard. She must please him. I pray she gives us a prince.

Soon after the royal army arrived John and I were invited to a
banquet at the abbey. I wore my most becoming gown of peach-colored
silk trimmed in saffron lace, with undersleeves of gold brocade. It was a
very elaborate gown; it took my maids half an hour just to fasten me into

the undershift, overskirt and tied-on sleeves, which were fastened at the wrist with rubies. I had an English hood to complement the gown, for I knew that our new queen Jane preferred the old-fashioned peaked English hood to the round French hoods Queen Anne used to wear.

Queen Anne! I was only too aware, as John and I were escorted to our places of honor at the king's banqueting table, that I must not mention her name or allude to her in any way. She had been swept from the face of the earth, and all that remained of her was her child, Elizabeth, the child no one dared speak of and no one at court ever saw.

The king was munching on a sweetmeat when we were brought up to the table. Apparently he had begun dining before his guests arrived.

"Ah, Lord and Lady Latimer! Our honored guests!"

The king motioned to us to sit down, waving us toward two high-backed carved chairs, a welcoming smile on his fleshy face. I saw now what had not been apparent when I admired him from a distance, on horseback: that he had grown very fat.

The slender, athletic hero-king I had seen on the tiltyard when I was a girl was no more; instead, here was a heavy, jowly warrior-king, muscular and strong but ponderous in his movements. The Henry I remembered was handsome and full of seductive charm. The man I saw before me now was middle-aged and had a sour droop to his mouth. Though he was being gracious to John and me his small eyes, sunken in their puffy sockets, were suspicious. And I noticed that the men around him were afraid of him. Their fear revealed itself in small ways, in the restlessness and slight trembling of their hands, in the way they stiffened to attention when he spoke, in the sidelong glances they gave him, as if watching for sudden unexpected movements, when he was silent and preoccupied.

"Here is the lady who saved the North for the crown," Henry was saying, his loud voice carrying easily throughout the large abbey refectory where we and a hundred or more others were about to dine. "Had she not acted to prevent the rebel march on York, we might be fighting today, instead of hanging rebels from every tree between here and the marches!"

I was acknowledged with enthusiastic applause.

"And here is her stalwart husband, Lord Latimer!"

Acclamation for John was hesitant (for it was well known that he had been about to lead the rebels into York, albeit under duress) until the king began clapping loudly. Then the noise rose in a crescendo. John smiled wanly in response. He knew that by sending the rebels into confusion and turning them against Prior Wulfstan I had saved his life; had he led the pilgrims into York he would have been executed by the king as a traitor.

Servants brought in the first course, shields of brawn and frumenty with venison, salted hart and a rich bruet. Musicians played as we ate, and for a moment I felt I was back in London, a young girl again, sitting beside my mother as she waited on Queen Catherine. But then I reminded myself that Queen Catherine was dead, she had died alone in her lonely exile at Kimbolton Castle. And that we had a new queen on the throne now, Queen Jane.

For some three hours the banqueting went on, with course after steaming course brought in and abundant wine to drink. The king, as ever the focus of all attention, talked on and on. But I couldn't help feeling tense, for there was such a strong undercurrent of fear and uncertainty in the room.

John grew tired and nodded over his plate of jellies and Lombard Milk.

"Rooms are prepared for you," the king said to me. "I hope you and Lord Latimer will stay the night."

I wondered for a moment whether King Henry was inviting us to stay the night so that he could visit my bedroom. He had always been seductive with me. But I saw no lechery in his expression. And it would be better for John if he did not have to ride back to Briarknoll until the following day.

"Thank you, your majesty." I got up and helped John to his feet. We were shown to a suite of small rooms, formerly monks' cells, and John lay down on one of the narrow hard beds.

There was a light tap on the door and when I opened it, a servant bowed and handed me a note.

"Walk with me in the garden, Cat," was all it said.

Of course I knew it was the king's message. I threw a coarse brown blanket from one of the beds over my thin gown and made my way to the inner courtyard where the king, with several tall guardsmen, was waiting.

The chill night was moonlit, and the air, though still wintry, smelled of damp earth and moss and pungent animal scents. There were no signs of spring yet, but they would arrive soon. Already the frost, when it came, left a thinner rime on the grass and melted in the early morning sun.

As soon as I came up to King Henry and his escort, he sent the guards away.

"I don't think I need to worry about any pilgrim assassins lurking in the shrubbery tonight, do I?" He smiled, and I smiled back, a tentative smile. "Do I need protection from you?"

"I am your majesty's loyal subject."

"Ah, but you are far more than that, and I think you know it. You realize I came within a hair's breadth of losing this northern region."

I shook my head. "It was a sort of madness, this rebellion. A contagion. People got caught up in the excitement of marching, and killing, and believing in the cause of defending the old faith."

"And attacking the evil Mouldwarp. Oh yes, I know what they say about me. Some of them really do want me dead."

"Only because they think you want to destroy their faith."

"To destroy their faith? Is that what I am doing? Or am I liberating them from the corruption and superstition of the church of Rome?"

We walked slowly through the old garden, the trees bare-branched and the shrubs leafless and low to the earth, as if clinging to the bare ground for comfort in this season of cold and darkness.

"I have great plans for this place," the king said as we rounded the corner of the herb garden and entered an orchard. "Oh yes, great plans. I need a strong fortress here in the North Country. St. Mary's Abbey will be dissolved. There will be no more St. Mary's Abbey. These grounds, these buildings will become my new palace. My Imperium." He waved one arm in a sweeping gesture.

"No king of England has ever built such a palace, on such a scale. I have ordered twelve hundred workmen hired. It will be magnificent. A monument to Tudor greatness." He stopped walking, paused in his talk, and looked over at me. "If only God is gracious, and gives me a son to inherit it."

"Yes. I was very sorry to learn of the Duke of Richmond's death." Henry's bastard son had died the previous summer, only the death had been kept secret for months. John and I had only learned of it recently. The king had ordered a quietly obscure burial for poor Henry Fitzroy, the boy who had never been good enough at sports to satisfy his father.

Henry shrugged. "I was fond of him, at one time I had hopes for him, but he was an embarrassment. Besides, my little Jane is pregnant. We will have a boy. I feel it." He reached into an inner pocket of his doublet and pulled out a silver-backed miniature. He handed it to me. The moonlight shone on the palm-sized painting of a woman's face, her hair hidden under her severe cap, her small brown eyes solemn, her small mouth held tight and rigid, as if she was making an effort to hold her tongue. It was the face of a girl, I thought, not a woman. And a girl no one would look at twice.

"She's very plain, as you can see. Nothing like the Witch." He looked over at me, his gaze searching. I did not know what, if anything, to say. He had brought up the unmentionable subject: Queen Anne. And he was looking to see how I felt about what had happened to her.

I dared not tell him, of course. I dared not say, you are a murderer. You tired of your shrill, demanding Queen Anne, and you grew angry at her when she did not give you the son you wanted. So you lied about her, and accused her of adultery, and forced her own uncle to serve as her judge and put her to death. I dared not say, you did something ugly and wrong, and you are a murderer.

I looked back at Henry, and saw, at that moment, the ruthless, calculating gaze of a man capable of putting a woman he had once loved to death. There was ice in his glance, ice in his heart.

"I am told that Queen Jane has a very sweet nature, and kind affections."

"She has, she has. Not like the Witch."

Once again there was only silence, as we walked on under the bare trees. I pulled my blanket around me. An owl hooted twice, and then I heard the beat of wings and the scream of a small rodent as the owl swooped down and caught his prey.

"She was one, you know," Henry was saying, his voice low and slightly tremulous. "No matter what anyone says. She put me under a spell. She forced me to love her." At the word "forced," the king's voice broke. "All that I did that was wrong, I did because she forced me."

I stopped walking, turned and looked up at him. "You don't really believe that. You are far too intelligent a man to believe that."

He laughed, and for a moment his somber mood lifted. "That's what I love about you, Cat. You have fortitude. Nothing frightens you."

"A great deal frightens me. You frighten me." I looked up into his face. A smile still hovered at the edges of his lips but his eyes were hard and glittering in the moonlight, the line of his jaw set and firm. Suddenly I felt the weight of my fear. I had an urge to run from him, yet I knew that if I ran, he would catch me before I had gone more than a few steps. I thought, we are like the owl and the poor creature it caught, the creature whose dying shriek I had heard only minutes ago. Wherever I go, whatever I do, he will always have the power to swoop down on me and catch me in his sharp talons, and I will be at his mercy.

"I would never harm you," he was saying. "I enjoy looking at you too much. But I see you are shivering. Come, let us find a warm posset, and a fire."

He led me back inside the abbey where we settled ourselves in front of the hearth in a room he was using as a guardroom. Four burly soldiers in red livery lounged at the opposite end of the room, rolling dice and drinking from large tankards. The warmth of the fire made my arms and hands tingle and I drank greedily from the cup of hot cider a servant brought me.

"Sire, I cannot help but wonder why you should be talking to me in this way."

"Shall I be gallant, or shall I tell you the truth?"

"The truth, of course."

"Because someone must believe me. I need someone to believe me. Someone with nothing to gain."

"I'll listen." That much, at least, I could offer. "What was the truth—about Queen Anne?"

"I despise that name!" He slammed his silver cup of hot cider down on the nearest bench, making the guardsmen jump up and start to walk toward us. With a gesture he stopped them and they went back to their dice and drink. "She never deserved the name of queen!" the king went on. "She was nothing more than a scheming whore. She knew the black arts. She was a witch. From the day I first saw her I was not myself. I felt like a man moving in a fog, wading through quicksand. My mind was not my own."

He called for more cider and drank deeply. "All those years I was in thrall to her, like a dog on a leash. She made me do terrible things. She disliked Wolsey, and of course he had to go. She hated Catherine and Mary. She tried to poison my poor boy, poor Fitzroy—did you know that? He was sick for weeks. She had a poison room, with all sorts of jars and ointments—a terrible place. Her own sister-in-law Jane Rochford came and told me about it. I had everything in it burned and buried."

He leaned closer to me, and spoke in a low tone so that the guards could not overhear. "I think she poisoned herself, by accident, mixing those potions of hers. I think that's why her babies were not normal. They weren't, you know. Those babies that came out early. One had no legs, just little stumps." He grew pale, clearly he was frightened. "The last one, I was told, had no eyes. I couldn't bear to look at it myself. They were freaks. She would have given me freaks for sons, if they had lived."

He looked around furtively, assuring himself that the guards were absorbed in their gambling. Then he turned back to me and rolled up one leg of his gold-embroidered breeches. There was a nauseating stench as he revealed his naked pale pink flesh, and a wide bandage stained with greenish pus. I drew back, taking a scented pomander of orange and cloves from the pocket of my gown and fastening it over my nose.

"She did this. Just as if she drove a knife into my leg with her own hands. She caused this—by witchcraft. I was riding at the tilt, and she cursed me. She made me fall. The horse fell on top of me. I've had bad wounds ever since."

He rolled his breeches down again and I took a gulp of fresh air.

"Witches have been burned for hundreds of years," I said, "by the church. Why didn't you let the priests judge Anne, and condemn her?"

"You forget, I am head of the church in England now. We have severed our ties to Rome. There has been no cardinal legate in England for many years. Our policies with regard to witchcraft, or heresy, or any other crime under canon law, are at present unclear. No, it was better to bring the Witch to justice for treason. And she was guilty of treason. She was desperate to have a son. She began sleeping with any man she could find, just to get a son, to save her life."

"You could have divorced her."

"And have her go on living and working her spells on me? And on my future sons? No Cat, I could not."

At length he rose, and I could tell, from the way he stood, that his leg was hurting him.

"I rely on your discretion, Cat," he said.

"John will want to know what we have talked about."

"And do you tell your husband everything?"

I smiled. "Most everything. But only if he asks."

"It does me good to talk. I've had no one to talk to since More and Catherine died."

But you killed them both, I wanted to say. You had Thomas More executed and you broke Catherine's spirit and hastened her death by your cruelty. You killed two of those you valued most in the world, and you cannot blame that on witchcraft. Or can you?

I wanted to say these things, yet I held my tongue. The king had confided in me. He had given me his trust, and even though I still feared him, he had brought me within the small circle of those he relied on. Someone must believe me, he had said. I did not believe him, I thought him dangerous and deluded, but I saw now for the first time that he himself believed what he had told me. I saw the frightened inner man that lurked within the frightening king. And I could not but feel that there had been formed between us, during that long and chilling conversation, a bond of honor.

18

I FIRST SAW HIM STANDING, TALL AND LEAN AND ARRESTINGLY HANDSOME, his reddish-blond hair tumbling down to his collar, one foot resting on a chunk of fallen stone, in the ruins of St. Mary's Abbey on the afternoon of Lady Day, in the Year of Our Lord 1538. He was wearing a leather jerkin and his long trousers were tucked into high riding boots of brown leather. I thought he was an architect or builder, standing there. All around him, amid the remains of stone arches and rough walls, were wooden sticks planted in the earth, marking the places where new walls and archways were to be erected, for the royal palace to be built where the old abbey had stood. He appeared to be studying these, thoughtfully, and I assumed he was in charge of the works.

A year had passed since my conversation with King Henry in the moonlit abbey grounds, and in that time much had changed. Hundreds of laborers had come to live and work on or near the grounds of the old abbey—the new Imperium. Men from nearby villages came to make bricks or tiles, or haul stones or timber, their wives and daughters hiring themselves out as cooks or laundresses or what the soldiers called camp-followers. The work never seemed to stop. The Imperium was like a giant anthill, with industrious creatures swarming throughout its labyrinthine depths, each bent on his or her own vital errand.

Yet when I saw him on that day, in the midst of all the activity, he was uniquely still.

"Pardon me, I wonder if you could help me?"

He looked up, saw me on my roan palfrey, and started toward me. He walked slowly, gracefully, a smile gradually irradiating his sun-browned face. There was an airy lightness about him. He was blithe. His eyes were very, very blue.

"Are you in charge here?"

For an instant he looked surprised, then laughed. "You could say that, yes. How can I help you?"

There were other men at work nearby. I heard the sounds of hammering and of sledges striking stone. Carts loaded with timbers and barrels passed by among the structures. But they faded out of my awareness as the man who spoke to me, his voice deep and rich, came closer, so close that he reached out to seize the bridle of my horse, steadying her.

"I'm looking for one of your stonemasons. A Frenchman. Monsieur Herbault."

"There are many stonemasons here. Hundreds I believe. They live in temporary quarters, on the other side of that hill." He pointed to a hillock on the far side of the Imperium grounds, some distance from where we stood.

The sound of his voice lulled me. I could not stop looking down into his eyes. He rubbed my horse's neck, his large brown hand gentle against her coat, and she whickered with pleasure. For a man responsible for a large and complex building operation, he seemed remarkably unhurried. He was looking at me with evident pleasure. My lips were parted. I was smiling.

"I'll take you there, if you like."

I slid down off my horse and he half-caught, half-supported me. Simply, naturally, a feeling came over me: I wanted to be in his arms.

"I'm Tom," he said as he took my horse's reins and, leading her, we began to pick our way through the expanse of stones and piles of bricks. A path led off across a meadow, with flowering hedges of dog-roses and veronica.

"Watch out for the nettles," Tom said. Strong sunlight warmed my face and neck under the broad-brimmed cap I wore, and the scents, sounds and colors around me now seemed heightened. The small blue flowers at the edge of the path were intensely blue, the green reeds that grew in the water-filled ditches were pungent in their rank odor, the crunch of Tom's boots as he took each step seemed particularly loud and distinct. I was caught up in each melodious bird call, each buzzing fly. The very rustling of my skirt as it swept over the stones of the path, catching on withered blossoms or fallen twigs, arrested my attention.

The slanting rays of the afternoon sun struck the leaves, the grasses, and our slowly moving bodies at what seemed a perfect angle, and we seemed to walk in a timeless moment, through the landscape of a dream.

We came to a stile and he led my horse around it, through the tall meadow grass, then came back to help me over the stone steps. His strong brown arm was bare almost to the elbow, with a fine dusting of reddish-brown hairs. I reached for it to steady myself. When I touched his arm it was rough but warm; touching it, I could not help but shudder slightly, as tremulous as the leaves of the dog-roses that shivered in the faint breeze.

I looked into his eyes, and what I saw there, in that long-ago moment, I can never forget. It was as if we had known each other for a lifetime—knew all, and understood all. We were complete. There was nothing more to do or say. Without hesitation I surrendered to the truth of that indescribable moment. I have never been the same since.

We spoke as we walked along, though our words had nothing to do with what we felt. They were only words, empty things when compared to the wordless tie between us.

"I am looking for Monsieur Herbault's cottage, but I am really on an errand of mercy. Father Croally from Grundleford sent me. He heard there was a woman in the cottage, a stranger, and that she may be ill."

"We must hurry then."

We quickened our pace for the last half-mile, though the path grew narrower and more stony, and Tom had to lead my horse through sweet-smelling waist-high grass for much of the way. At last we came to a row of newly built cottages, hastily thrown together (by the look of them) for the use of workmen constructing the Imperium. A few inquiries led us to a cottage at the far end of the row, somewhat apart from the others, screened by a row of shrubs.

Lean pigs rooted in a dung-hill only steps from the low doorway, and thin chickens pecked at the barren ground, watched listlessly by three small children in dirty shifts. The oldest of the children, a boy, I took to be five or six years old, the two girls perhaps four and two. The youngest, her fingers in her mouth, looked up at me as we approached, her gaze vacant as she wandered by the pigs and reached out to touch them.

Tom tied the horse to a tree and helped me down. His arms were warm where they touched me. I took my basket of food and herbs from the saddlebags and pushed open the cottage door.

The room was dim, the ceiling low. An odor of dirt and decaying food and unemptied chamber pots made me gag at first, though I managed to overcome my reaction and walked toward the narrow, uncurtained bed where a woman lay, her tangled and matted hair spread out around her. Her eyes were closed.

Except for the bed, there was no furniture in the cottage. Indeed it looked abandoned. A few candle-ends lay on the overmantel of the hearth, and an ancient kneading-trough stood against the single window. But there were no chests and no tables, no shelves for food—only a single string of onions hanging from a rafter. I wondered how long it had been since the children had had anything to eat.

I moved closer to the bed and saw that the woman cradled a sleeping newborn in her arms. The tiny infant was so still I thought at first it might be dead, but then I saw the merest flicker of movement in one of the small pink fingers and felt reassured. The baby was alive—but what of the mother?

Her face, half covered with hair, was pale and there were dark circles under her eyes. I looked around for firewood and, seeing none, went back outside where I found some sticks leaning against a hedge.

"How is she?" asked Tom as he helped me gather the bits of wood.

"Poorly. I think she's just had her baby. It's alive. There are loaves in my saddlebags. Would you give the children some bread? I'll try to make a fire and boil some tea."

I busied myself breaking the sticks and laying them on the hearth. Using a discarded bit of coarse cloth lit from the burning candle I kindled the fire, and hung a kettle of water over it into which I sprinkled a restorative herb. There was no sound from the bed. I could hear Tom talking to the children outside. His voice was cheering. He was making the children laugh.

When the tea was ready I poured some into a cracked cup and sat down gently on the bed. The woman heaved a sigh and opened her eyes. I saw fear in her eyes and held out the tea with what I hoped was a reassuring smile.

"You must be very tired. Here, drink this. It will restore you."

Her look of fear changed to bewilderment. Without waking the baby she raised herself up, painfully, until she could take a sip of tea from the cracked cup I held out to her.

"Thirsty," she whispered through bloodless lips. "So thirsty."

She drank again, then sank back into her thin pillow, eyes closed. Presently she opened them again, and looked at me, somewhat dazed.

"Are you my guardian angel?"

"In a way. The priest from Grundleford told me you might be ill and need some help."

I reached over and gently brushed the matted hair from her cheeks and temples. The firelight illumined her features. I blinked, then looked more closely.

"I've seen you before. But I can't remember where."

She turned her head away. "It doesn't matter." The baby woke and began to whimper.

"Were you employed at Snape Hall? Or in the household of the Duke of Richmond?"

I studied her face, the face of a woman who had suffered. Who was suffering.

"The Duke of Richmond!" she was saying, a note of contempt coming into her weak voice. "How the king used to cosset him! A weakling! Bessie Blount's brat!"

"Anne? Is it Anne?" I remembered that high-pitched, contemptuous voice, and saw, in the ravaged face, my once beautiful and imperious sister-in-law, Anne Bourchier Parr. The woman who had run away from my brother Will so many years before.

When she heard me say her name she began to weep. I could tell that she was struggling within herself, struggling not to give way to an overwhelming emotion. But she was too weak. The dammed-up feelings flooded out.

"Cat! Oh, Cat!"

I bent to embrace her, and for a long time neither of us could speak. She was so thin, so ill. I rocked her in my arms like a child.

The baby began to cry and Anne offered him her breast.

"Dear Anne, we had no idea where you were. We heard that you were living with a priest. What happened? Where have you been? What have you been living on, you and the children?"

She shook her head and swallowed. "There is too much to tell."

"Of course. Never mind all that now. The important thing is to get you well again, and taken care of, you and your children. I take it that Monsieur Herbault—"

She waved one hand dismissively, and I said no more about the absent Frenchman.

I went outside. Tom had one of the children on his knee, and the two others were at his feet, in the dirt. They were munching on hunks of bread.

"Is there a way we can get the family to Grundleford, do you think? The mother needs a midwife." Becca would take them in, I felt sure, until I could provide a place for them to live. There would be plenty of time to think about that later.

"Leave it to me." Tom lifted the child off his lap and set her gently down. He strode off purposefully toward the building site, his long stride swift.

By the time he returned, driving a workman's cart, the sun was low on the horizon. We laid Anne and her baby on blankets on the floor of the cart and I held the two girls on my lap. The boy sat beside Tom as he drove, whistling, along the cart track toward the village, with my horse bringing up the rear.

19

Y OU'RE HERE AGAIN. I'M SO GLAD." TOM REACHED FOR MY HAND, GRASPED it firmly in his, and led me off into the meadows again, where we had been the day before.

"I couldn't stay away." There was no sense in pretending, in inventing an excuse for coming again to the building site. I told Tom the truth.

He nodded. "If you hadn't come, I would have tried to find you." The air was sweet with the scent of gillyflowers, there were bluebells massed on the hillside and from somewhere nearby a blackbird shouted. I was exultant.

We walked along the same narrow path we had followed the day before, but instead of crossing the stile we turned toward a stand of old trees, and presently stepped into their shadow. Here the scents were of moss and fern, decaying leaves and fresh water. I leaned toward Tom as we walked beside a small stream for a ways and then he took me in his arms. His lips were warm. He kissed me gently at first, then with more urgency, until with the pounding of my heart and the great surging of my emotions I lost myself in the power of his kiss. I was lost—and I was found. For in that rapturous moment I felt utterly taken out of myself. I was a new being, the old self had passed away forever.

"You are in my heart," he said.

"And you are in mine."

A frown flitted over his brow. "Let's stay this way. No names, no ranks."

"I agree."

We kissed again, a lingering, unhurried kiss and I felt my heart expand. I had no defenses, and wanted none. I belonged to Tom, and Tom alone.

We sat on the bank of the stream and kissed and talked and kissed again. He splashed me and I splashed back and we ran through the wood, laughing and chasing each other like children. He picked up a small pinkish stone from the stream bed and held it out to me.

"A keepsake," he said. I took it and kissed it and put it in the pocket of my damp gown.

Watching him, I saw that in his reflective moments Tom appeared preoccupied, and I asked him what was on his mind.

He looked at me for a long time. "I'm thinking of getting married," he said at length. "It would benefit me a lot."

He knew that I was married already, for I wore my gold wedding band.

"Do you like the woman?"

"I barely know her."

Most men married for family reasons, or to gain money and standing. Everyone knew that. Tom was an artisan. Perhaps, I thought, he was pondering marrying a more prosperous artisan's daughter.

"Are you being urged to marry?"

"No. It is entirely my choice."

I thought of my two marriages. I had married Ned because we liked each other—and grew to love each other very much. But I had married him in part to avoid having to marry his grandfather. And I had married John in order to avoid having to serve Mistress Anne Boleyn. How wonderful it must be, I thought, to be entirely free, to have the choice be one's own.

"How fortunate you are to be so free."

"Fortunate—and now, after meeting you, unfortunate. The choice will be much harder to make now."

I kissed him then, a strong, possessing kiss. If I was his, I wanted him to be mine. Only mine.

We met the next day, and instead of going to the copse we went to the cottage Anne had been living in. When we got there Tom stopped me at the door.

"Close your eyes," he said, smiling. I obeyed. He lifted me into his arms, opened the door, and carried me across the threshold.

He carried me into another world.

A rich red silk coverlet was draped over a wide bed with embroidered hangings in red and gold. Gilded firedogs guarded the neatly swept hearth. A cupboard of carved oak was open, invitingly, waiting for our clothes to be deposited there. A bowl of red rose petals scented the entire room.

On a low table spread with a fine white linen cloth, plates of fruit and sweet loaves and comfits were laid out, and alongside them was a jug of wine. All was for our ease and comfort. The dingy room had been swept and scrubbed, and there was a basin of water and soft cloths for our use in washing. The room was lit by dozens of ivory candles that shed a warm glow over everything.

"Oh, Tom!"

He put me down and I circled the room, appreciating every object in it, all lovingly assembled by this mysterious, compelling man. I could imagine all the work that had gone into renovating the cottage, all the expense. How could a clerk of the works, even a master clerk, afford all this, I wondered.

I leaned against one of the carved wooden bedposts and allowed the scent of the rose petals, the soft light and warmth of the room to lull me. Through my half-closed eyes I saw Tom approach me, his bronzed face gleaming in the firelight. I trembled when he caressed my cheek. My body yielded to him when he kissed me. And when we lay, flesh to flesh and heart to beating heart, in the soft silken bed I was carried higher, deeper, further into realms of passion I had never before imagined. Even to try to set down here how intense were the pleasures and raptures we shared seems a desecration. Words are so feeble, actions so vital and strong. The merest touch of Tom's hand brought my body alive, the merest word he spoke, softly and lovingly, quickened all my senses and sent shafts of fire along my nerves.

I loved as I had never loved before. As I will never love again.

I loved Tom—and because I loved and needed him, I saw him nearly every day, saying that I was visiting my long-lost sister-in-law Anne in Grundleford when I was really with my lover. I did not count the days, the blissful afternoons of loving, the nights of longing when we were apart. I let the time flow, as spring turned into summer and the meadow grass grew high and the bluebells ceased to bloom. The days grew hot, the stream dropped lower in its bed and no longer churned and tumbled but murmured and trickled.

The stream is in no hurry, I thought to myself as we strolled along its banks, hand in hand, and neither are we. Such trivial fancies flashed through my untroubled mind, unburdened as it was by thoughts of duty or obligation. Tom's love freed me from such burdensome thoughts; he gave me the one thing I had never had: a carefree youth.

My birthday came. I was twenty-six.

"Never mind," I said when Tom kissed me and wished me another happy year. We had spent the afternoon lazily making love and I was gathering my things for the homeward journey to Snape Hall— something I always regretted.

"What does a day matter, or even a year? With you I feel ageless, the world feels timeless to me."

"Yet the season is changing," he remarked, looking out the cottage window. "Those old willows are growing grayer. Soon they'll meet the axe. The caterpillars have turned into butterflies, the birds' nests are empty. Life moves on."

Something in his tone alarmed me. I looked at him, his reddish-brown hair falling in careless curls over his collar (a collar that needed washing, I noticed), his linen shirt open at the neck, a faint stubble on his cheeks. I know nothing whatever about this man, I thought, except that his name is Tom and he is thinking about whether he ought to get married and that I love him.

I didn't even know where he went when we parted each time we were together. I supposed that he had temporary lodgings somewhere on the grounds of the building site, like the other workmen and supervisors. If so, he had never taken me there. No doubt he was ashamed of his quarters, I thought. He would not want me to see how humbly he lived.

"I am occupied tomorrow," he said as I took my leave of him. "But we can meet the day after. I'll wait for you as usual." He held me close and his parting smile was sweet, yet I sensed that something had changed. I was apprehensive.

That night, for the first time since I met Tom, I slept badly. Instead of dreaming of him I dreamed of a woman, young and alluring, a woman who remained just out of reach but was there, a beautiful and menacing presence, wherever I turned. I awoke with a start, frightened, and could not get back to sleep. For hours I lay in bed, waiting in vain for sleep to come, watching for the first light of dawn to appear outside my window, listening to the croaking of frogs and the sleepy twitter of birds. At last I heard the clanking of milk pails and the splash of wash water thrown from a window; the servants were astir.

I went to meet Tom at the cottage as usual but he was not there. The door was ajar. Leaves and dust from the garden had been blown inside, and the usually tidy interior was in disarray. The silk coverlet and bed hangings had been taken away, along with the carved cupboard and table. The bed was still there, covered by a simple straw-stuffed mattress, the stuffing poking through a rip on one side. Even the candles were gone.

Dismayed, I thought at first that thieves had taken the valuable furnishings. But as I waited longer, and Tom did not arrive, I realized that there had been no thieves. Tom had gone, taking all the fine furnishings with him—and taking my precious dream of love as well.

He is gone, I repeated inwardly. He has gone. I will never see him again. I have no idea where he is, or even who he is. And I dare not ask, for fear of revealing (for how could I conceal it?) that he was everything to me, that I loved him.

I sat down on the threshold of the cottage, the sun warm on my face and hands, and wept. My horse, tethered to the fence by a long rope, walked up to me and put her head down to be stroked. I buried my face in her rough coat.

How long I sat there, wretched and in pain, I cannot remember. But at last, my spirits very low, I got to my feet and managed to disguise my sorrow sufficiently to ride back to Snape Hall and pretend that my heart had not broken, my hope had not died and my world had not ended forever.

20

IN THE MIDST OF MY SORROW I WENT TO SEE ANNE, WHO AFTER recuperating in Grundleford had moved with her children into a cottage on my husband's estate. I had visited her several times before and was glad to see that she was getting stronger and that her baby son was growing plump and sturdy.

When I got to the cottage she was out in the garden, wearing an old brown smock and an apron of coarse cloth, pulling tall weeds out of the rose bushes. She smiled when she saw me, an open smile with no hint of the hauteur she had shown as a younger woman, before she left Will. Her once luxuriant auburn hair, thinner now and darker, was pulled back off her face country-style, making the deep lines around her mouth and nose prominent. She was only a few years older than I, but she looked like an aging woman of forty.

"If only Old Squibb could see me now," she said. "Remember how rude I was to him?"

"If he were here he'd probably help you with those weeds. He loved his roses."

"And I once had no tolerance for thorns, as I recall. Well, I've certainly been down a thorny path since then!"

"Tell me, what did happen to you, after you left Will?" I sat down on a bench in the shade of a cherry tree. Anne went on with her weeding while she talked to me.

"I ran. I got as far away as I could. I was afraid someone would find me and lock me up for the rest of my life, like Anne Boleyn's uncle did to his wife. I knew my father would be furious. He beat me when I was a girl, I was afraid he would beat me harder as a woman."

She turned to look at me, one hand on her hip. "I tried to convince everyone I was tough and brave, but underneath I was a coward."

"No one could call you that."

She laughed. "I know I've been called much worse names. And I've deserved them. Some of them at least. I hid in Paris for awhile. King Francis found me amusing—at first. He sent me into the country and there I met an outlaw who had once been a priest. Jean-Guillaume was his name. We had two babies. One died. I met an English pirate and came back to England, to Cornwall, with him. Then there was a sailor, and an Irish horse trader—what a good-looking brute he was!—and a hop-picker who dragged me all over Kent. I had three children by the time he came along. But I was tired of the rootless life. I thought many times of going back to Will, just to ask if he would give me shelter—for me and the children. But I couldn't do it. I had my pride."

"He would have done much more than just take you in. He was concerned about you. He wanted to make sure you had enough money to live on."

"I did—at first. I had my jewels, and my mother's. I sold them one by one. The sailor stole the rest when he left me. By the time I met Monsieur Herbault, the stonemason, I was desperate. I couldn't feed the children. No one would give me charity, not even the monks. They knew from the way I talked that I was wellborn. 'Go back to your rich relations,' they told me. 'Christ had no pity for the rich.'"

The pile of weeds she had pulled grew higher.

"I was an outcast, with nowhere to go."

"You could have come to me. I would never have turned you away."

"I know that now. And I'm grateful," she added, her voice low. "But at the time, the stonemason, repulsive as he was, seemed my only hope. He was willing to take me and the children. All I had to do was sleep with him, and cook and keep his house clean. He brought us all here to St. Mary's when the work began on the new royal palace. He got a good wage. When he wasn't drinking, he treated us well enough.

"Then I got pregnant with his child, and that angered him. 'I don't want to feed any more brats,' he said. He already had a wife and children somewhere in France. He tried to make me drink something to get rid of the baby but I couldn't do it. When I went into labor, he left. Just like that. He didn't even leave any food or money for us. I don't know what I would have done if you hadn't found me."

"The priest from Grundleford sent me. One of your neighbors, a woman, told him you were in need."

"So why didn't she come herself to help me?" Anne sighed. "Never mind. I know why. The women here shun me. I'm not one of them. They don't know what to make of me."

She wiped her hands on her apron and came to sit beside me. "I don't belong anywhere any more, Cat."

"You belong with us. With me. Or with Will."

She shook her head. "I could never live with Will again. Not with my children. As long as I stay away, the scandal I caused will fade in time."

"Then stay here. Call yourself by a new name. Start a new life. What was the handsome Irishman's name?"

"Bobby Daintry."

"Call yourself Anne Daintry. Put the past behind you. Say you were a nurse or a cradlewoman in a great house and that was where you learned to speak like a lady and walk like a lady."

"And read and write and speak French."

"Why not?"

I saw a light come into her eyes. It amused her, to imagine taking on a new identity.

"I'd have nothing to lose, would I?"

Only your noble heritage and your inheritance, I thought to myself. And you walked away from the former years ago, and have already lost the latter to Will, who was awarded all your property.

"No, nothing."

She slapped her knee, a most unladylike gesture. "I'll do it. As of now, I am Anne Daintry, of—of Antrim, but I've spent all my life in castles and great houses and don't sound Irish any longer."

Two of the children ran out of the cottage and Anne watched them with a soft look in her eyes. "To them I'm just mama. A new name won't make any difference." She spoke to the boy. "Is the baby still asleep?" He nodded.

"You look tired, Cat," she said, looking over at me. I hadn't been sleeping well. I awoke in the middle of the night, tried to read, tried to work at my tapestry frame, even tried to say my prayers. But nothing could distract me from thoughts of Tom. I kept remembering how he smelled, how it felt to yield to his strong embrace, how it felt when he touched me. My body had become so accustomed to responding to him that the mere thought of him made my muscles weak. Even in his absence I felt myself surrender.

I remembered every detail of him. The creased brown leather of his high boots. His long fingernails, which he neglected to clean. His untidy waves of hair. His very very blue eyes. His smile. The taste of his mouth, sweet like ripe fruit. His uneven moustache, fuller on the right side than the left. The small red birthmark beneath his ear, shaped like a scallop shell. His laugh, open and hearty and careless. How we both drank from the wine jug, passing it back and forth, and how he licked the drops of wine from the corner of my mouth.

Deep in the night, I remembered him, I longed for him, and nothing could assuage my longing.

"You look thinner," Anne was saying. "Are you eating enough?"

I shook my head.

"What is it?"

I took my time answering her. "Sorrow," I said at length. "Like you, I've been abandoned."

"That handsome Tom."

"Yes."

She nodded knowingly. "He was even better looking than Bobby Daintry. A man like that—well, a woman can't be too careful." She laughed. "Listen to me! As if I was ever careful!"

"I loved him," I went on, ignoring her light remark. "I know it was wrong, but I couldn't help it."

"Go to confession. You're not the first pretty young wife to stray. Your husband is an old man, isn't he?"

"Well, John is—aging—and we haven't lived as man and wife for a long time."

"Was your Tom married too?"

"He said he wasn't, but was thinking of marrying. But then, I don't really know if he was telling me the truth. I don't know anything about him. Not even his name. I thought he was in charge of the building works here. Now I realize he couldn't have been. He was a stranger."

"He deceived you."

"We had a bargain. No names, no ranks."

"No responsibilities, was what he meant!"

"But he loved me. I know he did."

"He hurt you. He was cruel to leave you."

I had turned this over in my mind so many, many times. I didn't want to accept the truth: that he had indeed hurt me badly.

"Maybe he had no choice." I spoke softly.

"Ha!" Anne exclaimed, getting up suddenly and turning to face me, her hands on her hips.

"Don't try to excuse him! He's a rogue and a liar! And he broke your heart."

She was right. I had no answer to what she said. Only the voice inside me that kept repeating, he loved me, he loved me. I know he did. The voice that would not be stilled, however many contrary words were said against it, for however long.

21

H E LOVED ME. I KNEW HE DID.

I kept faith with that love, and continued to believe, despite all, that one day we would be together again.

Anne laughed at me for clinging to my lost lover, and said I was even more deluded by men—or at least by one man—than she had ever been. At times I thought she was right. Yet deep in my heart I did not lose hope, and the memory of my lovely days with Tom remained fresh, unsullied by the shock and pain of his departure.

My lover was gone, but might one day return to me. The king's lover, his plain wife Jane, was gone for good. Once again King Henry was a widower, and we learned from my kinsman Cuthbert Tunstall, who spent a good deal of time in the capital, that the king pined for Jane and mourned her as he had never mourned anyone.

Their marriage had been cruelly brief, less than two years. Jane had borne a son, Prince Edward, and the boy had lived. But Jane herself, like so many women, had grown ill with childbed fever and not all the physicians in the realm had been able to save her. Now the king was alone again.

Not long after we heard of Queen Jane's death a ragged man came to Snape Hall and begged for food. I gave our steward permission to let him sleep in one of our barns and he was taken on as an under-groom. One day as I was riding to Grundleford to visit Anne, I was alarmed to see the man sitting at the side of the road. He got up when he saw me approach and removed his cap.

"Milady Latimer," he said politely, "I have a letter for you, from a gentleman at the royal court." He pulled a thick square of yellowish paper from his jerkin and held it out to me. I bent down and took it. "He sent me here. He said I was not to give the letter to anyone but you, and not to speak of it to anyone."

A letter—and from the royal court. A very private letter. Puzzled, I reached into my purse and drew out a few coins. "Here you are," I said to the man. "Thank you. Can I trust you not to tell anyone of this?"

"You can."

I put the thick packet in my saddlebag and rode on. Not until I reached the privacy of an orchard on the outskirts of Grundleford did I allow myself to read the mysterious message.

And when I read it, I could hardly believe it.

"My dearest Catherine," it began, "I am in agony. I miss you and want you near me. I believe that despite all, you want this too. I know you. I know that I am in your heart, as you are in mine. I did not tell you the truth about myself because I didn't dare. It would only have harmed us both.

"You must know of Queen Jane's death. The queen was my sister, and my heart is full of sorrow at her passing. I am Thomas Seymour, brother-in-law to King Henry and uncle to our future king, Prince Edward.

"I came to Yorkshire because the king sent me, to inspect the building of the new palace. I stayed because of you. I stayed too long. I left in secret because I am a coward. I was afraid I would never be able to leave you if I tried to say goodbye.

"The king wanted me to marry his niece Lady Margaret Douglas but I couldn't do it. My heart would not let me. One day you will be free. I will wait for you. When you are free, you will be mine. Please, dear Catherine, say you will be mine.

"Come to court, Catherine. Come and be near me. The king is going to marry again. Come and serve his new wife. He will send for you.

"I am the man who loves you,

"Tom"

My joy, as I read Tom's letter, was indescribable. I clutched the letter to my fast-beating heart. I danced around the nearest tree and ran through the orchard, shouting my delight, not caring who might hear me or see me. I do not think I was observed, but had anyone seen me, they would surely have thought me mad.

He loves me, I repeated again and again. He loves me. He wants me near him. He is going to wait for me to be free.

I could not put the letter out of my mind, not even after I returned to Snape Hall and went in to see John, to read to him as I usually did each evening.

"Ah, Gwennidor," John said when he saw me come through the doorway. I went up to the bed and bent down to kiss his dry cheek. He lay against a thick bolster, with red satin pillows behind his back. He was smiling but his voice was weak.

"Isn't—isn't—"

"No, dear, Margaret isn't with me. You know she never comes in to see you in the evening, only in the afternoon. You remember. In the evening she studies her French and Latin."

John frowned, his brow furrowed.

Lying there, his face crinkled and lined, he looked old enough to be my grandfather. I felt no wifely connection to him, only pity and affection. It was hard to believe I had ever slept with him.

One day you will be free, Tom wrote in his letter. One day you will be free. In truth I expected to be free before long. John's health was failing. He slept much of the time, and his hand shook when he reached for me. Often he could not remember my name, or Margaret's.

I had brought my Bible with me, along with several books of John's. He pointed to his favorite, the romance of Gwennidor. I sat down, opened the book and began to read. Within a few minutes he had dropped off to sleep, his mouth agape, his breath raspy.

I closed the book and took Tom's letter from my pocket. I reread it, the beloved phrases warming my heart. I miss you and want you near me. I know that I am in your heart, as you are in mine. When you are free, you will be mine.

When would the king send for me, I wondered. How soon? And who would his new bride be?

As it happened, the royal summons was not long in coming. Thomas Cromwell, the king's chief minister, sent a message to inform me that

I had been appointed as lady-in-waiting to the Lady Anne of Cleves, who would be coming to England early in the new year of 1540. I would be allowed to bring three servants with me, the message read. Two maidservants and a laundress.

"How would you like to go to court?" I asked Anne when I went to take her the news of my letter from Tom and the message from Lord Cromwell. "As my laundress?"

She wrinkled her nose. "Court! King Henry's court! I suppose it might be amusing, to see all those old faces again."

"You would go as my laundress, Anne Daintry. No one need know who you really are. I am allowed to bring three servants with me when I become lady-in-waiting to the new queen."

She raised her eyebrows in interest. Now I had her attention.

"Who is he marrying this time?"

"A German woman, I hear. A reformist no doubt, not a papist. Her name is Anne of Cleves."

"A German? But German women are mannish, and loud, and stubborn. Henry will never tolerate that."

"Perhaps he will if she is beautiful."

"In all my travels I have never seen a German woman who was beautiful. Not beautiful in the English way, with skin like alabaster and soft, sweet blue eyes and pink lips. Like you."

I shrugged. "King Henry is no longer young. It may be that his eyesight is failing." We laughed. "Besides, none of this matters to me. All I care about is that I will be with Tom again."

I read Anne Tom's letter, pausing for emphasis between each precious sentence.

"He's not a very eloquent man, is he? I've had my share of love letters, and they were full of flowery phrases. How my breasts were like two warm ripe pears, or my lips were like juicy red cherries, or my eyes—how does that phrase from Catullus go, 'Your eyes, my stars'?"

"A laundress that quotes Catullus! Now, that's a rarity."

"You know perfectly well what I mean. He's terse."

"And sincere."

"How can you believe him now, when he was so deceitful before?"

"But he explains that, here in the letter. He couldn't tell me everything before."

"He won your love under false pretenses. Nothing can excuse or explain that."

I thought over what Anne had said. "Love comes unbidden," I answered at length. "He didn't ask for it to happen, any more than I did. Love came over us."

"Like plague."

"You are a cynic, even if you can quote Latin love poetry."

"I'm merely seeing things as they are, instead of as I would wish them to be."

I went over to look into the cradle, to admire Anne's sleeping son. Will I have a son of my own, with Tom, I wondered. When John is no longer here, and I am married to Tom, will I be a mother at last?

"My laundress can bring her children with her, of course. We leave in three days, if you decide to come."

Anne smiled. "I will think it over."

22

WAVES OF RICH MUSKY SCENT ENVELOPED ME AS I STOOD UNDER THE canopy of cloth of gold. Perfumed coals were burning in a brazier, and their smell was almost overpowering.

"I dislike those heavy German perfumes, don't you?" the plump, short girl next to me whispered. "The scent of English roses or gillyflowers is so much sweeter."

I smiled down at her. "I agree. But I suppose we mustn't be too critical of the new queen or her perfumes."

"And we must kneel in her presence, and bow to her when she speaks, and bring her German beer whenever she asks for it. Yes, yes. I've been tutored in what I must do as maid of honor. They say she is very grand. She demands to be treated like a goddess, and not like the sister of the Duke of Cleves, whoever he is."

I looked more closely at the outspoken, opinionated girl. She was quite young, and pretty, with pale skin, dark eyes and auburn hair escaping from under her peaked hood. Her expression was piquant and engaging, the look in her eyes saucy.

We were standing under the queen's tent, with several dozen other ladies-in-waiting and maids of honor, waiting for the king's new wife-to-be to make her appearance.

She had only been in England for a week or so, but already crowds were gathering wherever she went, eager to glimpse their king's fourth wife. It was known that she was not King Henry's first choice as his newest consort. Other highborn women had been invited to share his bed and enjoy the title of queen. But they had all said no. Only this spinster German princess, Lady Anne of Cleves, had said yes.

In truth the crowds came, in part, because of the widespread belief that whomever King Henry married would die a terrible death. Queen Catherine of Aragon had died of loneliness and grief, imprisoned by her cruel royal husband. Queen Anne Boleyn had been executed on false charges (everyone believed they were false) of adultery with her own brother and others. Queen Jane Seymour, Tom's sister, had been killed through neglect after she contracted childbed fever—some even said that Henry had taken her to a village near Hampton Court where many villagers had the plague and left her there to die.

All the king's wives were cursed. What would happen to this new one?

"She's late," the plump girl was saying. "She's keeping us all waiting, choking on these fumes."

We moved away from the smoking brazier but then were too cold. The January day was raw. I felt chilly in my satin gown, though I wore woollen petticoats under it and woollen undersleeves as well. We were gathered on Hampstead Heath, under a gray sky weeping rain, to greet the Lady Anne. Our tent—the queen's golden tent—was one of many tents, spread over the wide heath in a long sprawl, each sheltering an array of dignitaries and nobles. Thousands of Londoners waited impatiently in the open, held back by guardsmen and soldiers, eager to see the Lady Anne and the king and to watch them all process in parade to the royal palace at Greenwich.

At last we heard, in the distance, the sound of trumpets and a golden coach came into view. Surrounding the coach was a mounted escort, the horses in gilded trappings and the riders in silver armor with plumed helmets and banners woven with the heraldic crests of Cleves and Guelderland. The roar of the cheering spectators seemed to fill the broad heath as King Henry stepped out from his own tent to await the arrival of the golden coach.

His massive body was awash in cloth of gold, and rubies and amethysts and garnets shone from his every garment. Ermine encircled his neck. He wore a velvet cap with many jewels and a white egret plume, and his fat fingers were weighted down with heavy rings, each of which held a great ruby or emerald or sapphire. Standing at the opening of his tent, the king leaned against a thronelike chair, so that some of his weight was shifted off his sore leg. I remembered him showing me the terrible wound on that leg, and imagined that it must still cause him pain. I wondered how Lady Anne of Cleves would react to the stench of the sore, and to the great wrinkled bulk of her aging husband when he made love to her. The thought made me shudder.

Beside the king stood Princess Mary, Queen Catherine of Aragon's fair daughter who, it was said, still clung to the old faith of Rome. She looked careworn and sour, I thought, much older than her twenty-three years. There was a good deal of gossip about her at court, and my plump companion was repeating some of it as we watched the royal figures emerge from the king's tent.

"They say Princess Mary still worships in the old way, and that the king punishes her by not letting her marry. She's very sad. She tried to get away across the sea to the Low Countries but she couldn't. I don't know why. Maybe the king caught her and punished her."

In her arms the princess held her half-brother, the baby Prince Edward. He was two years old but looked much smaller than a two-year-old ought to look, bundled in his golden blanket. The king barely took any notice of him. The king's other legitimate child, Anne Boleyn's daughter Princess Elizabeth, was not present; no child of Anne Boleyn was allowed to come within the royal circle on such an important occasion. But standing next to Princess Mary was a very beautiful young woman, striking and statuesque. Her gown of lilac silk flowed in becoming folds over her shapely body, slim-waisted and voluptuous; her fair skin was delicate, her blond hair abundant and curly, her features far more pleasing than those of Princess Mary, who had once been thought very handsome.

"Who is that young woman?" I asked the plump girl beside me.

"That's Lady Margaret Douglas, the king's niece. The one who was in the Tower for agreeing to marry one of my relatives without the king's permission. She was in disgrace for awhile, but now the king loves her again, as you can see." And indeed King Henry was smiling on his lovely niece, and talking with her, as he waited for Lady Anne's gold carriage to make its slow approach.

So that was Lady Margaret Douglas, the woman my Tom was

supposed to marry. The one he couldn't bring himself to accept, because of his love for me. I felt proud, gratified that his love for me was so strong—until I saw Tom himself come out of the royal tent and take his place beside the lovely Lady Margaret!

The look he gave her as he came up to her was one of affection and familiarity, far too much affection for my comfort. They smiled at one another, he leaned over to kiss her delicate pink cheek and she gave him her slender hand in friendship—or was it in love? I was too far away to see the look that passed between them, but their gestures were eloquent. Was Tom in love with Lady Margaret? Was he going to marry her after all?

My ungovernable thoughts ran wildly. Had Tom's decision about marriage changed since he wrote his letter to me? Was there to be a double wedding, of the king and Lady Anne of Cleves and Thomas Seymour and Lady Margaret Douglas?

I shivered, and moved closer to the perfumed brazier once again, trying to ignore the musky odor that poured forth from it along with thin columns of smoke.

Trembling, I returned to stand beside the plump girl. Bravely I asked her whether she had heard any rumors about Lady Margaret marrying Thomas Seymour.

She giggled. "Sir Thomas is afraid of marriage, they say. And the women won't have him, though he is handsome and rich and the uncle of the baby prince. My cousin Mary Howard, the one who was married to Fitzroy, said no to him. And Lady Margaret Douglas did too, so they say."

"Why?"

She shrugged. "There is a story. An awful story. Some believe it, some don't."

"What story?"

The girl pulled me deep into the interior of the large tent, away from the front where all the other ladies and waiting maids were clustered, watching for Lady Anne to alight.

"Something happened at his estate at Sudeley," she whispered. "It was said that a woman died because of it."

"What happened?"

"I heard from Francis—from a friend—that Sir Thomas was out hunting with one of the gamekeepers and the man's wife came along. She was very pretty, and Sir Thomas desired her. He had some of his servants hold her while he raped her, with her husband right there, tied to a tree so he couldn't help her. She screamed and one of her brothers came and attacked Sir Thomas and Sir Thomas killed him. Afterward, the woman fell into low spirits and stabbed herself to death. That's the story."

"I don't believe it."

"The gamekeeper swears it is true."

Tom? My sweet, gentle, loving Tom? Impossible!

"You shouldn't repeat such wicked things. Who are you anyway?"

"I am Catherine Howard. Queen Anne Boleyn was my cousin."

My eyes widened. "I have heard that the Howards and the Seymours are rivals. They spread lies about each other."

"I think that story is no lie. But I cannot be certain. No one can—unless she was present."

Angrily I left the girl and rejoined the other ladies-in-waiting. I tried to shut the awful image out of my mind, of Tom ordering his servants to restrain the woman while he—while he—

A blast of trumpets announced that Lady Anne of Cleves's carriage had come to a halt before the king's tent. Grooms rushed out to hold the heads of the stamping horses, the harness bells jangling in the wintry air.

A lady stepped carefully down out of the carriage, the heavy embroidered skirts of her gray gown cumbersome around her. A wide, strangely-shaped hood, made in a fashion I had never before seen, all but hid her face. From beneath it hung long fair hair. She was tall and strong-looking, confident and forceful in her movements. It was the Lady Anne of Cleves.

A shout went up from the crowd. The king stepped forward, took his future wife's hand and kissed her on the cheek—not on the lips, as was customary between husband and wife. His lips barely grazed her cheek. A murmur of astonishment spread among the ladies around me. They too had noted the chaste kiss.

We were summoned to the royal tent and one by one, we knelt before Lady Anne and were introduced to her, first the ladies-in-waiting, then the maids of honor among whom was my new acquaintance Catherine Howard.

As I drew near, taking my turn to be introduced, I studied the new queen. She was neither ugly nor beautiful, but something in between. Her small gray eyes were kind and surprisingly full of merriment—they made me think of my brother Will with his jokes and pranks. Her nose was straight, her mouth small and primly shut. But I was shocked to see that her skin was of a dull brownish hue, and covered with the marks and scars of the pox. The blemishes were unmistakable; as with all such disfiguring marks, they made one want to turn away.

When presented to Lady Anne, I was very near to the royal family—and to Tom, who kept his place next to Margaret Douglas. I did not look directly at him, but watched out of the corner of my eye. He seemed restless, uncomfortable, standing first on one foot, then the other, fidgeting with his long fur-lined sleeves, laughing nervously at a pleasantry of the king's. I thought, he's nervous because I'm near by.

Lady Anne spoke graciously to me in a very thickly accented English and then turned to the next woman to be introduced. My brief moment of royal attention was over very quickly. I watched as others knelt before her, murmured their greetings, and received hers in turn. King Henry, I noticed, was not watching his wife but the ladies who came before her, each in turn, and when Catherine Howard came forward to make her obeisance, he looked at her and smiled. She looked coyly back.

When at last we all had been introduced, together with the prominent clergymen and members of the king's council and the aldermen of London, we formed ourselves into a procession and followed the king and his new queen as they walked under the dark skies down the heath toward the royal palace of Greenwich, the members of Anne's German household alongside us. Near the king and queen walked my uncle William and his troop of guardsmen, the Calais Spears. My stepson Johnny was among them, looking lean and fit. I glanced at him but he did not smile in recognition; the spearmen were taught to show no emotion when on parade, as I knew, and I did not expect him to acknowledge me.

Besides, it was all the guardsmen could do to restrain the crowds that swarmed around us, calling out, clapping, reaching their hands out toward us as we passed in splendid parade. Entranced by the spectacle, they were wild with joy, like children let loose in a roomful of toys and sweets. Again and again they cried out to Lady Anne. "Welcome to our good queen! May she be fruitful! May she come to no harm!" Smiling, she nodded right and left as she walked along by the king's side, hurrying to match his long, uneven, limping stride.

From time to time she looked over at him, as if seeking reassurance. But he, when not gesturing broadly to the onlookers or flinging out golden coins to them from a bag he carried, was giving all his attention to his wife's maid of honor, the plump and pretty Catherine Howard. And I, my heart beating rapidly as I walked along, barely took notice of anyone but Tom, who had offered his arm to Margaret Douglas and was escorting her, as gallantly as a husband or a lover might, in the direction of the distant palace gates.

23

WHEN I FINALLY SAW TOM ALONE, AFTER MANY TANTALIZING WEEKS at court without him, we flew into each other's arms, heedless of everything but our need for each other. To kiss him was such rapture that it was almost painful. The feel of his warm lips on mine, the familiar smell of him, the comfort of his strong sheltering arms made me once again his, and his alone. All that had gone before, all my months of pain and sorrow before his loving letter arrived, all that I had heard about him at court fell away, forgotten, as he caressed me and once again made me his. I had no will, no thought, no self: we were one, and nothing else existed.

We met in a small damp room with a cot and chest, next to the wine cellar. It had been an under-steward's room, but Tom paid the under-steward to vacate it. The room became ours.

"How I've missed you, Catherine! How I've longed for you!"

I closed my eyes, listening to his tender voice as we lay, replete and more than content, side by side in the small candlelit room. "You cannot know what my life has been, these past months. How fast everything is changing. What dangers I have faced, and still face!"

"Dangers? From whom?"

He turned his face, so close to mine, away and stared up at the ceiling.

"When a man rises high, he is always in danger. And I mean to rise higher. Oh yes. Much, much higher, before I'm through."

"You would be much higher, part of the royal family, if you married Margaret Douglas."

Swiftly his mood shifted. He chuckled. "Has that been worrying you? I told you, I could not bring myself to wed her, because my heart is yours." He kissed me, and I yielded gladly to his kiss. But something in the lightness of his tone made me uneasy.

"Or because the lady said no?"

He pulled away suddenly, a strange glimmer in his intensely blue eyes. "Where did you hear that?"

"From the same person who told me that Henry Fitzroy's widow would not marry you."

Sitting up, and pulling his linen shirt around him, Tom swore, vehemently and loudly.

"Damn Howard whoreson villains! The lies they tell about me would fill one of your thick chapbooks! I suppose you've heard all the stories, about my thieving and whoring and lying—oh yes, and the one about how I raped a girl and killed her brother."

Surprised that he should mention the terrible incident Catherine Howard had told me about—an incident I had instantly dismissed as beyond belief—I nodded.

"None of it is true. You do believe me, don't you?"

He looked bereft. I sat up and put my arm around him. "Of course. I always want to believe you."

He sighed and, head bowed, ran his hands through his thick reddish curls.

"The Howards hate me and want to destroy me if they can. They will say anything, do anything, to bring me down. They lost the king's favor when Anne Boleyn was disgraced. We Seymours gained it when my sister Jane became queen. That much is clear. But, beyond all the lies—there is something else. Sometimes—sometimes I wonder—whether there is any good in me. Whether I was even meant to live at all." He spoke hesitantly, at the end of his words his voice dropped away almost to a whisper.

"Whatever can you mean?" It was so unlike him, this mood of

self-doubt. It was as if he felt a sense of doom hovering around himself. I felt a chill, listening to him.

Instinctively I ceased to hold him and moved away. He reached for my hand and held it.

"Something happened to me a long time ago. It was terrible. No one knows about it but my brother and me—at least I think no one knows. I have never told anyone. My brother Edward is a few years older than I am and as boys we were always at each other's throats. He is cleverer than I am and yet he always envied me because I was tougher and bolder. I wasn't afraid of a fight. It irked him that I wouldn't run away when he came after me. I stood and gave back blow for blow."

"Good for you."

"Ah, but there are many ways to fight—and I am only good at one of them. He found another."

"He drowned my favorite spaniel, and he made me watch while he did it. I was so enraged that I took a stone and tried to smash his head with it. He still has a scar. I became obsessed with killing him. I tried to push him off a high roof. When we went hunting I aimed at him with a crossbow and would have hit him but a deer got in the way. We fought a lot—until he was sent to live in Archbishop Cranmer's household and I went to sea for a few years. By the time we saw one another again, I had grown much bigger and stronger and he would never fight me again. But I still hated him. I still hate him now. I think, given the chance, I might kill him. So you see, I wonder whether I am worth very much. Maybe I ought to have been drowned along with my dog."

"That's a terrible thing to say."

"It is, isn't it? But you see, there is something more. My brother told me that he heard our mother admit once that after he was born, she didn't want any more children. She hated our father and wanted to leave him and enter a convent. So she went to an herb woman and got a poultice that was supposed to make her womb shrivel. Instead it made her fertile. She had me—and my younger sisters. So in a way, I should never have been born. Perhaps that's why I carry such sinful thoughts in my head."

"But Tom, surely you can see all this through a man's eyes now, and understand it—and understand and forgive yourself. To begin with, you know that boys are cruel, terribly cruel. What your brother did was wicked, and he should have been punished for it—not by you, but by your father. If he had been, you wouldn't have burned for revenge. Your need for justice would have been satisfied—or nearly so. Can't you see now that your brother was terribly jealous of you and did and said anything he could to hurt you? It was wrong—yet you can see why he acted as he did. Instead of wanting to kill him you can see that you need to protect yourself against him."

"I do protect myself—as well as I can."

"You think yourself unworthy, yet the truth is, you are no better or worse than others. Many people imagine themselves taking violent revenge on those who have hurt them, not just you. I know, I've heard them say it. And I'm quite sure that many unhappy mothers have tried to ensure that they would have no more children. That doesn't mean God didn't want you to be born, or that he cursed you with malicious thoughts."

"How can you be so sure?"

"Because God is our merciful father, who loves us."

"I have never known a merciful father."

I took Tom in my arms again. I had never felt so close to him as at that moment. I loved him beyond anything, and wanted to help him.

"I'm glad you told me this. Promise me that you won't reproach yourself any more."

"If you will promise to lend me your strength when I need it."

"All that I am is yours, you know that."

Our embrace turned once again to an embrace of desire, and the love that flowed between us was stronger and more intense than before. When we parted—all too soon—I returned to my duties in the queen's apartments with a full heart, feeling that Tom had entrusted something precious to me—not only his love, but his trust.

24

Hᴜᴍᴍɪɴɢ ᴀ ʙʀɪɢʜᴛ ʟɪᴛᴛʟᴇ ᴛᴜɴᴇ, ᴀ sᴍɪʟᴇ ʜᴏᴠᴇʀɪɴɢ ᴀᴛ ᴛʜᴇ ᴄᴏʀɴᴇʀs of her small mouth, Queen Anne sat at her large embroidery frame stitching a coverlet. Some of us, her ladies-in-waiting and maids of honor, were sitting with her around the frame, adding our own stitches and providing her with company. In addition to myself, there was my sister Nan, visiting for the afternoon, Lady Guildford, Lady Dorchester and the pretty young maid of honor Catherine Howard.

The windows of the queen's sitting room were open to the afternoon breeze, which brought in from the garden the sweet scents of roses and lilac, white star-flowers and freshly cut grass. It was spring, yet Anne was still dressed for winter. Though she had been in England for five months, she still wore her large, unattractive German hoods and her dressmakers continued to cut her gowns in the stiff, square German style and to sew them from heavy cloth suitable for a much chillier climate than ours. The dressmakers came often to fit her for new gowns, speaking to one another in their own harsh language and casting surreptitious glances at us from under beetle brows.

Anne's German servants had made no effort to learn any English, but Anne herself had an English tutor who came every other day to give her a lesson; she was able to converse in English after a fashion, with much stumbling and long pauses while she searched for words. She still swore in German, however, so that none of us could understand and take offense, and I often heard her muttering to herself in German under her breath. I could only imagine what those mutterings might mean.

"My dear mother would love this warm weather," Anne remarked to us, each of her words heavily accented. "It is so very cold in Düsseldorf at this time of year."

"Is it ever warm in Düsseldorf?" asked Lady Dorchester.

"Of course it is warm—in summer. That is when we have our fine weather."

"And is your summer very long, your majesty?"

"At least three weeks. Sometimes four," was Anne's tart response. The superiority of English weather to German was a frequent subject in the royal apartments, and Anne was always nettled by it. In truth, there were few subjects on which she could converse with anything like fluency, and weather was one of them.

We were silent for awhile, attending to our stitching. I was thinking of Tom, who I had not seen for several days, and wondering when we would meet again.

"Is this coverlet we are stitching meant to be a cradle blanket?" asked Catherine Howard with a sly look at the rest of us.

"No. It is for my bed."

"We do so hope that your majesty will soon be able to give us the good news that you are expecting a child." Catherine was persistent.

"You said the same thing yesterday. My answer is still the same. There is no child on the way. Nor is there likely to be." She muttered to herself in German.

"You must not despair, your majesty," my sister Nan ventured.

"Oh, I never despair. Despair is a sin. It leads to suicide. I am merely practical. I know what I know. My dear mother told me about men and women, and how babies are made. The man must have—must have—" She paused, trying to think of a word. The pause seemed endless.

"Manly force!" she said at length. "The man must have manly force. And your king is too old to have this."

All of us, save Anne, stopped stitching and looked at one another. King Henry, tall, broad-shouldered and strong, still magnificent despite his increasing girth and bad leg, King Henry with his Maiden's Chamber, his many seductions and his bawdy joking with his men friends, was the last man we would have thought would be lacking in "manly force."

"I think you must be mistaken, your majesty," said Catherine Howard boldly. "I believe his loins still stir—for the right woman." The meaning of her sly words was unmistakable, and my sister blushed.

"You forget yourself, Mistress Howard," said Lady Dorchester sharply. As the mother of the maids, it was her duty to reprimand the younger women when they spoke ill-advisedly.

"I am only repeating what I have heard," was the tart reply.

Anne glared at Catherine. "I think I know my own husband better than anyone else knows him. And if I say he has no manly force, then he has none. And that is the end of it." She lapsed into German then, and even without knowing any of that language I could tell that she was cursing the maid of honor whose bold words had stung her.

"Lady Catherine," Lady Dorchester said, "there are duties in the stillroom requiring your attention. Your immediate attention. Kindly ask your royal mistress permission to withdraw."

The smile on Catherine Howard's face told us all that, despite this reprimand, she believed she had won the skirmish. "With your permission, your majesty," she said, curtseying to Anne.

Instead of replying Anne waved her hand dismissively, and Catherine walked toward the door.

But before she could reach it, the door opened and in burst King Henry, his round face more joyful than I had seen it in months.

"Ah, here are my ladies! All my ladies!" His glance took in the five of us around the embroidery frame, and then lingered on Catherine Howard, who was only a few feet in front of him. She had knelt when he entered the room.

"How does my lady this lovely afternoon?" He reached for Catherine's hands, pulled her to her feet and kissed her on the cheek. "Well, I hope."

"I am just on my way to the stillroom, sire."

"Ah, indeed. I may pass by there later." He came toward us and Catherine scurried out.

"Henry, that Mistress Howard is a wicked girl. I will not have her in my service any longer. I want her sent away from court."

"And I say she stays, and that is an end of it. I caution you, wife. I command here, not you."

"In Cleves it is the wife who decides who will serve her."

"But you are not in Cleves—at least not for the moment."

I felt myself stiffen. The king's words were chilling, an obvious threat.

"And I don't believe your brother the duke would be very glad to have you back. From what I hear, he has threatened to kill you if you should return in disgrace."

"He speaks violent words, but he would never harm me. My dear mother would protect me."

"I caution you, madame, I have heard quite enough about your dear mother. I wish she were at the bottom of the sea!"

Lady Dorchester rose. "Sire, perhaps you and the queen would prefer to be alone."

"No. Stay. I am only here to tell the queen that the matter of her engagement to the Duke of Lorraine's son is being debated in the royal council this afternoon. It has come to the council's attention that she was pledged to the duke's son before she agreed to marry me, and if this proves to be true, then her marriage to me is invalid, under the law of the church."

"But it is not so!" Anne blustered. "I swear it is not so!"

Henry held up his hand, and she was silent, though she continued to gasp.

"The Lord punishes those who lie. They are stricken down like the grass under the mower's scythe, like the trees uprooted by the whirlwind. They are afflicted with the pox. They are barren—"

At these words he looked pointedly at Anne, and a long silence followed. Anne's gasps had turned to tearful sighs, though she was too proud to let her tears overwhelm her. She did not sob, the tears merely trickled slowly down her pockmarked cheeks.

"Ladies, I wish you a good afternoon." He swept out, leaving us all reeling with the shock of what he had said, and what it meant.

Lady Guildford, who had prudently held her tongue throughout the afternoon, quietly picked up her sewing things and moved to the window seat, away from the rest of us. Lady Dorchester bristled. "He should never have spoken to you that way, your majesty. I don't care if he is the king. He has no courtesy. And he treats women like his old broken-down horses, as things to be cast aside and sent away."

"I am not a horse!" Anne burst out, sobbing now, uncontrollably. "I am the Queen of England!" Nan went to her and spoke soothingly.

For a little while longer, I thought. You will be queen for a little longer—until the royal council can declare otherwise. Which the king has no doubt instructed them to do. This marriage has evidently been no marriage. And the king has his eye on a new lady, the ripe, pleasingly rounded, teasingly outspoken Catherine Howard.

25

"AH! OOH! GET AWAY FROM US, YOU OAF! GET AWAY FROM ME, ALL of you!"

King Henry, his swollen, bandaged leg exposed and propped on a cushioned bench, his face contorted and red with pain and furious anger, lashed out with his silver-tipped ebony cane at the servants who, gagging from the overpowering stench of his suppurating ulcer, were attempting to remove the bandage.

It was a ghastly sight: the pus-stained linen sticking to the sore, the dark red clotted blood, the fat, white fleshy leg with its red veins standing out like welts. The cruel instruments laid out on a table, sharp knives, tongs, pincers. More bandages, clean and white. Bleeding-bowls and salves in jars and bunches of juniper to burn and cleanse the air.

Dr. Chambers stood by, holding a pomander to his nose, watching the king's torment, waiting for the bandage to be removed so that he could cut open the angry crimson sore and release its poisons.

He had done it often before, and I had watched it before, for the king found my presence heartening when he was suffering and invariably summoned me when his pain was at its worst. He allowed me to govern him when others could not.

"Ayee!" the king wailed, taking aim at one of the hapless grooms who was bravely attempting to pull the bandaging off and whacking him with the cane.

"Can't you give him valerian to drink like last time, so that he will sleep through what you have to do?" I asked the doctor.

"He won't have it. He refuses. He wants vengeance first, then relief. Frankly, I am heartily weary of his tantrums."

"I heard that! Take care I don't send you to be tortured!"

"Serving you, your majesty, when you carry on in this way is quite torture enough."

The king opened his mouth to retort but was overtaken by a spasm of pain so severe that he screamed instead.

"Cat! Cat! You must help me, Cat! I am in extremis!"

I moved closer to him, careful to stay out of range of the long ebony cane.

"Sire, I have brought you a soothing poultice. But before I put it on you must let Dr. Chambers do his work. It is the only way. You know that."

He swore, a long and vehement oath, and the grooms went scurrying.

"Will you do as I tell you, as you did last time? Or do you want more pain?"

"Damn you to hell, Cat." He cursed me, but I saw his shoulders slump. He was giving in. I nodded to Dr. Chambers who handed me the cup of valerian tea.

"Drink this, sire. You know it will help you. Just drink it, and all will be over soon."

He glared at me, but reached for the cup.

"Drop the cane," I said.

Obediently he let it fall with a clatter to the floor.

I handed him the cup and he drank, swallowing some and spitting out the rest.

"This tastes of goat piss."

"The more you drink, the easier it will be for you to get through your ordeal," I said, handing the cup to Dr. Chambers who filled it again.

In the end he drank deeply, drowsed, still muttering curses, and at last snored. Swiftly the bandaging was removed, the twitching leg was held down by the doctor's servants and Dr. Chambers did his work. Fetid toxins spewed forth from the sore, making me want to run away, but I did not. I wanted to be there when the king awoke, to put the cooling, healing herbal poultice on his leg and receive his grateful and contrite thanks.

I was living at Richmond Palace now, still serving Anne of Cleves though she was no longer queen. As I expected, he had had their marriage officially annulled and within days thereafter had married Catherine Howard. He offered Anne a home in England, under his protection, so that she didn't have to return to Cleves to face the wrath of her unkind brother. Her dear mother came often to visit her, and as King Henry had given her a generous income she was entirely comfortable and wanted for nothing.

At my request John was brought from Snape Hall to Richmond also, and John, Margaret and I shared a suite of rooms overlooking the deer park.

John had not been capable of overseeing the running of his immense estate for a long time; all was left to stewards and managers. He had been removed from the Council of the North. He spent nearly all his time in bed, except for the hour or two when he was put in a wheeled chair and placed in front of the hearth.

He slept a great deal of the time now, a peaceful sleep. I thought it a mercy that he was not in pain. In his mind he seemed to dwell in the land of faery, the enchanted world where knights fought dragons and ladies saved their beleaguered lords from dark fiends who threatened them.

When he was awake he smiled at Margaret and me through misty eyes. Sometimes I felt that he knew us, at other times I wasn't sure. He rarely spoke, and when he did, his words made little sense. Sometimes he spoke gibberish.

Remembering the well-intentioned strong man he had been when I first knew him, a man capable of making thoughtful decisions and of being a good lord to his hundreds of tenants and the members of his large household, I cried at times to see him in his present state. Some of my tears, I knew, were tears of remorse. I was no longer his faithful wife, I was betraying him. He did not know it, of course, he could not know it. Yet he had a right to command my loyalty nonetheless.

We had been through a great deal together, John and I, and even though my heart was now Tom's, I still felt much affection for John and above all, I did not want to see him suffer pain, either in body or mind. I hoped that the comforts of Richmond Palace would ease his last years.

His last years! The thought made me shiver. I knew that Tom and I would marry when John died, and I often thought that I was in limbo, waiting for the end to come and for my glorious new life to begin, my life as Tom's wife.

In the meantime I was at the beck and call of two old men, my husband and King Henry, who often summoned me to Whitehall when his leg was causing him pain or when he needed someone to talk to—someone who was not a member of his royal council or an ambitious courtier out to get what he wanted through flattery.

I sat patiently through hours of the king's rantings and musings, occasionally answering when he asked me for my opinion but mostly giving the appearance of listening to him while actually thinking of Tom. I missed Tom. King Henry sent him away on diplomatic missions, and he was sometimes gone for months at a time.

"Crum," the king was saying one afternoon when I had been sent for. "Now tell me, Cat, what did you think of Crum?"

"I had the impression that Master Cromwell was a very efficient servant—though in the end he must have betrayed you because you had him executed."

"Hah! Betrayed me! He was the best servant I ever had, and the cleverest! They deceived me, you know. My councillors. They lied to me about my good, faithful Crum. They made me break him. I would give anything to have him back.

"The truth is, I don't know whom to trust any more. They're all a pack of deceivers, every last one of them. And they're all vultures, hovering over my head, circling endlessly there, just waiting for me to die! Yes, I know it. Then they'll move in and pick my carcass clean. My carcass, and all the gold in my pockets and the rings on my fingers."

He paused and looked at me. "You are not a deceiver though, are you, Cat? You read your Bible. You are a gospeller. You do what is right. I can trust you."

I felt uncomfortable. I did not want the responsibility the king appeared to give me. And I knew that if, even once, I gave him an answer that he disliked, he could send me to a dungeon or toss me aside, as he had the Lady Anne of Cleves, sending me away from court and away from Tom.

"Can you not confide in your wife, sire?" I asked hesitantly. "Can you not trust her?"

He laughed loudly. "Confide in an empty-headed twenty-year-old? An innocent, vacuous girl who knows nothing of life? No, Cat, I cannot confide in her."

He took my hand and, limping, led me into Queen Catherine's bedchamber. A huge bed filled much of the room, with a high headboard shimmering with iridescence. Hundreds of pearls were embedded in its lustrous wood, and hundreds more gleamed from the gauzy hangings that curtained the wondrous bed, that seemed to float in its own light.

"There, you see? That's where my innocent young queen belongs. In her great pearl bed, in all her naked loveliness, waiting for me to give her sons. That is what she was made for, that and nothing more."

He limped back into the adjacent sitting-room. I followed him. The oversize chair he sat in creaked under his immense weight.

"My wife is very dear to me. She will stay beside me, loyal and sweet, until I make my exit from this sorry world. Of that I can be certain. And she gives me pleasure, much pleasure. But as the whole court knows, it has been many months now since we were married, and she shows no signs of motherhood. None! Not even a miscarriage."

"Your majesty is fortunate in having a son and heir already."

The king looked at me balefully. "Do you know what the doctors tell me, Cat? About my son's fevers, that never seem to end? In private, behind closed doors, they say he is in danger of his life. He is a weakling. He could die at any time."

"I tell you, Cat, I MUST have a son! A strong, thriving, kicking and screaming boy. Sons like that are born every day to country women, strapping fat infants that grow up to be robust men. I must have one of those. Heaven knows I've worked at it, there in the great pearl bed. I've huffed and puffed and—"

"Sire! You forget yourself."

The king erupted into hearty laughter.

"Where's Will? Will could make a joke or two about it. In any case, I've made an effort. I've even hung my piece of the True Cross around my neck while I'm beavering away, so to speak—and still there is no result."

He paused, then went on in a resigned tone, his voice flat. "I fear God has cursed me, Cat. With my first wife I told myself she had a diseased womb, and could not conceive a healthy boy, only a girl. With the Witch I was convinced she was sent by the devil to put a spell on me, and was not worthy to bear the next king, so we had no son. Poor meek Jane lived just long enough to present me with a weak little runt of a boy, and no strong brothers. The German woman—ah! let nothing be said about her! And now my adored girl, my unsullied rose, my wife Catherine, is barren. Barren! I am cursed."

"We must all pray for the queen to conceive, and that the king may be granted patience."

King Henry sighed, a great heaving sigh, and closed his eyes.

"You are right, of course. Send me my chaplain."

"Before I do, sire, may I ask a favor?"

"Yes, what is it?"

"My stepdaughter Margaret is of an age to marry. I am hoping to find a good husband for her, but with your assistance I know I could not possibly do better. Do you know of some worthy man?"

He thought for a moment. "I'll ponder it, Cat. I'll give it some thought. In the meantime, come here and rub my sore leg. You give me relief when no one else can."

"Gladly, sire. I'll do what I can."

26

"I THINK THE QUEEN HAS A LOVER."

Anne Daintry, as she continued to call herself, nodded as she spoke, as if to underscore her conviction.

"I hope not," I replied, much dismayed. "Do you know for sure?"

Anne, officially my laundress, but in fact my trusted companion, came to sit beside me in the anteroom of Lady Anne of Cleves's sitting room, where I was in attendance, waiting in case Lady Anne summoned me.

"I would wager my inheritance on it—if I still had an inheritance. She's as devious as a woman can be, I've thought so from the first time I saw her. And clever. She was no virgin when she married the king, all her aunts and cousins know that—though they don't dare admit it openly."

I had always found Anne to be well informed, and shrewd. She had become my eyes and ears at the royal court, my primary conduit of gossip and information. She knew what was being said, and often what was being done, behind closed doors and in private closets. As my laundress, she mingled with the other servants in the queen's household whenever she accompanied me to the royal palace. Inevitably she learned a lot, and passed on to me what she learned.

"She had other lovers before her marriage?"

Anne nodded. "And now there are signs that another man besides the king is joining her in the great pearl bed."

"Someone ought to warn her."

Anne snorted. "That's just like you, Cat. Always thinking of another person's danger when you should be thinking about yourself! Can't you see, if the queen's a foolish layabout, then we all look guilty. It looks as if we've been keeping her secret. We're all guilty of treason!"

"All the more reason to warn her. To keep the rest of us safe."

"If I were you I wouldn't go near her. I'd take my leave and go back up north to Yorkshire, where it is truly safe."

"But the king and queen are about to go north themselves, on progress. They will be away for many months, it is said. Besides, we are not in the queen's household, we serve the Lady Anne of Cleves. And when I am summoned to Whitehall or Greenwich, it is to the king's presence, not the queen's."

"Say what you like, Cat, we are all in danger."

All that day I pondered Anne's revelations, and toward evening I spoke to her again.

"Tell me exactly what you have heard, and from whom."

Keen to tell me what she knew, Anne launched into her story, her eyes gleaming with pleasure.

"An old porter, the one they nicknamed Ganymede because he brings the queen her wine, got drunk late one night and stumbled into her bedroom. The king was away at a hunting lodge, but the queen was not alone. She was in bed, and the king's groom, Thomas Culpepper, was there in the room with her."

"Were they actually in bed together?"

"No, but the porter thought Culpepper was beginning to undress. He had his boots off."

"Go on."

"Well, you know how every time the king goes to the queen's bedroom there is a great ceremony about it. A dozen grooms of the bedchamber go with him, and pages carry torches as he walks through the rooms and corridors, all making a great deal of noise and laughing and the king laughing loudest of all."

"Yes."

"Now, he doesn't visit her every night, only one or two nights a week. Which nights those are are well known. Yet her washerwomen tell me that there are stains on her sheets nearly every night, the kind of stains only a lover leaves behind. They have to hurry up and wash the sheets clean every morning, before one of the busybodies from the royal council finds out the truth through his spies."

"What else?"

"Culpepper bribed one of Catherine's ladies, Lady Rochford, to keep silent about his coming to see the queen at night, and a chamber servant witnessed the whole thing."

"I gather there is more."

"Much more."

"But I have heard enough. I will talk to the queen."

Despite Anne's efforts to persuade me against it, I went on the following day to see Queen Catherine. I found her in her apartments, sitting amid her ladies-in-waiting while a chaplain read to them from the Book of Proverbs. I knelt when entering and a moment or two passed before Queen Catherine, who looked quite thoughtful as she listened to the Bible reading, realized I was there and indicated that I should join the others and sit down.

She looked older and paler than when I had last seen her, her dark eyes troubled. The splendid gown she wore, with its golden sleeves and skirt of ruby-colored velvet, set off her coloring to advantage, yet she lacked the animation to make her attractive face come alive. I took note of the costly necklace she wore, made entirely of table diamonds, and remembered what I had often heard about the extravagantly expensive jewels the king had showered upon her.

The chaplain was reading, his tone sober, admonitory.

"Stolen waters are sweet, says the wicked woman, secret bread is pleasant." "A woman comes, with the attire of a harlot, and a crafty mind. She says, I have decked my couch with coverings, colored sheets of Egyptian linen. I have perfumed my bed with myrrh, aloes and cinnamon. Come, let us take our fill of love till the morning; let us delight ourselves with love, for my husband is not at home; he has gone on a distant journey."

The text was shockingly apt, I thought. The queen sat still, listening without any apparent reaction. The chaplain turned the page.

"There are three things that are never satisfied," he read, "and that say not 'Enough' and one of these is a barren womb."

This passage stirred a response.

"Thank you," the queen said, rather tartly. "I believe we have had our fill of proverbs for today."

The chaplain bowed and left the room.

Queen Catherine turned to me. "Lady Latimer."

I knelt. "I beg your highness's attention for a few moments," I said.

"Yes? What is it?" Her gaze was skeptical.

"If we might speak privately, your highness."

"My ladies are quite discreet." Her eyes were steely. She had hardened, I saw. She had come a very long way from the chatty, bubbly girl who talked to me so openly on the day of Lady Anne of Cleves's reception on Hampstead Heath. She was guarded and wary. Lines of worry were beginning to etch themselves into her young brow.

"What I have to say is best communicated without being overheard."

There was the merest hesitation. I saw, or thought I saw, in that brief instant that the wary queen wondered how much I knew, and realized that she had to find out.

She rose and led me into a smaller room where tables held box upon overflowing box of necklaces, rings, earrings and bracelets, all with the soft gleam of gold, or the flash and fire of brilliant diamonds and sapphires, and the warm iridescence of pearls.

"I have just finished supervising the packing of my jewels for our progress journey. The king has been generous with me, has he not?"

"Generous indeed. He treasures you, much more than you treasure these gems."

She turned and fixed me with her narrow stare. "I know how you view me. I also know that you yourself covet the king's company. I am an obstacle."

"I covet nothing from the king, other than his continued good opinion. I cannot help it if he seeks my counsel. We have known each other quite a long time now."

She sniffed. "He doesn't ask *me* to rub his putrid leg."

"Perhaps if you offered—"

"Don't try to tell me how to be a good wife. You have no idea what it is like, being married to that—that monstrous thing."

"No, of course I don't. What goes on between husband and wife is beyond the understanding of any outsider no matter how sympathetic."

"Sympathetic! You think anyone is sympathetic to me! Never! They despise me. They want to destroy me, to bring me down, as they brought down my cousin Anne."

"I don't despise you, Catherine. I pity you."

She bristled. I had dared to call her, the queen, by her Christian name. Yet even as she stiffened with indignation, her eyes filled with tears. She turned away.

"Oh, if only you knew what I have endured from that horrible, twisted old man." Her voice shook.

"I am truly sorry. And I assure you, I am not among those who seek, as you believe, to destroy you. In fact, I am here to try to save you."

She turned toward me once again. "To save me?" I saw panic in her eyes. Swiftly she went to the closed doors of the chamber, flung them open, and peered out into the adjoining room. Lady Rochford and another of the ladies-in-waiting hovered near the door. Two pages scuttled away and another liveried servant, who had obviously been listening at the keyhole, muttered "Your highness" and backed off.

"You see how they hound me, pursue me. They drive me to earth like some wounded beast, so that they can finish me off! Now tell me, how do you intend to save me?"

I led her to the window, at the far side of the small room, as far as possible from the door and the listeners outside it. I whispered to her.

"I know you have a lover. Don't bother to deny it! But I don't believe you let him into your bed because you are wanton or lustful. I believe you know that if you do not give the king a son, he will put you aside. You hope to bear your lover's child, and say it is the king's."

The queen jumped and cried out as a knock on the door interrupted us.

"Yes?" she called out.

"Your highness, the king summons you."

"Tell him I am in my bath, making myself fresh and sweet-smelling for his pleasure."

"Very well, your highness."

She looked at me, willing me to go on. Her face was very pale, her eyes bright with fear.

"I have come to tell you that you stand in greater peril than you know. Your adultery is discovered. Master Culpepper has been seen in your bedchamber. There is evidence of your trysts. Your washerwomen have found it."

Catherine's hand flew to her mouth. "I never thought—I never suspected—"

"You have been foolish."

Her eyes were wide with terror. "Does the king know?" she whispered.

"No one dares to tell the king, he would refuse to believe it of you—and he would probably order the bearer of such horrible tidings to be killed or tortured or thrown into a dungeon. No, the king does not know."

Again there was a knock on the door.

"What is it?"

"The king is impatient to receive you."

"I am coming. Tell the king I am perfuming my body for him."

She turned to me.

"I am caught, like a rat in a trap. If I am a faithful wife, I will never have a child. The king is capable of making love to me, but there is no result. I think he is simply too old. I don't know for certain. None of the doctors will listen to me when I ask them. But if I am an unfaithful wife, I will eventually have a child—and the truth about who the child's father is will destroy me."

"And those around you. All your ladies are in peril. All your relatives too."

"What am I to do, Cat?" All her hardness, all her hauteur was gone. Only her guileless, thoughtless innocence remained—an innocence that was still appealing.

Flee, I thought. Flee while you can. Take your necklace of table diamonds, sell it, and go in disguise to France or Rome or Spain—any place where the long reach of the king cannot snatch you—and hide there until he dies.

I thought this, but I did not say it. What I said was, "I don't know. But I do know this. You can pray for a child. You can be a faithful and loving wife. You can send Master Culpepper away."

She lowered her eyes. "I cannot do that. Without his love, I would throw myself into the river."

I saw then that Catherine's lover meant more to her than I had imagined. Not only could he give her the child she desperately needed, her love for him gave her the strength to go on from day to day. Her love for him was her salvation—and her ruin. I knew what it meant to love that deeply. I realized that she would never give her lover up.

I took her hands. "Catherine, be careful!! If you care nothing for your own life, at least spare those of us who know your secret, and may be brought to die for it!"

27

IT WAS A COLD, DREARY FEBRUARY DAY, THE DAY OF QUEEN CATHERINE'S execution. I stood shivering as an icy wind off the river swept through the Tower courtyard where the scaffold had been erected, hugging myself and wrapping my felt cloak around me as tightly as I could. I was shivering with cold, but also with fear, for King Henry's wrath had fallen not only upon Catherine, but upon all the women who served her, and one of them was to die with her this day.

As I watched, a company of tall guardsmen wearing somber black livery marched in and took up their positions around the scaffold, each man carrying a long pike with a sharp point at one end. Three burly laborers carried in the thick flat block of wood on which the queen would lay her head, and placed it at the center of the scaffold where all of us in the waiting crowd could see it. Another man, walking slowly and solemnly, brought in the heavy axe, its razor-sharp blade gleaming, and placed it beside the block.

A murmuring ran through the crowd at the sight of the axe, and I overheard some of those around me whispering that a queen, even an adulterous one, deserved a more merciful death by a sword. Anne Boleyn had been killed swiftly and efficiently by one blow from a heavy sword.

Everyone knew that to die by the blows of an axe was bloodier, and far more painful. The first stroke did not always fall squarely upon the neck, and the victim suffered horribly before dying.

Soon the murmurs ceased. It would not be long now before the queen appeared, to meet her fate.

Poor Catherine! I had tried to warn her, but she had not heeded my warning. She had gone on progress with the king, the journey a difficult one, plagued with delays. She had gotten sick while on the journey, and when those of us who served Lady Anne of Cleves heard that, we all hoped and prayed that she was pregnant at last, though I worried that the child, if there was a child, would be the son or daughter of Thomas Culpepper, and not the king. But after a few weeks she improved, and we heard no announcement of a pregnancy. When the king and queen returned to London at the end of their long journey, there were fresh rumors, including the persistent rumor that the king was dissatisfied with Catherine and meant to take a new wife. Others said he continued to be enamored with her and had given her more costly gifts.

Then all the contradictory rumors were stilled. We heard that the queen had been shut away at Syon House, and that the king meant to do away with her. People nodded and repeated the old truism that all King Henry's wives were cursed, doomed to die a horrible death.

As I feared, she had continued to sleep with her lovers, not only Thomas Culpepper but another man, Francis Dereham, who, it was said, had been her lover before she married. One of the servants betrayed the secret, and it was soon brought to the ears of the king. At first he had refused to believe it, but eventually, after many of Queen Catherine's servants were questioned and threatened, it became evident to him that his beloved unsullied rose had sharp thorns indeed. He wept, and swore, and wept again, and ordered the great pearl bed to be chopped into little pieces and used for kindling. Finally he ordered that the queen be executed.

I had not seen Catherine since the king shut her away, first at Syon House and then in the Tower. I was told that she was melancholy, filled with remorse. That she wrote to the king, pleading with him to forgive her, but he threw her letter into the fire unread. And that, knowing that she could not escape death, she rehearsed for the day of her execution, having the fatal block of wood brought to her prison room and practicing laying her head upon it, so that when the time came she would do what was necessary with dignity.

Four black-clad drummers emerged from the nearby barrack and mounted the steps to the scaffold. They began a low muffled beat, solemn and mournful. I heard the throaty croak of a raven. From the river came the loud call of a bargeman, "Bridge, ho!"

Then a door opened, and the queen appeared.

She had grown terribly thin over the months of her imprisonment. Her plain black gown hung loose around her now slender torso. Her chubby cheeks and double chin were gone. Now her face was gaunt and very white, her eyes wide with fright. When she walked toward the scaffold steps her legs would not support her, and two of her ladies had to take her arms to help her climb the stairs. When the headsman joined her on the high platform, his large muscular frame covered in a close-fitting black tunic, a black hood with eyeslits covering his face, Catherine nearly fainted.

The crowd was completely silent as she stepped forward and began to speak.

"I am thankful—" she began, her voice too low to be heard even by those closest to her, her face completely drained of color. "I am thankful to my lord and master, our sovereign King Henry, for his gracious mercy to me, an undeserving sinner." Her voice, still trembling, became audible. "I confess before the Lord God, my lord the king and you his good people here assembled, that I am guilty of those crimes with which I am charged and convicted. I am unworthy to stand before you. I am deserving of a worse fate." Everyone present knew what she meant. Traitors were hanged, then cut down still living and disemboweled, their steaming intestines sometimes stuffed into their mouths to suffocate them. Catherine was guilty of treason, yet the king had not ordered a traitor's death for her.

"Let my punishment be an example to all who would betray our lord the king," Catherine was saying, "and may God have mercy on me, a sinner." She bowed her head. "Into Thy hands, O Lord, I commend my spirit."

Her voice broke on the last words, and I became aware that many of those around me were in tears, for Catherine was indeed a pitiable figure, so young and so alone, and about to be killed. I whispered a prayer for her.

Her hands shaking, she took off her hood and knelt down, crossed herself, and laid her head on the cold wooden block. The headsman took the heavy axe, lifted it, and brought it down with a loud thwack.

I shut my eyes. I couldn't watch.

When I opened them I saw a ghastly sight. Blood was spurting out from the wounded neck, flowing down over the wooden block and onto the black gown, staining it crimson. The body was heaving, the hands and arms twitching and fluttering like the wings of a dying chicken. But the head hung, limp and all but lifeless, mouth agape and eyes staring, still attached to the body.

The headsman lifted the axe a second time, and struck, and then a third. Finally the head fell onto the planking of the scaffold with a soft thud, the queen's beautiful long auburn hair reddened with gore.

I turned away, I felt nauseous and dizzy. Gulping in deep draughts of the chill air, I managed not to be sick. Slowly I recovered, as two of Catherine's ladies threw a black cloak over her body and dragged it away. The head, I noticed with a frisson of horror, was lifted by the wet hair and tossed into a bucket.

But the headsman's grisly work was not yet done. One by one the dead queen's chamber servants were brought to the block and executed. Among them was the old man Anne Daintry had told me about, the one they called Ganymede, who had witnessed Thomas Culpepper with his boots off in the queen's bedchamber. Grizzled and bent, he managed to climb the steps of the scaffold, mumbling to himself. He looked dazed, glancing out over the sea of faces in the courtyard. Then he was seized by two of the guardsmen and forced to his knees, his torso held down so that his head could be severed.

Then came the final act in the morning's bloody drama. Lady Rochford, who according to gossip had been the dead queen's chief ally in arranging her adulterous meetings, was brought, screaming and weighed down with chains, to the block and turned over to the executioner. Her high-pitched screams, moans of dread and animal howls caused an uncomfortable stirring in the watching crowd. Clearly Lady Rochford had lost her reason. She belonged in a madhouse, or locked in an attic, not here on a gory killing ground amid the blood of traitors. Besides, she was only a wretched aging woman. An object of pity.

Her chains were unlocked and she shrieked afresh, rubbing furiously at her wounded wrists where the cruel metal had bit into her flesh. Then she did such a startling thing that I almost cannot bring myself to record it. She tore at the dark, dirty rags that covered her thin body until she was nearly naked.

So quickly did she act that those who were guarding her could not immediately cover her nakedness. For what seemed an eternity she stood before us all, her shrunken breasts, distended belly, nearly bald female parts and wrinkled thighs fully disclosed to our view, while the guardsmen scrambled to find a cloth to cover her. At length someone produced a shroud, and her nakedness was concealed beneath it.

Yet the sudden, grotesque spectacle had had its effect. And Lady Rochford, mad though she was, knew that she had succeeded in shocking and revolting us all. Because as she stood there before us, in all her hideous bareness, she opened her toothless mouth and laughed. A high-pitched, frenzied laugh, ghoulish and unearthly.

"Fools!" I heard her cry. "Fools, fools!"

When the shroud was thrown over her and she was held down upon the chopping block her words were muffled and a moment later the axe put an end to her life. But as I stumbled, aghast and in tears, out of the courtyard and toward the river, desperate to get away from the stench of blood and death, I was haunted by the sound of Lady Rochford's croaking accusation.

"Fools, fools" rang in my ears as I walked quickly, then all but ran to the riverside in search of a wherry to take me home.

28

THE KING HAS SENT YOU ANOTHER GIFT," ANNE DAINTRY ANNOUNCED, indicating a large carved rosewood box that sat on a nearby table. "How many is that now? Five?"

It had been almost a year since Queen Catherine Howard's execution, a lonely year for me as Tom had been kept away from court on one foreign mission after another. And a lonely year for King Henry, who had been melancholy and disillusioned ever since he discovered that his cherished young wife had been faithless.

"Six, I think."

"He is courting you."

"I'm married."

"To a dying man."

"John may live a long time yet."

It was true. Feeble as he was, and largely insensible to the world around him, John lived on. I made him comfortable, heaping warm furs on his bed and making certain the hearth fire in his room was always bright and crackling. I supervised the servants to make sure his linen was changed often and that he was kept clean. When sores erupted on his legs and back I spread healing ointment on them, the same healing ointment I used on the king's ulcers.

Once in a while I saw John smile, especially when Margaret came into the room or the kind and skilled young German doctor, Philip von Lederer, who attended him. Philip, who had come to England in the entourage of Lady Anne of Cleves, was a gentle, soft-spoken man, cultivated and thoughtful, who in addition to caring for his patients took time out to tutor Margaret in Greek. I enjoyed him. Sometimes, when we were watching by John's bedside, the three of us, Margaret, Philip and I, played hazard or he talked to us about life in the duchy of Cleves.

"Open your gift." Anne was insistent.

"Whatever it is, I don't want it." I pushed the rosewood box away. The last thing I wanted to be reminded of, today of all days, was that the king admired me and was thinking of me fondly. For Tom was coming home at last, and I wanted nothing to mar the joy of our reunion.

I watched and waited for him, hour by hour, wondering what was keeping him and praying that his ship had not foundered in the Channel. He had been in Hungary for a long time, at the court of Emperor Ferdinand. His journey back to England was long and difficult.

At last, late one night, he arrived. Because it was nearly midnight the outer gate was locked and most of Lady Anne's servants were in bed. I heard the dogs barking and then there was a tap on my bedchamber window. It was Tom. With a joyful cry I flung open the window and Tom climbed nimbly in.

"Cat! My Cat!"

And then we were in each other's arms.

Our loving was all the sweeter for our long separation, and it was several days before we could bring ourselves to speak of anything other than our joy at being together. Finally, however, we managed to talk of mundane things.

"I've been to see the king," Tom told me. "He's aged. And grown fatter and grayer."

"And more irritable."

"Someone should put him out of his misery, like an old bull."

"Hush! You know better than to talk of ending the king's life! What if one of the servants were to hear you?"

"I've been away so long I've almost forgotten the dangers of this godforsaken court. Almost, but not entirely." He looked at me, hesitant to go on. I knew at once that something was troubling him. He smiled, a rueful smile I thought. He came up to me and brushed his hand tenderly against my cheek, stroking it as he spoke.

"So soft, so soft," he murmured, following the trail of his hand with kisses. "I have been dreaming of you, Cat. Dreaming of the day when you would be free to become my wife. But now—"

"Now what?"

He sighed. "I may as well tell you straight out. The king has told me that he intends to marry you once you become a widow."

The words struck me like a blow. Even though I had been nervously aware that I was becoming more and more the focus of royal attention, I allowed myself to go on believing that King Henry valued me as a trusted friend and as someone to confide in, not as a future wife. Besides, I had heard him swear dozens of times that he would never marry again.

A sudden thought made my stomach clench in fear.

"Does the king know about us?"

"No, I don't think so. Unless he is much more devious than I take him to be."

"He is very clever you know. Much cleverer than those around him. And he has grown very suspicious."

"Surely if he had any suspicions about you, he would never dream of marrying you. He has to think you are blameless, faithful to your husband."

"But why tell you that he wants to marry me? Why you?"

Tom shrugged. "Because I was there. Because I remind him of poor Jane—and marriage. Because he likes to boast about his amours. Also because he is always after me to get married. The uncle of a future king must have a wife, he said. A young and fertile wife."

"And what did you say?"

"I laughed and told him about King Ferdinand's eleven ugly daughters, in Hungary. Let me see, there was Greta, Elizaveta, Amelia, Sofia, Carlotta, I can't remember them all. Plain as a pig's backside, every one of them. The king kept insisting that I choose one and marry her."

I sat down on a cushion in the window seat. All at once the full import of what Tom had told me about King Henry settled like a leaden weight on my heart.

"So he means to marry me, after all. That explains all the gifts he's been sending me. Beautiful things, quite extravagant. I thought he was just thanking me for all I do for him. I haven't even opened the most recent gift yet." I indicated the carved rosewood box that sat on a table in the corner. "Now I understand. He has been wooing me."

My lip trembling, I got up and ran to Tom, who held me tightly while I cried.

"There there, dear. My sweetest Cat, don't cry. It's all for the best. Everything will come out all right. Even better than we planned."

"No, it's terrible! I don't want to be the queen, I want to be your wife!"

"And you will be, beloved, very soon. The king can't possibly live much longer."

"Why not? John has survived far longer than any of us thought he would. Dr. von Lederer keeps shaking his head in disbelief, and joking that he will live to be a hundred. Maybe King Henry will be just as tough."

"King Henry will not live to be a hundred. I doubt he will last more than a year or two."

I shuddered at the thought of joining the ghastly parade of the king's unlucky wives. "He may well live longer than I do—if he shortens my life."

Tom's face grew closed, his eyes narrowed.

"That won't happen."

"How can you be so sure?"

"Because I'll be there to protect you. I won't let him harm you."

"He'll send you back to Hungary or somewhere, to a place so far away you could never come back in time to save me, if I were in danger."

"Then I will refuse to go. Cat, can't you see this is a benefit for us? Think about it! You will be queen! The highest ranking woman in the land. The one who holds the king's regard and love. Think of the power that will give you!"

"I have never sought power."

"It will greatly benefit us nonetheless. You will be the stepmother of Prince Edward. In time, when King Henry dies, you will become the closest relative of the new king Edward VI. The Queen Dowager. Wealthy, titled, privileged—"

"And your wife?"

"Yes, of course. After a suitable mourning period, you will marry me. Together we will reign for Edward, as joint regents."

His bright blue eyes shone with anticipation. All that he hoped for seemed, in that visionary moment, to lie within his grasp. I was far less sanguine.

"Open the king's gift, Cat," Tom said after a time. "I'd like to see it."

With reluctance I went to the table where the carved rosewood box rested and lifted the lid.

Inside, resting on a fold of black velvet, was Catherine Howard's necklace of table diamonds.

I drew in my breath with a sharp sound. My knees felt weak. What did it mean? Was it the king's way of telling me that he meant to put me in Catherine's place? That I was worthy to be queen? Or was it a darker message, a reminder that while precious, priceless gems endure forever, the necks they encircle can always be replaced?

29

LATE ONE NIGHT I WAS SLEEPING ON A COT BY JOHN'S BEDSIDE WHEN I felt a gentle touch on my arm.

"Milady, milady, wake up." It was Philip von Lederer's voice, rousing me. "He's going, milady."

Quickly I threw my wrap over my silk nightgown and went to stand by my husband's bedside. His breathing was ragged, his breath catching in his throat and a horrible gurgling sound rising with every breath. His eyes were closed.

Margaret, looking thin and fragile in her nightclothes, stood on the other side of the bed, her tearstained face a pitiable sight. Philip stood beside her, a protective arm around her shoulders.

I held John's limp hand and kissed it. I had told him so often that I loved him that there was no need for us to communicate, and in any case I didn't know whether or not he could hear anything that was said to him. In the midst of the overwhelming solemnity of the moment I had an odd thought. Here I was, on the verge of widowhood, already mourning my husband of many years—and at the same time I was longing for the comfort of my lover's arms and also dreading the king's marriage proposal, which could not be long in coming.

John began to cough, then to choke.

Alarmed, I looked over at Philip. "Can't you help him?"

Philip shook his head, slowly and sadly. "There is nothing more to be done. He is drowning."

I put my face close to John's and his breathing seemed to ease slightly. The spasm of coughing passed.

"Merciful Lord," I prayed, "take the soul of my dear husband John without pain. Spare him, for Jesus' sake."

As I prayed, the room grew still. All I could hear were Margaret's quiet sobs. Then there came one last, long rasping sigh from the depths of John's ravaged chest. It was over.

With John's passing my life changed, as if overnight. Hardly had we held John's funeral and arranged for his burial when I began receiving royal commands to attend the king at banquets and ceremonies, christenings and weddings, small suppers to which only those closest to him were invited.

My sister Nan was nearly always invited along with me, to serve as companion and chaperone, and Nan was only too delighted to be so favored. For years she had looked on me as an oddity, a renegade with eccentric, independent views; now, at last, I had gained her respect by rising high in the king's estimation. She was only too glad to accompany me on royal picnics, to ride with me in the royal barge, to sit through concerts at court and to bask in the king's largesse.

"You see how they kneel to you, Cat," she remarked when the king's servants came to bring me messages or deliver gifts. "It is as if you were already queen. They know the future."

"He has not yet asked me to marry him, Nan."

"But he will. Everyone says so. Even the Lady Anne of Cleves, who I hear was hoping he would take her back. And when he asks you, you can't very well say no."

"Others have."

"Princesses from foreign courts, yes. But not Englishwomen." She sighed. "If only our mother had lived to see you marry the king! How proud she would have been! And just think what you can do for our entire family, once you are the highest lady in the land. Why, the Parrs will rank with the Seymours and the Howards! We will be the richest family in the kingdom!"

"I think that distinction will continue to rest with the Tudors."

"Oh, of course. The Tudors. But Cat, when you have children by the king, they will be Tudors! Think of that."

Day by day it was becoming more evident that Nan's optimism was well founded. Messengers from Whitehall arrived with costly gifts. One day it was a gentle mare for me, a fine riding horse, light in the mouth and responsive to the slightest touch of my heels. Another day it was a sleek, shy greyhound, swift on her delicate legs and eager to push her soft wet muzzle into my hand. There were chests of new gowns, in the stylish colors of lady blush and gosling and peas porridge tawny and a dozen other hues.

Officially, of course, I was in mourning for John and as a new widow I was obliged to wear black as a sign of mourning. But the king ordered me to ignore that obligation, in the service of a higher one: my obligation to please him, my sovereign.

Henry knew that I had a weakness for beautiful gowns and kirtles made in the latest styles, so he instructed his envoys in Spain to send me Spanish farthingales, their full, wide skirts stiffened by hoops made from whalebone. As soon as Nan and I appeared at court in these uncomfortable but strikingly handsome gowns (for Nan kept pace with me in all my new gowns) all the other ladies had to have them too. Nan and I became leaders of fashion—a new role for me and one that I confess I enjoyed.

There were gowns from Milan and Venice also, curiously made with pleats and wide sleeves, and charming Dutch kirtles and French hoods with fine jewels sewn around the edges to frame my face.

One afternoon Sir Thomas Heneage, King Henry's chief body servant, came to meet me. He escorted me by barge to Baynard's Castle, the old fortress on the river now used to store the costumes and props for the court masques and pageants, along with arms and weaponry. Heneage was pleasant, courteous and respectful as always, but I sensed that there was more to his mission than he was telling me. I knew there was no use in asking what lay behind our expedition; I knew him well enough to realize that he invariably kept his own counsel.

When we entered a large, musty-smelling room filled with wooden trunks I began to feel uncomfortable, though I couldn't have said why. Heneage walked over to one of the trunks, produced a large key and opened it, throwing back the lid to reveal a multicolored froth of silk and lace and damask.

"The garments in these trunks," Heneage said, lifting out a purple petticoat trimmed in gold, "belonged to her late majesty Queen Catherine Howard."

Involuntarily I drew in my breath and took a step backward. Hearing the name of the late queen frightened me. I wanted nothing to do with her—or her clothes. I had already been frightened by the gift of her diamond necklace, which I could not bring myself to wear.

"The king has made you a gift of these garments. Many of them, he says, have never been worn." He began lifting the shimmering gowns and kirtles, petticoats and sleeves out of the trunk, one by one, and laying them on a table under the room's rose window. His voice was as expressionless as his face.

I shuddered. "Stop!" I cried out, nearly shouting. "Take me back to Richmond at once!"

Heneage paused in removing the garments from the trunk.

"And what shall I do with these?"

"Burn them!" I turned to go, then hesitated. "No, I'm wrong. It would be wasteful to burn such valuable things. See that they are sold, and that the money is given to the poor."

"Very well, milady. But if the king finds out—"

"I trust you to ensure that he does not."

Heneage bowed, a slight smile on his face. We understood one another. "Naturally I will see that your discretion is rewarded." I knew that to have Heneage on my side would be vital once I became queen.

Once I became queen! I still found it hard to believe that it would ever happen, even though each passing day's events continued to point in that direction. Nan alluded to my future royal status constantly, the palace servants continued to show me a degree of deference I hardly felt I deserved and even Tom, somewhat to my dismay, was much in favor of my becoming the third Queen Catherine to marry our sovereign. As the weather warmed and the court began to prepare for the feastings and revelings of summer, I tried to prepare myself for what everyone believed was inevitable: a proposal from the king.

30

THE KING HAD CELEBRATED TOO LUSTILY THE NIGHT BEFORE, STUFFING himself with his favorite mugget and sturgeon's liver and drinking far too much sugared wine. I knew it better than anyone, for I had been sitting across the banquet table from him while he ate, observing how his small bright eyes grew more and more dull as he drank, hearing him belch, turning aside when he vomited into a silver ewer held by the ever faithful Thomas Heneage.

I was not surprised when he sent for me on the following morning. I knew he would be ill. I had my basket of remedies ready.

I found him sitting up in bed, intent on reading a gilt-embossed book. He had on his new reading glasses with gold frames, and they gave him a scholarly look. His swollen leg was elevated, and draped in a light cloth of silver tissue.

As soon as I was admitted to the room he waved the servants and other attendants away.

"Come in, Cat, and give me some of those licorice pastilles you always carry."

"Good morning, your majesty," I said, curtseying and handing him the bag of pastilles. "I have your olive oil suppositories here as well in case you need to take a purge."

"Not yet, not yet. Listen, I've just been reading Melanchthon on grace. A fine passage. Sit down, here on the bed. Let me read it to you."

I sat patiently while he read me the long Latin passage, loudly emphasizing the parts he agreed with and shaking his head here and there over points he found objectionable. He quite often discoursed to me about theology, a subject that fascinated him. As he read, I wondered at his evident clear-headedness. He had drunk so much the night before that it seemed he would require at least half a day to recover his wits. Yet here he was, early the following morning, deep into a difficult set of arguments.

"Tell me, what do you think of this?" he asked when he finished the passage.

"Sire, you know my views well. We have often discussed them."

"Remind me."

I gathered my thoughts. "Philip Melanchthon is an able theologian and an eloquent writer. I agree with him that we are saved through grace alone, and not through our own efforts or our own merits."

"And by the sacraments, of course. The sacraments are the means of grace."

"The sacraments have always been a part of church tradition, though as you know they are not mentioned as such in the Bible."

"But they are implied."

"If you say so, sire."

"Ah, Cat, I will not let you squirm so easily out of an argument." He looked at me over the tops of his glasses. "I know the opinions of you bold gospellers." He laughed.

"And I, as a good daughter of the church and a loyal subject of your majesty, know that I must conform to the Six Articles, which is the law of the realm. Thus I subscribe to the doctrine that the sacraments convey grace."

The Six Articles, drawn up by the beetle-browed Bishop Gardiner and others who thought as he did, had been the governing points of belief—and the law of the land—for several years.

"You are clever, Cat." He sighed. "You remind me of my first queen, your namesake. The Spanish Catherine. Now, there was a well educated woman! She taught me a great deal—she was older than I was, did you know that? Though I never admitted it. I looked up to her, in a way. She had spirit, and heart, and a well trained mind."

And you sent her away to die, I wanted to say, but held my tongue, as I so often had to do when the king conversed with me.

"Well then, Cat, don't let's argue. Take the Melanchthon book and read it and we will talk further." He handed me the book and I dutifully put it into a pocket of my kirtle, omitting to mention that I had read it already.

He reached for my hands and took them in both of his, and smiled, not a lecherous smile or a smile of gloating triumph (both of which smiles I had often seen on his round face) but a genuinely loving and tender smile.

"Now, let us talk of more important things."

I began to shiver. Had the moment I had been dreading come?

"Tell me truly, dear, could you find it in your heart to share the rest of my life, as my loving spouse?"

I lowered my head. I felt as if I were putting my neck into a noose.

"If your majesty wishes it." My voice was so low it was almost a whisper.

"I do. I have always wanted you. You know that. You arouse my lust, you intrigue me with your intelligence and you have honored me with your loyal friendship. I cannot imagine a better or truer life companion."

His sincerity, at that moment, was genuine. I would have bet my life on it. Yet I knew him; I knew how easily his enmity could be aroused. The pain in his legs, the machinations of his councillors, the disloyalty of his servants—anything could make him snarling and hostile or even send him into a frenzy of anger.

"I fear, sire, that you think too highly of me."

"Here is how highly I think of you." He reached into a drawer beside the bed and extracted a small pearl-encrusted golden box made like a scallop shell. He handed it to me.

Inside was a ring with an emerald the size of a pigeon's egg.

"It belonged to my grandmother, the Venerable Margaret. She would have liked you. She liked me, very much, when I was a boy. If she saw me now, she'd scold me. Even when I was young she got after me for eating too much and chasing the little girls—when I slipped away from the jailers my father hired to keep watch over me, that is." He laughed.

I had put the ring on my finger as he was talking. Its weight made lifting my hand an effort. In its clear green depths I saw shafts of light and flashes of fire. It was magnificent.

"It's very beautiful," I said. "You have given me so much."

"How else was I to woo you? An old man who needs pastilles to settle his stomach and suppositories to clean out his insides can hardly gain a bride by his good looks alone."

"As your majesty's loyal subject, I am in duty bound to obey your every request, as long as I am free to do so."

"Cat!" he cried out, exasperated by my subjection. "Have you no feelings for me, none at all?"

"Oh yes, I have strong feelings!" I stood up, still wearing the great emerald, and spoke my mind. "I still feel fear and revulsion at the memory of you putting your hands on me, kissing me, when I was a young girl. I still feel the fury and anguish I knew when my beloved Ned died, a victim of the heartless demands of your court! I feel sorrow for poor Queen Catherine of Aragon, that noble and gracious lady, and for poor foolish Catherine Howard, and even for the one you call the Witch. They all got entangled in the deadly web of the court, and in the end the great spider at the heart of the web devoured them! As he will no doubt devour me!"

Terrified at my own outburst, overcome by the fateful answer I knew I must give to the king's request, my heart torn by having to yield myself to the bloated old king while all my love was Tom's and Tom's alone, I wept, openly and bitterly.

For a long time the king said nothing, but simply let me sob. I was raw and naked before him, stripped of all pretense of willing compliance. After awhile, feeling drained, holding a lace-trimmed silk handkerchief to my nose, I began to be calmer.

"Don't you know, Cat, that it is because of your honesty that I cherish you?" His voice was gentle and caressing. "For all past hurts, I most humbly ask your forgiveness."

I was moved, as he knew I would be, by his words. The humble words of a great king, offering me his love.

I composed myself. "I forgive you," I said simply, not knowing what else to say. The Bible teaches us to forgive, after all. Yet in my heart my grievances still rankled.

Ignoring the quavering in my voice, the king took my hands in his.

"Then are we agreed, sweetheart. Six weeks from today will be our wedding day. Heneage will arrange everything."

He kissed my hands, and admired the great emerald on my finger.

"That ring," he said, "cost me all of last year's revenues from Cornwall. Including the smuggled goods we took back from the pirates."

"I have heard many a compliment, sire, but none as grand as 'You are worth as much as Cornwall.' It is a very romantic sentiment."

His loud guffaw brought the servants back into the room.

"Never mind, never mind," he called out to them. "I was only laughing. She makes me laugh, you know. Just like her brother. Bring us wine, then, and cakes, for we have rejoicing to do!" One of the grooms bowed and went out.

"Speaking of your brother, he will enjoy the first fruits of your elevation. The queen's brother must have many honors and emoluments. I am appointing Will to my Privy Council and making him a Garter Knight. He will have the wardship of the Cinque Ports and three fine estates in Cumberland. We must think of a suitable marquisate for him as well, what do you think?"

"I think he will be delighted."

"Oh, and one more thing," Henry added as the groom brought in a flagon of wine and a plate of honey cakes sprinkled with sweet almonds.

"Your stepdaughter Margaret. I know you have been wanting to make a good match for her." He stuffed a cake into his mouth and wiped his hands on a linen napkin. "I have just the right man. He's rich, well connected, ambitious, and handsome."

"Who is it, your majesty?"

He fixed me with an enigmatic stare. "An acquaintance of yours— and my brother-in-law. Tom Seymour."

31

Tom! TO BE MARGARET'S HUSBAND!

I felt my face grow warm. My mouth dropped open. Fortunately King Henry had shifted his attention to the honey cakes and was devouring another one.

Tom to become my stepson! And Margaret to be married to a man who was very much in love with her stepmother! It was unthinkable—and yet the king had spoken. It was his wish.

Having felt hot, I now felt a sudden chill. I looked over at my future husband, his expression bland as he munched on the sweet confection, crumbs of cake dropping into his graying beard. Yet again I wondered, how much did he know about Tom and me? Did he know that I longed for Tom, night and day, that I would give anything to be with him? And that Tom had pledged his love to me again and again, ardently and with the most impassioned kisses and lovemaking? Was the king hoping to remove Tom as a rival, by binding him to me with ties of family rather than of romantic love? Or—and this was the most chilling thought of all—was Henry punishing me for loving Tom by placing me in the agonizing position of becoming Tom's stepmother?

I didn't know what to think, or to say. I reached for a honey cake and ate.

Fortunately, the king did not bring up the subject of Tom and Margaret's marriage again that day. He seemed to regard it as settled. That night I spent long wakeful hours anxiously turning over in my mind all the worrying aspects of the king's plan, and wishing that I could share my worries with my beloved. On the following day I remarked to the king, in as casual a tone as I could manage, that Margaret was still in mourning for her father (as I was myself) and that any announcement of a betrothal ought to be put off for at least a few months. Henry grunted in agreement and we went on to talk of other things. Inwardly I felt a great wave of relief and joy. At least there would be no wedding any time soon—except my own, of course.

With only six weeks until the day King Henry had chosen for our nuptials there was a great deal to do, and I distracted myself with the wedding preparations, and the forming of my new household as queen.

Queen! I repeated this word to myself, again and again, but could not get used to it. I was still plain Cat Parr, no matter what titles and privileges might be showered on me, and I vowed never to forget it.

Anne Daintry was of the greatest help to me in choosing the hundreds of people who would serve me in my new role. I told her that I wanted my uncle William, now elderly, to serve as my chamberlain (he had come to me and respectfully requested the post), Daniel Frith, my former steward from Gainesborough Hall, to be steward of my household, Mrs. Molsey to be my cook and Avice Odell, my friend from the days when I was in Henry Fitzroy's household, to be my mother of the maids. My sister Nan would be my principal lady-in-waiting. There were dozens of others, a sprinkling of villagers from Grundleford, some of John's former gardeners and grooms who I wanted to have near me as queen. It made the new life I faced seem less formidable, to have familiar people around me.

My stepson John Neville (no longer Johnny) was to be the captain of my guard while Philip von Lederer would be appointed as my physician and Gwillim Morgan my apothecary. I had been entertained many times at Lady Audley's house by her fool Ippolyta the Tartarian. I now sent Anne Daintry to request that Ippolyta come to court, to make me and my friends laugh with her wild dancing and japes and mimicry.

I relied on Anne to supervise the sewing of the new liveries in my colors of tawny and popinjay blue, and to make certain the ten seamstresses who were stitching the thousands of seed pearls onto my wedding gown did not fall behind in completing their laborious task.

My sister resented the authority I gave Anne.

"A laundress! A lowly, despised laundress is running your household! It's a disgrace. An insult to us all."

"May I remind you Nan that that laundress was born an earl's daughter? And that she is still, in law, Will's wife?"

Nan snorted. "She forfeited her birthright when she turned her back on her husband and family and took up a life of degradation. She dishonored her father and the rest of us. With those bastard brats of hers, she's no better than a whore! Will's wife indeed! Will's shame, more like it."

"Nan! She's my friend. And she's Will's friend too, you know. He met with her when she first came back to court with me. They talked everything out, and he's made her a generous allowance. They are on quite good terms."

"Will has no more sense about these things than you have."

"What things?"

"Who ought to keep company with whom. Who ought to know their place and not try to rise above it."

"As I have?"

Nan gave me a long look. "You have been raised up by the king. By royal command. You have done nothing to attempt to advance yourself."

"I'm glad you approve." The sarcasm in my tone was lost on Nan, who merely nodded and went on to talk of another matter.

"I believe the Lady Mary is to live at court, with an apartment near yours."

"Yes. I will be glad of her company."

"Everyone says she will wind up an old maid. She's nearly twenty-seven. And what with her bad health, and her Spanish blood, and that stubborn will of hers, what man would want her? And she refuses to marry a husband who is of the reform faith. She still clings to the Romish belief."

"I admire her strong character."

"You confer your admiration much too freely, in my opinion."

I said nothing to this. It did no good to argue with Nan. Arguing was tiresome, and Nan never changed her views no matter what anyone said to her. I accepted her as she was; after all, she was my sister, and family ties are very important. I wished that I could confide in Nan the way I confided in Anne Daintry, but it was no good wishing. Things were as they were.

About this time, not long before my wedding, Henry's daughter Elizabeth was brought to court by her lady mistress, Catherine Champernowne, and because she had been disobedient, Henry insisted that the child abase herself and seek his pardon.

We received her in the watching chamber, a large long room with an immense hearth. Royal guardsmen stood at attention, halberds at the ready, and along the walls, surrounding the hearth, were hung gleaming swords and muskets and pikes, embossed shields and long knives whose hilts were ornately decorated with filigree designs in silver and gold. Henry and I were seated in high-backed thronelike chairs at one end of the room, and at the other end, the double doors were opened to admit a small figure in a light blue gown, a lace cap around her pale face, a starched white collar around her slim neck.

She took a few slow, tentative steps into the room, then got down on all fours and began crawling toward us, her progress slowed by the full skirt of her gown which became entangled between her legs.

I watched, disturbed at the sight, as she inched along, head down, concentrating on dragging herself across the many yards that separated us.

Children were often punished in this way—in my childhood I myself had been made to crawl to my father when I disobeyed him—but I wondered how grievous Elizabeth's disobedience could have been to condemn her to crawling the entire length of this chamber.

"What did she do to offend you, sire?" I asked Henry, who was watching his daughter with a sour look on his face.

"She's sly and willful, just like the Witch."

"But she can't be more than nine or ten years old. Surely with the guidance and encouragement of loving parents, she will learn truthfulness and submission."

Henry looked over at me and grinned. "That's what I love about you, Cat. Your optimism. Even about the Witch's Brat here."

Little Elizabeth had covered only half the distance from the doorway to where we sat, yet already she was scraping her knees and palms raw on the rough tiled floor. As she came closer I could see that there were bloodstains on her kirtle and sleeves. Yet she made no outcry or complaint; to endure the pain in silence was part of the punishment.

On she came, doggedly as I thought. When she lifted her face I saw that she was gritting her teeth and that her small white brow was furrowed in effort. So this is Anne Boleyn's child, I said to myself. I had never seen her up close before, as Henry had kept her away from court at Hatfield and various other royal manors from the age of two on. I had glimpsed her once or twice from a distance, on one of the rare occasions when she was brought to Whitehall or Greenwich, but that was all. Now I saw that she had her father's coloring and features—except for a resemblance to Anne around the eyes. I thought, she will be a beauty when she is older, with her fine white skin and delicate face, her long neck and tapered limbs.

Just then she reached us, and, still kneeling, lifted her eyes to meet the king's stern gaze.

"Father," she said, "I beseech your blessing, for charity." Her childish voice was even, her words distinct. But the look she gave her father was anything but deferential. There was a furious stubbornness in her eyes, an unmistakable pride in the tilt of her chin and a disdainful set to her mouth. When, ever so briefly, she turned her glance on me I saw there a flash of venom.

"I have been told that you are disobedient. That you challenge your chaplain on points of theology and correct your Latin tutor's grammar."

I saw Elizabeth press her lips together. The muscles in her neck grew taut. She wants to answer him back, I thought. But she knows she doesn't dare. How clever she is, and what self-restraint she has developed! Though she was far from being a lovable child at that moment, still my heart went out to her.

"Disobedient children are unnatural beings," the king was saying, "cruel murderers of their parents. Theirs is a special hell."

"I am heartily sorry for all my misdeeds," came the childish voice again, the timber slightly stronger.

Impatient and uncomfortable, Henry was fidgeting in his seat.

"Very well then. Come here." He held out his hands and Elizabeth came closer, placing her head beneath his palms.

"Bless you, my child," he said curtly, and removed his hands quickly, as if they had inadvertently touched a snake or a hot coal.

"This is Lady Catherine, your stepmother-to-be. Ask her blessing, out of respect."

"Yet another?" I heard Elizabeth whisper to herself as she came over to me and submitted her head to my outstretched hands.

"Stepmother, I beseech your blessing, for charity."

"Bless you, my dear child."

"Champernowne!" Henry called out, his loud voice echoing in the long room. "Take her away!"

From out of the shadows stepped Elizabeth's lady mistress, Catherine Champernowne, a serious-looking woman in an unadorned dark gown. She came forward briskly, took Elizabeth by the arm, and both made respectful exits. As Elizabeth left I was again disturbed at the sight of the bloodstains on her kirtle and sleeves.

"Don't you think, sire, that it is a mistake not to restore the Lady Elizabeth to the succession? She and the Lady Mary both. If, God forbid, the prince should die—"

"Yes, yes, I know." He reached for the goblet at his elbow and drank deeply. "We must make another prince, you and I. And soon."

When, a few days later, my stepdaughter Margaret came to see me, bringing with her Philip von Lederer, I could not help contrasting Margaret's open, joyous face with that of the haunted, guarded Elizabeth. Even before she spoke I could tell that Margaret had a delicious secret—and I was glad, because ever since John's death she had been somber. I kissed her and invited both young people to sit down.

"Mother Catherine," Margaret said, "Philip has something he wants to say to you."

"Yes, Philip, what is it?"

"Lady Latimer, I must speak plainly to you. If your late husband were still alive I would approach him, but sadly he is not. So I come to you."

"Say what you have to say, Philip."

He cleared his throat. "I love Margaret and we are pledged to one another. I know that I am unworthy of her, both by birth and merit." Here he glanced at Margaret with a look of fond devotion that I found very touching. With a pang I remembered how Ned appealed to my mother to let us marry, all those years ago. My dear Ned, how I loved him! "But she says that she loves me," Philip went on, "and that is what matters most."

"Yes, that is what matters most. But I may as well tell you both, the king has other plans for Margaret."

"I thought he might," Margaret said, beaming. "That is why Philip and I went to Woodsetton last week, where Philip's friend James Himley has a small parish, and were married."

32

WILL LED ME DOWN THE AISLE OF THE CHAPEL AT HAMPTON COURT on my wedding day, joking with me and winking at Prince Edward who stood with his sisters at the front of the church. I was glad of Will's comforting presence, my arm resting on his, as I walked past the rows of courtiers and officials whom the king had invited to the small ceremony. I knew that many of them disapproved of his marrying me, others pitied me and whispered the old curse that anyone who became King Henry's wife would die, soon and miserably.

I wobbled a little on my stiff cork-heeled shoes trimmed in gold, and hoped their gold ruching would not get caught in the folds of my three satin petticoats, with their delicate loops of silver-gilt thread and heavy hems stitched with green glass beads. My gown was of pale ivory silk with bone-colored lace at the neck and oversleeves of sheer cypress cloth, so thin it was like gauze. A caul of fretted gold covered my coiled and plaited hair. On my hand was my beautiful wedding ring, and another gem Henry had given me that morning, an acorn-sized diamond called the Mirror of Portugal that flashed its myriad facets around the room as I walked. At Henry's insistence I also wore Catherine Howard's great necklace of table diamonds, hoping it would not prove to be an ill omen, and a small gold cross on a chain that he told me had belonged to his mother.

Tears came to my eyes when I walked past Tom, standing with his brothers Edward and Henry and looking extremely handsome, and I grasped Will's arm more tightly to make certain I did not break down. I forced myself to glance at the other wedding guests, all resplendently dressed and solemn, as I passed: Prince Edward and his sisters, Margaret and Philip von Lederer—beaming happily at me and at one another—my sister Nan and her husband, my uncle William, and my ladies-in-waiting. Among these the dark-haired, strikingly beautiful Kate Brandon stood out, her vivacity apparent even in repose as she turned her laughing eyes toward me and made a wry face, making me smile.

Kate was the very youthful bride of King Henry's closest friend Charles Brandon, who like the king was aging rapidly, his once muscular and athletic frame now bulky and cumbersome and his face jowly and wrinkled. Kate sympathized with me, a much younger woman marrying an elderly man; she knew the tediums and deprivations such a marriage entailed, and had lightened my hours of wedding preparation by laughing with me over our mutual burden.

My bridegroom, massive and dominant as he stood before the altar in his doublet of gleaming cloth of gold, his balding head bare out of respect for his surroundings, leaning for support against the altar rail, smiled broadly at me as he watched me approach. In me, he believed, he had what he wanted. I would complete his life, and give it ease and peace.

"You will be my last wife, Cat," he had often told me as the day of our wedding came closer. "You will be the wife I should have had from the beginning. The one who will give me lasting happiness in every way."

I saw the contentment on his round face, and tried to mirror it as I let go of Will's arm and took my place beside Henry. Together we stood before the beetle-browed, hook-nosed Bishop Gardiner, who regarded us without enthusiasm and began to read the service in his rather high-pitched tenor voice.

He spoke the words in English—the language of the reform worship—not Latin, the tongue of the Roman faith. Yet in most other respects Bishop Gardiner was a traditionalist, skeptical of all innovation in matters of belief and highly vocal in his loud denunciation of gospellers such as myself who tended to question church authority and seek answers in the Scriptures.

It had been Bishop Gardiner who expressly forbade all women from reading the Bible, lest they presume to form judgments of their own and challenge the views of men—specifically, the views of the clergy. Women were inherently sinful, as everyone knew; as daughters of Eve, who led Adam astray into wicked disobedience and so brought about the fall of mankind, women ought not to profane the Scriptures by their vain studying and conjecturing about the truths of faith.

Reluctantly, the bishop had conceded that noblewomen like myself could, when alone, peruse the gospels, as long as they did not attempt to read to others or teach them. Yet whenever Bishop Gardiner and I encountered one another (which was rarely, as I avoided him as much as I could), I thought I detected disapproval in his eyes, for he knew that I not only read the Scriptures but held discussions about them with other women, and had I not enjoyed the king's special favor and protection, I would most likely have felt the force of the bishop's wrath.

"Does anyone here present know of any reason why this man and this woman may not lawfully be joined in matrimony? If so, speak now, or forever hereafter hold your peace!"

The words rang out sharp and clear in the echoing chapel.

Tom, I thought. Tom knows plenty of reasons. But of course he will say nothing.

I thought of the anxious hour, five days earlier, when I had been forced to swear, on oath, that I had been pure during my two marriages and that I had never known any man but my two husbands. The oath was necessary, Henry told me. It was the law; any woman who married into the royal family would have to take it.

I hated to lie—yet of course I dared not admit that Tom was my lover. If I did I would be guilty of treason, for deceiving the king and agreeing to become his wife while deceiving him. I would be no better than Catherine Howard, and like Catherine, I would surely be executed.

I held my breath anxiously. The moment passed.

"Henry Tudor, do you take unto wife this woman here present, Catherine Parr Burgh Neville?"

"Yes!" The king's response was quick and so loud he almost shouted.

"Catherine Parr Burgh Neville, do you take unto husband this man here present, Henry Tudor?"

"Yea."

We joined hands, repeated our vows, and then I felt the wedding ring slip onto my finger.

It was done.

Even at a court known throughout Christendom for its lavish banquets, our wedding banquet was a feast to rival all feasts.

"This is my last bridal banquet," Henry said to me, taking my hand and kissing my wedding ring. "I want it to be my best."

He waved in the first course and all the guests gasped at the sight of huge Muscovy salmon, as long as a man's leg, carried in on large silver trays. Larks in ambergris were followed by three suckling pigs, roasted whole, and jellied galantines, stewed sparrows and haggis (a horrid dish I could never force myself to eat, though John had loved it and we often served it at Snape Hall).

On and on the massive trays of food were brought in and set before us, while grooms served canary wine and sack, claret and malmsey.

My viol players from Modena played lively gigues and stately allemandes, sweet serenades and some music of the king's own composition, which everyone took note of and politely applauded. The boys of the royal chapel performed, as did my fool Ippolyta the Tartarian, her fat, doll-like face painted thickly with white lead and her lips crimsoned with madder, who joked endlessly about the wedding night to come and sang and whirled about in a vigorous Russian dance.

We were at table for over three hours, and midway in that long siege of gluttony the wedding gifts were brought in at the king's request and shown off to the guests. There was gold and silver plate in abundance, each piece a gem of fine craftsmanship, and drinking glasses with gold rims and goblets of pewter from the Rhineland—a gift from the former queen Anne of Cleves. From the French court came multicolored tapestries representing the Judgment of Paris. ("An ominous gift," Henry muttered. "Are you supposed to be Helen of Troy, Cat? And are we going to war with the French?")

For me there were many treasures: embroidered petticoats and white gloves trimmed in leather, silk and gold thread, bracelets of rubies and sapphires from Goa, jeweled scent bottles and silk cushions with my initials outlined in mother of pearl.

From among these beautiful ornaments I chose a pair of jeweled slippers and handed them to Lady Mary, a bodice of silk damask for Lady Elizabeth and a pair of ivory combs and a gold bodkin for Margaret. All three rose from their benches and came to kneel before me to thank me for their gifts.

Prince Edward, sitting next to his father, had seemed subdued throughout the evening. He stared down at his plate, which was heaped with food, and could not be coaxed into laughter by Will, who usually amused him greatly. However, when the prince caught sight of one of my many gifts—a crossbow ornately decorated in silver—he fixed his attention on it.

"Stepmother," he called out to me in his reedy small voice, "since you are sharing your gifts, I should like you to share this one with me."

I was caught off guard. The crossbow was a gift to me from the king, something I had been coveting for many months, made by a master armorer, Giles Bateson. The king had ordered Bateson to create the bow especially for me, to fit my size and strength. The thought of parting with it both saddened and vexed me.

"Stepmother!" The reedy voice came again. A hush fell. The wedding guests were listening. Even the viol players, sensing the tension in the room, let their instruments fall silent. "Did you not hear my request?"

"Yes, Neddy," the king said to the prince, hugging him. "You shall have it—and anything else you want. What about a new pony?"

"Uncle Tom brought me one from Hungary."

"A dog then. One of my bitch pointers. You like dogs, I know you do."

"I have ten dogs. I want the crossbow. And the case, and the strings. Everything." He folded his thin arms across his narrow chest and stared at me.

"Have you ever hunted with a crossbow, Edward?" I asked. "Most boys can't draw the bow until they are nine or ten—and you are only six. Here, let me show you." I got up from my chair, took the beautiful crossbow with its inlay of etched silver from the servant who held it and went around to Edward on the other side of the table.

"Now then, stand up and see whether you can hold the bow, and pull the trigger." I held the heavy crossbow out to him but he made no move to take it. Instead he turned on his bench, deliberately turning his back to me, and motioned to the gentleman attendant nearby. "Take the thing to my rooms."

I wanted to chastise him for bad manners but I bit my tongue. He was the future king. I handed the crossbow to the attendant and, with as much dignity as I could manage, returned to my seat, aware that everyone was watching me.

Henry, apparently oblivious to the exchange, was eating stork pie and pears in clotted cream. Sensing the uncomfortable silence, he looked up from his plate.

"Where are the rest of the gifts? Bring them in."

The gifts were brought, the talk resumed. Gradually the former mood of pleasure was restored, and the eating, talking and drinking went on with interludes for dancing and masquing, until it was time for Henry and me to retire to our bed. We did so amid a chorus of bawdy comments and rude noises, jokes that made me blush and showers of rice that rained down on my lovely dress, caught in my hair and disappeared into the fresh green rushes under my cork-heeled shoes.

33

WHEN I ENTERED OUR WEDDING CHAMBER, WEARING MY NEW nightgown of thin black satin with wide sleeves of Burgundian velvet and very aware that the king would be eagerly awaiting me, I found him burrowing beneath the pillows on the bed.

"It's a thigh bone of Saint Cuthbert," he said, holding up a dark brown length of what looked like rotten wood and then placing it underneath one of the cushions. "It's sure to make you fertile. There's a finger of Saint Agatha under the mattress and I know of your devotion to Saint Agatha. I meant to put my relic of wood from the holy manger under your pillow but I can't find it."

His words were slurred. He had drunk a good deal of wine and spirits at the wedding banquet, and he seemed unsteady as he walked to the immense stone hearth. An applewood fire had been kindled there, and the air in the room was sweet with its fragrance, though pungent smells from the kitchens on the floor below also drifted in from time to time.

Henry was hanging a charm from the capstone of the hearth.

"A sailor who rounded the horn sent me this. The heathens there believe it drives off evil spirits."

"What is it?"

"A monkey's claw, I think."

I made a face, and Henry held up a warning finger.

"No use tempting fate on our wedding night."

My mother's great bed with purple hangings had been prepared for us, the bed she left me in her will, piled with fur rugs and a costly coverlet trimmed with ermine. Soft candlelight and the red glow of the fire turned everything in the room a warm pinkish-orange.

Henry, his wide bulk encased in a linen nightshirt, lay down on the bed, making it creak loudly, and looked at me. His gaze moved slowly down the length of the satin nightgown, then upward to my face, framed by the long cascade of my reddish-brown hair, which my chamberwomen had brushed until it glowed. His eyes grew heavy with desire.

"Take off that gown, Cat. Slowly."

I reached up and unfastened the sleeves, one at a time, and drew the soft velvet down over each bare arm, letting it fall to the floor. As I undid each button of the satin bodice I heard the king sigh with satisfaction, until the bodice too lay on the flagstones at my feet.

"Why, you're still fresh as a girl, Cat. Such fine, dewy skin. Such a trim waist. Oh, your pretty little bosoms! Such pink little nipples, like a schoolgirl! Like a young wench from the dairy! Quick! Take off the rest!"

I did so, until I stood naked before him, and heard his deep sigh of satisfaction.

I stood still, letting him savor the look of me, seeing the dull glow of lust in his small eyes, the parting of his thin red lips. He was my sovereign, I knew I had to obey him. That was all I could think or feel. I was his to command.

He beckoned to me, and I moved closer. He ran his hand slowly down from my waist along the curve of my hip, then across my smooth belly with its slight swell.

"As soft as an angel's skin," he murmured. "Heavenly soft."

With the tips of his fingers he brushed the reddish hair that circled my woman's cleft. I trembled.

And I gagged. For in the next moment he pulled up his nightshirt to expose his enormous, wrinkled red-veined legs, with their hideous stinking sores, and the gush of putrid air that reached my nostrils was so foul that I nearly fainted. I saw that he had fastened scented pomanders around his ankles in hopes of counteracting the terrible stench, but I could not smell their rich, spicy scents at all. They were useless.

"Sit astride me, Cat," he said, his voice thick. "Ride me like you ride your speckled roan, when you bunch your skirts up and ride like a man."

I held my breath and climbed onto the bed and up atop him, avoiding looking at his diseased flesh, white and wasted, at his wrinkled neck and few remaining yellow teeth, at the sparse white-gray beard he had oiled to make it shine, at the rakish pearl he wore in one ear, a last vestige of his once youthful, virile manhood. I closed my eyes and reached for his small, soft penis, trying in vain to put it within me.

"Pretend you are a virgin, Cat. You know how virgins excite me. Pretend you are a frightened young virgin who never had a man before, who is afraid—afraid—"

His voice began to falter. I saw that his tired eyes were closing. The wine and the exertion were dragging him down into sleep. I could see that he was fighting to stay awake, willing himself to go on with his futile effort at lovemaking, trying to make himself talk for as long as he could, until at last the words would no longer come.

He twitched, grunted, and then became still. In a moment he was snoring.

Greatly relieved, I climbed off his reeking body and lay down at the far side of the bed, as far from him as I could get, and covered myself with a fur blanket. Laying my head on the pillow I felt something hard and unyielding that poked up under my cheek.

Saint Cuthbert, I thought. Please forgive me, Saint Cuthbert, if I move your thigh.

34

THAT SUMMER, MY FIRST SUMMER AS QUEEN OF ENGLAND, WAS THE hottest anyone could remember. I sat with my ladies in the palace rose garden, sipping cool cider and fanning myself with the ivory fan Kate Brandon gave me for my wedding—a fan that was precious to me because it had belonged to Kate's mother, and before that to the first Queen Catherine, Catherine of Aragon.

I was idle. Everything was done for me, now that I was queen. My slightest wish, once expressed, was obeyed. People knelt to me (which, I confess, made me uncomfortable; I am only Cat, after all), no one except my family and closest intimates dared speak to me without permission. If I wanted a new gown or a new billiment, I had only to summon the dressmakers and jewelers and describe the thing I wanted; it was soon supplied.

On long hot afternoons my ladies, Margaret, Anne Daintry and I went out on the river in my own royal barge, gilded and painted in bright red and blue and with a carving of a black panther, poised to strike, at the prow.

The viol players serenaded us, servants brought us comfits and spiced wine and we sat, talking and drowsing, under the shade of an awning while the green shore drifted by.

Henry grew restless in the heat and announced that we would go on an extended progress through the countryside. With a traveling party of fifty servants and a hundred carts heaped with bedding and furnishings, clothing and hunting gear, we set out on a hot July afternoon for the country.

Our way led along dusty roads and through fields of parched crops. The haymaking was past but many cattle had died of thirst and the poppies and yellow hawkweed that ought to have been blooming in the meadows were nowhere to be seen; they had all perished under the searing sun. The hedgerows were withered and the trees drooped, dying slowly for want of rain.

We settled in at a hunting lodge near the village of Dunham Oak and Henry rode out each morning with his huntsmen. He rode a big bay gelding that could carry his weight—with difficulty—if he didn't try to ride him uphill. The effort exhausted both man and horse. Yet Henry went out every day, in the brilliant sunshine, and did not return until he had killed a wagonload of game, most of which he had distributed to the villagers of Dunham Oak.

He stopped sending the game, however, when he learned that there was plague in the village. I wanted to send herbal remedies at once (for plague can sometimes be cured, if the sufferer is strong and the herbs are taken as soon as the first symptoms appear) but my husband stopped me.

"No!" he said. "Let the dead bury their dead, as it says in the Scriptures. We will stay as far from Dunham Oak as we can."

I was horrified to learn that he actually sent a troop of guardsmen into the village to collect every single person afflicted with plague, even the babies, and to lay them out in the dry fields to await death. No one was allowed to come near them, and their pitiful cries, as I learned later, were truly heartrending, especially the wails of the infants.

"How could you?" were the only words I could choke out when I learned what Henry had done. (He had given orders that the truth be kept from me until after the plague victims were dead and buried.) "How could you, a Christian, withhold charity from those poor people?"

"Compose yourself, woman!"

They were the first harsh words he had spoken to me since our marriage, and they startled me into silence.

"What would you have had me do?" he barked. "Would you rather we had nursed the poor wretches while they died, and caught the plague ourselves, and died along with them? What good would that have done? Think sensibly. It was necessary for a few to die so that many could escape death."

So that you could escape death, I wanted to say. So that you would feel safe. Never mind others. Only you matter to yourself.

"Cruelty is always wrong," I said. "Jesus was never cruel."

"Jesus was never King of England."

I had no answer to that, and so our quarrel was broken off. But for weeks there was an uneasiness between us, and I knew that, in his heart of hearts, Henry recognized that what he did was wrong, and his conscience troubled him.

Word rapidly spread of what the king had done in Dunham Oaks, and there were murmurs of discontent. The king was evil, people whispered. It was his wickedness that brought on England the wrath of God, and God's punishment, the drought. Old prophecies about the Mouldwarp were revived, prophecies that had been repeated at the time of the Northern Rebellion. Alarmed, Henry gave orders to local officials that anyone overheard slandering the king should be executed. But these orders, and the fears they provoked, only led to more whispering, more rumors, and more discontent.

To evade the atmosphere of criticism we went north, hurrying past villages where fresh trenches had been dug to receive the bodies of those who died of plague. There were feral dogs on the roads, savage and masterless, and orphaned children (it pained me to see them) and clusters of ragged-looking laborers in search of work.

"It can't be helped," Henry said. "The sickness disrupts everything. Every summer it is the same. The plague comes, people die, crops are neglected, and when harvest season comes, there is no work." He sighed and crossed himself. "Lord deliver us from the pestilence."

We were to meet Mary, Elizabeth and Edward—each one of the royal children brought from his or her separate residence—at Ashridge for a prolonged visit.

"They irk me, Cat," Henry admitted as our carriage entered the courtyard of the great house. "Edward is frail and reminds me of the loss of my dear Jane. Mary is a stubborn papist, like her mother. And as for the Witch's Brat—" he made a gesture of vexation. "The worst of it is, she's the only one that has the brains and the stomach to be a true king's child."

We sat down to supper and were joined by Edward, sullen and pale, Elizabeth, subdued and nervous, and Mary, composed and glad to see her father. There were awkward silences during the first courses, but then I called in my fool Ippolyta the Tartarian and soon we were laughing together, and Mary, who could be quite witty and loved to make puns, was challenging Ippolyta with riddles and learning the steps of a Russian dance from her.

After supper we played hazard until quite late and let Edward win, as he always sulked when he lost.

The next day I took the girls hawking (Henry would not allow me to ride, lest I damage my womb) and afterwards we fed the hawks with horehound water and rhubarb. Henry took Edward out to shoot deer and then, while Henry napped, the rest of us picnicked.

Each day we found more to do—gathering the few small strawberries we could find among the dead and dying weeds, watching the farmers bind the grain in preparation for threshing, wading in the shallow streams for relief from the August heat. Gradually Edward seemed to gain color in his cheeks, to lose some of his affected hauteur and become a happy six-year-old. Mary thrived, though she annoyed her father by hearing mass—a privilege he reluctantly granted her—and saying the rosary each night for the soul of her mother.

"Let's gather some herbs to fill the pouncet box," I said to Elizabeth one afternoon when we found ourselves alone. I had bought her a lovely silver box with a domed, perforated lid meant to hold aromatic herbs and flowers; when worn at the waist, it was believed to guard the wearer against the plague.

Putting on our wide hats to shelter our complexions from the sun, we walked through the fields collecting plants. Elizabeth was very quiet at first, and we exchanged few words. But after a time she spoke.

"Mary says they are looking for a husband for her. The old men I mean. My father's advisers and secretaries."

"Yes, I imagine they are."

"There won't be any wedding for me, I know."

"Not until you are older, dear."

"Not even then." Her small face with its intelligent eyes and pointed chin was grave and thoughtful as she looked up at me. "No one will want me. Because of my wicked mother."

"Your very unfortunate mother."

"Did you know her?" Her voice was timid.

"Yes—a little."

"Tell me what she was really like. No one will talk to me about her. They won't even say her name."

"Anne. There. I said it. Queen Anne. Your father called her Brownie, did you know that?"

Elizabeth shook her head, a small smile dispelling her seriousness.

"Men were always drawn to her. She was compelling. The portrait-painters could never quite capture her charm."

"My father ordered all her portraits burned. But my aunt Mary saved one and had it sent to me."

She reached into a purse that hung from her belt and brought out a silver locket. She opened it and showed me the two pictures inside. One was a miniature of Anne, the other of a young boy.

"Who is that?" I asked, indicating the boy.

"My sweet Robin. Robin Dudley. We were born on the same day. We are pledged to each other. Don't tell anyone."

Now it was my turn to smile. I remembered a boy I had known many years ago, a distant Fitzhugh cousin. How intensely I had loved him when I was not much older than Elizabeth. How I had dreamed that we would be together always.

"I won't. I promise."

We had nearly filled our baskets with rose petals, forget-me-nots, wild thyme and hartshorn when we heard shouting. I looked up and saw, over the hedge, my husband making his way with surprising speed in our direction. He walked with the aid of a tall golden staff, and he was clearly agitated.

"Cat! Cat! Come quickly! Edward's been taken ill! He needs a plaster for his chest. Hurry!"

I dropped my basket and ran back at once toward the house, leaving Henry and Elizabeth to follow along behind.

I had seen Edward's sudden crises before, and they were truly alarming. A high fever made his normally pale face brick-red. His breathing became shallow and he started to choke and cough. Eventually he collapsed into a helpless, gasping heap on the floor and flailed his arms and legs so violently that no one could go near him. Once he reached that stage there was nothing anyone could do but pray, and wait for him to faint so that he could be put to bed.

As I ran toward the house I thought, what can I do? There's no time to prepare a plaster. What will calm him? What will restore his breathing?

Lavender. Lavender will relax him. And for his chest—what? I remembered Will telling me that when our mother's health was failing, and she was having trouble breathing, it helped her to go into the old Roman baths near his estate where hot water gushed from an underground spring and vapor rose in dense clouds.

The kitchens, I thought. We'll get him down into the kitchens where cauldrons are kept boiling and steam rises in clouds.

I hurried to where Edward lay, coughing and choking. The three physicians who constantly accompanied him stood in a half-circle around him, staring at him and looking extremely frightened.

"Quick!" I shouted to a strong-looking footman. "Take him to the kitchens!"

My orders were followed and the footman ran with the prince in his arms into the large, smoky room where whole calves and piglets were turning slowly on spits. A vat of broth was bubbling in the center of the room.

"Take him there," I said, pointing to the huge black cauldron from which steam rose in a thick mist. "Hold him in the steam."

Struggling, protesting, Edward fought for breath while the footman did as I bade him. The heat of the steam frightened him at first, but as he breathed it in, and began to feel relief in his painful chest, he let the vapor do its healing work. His coughing eased, he began to draw deeper and deeper breaths.

My own relief was immense. What if Edward had choked to death? Henry's wrath and frustration—somehow I did not imagine that he would feel much grief, he had been accustomed for so long to the likelihood of the boy's death—would surely have been monumental. I did not want to face that storm of emotion.

But Edward was not only alive, and drawing breath more easily. He was speaking to me, in a low rasping voice, almost a whisper.

"Stepmother, I'm sorry," he was saying.

"Don't talk, dear. Rest your voice. You're going to be all right now."

"I broke the crossbow. You were right. It was too big for me. I threw it down and it broke."

"We'll get you another one."

"I broke it. God is punishing me."

He closed his eyes, exhausted from the fearful exertion he had been through, and I sang him a lullaby as he dropped off to sleep.

35

A H, SO PALE," SAID THE SLEEK, MOUSTACHIOED DUKE OF NAJERA AS HE took my hand to kiss. "I trust your majesty is not in poor health."

"I confess that I am in indifferent health, milord duke," was my response. I took note of the Spanish nobleman's keen brown eyes that swept down the length of my gown, lingering at the region of my belly. I had become accustomed to being scrutinized. Everyone was watching for the least sign that I might be pregnant.

"May we hope that this indisposition betokens the arrival of an heir?" His tone was polite and his words formal, but the question was overly bold, even rude. He presumed too much. Just because he was the emissary of the Emperor Charles V, and charged with a very important mission to our court, he imagined that he could ask me bold questions and ignore the ordinary rules of courtesy.

"Milord, you forget yourself," said my friend and lady-in-waiting Kate Brandon, coming to my rescue. "The queen's health is a matter of state and cannot be talked of lightly."

In truth I was not feeling at all well, though I did not dare absent myself from the grand reception we were holding to welcome the Duke of Najera. My stomach was so upset that I tasted bile in my throat, and when I walked I felt dizzy, as if I had drunk too much wine.

I was nervous, because I knew that my husband intended to declare to all the guests, and most especially to the duke, that he intended to turn over to me the task of governing the kingdom.

Henry was going to war. He was about to invade France, and would be away leading the army for many months. In his absence I would be his deputy, as regent in his stead. And if he died—as well he might, given the rigors of campaigning and the condition of his seriously infected legs—then I would be regent during Prince Edward's minority, a weighty responsibility indeed, and one that others would envy greatly.

I was also nervous out of sheer excitement, for while Henry was away I would be able to see much more of Tom, and if we were careful, we would be able to enjoy many blissful hours together.

I saw that the king, who was in high spirits, had thrown one arm around the slight little duke's shoulders and was leading him back in my direction.

"Do you know what they say about the emperor?" Henry was saying, his face merry. "That he speaks four languages. He speaks Spanish to God, Italian to women, French to men and German to his horse!" He laughed, a hearty, throaty, young man's laugh, ebullient and uninhibited. And the duke, who had no doubt heard the old joke about the emperor and his four languages hundreds of times, managed a pained smile.

"Did you know that my wife," Henry went on as the two men neared me, "speaks four languages too? English to me, French to the diplomats and the dancing-master, Greek to the scholars and Latin to the clerks. I don't know what language she speaks to her horse." He guffawed. "In all seriousness, she is a very wise and learned lady, is she not? As wise as she is beautiful."

He looked at me with satisfaction, and the duke followed his gaze. I was indeed the star of the court in those early months of our marriage—and the object of much envy. Only a few weeks earlier the king had made me the richest woman in the realm by granting me all the many valuable lands Queen Anne Boleyn and the second Queen Catherine had once owned, plus a number of estates and castles that had been confiscated from traitors to the crown. (Was there blood on my hands as I accepted these gifts? I shuddered to think so, yet I could not refuse them.)

My relatives had all been elevated in status. Will became Earl of Essex, taking the title Anne Daintry's late father had held. My uncle

William became Lord Parr of Horton. And my proud sister Nan received ten manors and an increase in wealth from her husband's appointment as one of the commanders of the coming campaign.

We Parrs were all indeed to be envied, and I most of all. How I wished that my dear mother had lived to see our prosperity and power! Yet I was uneasy in spirit, and my stomach churned as my husband and our guest of honor came nearer.

The duke was smiling. An ingratiating smile, I thought. A false smile. I did not trust him. But then, are diplomats ever to be trusted? He had come to our court for one purpose: to make the final plans, with the English commanders, for the invasion of France. The emperor's soldiers and the English soldiers had to coordinate their strategies, and to ensure that they would have enough provisions and arms ready when the campaign began. And, of course, to ensure that the bond between our court and the imperial court remained strong, with no petty enmities or misunderstandings arising to threaten it.

"I have been waiting until your arrival, milord duke, to make an important announcement," Henry now said. "It is my decision that during my time away from this realm, my trusted spouse Queen Catherine will reign in my stead."

A murmur of surprise ran through the room. The duke raised his eyebrows, but said nothing.

"But sire"—it was Bishop Gardiner's high voice, raised in protest—"it would be unseemly to confer so significant a responsibility on a mere woman."

"Queen Catherine of Aragon was regent for me when I fought in France years ago."

"If I may say so, sire, Queen Catherine was much more experienced in governmental matters, having been brought up at the court of her illustrious mother Queen Isabella of Castile. And as I recall, there were some on the royal council who objected to Queen Catherine's regency."

"All objectors were silenced—as they will be now." My husband looked at the bishop, who met his gaze unflinchingly.

"We of your majesty's council are charged with the responsibility of advising your majesty on all important questions."

"And you will be consulted as needed."

Now Bishop Gardiner glared at me, and I ignored him. I saw, out of the corner of my eye, that he was fidgeting and growing red in the face.

Attempting to compose himself, but still agitated, the bishop spoke up once again.

"This warmaking! It will cost the earth! I'm sure our distinguished guest from Spain will agree with me," he went on, hoping to gain some sign of allegiance from the duke, who studiously avoided giving any such sign. "All those barrels of flour and bales of hay, all those carts and wagons, and the horses! Where will you find enough horses? They have to be shod, you know. You will have to carry thousands of horseshoes and the nails to fasten them on with. No one ever thinks of these details. Of how many different sizes of horseshoes are needed, and how many different kinds of nails."

"Apparently you do, milord bishop," I said, suddenly interested in Bishop Gardiner's catalog of complaints. Could he be useful to the army? "Have you any experience of supplying armies?"

"My father and uncle were provisioners to King Henry VII, I grew up with the trade, before I took holy orders."

"Well then, let us enroll you as a purveyor of armor and armaments. The king was just telling me yesterday that we lack cuirasses and Flemish halberds. Can you find us suppliers for these among the London armorers? Your clerical duties could be handed over to others for the duration of the campaign, couldn't they? You would of course remain a member of the royal council."

"You see!" Henry cried. "Isn't she splendid! She thinks of everything." He patted my arm lovingly, brimming over with praise.

Bishop Gardiner, more uncomfortable than ever, was at a loss for words.

"We will count on your help," I said to the bishop at length, and in response he gave me such an icy, furious look that it made my blood run cold.

"And I on yours," was his cool reply. "There is something of importance I have been meaning to bring to your attention." He spoke loudly enough so that all those around us could hear—except my husband, who had left my side and was talking with Charles Brandon. The Duke of Najera had also wandered away, and was talking to two of my maids of honor.

"I believe there is in your household a woman of ill repute," the bishop said. "She must be removed."

"You are mistaken."

"I refer to the laundress who has taken the name Anne Daintry."

Now I was the one at a loss for words. Questions whirled in my mind. How had the bishop discovered Anne? And why was he using her to exert his power over me? Was it because of my appointment as the king's wartime deputy? What else did the bishop know? Did he know that Tom and I loved each other, and that the oath of marital purity I swore before I married the king was false?

I was trembling. I could not keep my voice from shaking as I answered.

"The lady you mean is my friend. She is married and has four children, all of whom are in my household and under my protection."

"She has dishonored her marriage vows and her presence in your household is scandalous and reflects poorly on your own moral character."

"Jesus befriended Mary Magdalene. I may befriend Anne Daintry."

"Are you comparing yourself to Our Lord and Saviour?"

"I am attempting to follow his example, as should you, lord bishop, in showing forgiveness and compassion."

"I have the cure of souls. It is my mandate from the Lord to reprove sin."

"Judge not, that ye be not judged. Matthew 7:1."

My consort of viols began to play a lively volta and Will, who loved to dance and was a graceful and skillful dancer, came up to me and held out his hand. I gladly took it and let him lead me out onto the bare tiles where the rushes had been swept back and a space cleared for dancing.

For a few carefree moments I lost myself in the pleasure of whirling and leaping in the intricate steps of the dance, even though my pulse raced and my dizziness and queasiness increased. When Will and I danced together we were always applauded, and Will's nimble jumps met with shouts of admiration. Soon other dancers joined us until all the guests were caught up in the joyful commotion. Even the Duke of Najera was jumping high and twirling his partner with skill and finesse.

When the dance was over I went and sat down next to Henry, whose energy and high spirits, I could tell, had begun to flag and who was in evident pain.

"Here, my dear," I said, smoothing out my embroidered damask skirt, "rest your leg on me."

With difficulty he lifted his heavy, stinking leg up and heaved it onto my lap. I braced myself to receive the weight. With a sigh he leaned back in his great high chair and closed his eyes while I massaged the soreness away as best I could.

We stayed as we were, content to watch the others dancing and feasting, for an hour or more until the guest of honor took his leave and came up to us to say his farewells. He bowed and kissed my outstretched hand.

"Is your majesty feeling any better?" he asked.

"Enjoyable company always lifts my spirits."

I smiled as graciously as I could while the Duke of Najera took his formal leave, bowing low to my husband and assuring him of Emperor Charles's continuing brotherly fidelity.

I had not answered the duke's question directly, I had evaded it. In truth I did not feel better, nor were my spirits improved. If anything I felt worse. My husband's approaching departure, the duties that would fall on my shoulders after he left, Bishop Gardiner's challenge to me over Anne Daintry and above all, my trepidation and excitement about being with Tom combined to increase my biliousness. For a moment I stopped rubbing Henry's leg and rubbed my own stomach instead, hoping to ease the increasing discomfort I felt and the taste of bile in my throat.

36

WITH A FLOURISH OF TRUMPETS AND THE BEATING OF A THOUSAND drums the great army embarked for France.

First came the archers and bowmen in their leather jerkins, longbows of polished ashwood slung over their arms, then came the gunners, their huge guns drawn in carts behind them pulled by straining oxen, then the tall, stern-featured morris pike men, muscular as wrestlers, then the guardsmen in red tunics with blue and gold banners flying, and in the vanguard, the sappers and miners, mortar-makers and coopers, smiths and surgeons and butchers.

Gentlemen officers in doublets and hose of white satin commanded the feudal levies, armed tenants formed into hordes of marching men, carrying bills and pikes and with gleaming knives at their waists.

Armed at all points, and wearing special armor that did not chafe his throbbing legs, the king rode up to his flagship surrounded by the Calais Spears. It was his hour of glory, I thought, watching the embarkation from a specially built platform on shore with a huge crowd of onlookers around me. The start of his last campaign. Even though he had to be lifted up onto his huge warhorse by a winch, Henry was still a formidable warrior, who commanded loyalty from his troops and

admiration and affection from all those who remembered him in his
younger days.

Henry waved his plumed hat to me from on board his flagship, and I
waved back. We had said our goodbyes earlier that day, and I had given
him a gift, a gold-hilted sword made by his armorer Erasmus Kyrkenar
engraved with an encouraging message.

"Rejoice Boulogne," it read, "in the rule of the Eighth Henry! Thy
towers are adorned with crimson roses, now are the ill-scented lilies
uprooted and prostrate, the cock is expelled and the lion reigns in the
invincible citadel."

The French-held town of Boulogne was the army's destination; to
besiege it successfully was the principal object of the English campaign.
Henry received his gift with delight, and ordered the sword carried
alongside him by servants, who also carried his heavy musket and long
metal lance.

I continued to watch as the ships were loaded and then as, with the
turning of the tide, they sailed out of the harbor and were soon lost over
the far horizon.

"Someone ought to put the old man out of his misery," Tom muttered
as we lay in each other's arms, replete from lovemaking. We were at
Sudeley Castle, Tom's lovely rural estate in Gloucestershire built of
weathered golden stone quarried from the surrounding hills. We were
enjoying the first true privacy we had known in many months, though
Tom was clearly nervous and he kept listening for footsteps in the
corridor outside our bedchamber.

"If he doesn't die of the heat and the camp fevers first."

"He's flourishing. This campaigning seems to invigorate him.
They've already taken some of the smaller towns and according to the
last despatch I had, the army is assembling in the vicinity of Boulogne."

I looked over at Tom, his long reddish-blond hair tangled against
the lace-trimmed pillow, his handsome face more stern and set than I
remembered it in the past.

"Old men die in war—and usually not from wounds." His voice,
normally so soft and deep and rich, was grating, his words harsh.

"Did you want very much to go on this campaign?"

"What do you think, Cat?" he said, raising himself up on one elbow and looking down at me. I could not help but flinch under his gaze. "Do you imagine that I am finding it easy to stay here in England, fiddling with accounts and dealing with Italian bankers, while my brother and your brother-in-law Hertford and old Brandon are leading the men into battle? I resent it every day."

"But with you here, we can be together."

"When old Harry dies we can be together permanently. And without any fear of meddling by that self-righteous demon Gardiner or his spy Thomas Burgh."

"My former father-in-law?"

"Yes. Didn't you know? The two have become as thick as thieves. Burgh has been poking his nose into everything, looking for sins against the Ten Commandments so that the good bishop can burn more people at the stake."

I looked at him, admiring for the hundredth time his fine profile, smelling his rich masculine smell, and once again my heart melted. He could do no wrong, say no wrong. I tried to snuggle closer to him and reached up to kiss his cheek with its bristling stubble.

"All that matters, dearest one, is that we are together now. This is our eternity."

"And all I know is that it is taking an eternity for the king to die." He got up and began putting on his clothes.

Dismayed, I watched him. I knew better than to try to make him stay longer. He was restless these days, watchful and with an underlying anxiety that troubled me.

When he was dressed, he turned back toward the bed.

"I need a loan, Cat. Ten thousand pounds."

"I've already loaned the king seven thousand, for the war."

"It's only for a few weeks. You can get a loan against your rents."

"This is July, Tom. My rents are not due until October, after the harvest is in."

"I know, I know. But the bankers will lend to you, you are the queen. They wouldn't dare refuse you as they do me. Besides, if I know you, you have never been late in repaying your accounts. You keep your heart pure and your silken petticoat clean and pay your debts on time."

He was right, of course. I was conscientious about everything. Everything but my love for him, that is; where my love for Tom was concerned, I was careless, reckless, daring. As well he knew.

"Well? Can you get me the money?"

"I'll send Uncle William's deputy to London in the morning." My uncle William was the controller of my household, and in charge of overseeing my accounts. But he was in France, with the Calais Spears. In his absence one of his servants would have to go to see the Flemish or Italian bankers in the capital.

"What is it for, Tom?"

"What is it for? You've seen this place of mine. It's crumbling. It was built in the time of Ethelred the Redeless, you know, about a hundred centuries ago, and old Ethelred was no builder. The roof has fallen in, the walls have holes in them, the tenants don't pay their rents—yes, I know, I must get a new steward to look after all that, you remind me often enough!"

I sighed. "All right, Tom. I'll see to the money. And you will let me have it back in a few weeks?"

He nodded impatiently. "I must be off."

"When will I see you again, dearest?"

He shrugged. "Soon," he muttered, and was off out the door, leaving me crestfallen and with a hollow feeling just behind my ribs, near my heart.

37

"YOUR HIGHNESS, WHAT ARE WE TO DO WITH THE SCOTS PRISONERS? There are too many of them to feed, and they are dying."

I sat at the head of the council table in the painted chamber at Whitehall, wearing my purple velvet gown whose royal color gave me strength to face the unruly council members, and listened to the question.

"I would hear more of this matter," I said.

"Your majesty is aware that Lord Hertford's army took some two thousand Scots prisoners after the latest border raids, and they are being housed in the jails of Durham and Newcastle and the nearby towns. Some have the jail fever. None have enough to eat."

I opened my mouth to respond but Bishop Gardiner was too quick for me.

"The Scots are false, deceiving wretches who defy the king's authority. They deserve to die. Let them die."

There were outcries of protest from others around the table and wrangling broke out. "Kill them all! Burn their crops," said some harsh voices. "We must not be as savage as they," said others. "They have not all been tried. Some may be innocent."

I held up my hand and the commotion died down. "By the queen's authority," I said, "and in the king's name, let the most villainous of them be sent to our jail at Alnwick, and let those closest to death be fed at our royal charge." I nodded to my comptroller who began counting out coins from a small chest at his feet and putting them into a leather pouch. "The rest can be released if they put up a bond to guarantee their good behavior."

Bishop Gardiner snorted. "Good behavior! No Scot understands good behavior!"

The council secretary wrote down my decision and passed the writing to me. I signed it, in my large broad hand, "Kateryn the Queen Regent," and he sealed it.

"Take this letter and the purse of coins to the jails and see that my orders are carried out."

"Foolishness," the bishop said, but no one echoed him, and we passed on to the next matter to be discussed.

It had been like this ever since the king left for France. Fractious councillors, emergency decisions to be made, petitioners coming to me at all hours of the day and night with papers to sign and messages to deliver. I had no idea the tasks of rulership were so many and so demanding.

"With your highness's concurrence, we must take another loan, for forty thousand pounds." It was Wriothesley who spoke, dark-faced and unsmiling.

"Didn't we just take a loan last week?"

"We have another urgent request from my lord of Norfolk."

"Very well, if we must. But each time we borrow, the usury rates rise."

"No one profits in war but the bankers," was Archbishop Cranmer's remark, his gentle voice a contrast to the shrill and strident tones of the others.

"Even as we debate here and borrow money to aid the killing in France, let us bow our heads to remember all those who are dying."

"Amen. Let the council be silent for the space of the Lord's Prayer."

A silence fell. All bowed their heads. I prayed for the dying—and for strength and wisdom to carry out my task.

"Now let us resume, my lords."

An hour later the wrangling and debating was still going on, and my head had begun to ache from the effort of keeping control over the pace and direction of the meeting. A quarrel had arisen over some French sailors captured by the fishermen of Rye after the French ship they were sailing in foundered. Should they be executed as spies or put to the rack and tortured until they revealed all they knew about a plot to invade the south coast?

"My lords, we will be prudent in this matter," I said at length. "I will write to the king about the Frenchmen and let him decide what should be done."

At that moment the doors to the council chamber burst open with a violence that made them crash against the painted walls.

"LET him decide? Let him decide? He decides now: the French will die. Every last man. If I have to kill them myself!"

It was King Henry, scowling angrily and wielding the heavy sword I had given him when he left for France nearly five months earlier. Grunting with effort he lifted the immense sword and brought it down in the center of the council table, smashing the thick oak in pieces and sending the panicked councillors running to the corners of the room. I stayed where I was, too startled to move and hampered in any case by the bunched folds of my long purple skirt.

"My lord king!" I cried when I found my voice. "My dear husband! We did not expect your return for another ten days at the earliest!"

"That is quite evident. I see you are taking my place very competently. I hope you are not expecting to replace me permanently any time soon." With an agility remarkable in one so stout he picked up the heavy sword and ran his finger over the blade, whose smooth metal edge had been chipped and broken in places by the force of his blow.

"How can you say such a thing, husband, when it was you yourself who placed on me this burden of governance? A burden I gladly relinquish as of this moment. Very gladly indeed."

I rose from my place at the head of the smashed table and knelt at the king's feet.

"That is not what I have been hearing. I have been hearing that you have been enjoying your role immensely. That you have played the king with a sure and firm hand. An overly firm hand. You are even wearing the royal color, purple. Clearly, like so many others at this court, you are waiting impatiently for me to die, so you can take over."

Bishop Gardiner was smiling and nodding. Archbishop Cranmer, to his credit, looked dismayed (he knew me to be a woman without worldly ambition) but was too reticent a man to oppose the king openly.

"Milord, you do me an injustice. I have been exhausted by this thankless task of being regent. You read the letters I sent you. I told you how impatient I have been for your return. Only you can govern this realm—you and your councillors. I am a poor substitute."

Ignoring my protest, the king motioned to a groom to take his sword and asked for his chair of state. When it was brought he sat down with a sigh of relief and looked around the room.

The councillors, standing in little knots of two and three against the walls, ceased to cower and, following the king's beckoning finger, seated themselves on their long benches amid the wreckage of the council table. I remained kneeling.

"Bring a chair for the queen," Henry said and a chair was brought.

"Now, Cat," he said when I was seated, "what's this I hear about you leading your women in Bible reading and theology? Have you really been telling them that they need no priests or church to be saved? And that there is no such thing as purgatory? That is heresy, Cat. Are you a heretic as well as a would-be ruler?"

"I thought the Inquisition was confined to Spain and Rome, sire. It appears to have taken root in England as well."

"Mind your tongue, woman, and remember that you are addressing your sovereign, who is head of the church in these realms." It was the high, unpleasant voice of Bishop Gardiner.

"I am addressing my husband, milord bishop. The man who chose me as his wife—so he confided to me—for my piety and goodness. Sire," I went on, turning to Henry, "someone has been misleading you. I am no heretic, but a true daughter of the church."

"Ah! So it is only that those around you are leading you into heresy."

"There are no heretics in my household, as far as I am aware."

"And is it true that you have been writing a book on matters of faith?"

"Only a small devotional work, sire, in which I call attention to my faults."

I noted that the king's voice was lower and his tone much less wrathful than earlier. As usual, his outburst of violent anger, while severe, passed quickly, leaving him fatigued.

"I will talk further of these matters," he said. "But for now, the council meeting is at an end." He waved the men away and they left the room, all but Bishop Gardiner. A few of them glanced at me as they left, some in concern, most in apprehension, for the king's suspicion, once kindled, was inclined to spread.

"I must have the truth," Henry said when only the three of us were left in the room and the bishop had closed the thick doors with a fateful-sounding click of the lock. "Is it true that you have an ill-living woman in your service, the laundress Anne Daintry, and that she has led you into heresy?"

"No, my husband, it is not true. She reads her Bible daily, and says her prayers, and is reformed in her manner of living. She seeks only a return to modest respectability. She and her children have been under my protection for several years."

"Your generous impulses lead you into error, madame, as I have pointed out to you often in the past."

"May I remind your highness," the bishop put in, "that there can be no protection for those who espouse blasphemy and error? And that anyone in the queen's household who lives sinfully brings dishonor upon her mistress?" The bishop was skillful with words. His accusations stung.

I felt the blood rising to my cheeks and resisted the impulse to give in to anger. Instead I knelt once again at Henry's feet, and this time I sensed a response from him. For the first time since he made his startling appearance in the council chamber I felt his presence as a man—and a man who loved me.

"Your majesty," I said in the most tender tone I could manage, "I ask your humble pardon for any wrongs I may have done you. I meant nothing but your good, and England's. If I am in error teach me the truth. But I beg you to spare my laundress, and show her mercy. She is of the greatest help to me. She is reformed, I swear it. Many years ago she lived a thoughtless, wanton life, but no longer. I will vouch for her sinlessness. The bishop knows this well, for I have told him."

"Is this true?"

Bishop Gardiner shrugged. "Both are at fault. Each vouches for the other."

I felt Henry's back stiffen at the accusation aimed at me. "Until I received your letters telling me how she was conducting herself as regent, and warning me that she was attempting to take power for herself, I never thought ill of my Cat. She has always been blameless. She has never been self-seeking. Look at her, kneeling there like a penitent child! Does this look like the posture of a woman who wants to take power?"

"Often those we trust most are devious. Remember your last wife, Catherine Howard. Remember Mistress Boleyn!"

Henry rose to his feet, his anger crackling once again.

"Get out! Get out! How dare you mention those hateful names! How dare you compare those women to my faithful Cat!"

My head was bowed, and I could not observe what was going on in the room, but I heard the rapid shuffling of feet and surmised that the bishop was leaving. My heart was pounding. Henry was acting erratically, first suspecting me and trusting Bishop Gardiner's warnings, now defending me and turning on the bishop in fury. I thought, yet again, what a very dangerous man he was.

I heard the doors click open, and then the noise of the shuffling feet ceased. The bishop had paused in the doorway.

"Just remember, sire, that I have observed sin in the queen's apartments. I have prayed about it, and the Lord is leading me to speak out against it, lest the punishment of barrenness fall upon this queen as it did upon the last one."

Barrenness! The word fell with chill force upon us, as startling and as frightening as the king's sudden appearance in our midst. Bishop Gardiner had implanted a fearsome new suspicion in the king's mind: that the reason I had not given him a son was that I was sinful.

From now on, I sensed, Henry's superstition and fear of divine punishment would work with even greater effect on his unsettled mind, a worm of doubt boring deeply into his every thought. And I knew, in my heart, that as long as Henry lived, I would never again know peace.

38

THEY CAME FOR ANNE ONE NIGHT IN THE DARK HOURS JUST AFTER midnight, twelve armed guardsmen and a pitiless jailer who entered the wing of the palace where my servants slept and made their way to the small chamber under the stairs where Anne had her modest room. Her children were not with her, fortunately. They stayed in the country, and she visited them when she could. She was alone in her room when the men càme for her, bursting in and waking her, seizing her roughly and binding her hands and forcing her out into the night to take her to the dungeon.

I awoke to the sound of cries of protest and doors opening and shutting and commotion in the corridor. My first thought was, has the king died? He was away at Romford on a hunting trip, staying at a manor house two days' ride from the palace. Had he fallen from his horse, and had a messenger come to give me the dire news? Or was Edward ill? He had been sickly all winter. Was he having trouble breathing again, and did he need my help?

Hurriedly I threw a cloak over my nightdress and went out into the corridor, where my sister and some of my other maids and ladies-in-waiting had gathered.

"They have taken away that woman who calls herself your laundress," Nan said. "She is seized for heresy. And about time too."

Ignoring Nan's scornful remark I rushed along the passage and down two flights of stairs to the old section of the palace near the scullery where Anne's room was. The door was wide open. No one was inside.

"Oh, your highness," cried a young maid from the kitchen nearby, her face tearstained, "they've taken her away. She tried to fight them but they were too strong for her. Oh, how she screamed! She's so brave. And now we'll never see her again."

"Hush! The king won't let anything happen to her. I promise. Say your prayers."

I rushed down the long cold halls toward the exit to the inner courtyard. But I was too late. A party of horsemen was going out the far gate, at a gallop. I had no doubt that Anne was with them.

I knew where they were taking her. Bishop Gardiner's London residence had a dungeon deep below ground where suspected heretics were interrogated and tortured. For years I had heard stories of men taken there—strong men—reduced to gibbering wretches by the terrible pain of the cruel mechanical devices that rent their flesh and drove them out of their minds with fear.

I returned to my own apartments, called for my chamber women and dressed quickly in a simple gray gown and black cloak. Taking my basket of medicines I went out into the night—sending away my usual escort—and told the driver of the waiting coach to take me at once to the episcopal palace.

It was dawn when I arrived.

"Open these gates in the king's name," I said to the liveried gatekeepers who stood barring the entrance.

"Who asks?"

"Catherine the queen."

The sleepy gatekeeper nearest me blinked and stared at me. I did not look like a queen, modestly dressed as I was and without an escort of soldiers in the red royal livery. I had arrived in a coach, however, and that was evidence enough that I was a woman of rank.

After a delay they admitted me. I insisted upon being taken to the dungeon but was shown into a salon draped with gold curtains bearing Bishop Gardiner's escutcheon.

I was not kept waiting long. An elderly priest came in.

"Your highness," he said in an oily voice and with a bow, "you honor us with your presence in this house."

"Take me to Anne Daintry at once."

"To whom, your highness?"

"You know perfectly well. To the servant from my household who was taken from the palace an hour or two ago."

The priest spread his hands. "But your highness, I have no idea who that is. You must be mistaken."

"Where is Bishop Gardiner?"

"I believe he is detained on the king's business."

"Tell him the queen requires his presence here immediately."

"I will do my best, your highness, but I'm not certain I can find him. He may be at his prayers, or he may be breaking his fast—"

"Where is his oratory? We will go together."

With a grimace the priest led me to a small dark chapel, empty of worshipers, and then to a grand salon where, at the head of a long table of polished wood, the bishop sat eating. When he saw me come in he was so startled that he practically jumped from his bench.

"Casparo! What are you thinking! What is she doing here?"

"I have come for Anne Daintry."

"For whom?"

"Don't pretend that she isn't here. Your men came for her at the palace last night."

"Whether this woman is here or not is a matter of church law and church jurisdiction. It does not concern you."

"I will decide what does and does not concern me, especially in the king's absence."

"I am acting on the king's orders."

"I don't believe you."

"Casparo, show her the order."

The oily priest went out and, after a few moments, came back into the grand room with a document, which he handed to me with a fawning smile. It was signed by Chancellor Wriothesley and stamped with the king's seal. It authorized the arrest of Anne Daintry on a charge of heresy.

As I read it, my heart was in my throat. Had the king truly done this without telling me? Or was it a plot by Gardiner and Wriothesley, using the royal seal but in fact acting on their own?

"I am going to confirm this by sending a messenger to the king."

"As you wish," Gardiner said, and went on with his breakfast.

"For now, I demand to be taken to see Anne."

"She is not here."

"Where is she then?"

"She has been taken to a place of safety."

"A dungeon, you mean."

The bishop said nothing, but wiped his mouth on a linen napkin edged in gold.

I remembered the strength I had summoned to preside at council meetings, and drew myself up to my full height. In my most commanding voice I said, "If you do not take me to Anne Daintry immediately, I will send for my own guardsmen and have your lackey here arrested for offending my royal person."

It was an empty threat, for I had no guardsmen outside and it would have taken me at least an hour to send to the palace for armed men. But the bishop capitulated. With a look of extreme annoyance he threw down his napkin and got to his feet.

"Send for my coach." Rudely he walked past me without any further acknowledgment and turned his back on me as he left the room. Before long he returned, dressed for travel and wearing long black boots.

"Bring her," he said to the priest he had called Casparo. Together we made our way to the courtyard and entered the bishop's spacious, beautifully painted and gilded coach with the carved red episcopal hat at its apex. Six matching grays pulled the coach, and two postilions rode out ahead of it.

By now morning had broken and dull sunshine illumined the road we were traveling. Neither the bishop nor his oily acolyte spoke during our journey, not even to answer me when I asked how far we had to go. I realized, too late to take any action, that if he wanted to, Bishop Gardiner could confine me in some obscure dungeon along with Anne, and leave both of us to die there. No one would know where we were. We would never be found, not even after our bodies had decayed. No doubt our lifeless bodies would be thrown into the river secretly at night, along with the household slops.

I tried to keep such thoughts from my mind as we went on, traveling west as I could tell from the position of the sun. Henry, in his hunting lodge, was away to the east of the capital. With every mile I was going further away from him. Further away from any potential help. Yet I had to do what I could for Anne, I had no doubt she was in grave danger, and I had to go to her, to rescue her, if I could.

Eventually the coach pulled into a courtyard and we alighted. I could tell at a glance that the building we entered had once been a monastery. It had the look of a cloister, a haven from the world. Yet it appeared neglected and unoccupied, and there were few servants in the courtyard—a sure sign that no one of importance had been living in the main house or adjacent buildings for some time. There were broken windows and crumbling masonry, untrimmed bushes and hedges, paving stones missing and a pond covered in green scum.

I followed the bishop and the priest in through the high carved doors and along dusty corridors that led to several flights of stone steps. Lanterns were lit and we made our way in semi-darkness. I stumbled, and cried out, but no one helped me.

The deeper we went the more cold, frightened and alone I felt. The fearsome thoughts that had come to me in the coach now rose again in my mind. What if I was being led to my own imprisonment? What if I never saw daylight again?

If I did come to harm, would Tom ever find me? Would he liberate me? Or if he did find me, would it be too late?

I became aware of a powerful smell that grew stronger the deeper I descended, until it made me cough. My eyes watered. I was thirsty. And very cold.

I had smelled the strong and terrible odor before, of that I was certain. But where? Now Bishop Gardiner and the priest were coughing as well, and I saw both men produce scented pomanders and hold them to their noses. The scents of cinnamon and rose leaves came to me, faint odors within the all-encompassing stench.

With a shock I remembered where and when I had encountered that smell before. In the slaughterhouse at Gainesborough Hall, in the fall when the pigs were driven in to be killed and their flesh salted in brine for the winter.

It was the stench of blood. Of pain. Of death.

39

"HERE IS YOUR LAUNDRESS," BISHOP GARDINER SAID IRRITABLY AS A heavy door was unlocked and thrown open. A lantern was hung from a peg protruding from the wall and the door was slammed shut and the lock refastened.

The tiny room was freezing cold. I rubbed my arms, my teeth were chattering. By the meager flickering light of the lantern I could see walls of crudely cut uneven stone, damp with slime, a pile of filthy straw and, in the far corner, a human form.

"Anne?"

She screamed in fear, blinking against the light, one hand in front of her face.

"Anne, it's Cat. It's only Cat."

"Water?" she asked, her voice faint. "Have you brought me water?"

"No, dear. But I'll get it for you."

I pounded on the thick door. "Jailer! Come here!"

I waited. There was no response. I called out again. My God, I thought, are they going to leave me here, just as I feared?

My pounding brought a chorus of feeble cries from other unseen wretches, confined like Anne.

"Help! Help!" came the pitiful voices. "For the love of God, help!"
Jesus have mercy on them, I prayed silently.

"It's no good," Anne said. "I've pounded on that door till my fists
were bloody. No one ever comes."

"We must get you out of here." I went closer and knelt down beside
Anne, and saw that she was covered in bruises. Her face, her neck and
bare arms were a mass of blue and yellow marks and weals.

"What have they done to you?"

"I am condemned. I am condemned as a heretic." She swallowed.
"They said that I denied that Jesus is present in the bread and the wine.
That I am guilty of reading heretical books. Books you gave me, Cat."

She raised her eyes to my face. She did not have to say any more.

"Never mind that. It is only a wicked plot. The king will see
through it. He is not easily deceived. He will free you and punish your
captors."

I tried to sound confident but my cold hands shook as I uncovered
my basket of medicines and, taking out a pot of salve, began spreading it
on the worst of Anne's bruises and sores.

"Where is the king? Why have you come alone?"

"He is hunting in the country. But he will return shortly. In a few
days at most."

Anne's head drooped. "They will never let me go."

"Of course they will. They must."

"I am condemned," she whispered. "And you are condemned
with me."

"What?"

She nodded, swallowing again in a vain effort to assuage her severe
thirst.

"They tried to make me tell them things about you."

"What things?"

"That you do not believe in purgatory."

"It's true, I don't."

"That you read heretical books."

"I read the writings of the reformers, yes. As the king well knows.
He reads them too, and we discuss them."

"They know about you and Tom Seymour."

My stomach heaved and my mind reeled.

"They don't. They couldn't."

Anne swallowed. "They said to me, you will tell us what you know of the queen. Of her disloyalty to the king."

Now it was my turn to swallow. My mouth was suddenly dry. "What did you say?"

"I can't remember. They were beating me so hard I think I fainted."

I tried to think. If Anne had been forced into telling the truth about me and Tom, would I be allowed in to her cell? Wouldn't I be manacled and put into a cell of my own?

Quietly, I moved toward the door and stood with my ear to the scratched and scarred old wood. I thought I could hear breathing on the other side. They were listening to us talk. They hoped we would say something that would betray me.

Suddenly I pounded as hard as I could on the door once again and was gratified to hear someone cry out in surprise.

"Jailer! I demand to see the jailer!"

I heard footsteps retreating outside. Presently the footsteps came closer. Several pairs of footsteps.

A key was put into the lock and the door was flung open. Chancellor Wriothesley stood there, looking much as he had at the council table when I was regent. Grave, unsmiling, forceful even in his silence.

"I demand food and water for the prisoner. At once."

Wriothesley turned to the servant who stood behind him. "See to it."

"And I demand that the prisoner be released, once she has slaked her thirst and satisfied her hunger."

"Your highness may leave at any time. The prisoner is in the hands of the Heresy Commission. She has been examined and found guilty. She is condemned."

"And if the king orders otherwise?"

"When I see an order from the king, I will obey it."

"Take me to the king at once."

"Your highness may go anywhere you like, though I cannot spare any men to escort you just now. But if you leave, you will not be allowed to return. Condemned heretics are not allowed visitors, lest they infect them with their dangerous beliefs."

I opened my mouth to retort but before I could get my words out Wriothesley interrupted me.

"And those who attempt to interfere with the just punishment of heretics are subject to the condemnation of the court."

The threat hung in the air between us like a malignant vapor. In the silence I heard the drip, drip, drip of rank water running down the walls of Anne's cell. I knew that I ought to leave, yet I couldn't bring myself to abandon Anne. The minute I leave, I told myself, they will do their worst.

A servant brought in a small pitcher of water and a stale-looking loaf of bread. Anne drank the water greedily and noisily. Wriothesley watched her, his face impassive, then took his leave. Once again I heard the heavy door shut and lock, and my heart sank. Was I making a terrible mistake? Ought I to have left?

The sight of Anne smiling slightly told me the answer.

"You are good to come for me, Cat. I always made fun of you for being so good. Now I'm grateful."

"Forgive me for what I'm about to do," she said a moment later, lifting her skirts over the dirty straw on the floor. I turned my head while she relieved herself. The sickening smell made my already queasy stomach lurch and before I knew it I was throwing up. I couldn't help it. I wiped my mouth with my handkerchief, and saw, by the light of the lantern, the crown embroidered on it in shining gold and silver threads. If only I could get word to the king, I thought. I don't belong here, and neither does Anne.

"Before they come back, there is something I need to tell you, Cat. No one knows. I want you to know."

She was interrupted by the return of Wriothesley. He had Bishop Gardiner, a priest and several other men with him.

"Bring her."

Over my protests two burly men took Anne to a large room, lit by smoking torches. I was held back from aiding her as she was stripped of her dirty gown and laid on a coffin-shaped plank of wood hollowed out in the middle. She screamed and struggled uselessly while her wrists were tied with ropes attached to a wheel, and the same was done to her ankles.

"Heretic!" Bishop Gardiner called out in his high voice. "Before you are subjected to the pain of your due punishment, will you tell us who instructed you in the vile beliefs you hold?"

Anne cursed. One of her captors slapped her, making her moan.

"Will you describe the disloyalty of the queen?"

"I am not disloyal!" I shouted, but the man who stood behind me, restraining me, only tightened his grip on my arms, pinning them behind my back.

The bishop ignored my outburst. "One last time, I ask you. Will you tell me the names of your teachers in heresy and of the queen's partners in disloyalty?"

Feebly Anne spat, her thin spittle falling harmlessly on the stone floor.

The torturers—for that is what they were, inhuman-looking muscular creatures with leather hoods masking their faces—positioned themselves at the head and foot of the long plank on which Anne lay. At Gardiner's nod they began slowly turning the wheels to which her wrists and ankles were tied, and I saw her arms and legs grow longer until they were stretched to their full length.

She grimaced at first, then swore.

"Stop! Stop in the king's name!" I yelled again and again, as Anne, yielding to the increasing pain, began to scream.

Gardiner raised his hand and the wheels stopped turning.

"Will you tell us now?"

I prayed, let her tell them something. Anything, just to make them stop.

"Go to hell," she said faintly, trying to catch her breath, gearing herself up for another onslaught of pain. "Or to purgatory, if you prefer."

Once again Gardiner nodded to the torturers who resumed their turning of the wheels, faster this time.

A long thin wail of agony came forth from Anne's throat, and her eyes rolled back in their sockets. Then the wailing stopped, and she lay still, her eyes closed.

"Oh my God! She's dead! You've killed her!"

A bucket was brought and a strong-smelling liquid ladled from it over Anne's face. It was vinegar. She choked, her eyes flew open and once again the cruel wheels were turned. Now her screams were hoarse, desperate. Animal cries. Her agony went on, minute after minute, until I felt I could no longer stand to watch.

"No! It is too much! It is all too much! Can't you see she knows nothing!"

I tried with all my strength to free my pinioned arms and kicked out at the man holding me. He immobilized my legs by locking them between his. I could smell his sour breath. I thought I could hear him chuckling to himself.

Now Anne, in her extremity of pain, was no longer cursing her captors but repeating the names of her children again and again.

I heard a dull crack, and then another and another. Her bones were breaking.

"Deliver her, O Lord, from her enemies," I prayed. "Send your angels to stand between her and the pain." My cheeks were wet with tears.

Anne fainted again, and again was revived with vinegar. The sounds she made were inhuman. Then one clear sentence stood out from the rest.

"For the love of Christ," she sobbed, "kill me."

"Speak, heretic, and you will be spared. Tell us what you know."

But she had drifted away into unconsciousness again, and this time the vinegar seemed to have no effect. She was unfastened from the rack and carried back to her cell. I was released. I turned and slapped the man who had restrained me.

"Little hellcat!" he muttered as I passed him, following Anne's limp body being carried along the corridor.

We were left in the putrid cell, where I did my best to ease Anne's pain with my herbs.

She slept, and I lay down beside her, exhausted and wretched. I laid my cloak over her shivering body and offered her the only comfort I could: the comfort of my presence.

In one terrible moment I thought, I could ease her pain permanently. I could give her enough of a sleeping draught to release her from life. She had begged for death. Shouldn't I be merciful to her and relieve her of more hours of agony? For I had no doubt, after what I had seen, that the torturers and those who commanded them would never relent.

But we are taught that it is a sin to take life, and so I tried to put the dark thought out of my mind. I closed my eyes and eventually went to sleep.

When I awoke I was immediately aware that Anne was whispering to me.

"Cat."

"Yes."

"I need—to tell—you—" Every word was a painful effort.

"I am—carrying—"

"A child? Are you carrying another child?"

She nodded slightly. Her eyes were clouded, unfocused. I thought, I can't possibly imagine her suffering. It must be far beyond anything I have ever known. Once again my cheeks were wet with tears.

"Will you—look after—the—others?"

"Yes, dear. Of course I will. But you will recover from this. Your strength will come back."

I took her hand in mine and gripped it as hard as I could.

She shook her head.

"Care—for my—little ones—"

She appeared to faint once more, only this time, in the dim lantern-light, I saw her lined brow grow smooth and her taut mouth relax. There was a look of peace on her face, and I thought I felt her fingers tighten ever so slightly around mine. Then she was gone.

40

IT WAS SCARCELY A MONTH AFTER ANNE'S DEATH AND I WAS STILL defiantly wearing mourning for her, despite the king's warning that to mourn a heretic was practically to be one oneself. I was going down the privy stairs from my apartments, using the back staircase in an effort to avoid Bishop Gardiner, who seemed to be everywhere in the palace at all hours, looking for suspects to bring before the Heresy Commission.

I paused on the landing and heard the high-pitched, excited voices of boys, young pages, gambling with dice.

"Six it's the widow Brandon, four it's the widow Fitzroy!"

I heard the clattering of the dice along the stones, then a cheer. I started to go into the corridor—for I always discouraged the pages from gambling—but then I stopped. I listened.

"Four again! It's the widow Fitzroy for sure."

"Brandon's the one I'd want, if I were king. Such big titties! Six! Six!"

The clattering and shouting went on, with more boys joining in. They were betting, I realized, on who would be the king's next wife.

I had known for weeks that a plot against me was taking shape, and that Bishop Gardiner was behind it. Or was he? The king's behavior toward me had changed, and in my most anxious hours I thought he might be the one moving against me after all, with Gardiner as his cat's-paw.

What I knew for certain was that my servants had begun deserting me, leaving their posts because of illness, or the promise (so they said) of a better position in the king's household or for some other invented reason. The exodus was alarming, for it could only have one cause: the servants believed that soon I would no longer be queen.

The defections were spreading. Ladies who had formerly been glad to join me in my apartments for devotional reading or games of backgammon or to sew garments for the poor began shunning me, and whispering behind my back what a shame it was that I had no son.

Kate Brandon, long my friend, now became my rival for Henry's affection. Lively, blond, full-figured Kate, quick-witted and sarcastic, her clear blue eyes filled with a saucy, almost wanton joyousness. Kate who named her spaniel "Gardiner" and her parrot "Wriothesley." Kate who had two young sons and, it was said, would be ripe to give King Henry the heir he needed once I was out of the way.

Even Kate, who I knew wanted to be loyal to me, was caught up helplessly in the wide net of royal intrigue. She did not dare refuse the king's attentions, and now that she was a widow—for her husband Charles Brandon had died not long after returning from the French campaign—she was available to marry again.

I did not distrust Kate, only the capricious king and his ruthlessness in going after what he wanted and needed. He had been married to me for several years, and I was not pregnant. I was thirty-three, nearly thirty-four. Soon I would be too old to have a child. While Kate was young, in her twenties, and had already proven herself as the mother of sons.

One day the king's servant Thomas Heneage came to my apartments and asked, on the king's behalf, for my necklace of table diamonds.

Right away I felt a flicker of worry. The necklace he was asking for was the one that had come to me when Henry was courting me. It had belonged to the ill-fated Catherine Howard, and because of that I rarely wore it.

"Why does the king ask for this necklace, Thomas?"

"He does not confide in me, your highness."

"But you know all that is going on with him, don't deny it."

"If your highness says so." He did not meet my gaze.

"I want to know, Thomas. Is this necklace going to be presented to the Duchess of Suffolk?" I demanded, giving Kate her title.

Heneage hesitated. He dared not be disloyal to his master, yet I knew that he had always had a particular regard for me.

"It would not surprise me if it were, your highness."

"So he has been giving her other gifts."

Heneage looked uncomfortable.

"Other jewels. Gowns. Gold plate. Perfumes." I paused between each thing I named, long enough to allow Heneage to frown slightly and look troubled. I knew that I was right.

"And the rose bushes," he said.

"What about the rose bushes?"

"She loves roses. He has ordered four thousand rose bushes to be planted in the privy garden at Westminster, so that fresh roses can be brought to her each day."

I sighed. "So it is true. He plans to do away with me and marry wife number seven."

"She may not have him."

"How can she refuse?"

Heneage lowered his voice to a whisper, and bent down so that his head was near mine. "I have heard that she keeps a trunk packed and ready to go and always has a Spanish ship waiting at the docks, to take her to Porto. From there she will go to her mother's family in Tordesillas."

"I see."

I decided to confront Kate and, as I hoped, I found her completely open about the very awkward situation in which she was placed, and about her plans to extricate herself from it should the need arise.

"I haven't told you before because I keep hoping nothing will happen," she confided to me with a rueful smile. "Yes, it is true that the king is paying a great deal of attention to me, and giving me things—just as he did to you right before he married you. Yet I am convinced that he retains a high regard for you. I keep hoping that you will be spared. In any case, whatever happens between you and King Henry I will not become his wife. I am prepared to leave on an hour's notice should he propose marriage to me. And I assure you, I will do just that. Leave."

It was a chaotic time at court, with everyone waiting for the king to die and trying to position himself or herself to benefit—or at least, not to be harmed. Henry himself was at a loss, physically declining, given to fits of violent anger, occupying himself with hunting yet unable to ride any more, so he had to content himself with watching others hunt. He spent hours soaking his legs in thick oatmeal baths. Fevers and colds laid him low, and his face, once fat but now flabby and woebegone, had turned a sickly pale yellow color.

He clung to life, but had to be carted from room to room in a wheeled chair upholstered in velvet. His accustomed vigor had left him—for good.

His only enduring pleasures, apart from paying court to Kate Brandon, were eating green artichokes (which upset his stomach), playing with his caged ferrets and toying with people's lives.

He had sent Anne Daintry to her death, and others in the royal household as well—a singer from the palace chapel, a tailor from Greenwich, a printer suspected of printing heretical books. He even signed an arrest warrant to be issued against the the mild, inoffensive Archbishop Cranmer. But before the arrest could be made he gave the archbishop a ring which, he assured him, would protect him if the chancellor and his soldiers came for him. And when it turned out just as Henry had predicted, when Chancellor Wriothesley tried to arrest the archbishop and he held up his royal ring, saving his life, Henry laughed so heartily that he choked, and turned purple before Dr. Wendy could revive him.

I tried to talk to him about Anne Daintry's death, but realized very quickly that I was making a mistake. All he said was, "Blood must flow! Flesh must burn!" and then reminded me that the true faith was in peril.

"Are you aware, madame," he asked me, "that a proclamation has been issued prohibiting the possession of heretical books? And on that subject, what of your new book? Is it heretical?" He smiled a sly smile.

"I am assured that it is not."

"Has it never troubled your conscience that in publishing this book you may be inflaming erroneous views in others?"

"No, sire. What I write comes from the Scriptures, and from my own private meditations."

"I must read this book of yours. I'm told everyone else is reading it. I will decide whether it is full of error or not. Or perhaps"—he showed his decayed teeth in another sly smile—"I should command Bishop Gardiner to read it."

The bishop and I were at odds over many things, especially Prince Edward's education. I favored the learned Richard Cox as the prince's tutor, but the bishop thought Cox was too close in his thinking to the reformed faith. When I added a second tutor for Edward, the Cambridge scholar John Cheke, Gardiner was incensed.

"The man doesn't even speak Greek properly," Gardiner cried out.

"His is the authentic pronunciation," I said. "The clerical pronunciation is distorted, a product of centuries of ignorance."

"Are you calling me ignorant?"

"I am saying that Dr. Cheke and his colleagues have resurrected the true sound of ancient Greek. We can all learn from them, and benefit."

"A woman! Teaching me Greek!" Gardiner sputtered, making Henry laugh.

"If she can teach me theology, she can teach you Greek," Henry said, adding in a darker tone, "though I don't like it much when she wins our arguments. And I do mean to read that book of yours, Cat, to see just how much it has in it of reform doctrine."

To add to all the executions, all the gossip over the king and Kate Brandon (or the king and Mary Howard, Henry Fitzroy's widow, who some said would be the next queen), all the excited commotion over what posts were likely to be the most valuable ones in the coming reign, we woke up one morning to find that there was a madman among us.

A wild-eyed man in the brown robe and hood of a monk began running through the palace corridors proclaiming that I would not be queen much longer.

"The queen is not long to reign! The queen is not long to reign!" he shouted over and over, darting here and there, opening doors, peering into closets, interrupting ambassadorial receptions and romantic tête-à-têtes in small rooms.

"The fellow's insane!" Tom cried out when the mad monk accosted him as he was playing hazard with Prince Edward and me in the prince's apartments. "A new queen is coming in! And not one of yours!" said the stranger, coming up to Tom and lifting the flap of his dirty hood so that he could look right into Tom's disgusted face.

"Get away from me you filthy lunatic!" Tom pushed the man so roughly that he fell against a table of inlaid wood and hit his head. He got up, dizzy but apparently unhurt, and began cackling to himself.

"Guard your lady, guard your lady," he repeated, parrotlike, as he half-jogged, half-leaped around the room, stumbling again and again.

"You," he shouted then, pointing at me, "you shall not reign long. Soon it will be all over for you!"

Tom rose and drew his sword, which he wore in spite of the strict prohibitions against bringing weapons into the palace. He slashed at the air and the madman turned and ran out.

The king, annoyed when the mad monk interrupted one of his oatmeal baths, ordered him caught and expelled. But it took days for the guards to hunt him down and capture him, and by then his message had been spread to every room in the palace. The gossip and the betting reached new levels of excitement, until everyone was speculating on who would be the next queen.

41

T OM WAS COMING INTO HIS OWN. KING HENRY HAD APPOINTED HIM Lord High Admiral, and his first duty was to preside over a grand spectacle on the Thames.

Two barges floated on the river at Westminster, one the king's barge, red banners and pendants flying bravely in the afternoon breeze, the gilded roses carved into the prow agleam in the sunshine, the other painted to look like a papal barge (though no vessel belonging to the pope had appeared in English waters in many years).

In the king's barge stood the Lord High Admiral himself, tall and very handsome in his red and gold doublet and heavy gold chain of office, and Prince Edward who stood at the wheel, and Princess Elizabeth, who had been allowed to join in the make-believe by wearing the jerkin and breeches of a gunner, her bright red-gold hair tucked into a gunner's cap. The king sat in his wheeled chair on a raised platform just behind Edward, shading his eyes from the sun and shouting orders to the crew. I sat beside him, making myself as inconspicuous as possible.

In the papal barge were Will, dressed like the pope himself in a long red gown and tiara and blessing everyone in sight, and Princess Mary, dressed as a nun and clutching her jeweled crucifix in excitement. Mary, devout as she was, continued to surprise and delight me by her sense of humor, and she was happy to take part in the race that was about to ensue. A group of servants dressed as cardinals manned the guns of the papal boat.

At a signal from the shore the two vessels began racing downriver, the oarsmen straining, the hundreds of spectators making a noisy clamor on shore. Drums were beating and martial music playing, and the king happily beat time, merry as a schoolboy, and clapped as the boats sped toward the King's Bridge, their destination.

At a prearranged signal the gunners on both barges began firing blank charges, smoke billowing out over the water with angry shouts and taunts flung back and forth between the crews. Edward turned the wheel and tried to ram the papal barge, whereupon a loud volley of explosions was heard and the mock cardinals began to fall as if wounded. Finally Will, as the pope, pretended to be struck by a musket ball and leaped headfirst into the river, followed by his cardinals and crew. Amid much laughter and applause, the prize was awarded to the king's barge and all the actors were rescued.

Later, at a banquet celebrating the royal victory, Tom sat next to Princess Mary—now shorn of her nun's costume—and showed her much attention. King Henry favored Kate Brandon as his dining companion, and I found myself seated between my stepdaughter Margaret and her husband, the German physician Philip von Lederer.

"Princess Mary is much in favor tonight," I remarked, hoping my envy was not apparent in my voice. "That ought to put an end to those stories about Princess Elizabeth having the admiral's child."

"Edward wants his sister to marry the admiral, Mother Catherine. And since Edward will be king any day now, Tom Seymour is acting in obedience to Edward's wish."

Margaret was sensible and shrewd. I supposed that what she said was correct, though this was the first I'd heard of it. Without Anne Daintry to be my informant, I was no longer in possession of all the latest news. And Tom had been avoiding me, just like my servants and the court ladies.

I watched in increasing depression of spirits as Tom made Mary laugh and blush, and lifted his glass to drink to her. He served her from the plates of food brought to the banquet table in ceaseless succession. He's all but wiping her mouth for her, I thought bitterly—only to see him do just that, with a gallant flourish of his own napkin of fine white lawn.

I despised Mary then, despite our ongoing friendship, and envied her her rank as the future king's sister, and quite possibly the queen herself, should Edward die young. She had to marry someone, I realized. True, she was a papist, and Henry had been unable to find a foreign prince who would agree to marry her. But she could not reign alone. She had to have a husband. Why not Tom?

Suddenly feeling ill, I got up from the table and went into an anteroom. A group of dancers were assembled there, dressed for their role in a pageant. The women were gowned as the Nine Muses in flowing Greek robes, the men attired as Art, Music, Poetry and so forth in whimsical finery adorned with symbols of their crafts. The dancers were rehearsing their steps, and paid little attention to me as I stood in an alcove by one of the room's tall windows, looking out into the torchlit garden. The garden where the king had planted four thousand rose bushes to please Kate Brandon.

In a moment Philip von Lederer joined me there.

"Are you feeling unwell? Is there anything I can prescribe for you?" His gentle smile told me that he knew what was troubling me, and that it wasn't only a passing stomach pang.

I returned his smile. "If only you could prescribe something that would make me pregnant with the king's son. That would solve everything."

Philip shook his head. "It's no use. He's too sick to become a father."

"Not even with Kate Brandon?"

"Not even with her. Not with any woman."

"Have you ever tried telling him that?"

"No. He has never heard the truth from his other doctors, and if I told him the truth he would reject it as a lie. He would probably send me to my death."

After a pause I said, "He may well send me to the stake, and soon. I have had ample warning. Some days he threatens me, other days he laughs and says he would never dream of letting me come to harm."

"Unfortunately he allows himself to be too easily led by those around him. The weaker he gets, the more frightened he becomes. He lets Bishop Gardiner persuade him to do whatever Gardiner wants. And all Gardiner wants is power."

"And I stand in his way."

"Yes. You must protect yourself, in any way you can."

I needed to protect myself. That I well knew. But how? Should I keep a ship waiting at Greenwich to take me to Spain, like Kate Brandon? Or to the Low Countries where there were many adherents of the reform belief like myself and I would not be hounded for my views? Should I go to the New World, where the Spanish and Portuguese were said to have colonies, or to the Spice Islands where the cannibals lived? Or should I simply go back up north to Yorkshire, where I felt at home, and hide myself away until Henry died? I could go on a pilgrimage, as so many did before the monasteries were destroyed, and never come back.

But I was no coward. I would not run. I would stay at court and face whatever fate awaited me. But I would not face it alone.

A few days later I sought out Tom and found him, after much difficulty and many inquiries, at Deptford where a new ship was being prepared for launching. He drew me into a dockside workshop full of workbenches, tools and lengths of lumber—a shipwright's workshop. Once he had shut the doors he embraced me.

At once I was enveloped in the warm, musky, sweaty scent of him and my blood quickened, my heart beating faster and my breath coming in uneven gasps.

"Tom!"

"Darling! I've wanted so to be with you!" He kissed my cheeks, my forehead, my lips. This was the old Tom, my dearest lover. At his touch my fears about Princess Mary almost melted away entirely.

"I've longed to be with you. I've missed you so!" I clung to him, reassured by the feel of his strong arms holding me tightly.

When at last he released me he held my hands and looked down at me, his face alight with love.

"You know we can't be together. We can't risk being seen together. Even now, if we aren't careful, one of Gardiner's spies will find us. Are you sure you weren't followed here?"

I shook my head. "I don't know."

Tom let go of my hands and walked noiselessly to the door. He opened it a crack and peered out, then shut it again.

"There is another way out. I'll show you. You mustn't stay here very long."

"Isn't there anywhere we can meet, even for a few hours? The king has given me a manor at Chelsea. Could you come by boat, at night, and meet me there?"

"Every house that belongs to either of us is sure to be watched. Don't you know how much gossip there is about us? We mustn't do anything to confirm the stories. I must stay away from you, and you from me. Now, you must go."

He led me into a smaller room and opened a cupboard to reveal a hidden flight of stairs.

"At the top of these stairs is an attic. Walk along it and you'll find another door. It leads into a room where my servants sleep. Wait until one of them comes. He'll show you how to get back to the palace without being seen."

I started up the narrow stairs, then turned to look at Tom once more.

"Tell me the truth. Are you going to marry Princess Mary?"

He shrugged, looking pained. "Young Edward wants me to. But I doubt if he will actually order me to, even when he becomes king. In the meantime, courting Mary is the best way to convince everyone that I am not enraptured by you! You do see that, don't you?"

I wanted to believe him. What he said made sense. "Yes, of course. It's just that I miss you."

"I miss you too, beloved. Never doubt that. Oh, and as to our friend Gardiner, there is something you might pass on to the king. When I was in France Commander Hertford told me that all the shipments of arms the bishop sent were late, and that half the supplies were missing."

"Were the sailors stealing the arms?"

"No. The cartons and chests were nailed shut, and sealed. They were only half full when they left London."

"Surely the bishop would not deliberately weaken the royal army!"

"He would if he was in the pay of the French. Hertford's men saw Gardiner's men taking bribes from a French seneschal."

"And the king doesn't know."

"Everyone is too afraid of Gardiner to tell him."

"Not everyone," I said, and mounted the stairs.

42

D R. WENDY, ONE OF THE KING'S YOUNGER PHYSICIANS, CAME TO GET ME as I was preparing for bed one evening.

"He's worse again," was all he had to say. I knew that the king had been ill for several days. He had kept to his room, seeing no one. I felt sure he would send for me eventually, and I was ready. I put on a velvet gown in a dark garnet color—Henry liked me in deep red shades—and dispensed with my elaborate coiffure and French hood. I was careful never to wear purple, as it angered him and led to accusations that I was trying to usurp the throne.

Calling for my fool, I took my herbs and poultices and followed Dr. Wendy to the king's apartments.

"Are his hounds in the room with him?"

"Two of them, your highness."

"Good."

We went in quietly. A lutenist was strumming in one dark corner of the vast room. On the big bed with its carved posts and curtains of cloth of gold lay the old man, his legs resting on cushions, his hands moving restlessly across the satin bedclothes.

In the candlelight his wrinkled face was a grotesque mask, locked in a grimace of pain, and I could hear him alternately holding his breath, then releasing it with a groan. His head was bald but long gray wisps of hair hung from just above his ears, giving him the look of an aged derelict from the London streets. The costly furnishings of the room did nothing to dispel the impression he gave, as of a man without comforts, abandoned to the inevitable decay of the flesh.

He brightened slightly when he saw me.

"Cat! It hurts so much, Cat."

I went to the bed, willing myself to overcome the nausea that always came over me when I smelled his putrefying sores.

"Shall you take a cordial, sire, to ease the pain?"

He nodded and closed his eyes and I signaled to Dr. Wendy to prepare the opiate drink.

"He hasn't slept in two nights," the doctor murmured to me as I held the goblet to Henry's lips.

"He will."

When the king had drunk the draught I whistled to the dogs and they came to the bedside, pushing their warm muzzles under the satin coverlet.

"I've brought you some licorice for Tostig and Gundred." I put the sweet soft pastilles in his thin hand and let the dogs take them, licking the hand that fed them.

"Good dogs. Faithful dogs." The words uttered in a rasping voice.

"Now then, husband, shall we attend to your legs first, or would you like a song and dance or two?"

"Both," he said, trying to smile.

I looked over at Ippolyta, who told the lute player to play a galliard and began hopping around the room, twirling her bright skirts with their silver spangles and banging on a little drum that hung from her belt.

When the dance was finished she sang a Russian song—her singing and the harsh gutteral Russian sounds always amused Henry. Then she began telling a bawdy story, and Henry snorted, though I could tell that the effort to laugh hurt him.

I had long since used every poultice and healing compound I knew of on my husband's tortured legs. But I had recently learned of another form of treating the sores. It seemed very odd, yet I reasoned that it could do no worse than the outworn remedies that no longer seemed to have any effect.

"What are those?" Henry asked when I extracted four earthworms from a basket.

"Just what they look like. Garden worms."

"You're not going to feed me those, I hope."

I laughed. "No. They feast themselves on the corruption in your legs. Or so I'm told by a healer from Hispaniola."

I held the wriggling creatures close to the sores and they obediently began to burrow into the rotting flesh.

Henry shuddered. "I can feel them," he said, closing his eyes.

"They bury themselves deep. Like the traitors in your armies."

Henry's eyes flew open. "What? What traitors?"

"You mustn't agitate him, your highness," Dr. Wendy cautioned.

"But I am already agitated." No longer moribund, and suddenly oblivious to the pain in his legs and the worms I had attached to them, Henry struggled to sit up. "Tell me. What traitors?"

"I am told that the chests of arms and ammunition sent to the royal armies in France were only half full, or less."

"Yes, that is so. We could have conquered all of Normandy if those chests had been full. We were told the sailors were thieves."

"I have it on the best authority, sire, that the thieves were not sailors, but our own provisioners. One in particular."

"Which one? Tell me and I'll have him broken on the wheel. I'll have him spitted and roasted. I'll have him eaten alive by rats!"

"If I tell you, will you promise to believe me? I swear by the holy Scriptures that what I say is true."

He regarded me solemnly, his angry eyes intent on mine.

"I promise."

"Well then, it is Bishop Gardiner."

My words had a curious effect. At first the king's yellowish forehead wrinkled in confusion, then disbelief, then renewed anger.

"Yes," he said, staring in front of him, his voice low. "Yes, I can believe that. Gardiner has enjoyed a sudden increase of wealth. Now I know why."

"There is more."

He looked at me intently once again, with an almost feral curling of his lip.

"Gardiner's officers were seen taking bribes from the French."

The howl that came from the king's throat was agonized.

"Boulogne! My Boulogne! Oh my good fallen gentlemen!"

He wept, crying for the loss of the town, which had been seized by the enemy because the English had run short of arms and ammunition. I did my best to comfort him, pulling his head down to my chest and wrapping him in my arms while Dr. Wendy, made uncomfortable by the king's raw show of emotion, quietly left the room.

For many minutes neither of us spoke. Then, gradually recovering, the king sat dazed, drained and spent.

"Worms," he said. "All of them, Gardiner and his traitorous men. Worthless worms. Burrowing deep into their chests of French gold just like those horrid things that are eating into my legs. And to think Gardiner almost had me convinced that you were a traitor, and a heretic, Cat. But I should have known. You were the faithful one."

He reached over and patted my hand. "It was you who were faithful all the time."

As if on cue the dogs came up to the bed once again, wanting to be petted. At the sight of them the king's eyes glistened once again.

"I know who loves me," he said, stroking the dogs' heads and scratching their ears. "I should no more have doubted you, Cat, than these loyal friends. Forgive me."

"I didn't realize until today that there was anything to forgive."

It was a lie, of course, and we both knew it. But it was a comforting lie.

Henry rummaged in the drawer of a small chest next to his bed. "Now then, Cat, I want you to wear this. It's my signet ring. I gave it to Cranmer when Gardiner went to arrest him. It saved him. It will save you, if I cannot." He put the ring on my finger and clasped my hand in both of his. Then, weary, he sank back onto the cushions of the bed, his eyes closed, his face gaunt and tired, the marks of tears on his sunken cheeks.

43

I WAS WHEELING MY HUSBAND IN HIS UPHOLSTERED CHAIR IN THE ROSE garden at Westminster. All around us were blooming rose bushes, their scent so sweetly pungent it was nearly overpowering. As we passed through the densely planted bushes Henry reached out and plucked a bloom. He inhaled its fragrance, then handed it to me. Smiling, I tucked the flower into one of the loops in the sleeve of my gown.

It was midday, and the warm sun beat down on the flagstones under our feet. Henry was humming a tune he had written in his youth, a tune I knew well, "The huntsman and his snare."

Before long we heard the ominous sound of booted feet marching in unison. The sound became louder, and soon a large detachment of guardsmen came into view, tramping through the roses, with Chancellor Wriothesley at their head.

"Milady Catherine, I have a warrant for your arrest. You are accused of heresy, and of being a traitor to the crown."

I stood still, not flinching, though there were many guardsmen and the swords at their sides flashed menacingly in the sunlight.

I held out my hand, to show the chancellor the king's ring.

For a moment no one spoke or moved. Then the king got up out of his chair, supporting himself with his gold-headed cane.

"Wriothesley!" he called out. "Come here."

The chancellor, shaken by the sight of the ring, obeyed. When he reached the king he fell to his knees.

With a loud thwack King Henry brought the cane down across Wriothesley's broad shoulders, while the guardsmen, their expressions impassive, looked on.

"Fool!" he shouted. "Villain! Did you really believe I would let you arrest the queen? Vile whoreson dog!" he went on, bringing the cane down again and again. "Beast and traitor! If you ever threaten the queen again, I'll put you and Bishop Gardiner in the stocks! I'll have your heads! I'll hang them high on the King's Bridge, till they rot black and stinking like your foul black souls!"

44

Not all the worms, not all the poultices or pills I or the apothecaries could supply could save Henry, who finally succumbed to the decaying of his wretched body in midwinter of my thirty-fifth year.

I mourned him. Yes, I mourned him—though I certainly did not want him back, and when the surgeons embalmed him with clove oil and myrrh and wrapped his corpse in cerecloth and velvet and laid it in his elmwood coffin I was relieved. I no longer had anything to fear from him.

On the contrary, I had much to rejoice in, for the king had left me many chests of gold coins and jewels and more property than any one woman ever deserved. Having been very rich before, I was now twice as rich, so rich I could not comprehend my wealth, and in addition to being rich I continued to enjoy preeminent rank among the ladies of the court, though Tom's sister-in-law Anne Seymour—now very grand as Duchess of Somerset—did not think I deserved my high status.

In honor of Henry I wore his signet ring, the ring that had saved me from a heretic's death, and with it another ring I had ordered my goldsmith to make, a death's-head that resembled the king in his last years.

I did not attend my late husband's funeral but I did stand quietly beside his coffin as it lay in the candlelit presence chamber, under its golden pall, the Privy Chamber gentlemen standing guard nearby. And I wept for the old king, and all that he represented, good and bad. He was, after all, the only sovereign I had ever known, and I had known him very well indeed. With his death something solid had passed out of my life, and there was as yet nothing to replace it.

The old king died in January, and by February the new king was crowned.

Edward, nine years old but looking more like a boy of seven, put on the ermine-trimmed robes of a king and held the orb and scepter that Archbishop Cranmer offered him at his coronation, his teeth chattering from cold—or was it fear?—in the vast cathedral. Tom was among those who held the boy-king's long train as he walked slowly along the aisle, trumpets blaring and choirs singing, at the conclusion of the long coronation service. Tom's expression was unreadable, his face a mask of dark reserve. But I knew what he was thinking, for he had come to see me only days before at my riverside house in Chelsea, and he had been very upset indeed.

"I'm being kept back from power, Cat! Held back by my hateful brother! Imagine, he calls himself Protector! Not regent, but Protector! As though all England lay under his sole care. No one chose him for this role, he chose himself."

Tom strode from one end of the large room to the other as he talked, his boots striking forcefully on the stone floor, his head thrust forward in anger. He barely glanced at me.

"Henry wanted the entire royal council to hold the regency," I reminded Tom. "He told me so. He said it was in his will. Of course," I added, "he might have chosen to make me regent. I have had some experience in that role."

"You, Cat? Do you imagine that you could keep my domineering brother in line? He would cut you with his words."

"I can cut back, if need be."

"You haven't seen him at his worst. He's cold. Cruel. There's no humanity in him. Sometimes"—Tom clenched his fists—"sometimes I think I could kill him."

I thought of Bishop Gardiner, who had been capable of such ruthless lack of feeling—not to mention treachery. Having escaped a traitor's death because of his clerical status, the bishop survived—but was out of favor in the new reign, his conservative religious beliefs at odds with the more reform views of the Protector and the others on the royal council. And of the new king.

Tom stopped pacing and sat down beside me, still talking of his brother.

"Do you know what he did? He ordered me to appear before him—just as if he were king himself—and shouted at me as if I were a stable boy. He accused me of bribing Edward to win his affection. Can you imagine?"

"You do give him money. You always have," I said mildly.

"Of course I do. He's my nephew. I indulge him. But he loves me—not because I give him a few coins from time to time, but because he's always loved me, ever since he was a baby. He always hated his uncle Edward. Nobody loves Edward, not even that haughty wife of his. You should hear her berate him!"

I suggested that we walk in the riverside garden, hoping that the brisk air and delicate colors of the winter sunset might abate Tom's indignation. But as we walked along the garden path between the leafless trees, his stride lengthened and the bitterness he felt rose in him again.

"I can't endure Edward much longer. I've reached my limit—and beyond. It's time for action."

"Action?"

"To rid England of the Protector."

I swallowed hard. "This is the first I've heard of your plans."

"What did you imagine I did with the money you lent me?"

"You didn't tell me. But I did think you would pay me back."

"I'll tell you now," Tom responded, ignoring my reference to his paying me back. A gleeful look came into his eyes. "I've bought a cannon foundry."

I was speechless.

"Ten German armorers are at work even now, in Greenwich, making cannon for me, and having them transported to Sudeley Castle. I have established my armory there."

There was a long pause while I took in this astounding information.

"You intend—to overwhelm the kingdom?"

"There will be no need for that. Once my brother and his allies see that I am prepared—for anything—they will step aside and let the right man serve as regent for the king."

Tom smiled. His bitter anger had begun to dissolve. "All I need is another twenty or thirty thousand pounds in gold. To pay soldiers."

I shook my head. "If I gave you the money it would get us both killed."

He bristled.

"I am a soldier, Cat, and you are not. I assure you I know what I am doing."

"Nevertheless I prefer to go on living."

He frowned at me, then sighed.

"As you wish then. I'll get the money another way."

"How?"

"There are always ways of getting money, if you want it badly enough."

His words hung in the air, an implied threat. If I did not give Tom what he wanted, he would do something that would put himself in peril. But then, hadn't he already taken drastic steps in recruiting a private fighting force from among his tenants and equipping them from a private armory?

He took me in his arms.

"Don't desert me now, Cat. Not when I need you more than ever."

I felt myself yield to him. My body knew no other reaction. I was his, always his. Yet my mind resisted, faintly at first, then more strongly.

"It would be a mistake—for us both."

For an instant he hesitated, then he relaxed his grip on me.

"Perhaps you are right. I would not want my enemies to pursue you. Dear Cat, you must be my guide when I am led away by my passions. I know I am not prudent."

He kissed me, and for the first time that afternoon I felt I had my familiar Tom back again. But soon afterward he left me, eager to return to his dangerous plans, and I felt a stabbing at my heart, a warning, as I thought, that even the noblest of plans can fail and that Tom was far from being the noblest of men.

45

ELIZABETH, RED-CHEEKED AND SHINING-EYED, CREPT INTO MY HOUSE AT Chelsea by the scullery entrance just before dawn, with her dubious protectress Mistress Ashley trailing behind.

Elizabeth was staying with me and I felt responsible for her. I had become aware, a little before midnight, that she was not in her bed and one of her bedchamber women had admitted to me that the princess had gone out in a barge and was last seen floating downriver.

I had been waiting up for her to return ever since.

"Elizabeth!" I called out as she tiptoed across the scullery floor. At once her body went rigid, and I heard her sharp intake of breath. In the same instant Mistress Ashley let out a little scream and attempted, so clumsily that she almost fell, to bow to me.

"Wait in my bedchamber, Ashley," I said. "I'll deal with you later." Too alarmed to protest, the frightened Ashley fled, leaving Elizabeth and me to confront one another.

"Where have you been?" I asked the girl.

Instead of responding the princess turned toward me, regarded me coolly, and drew herself up to her full height—which was nearly the same as mine. I saw a glint of stubbornness in her eyes and took note of the willful tilt of her chin.

She has her father's strength, I thought to myself. And her mother's wantonness.

In that moment, by the light of the smoking candles guttering in their sconces, I saw that Elizabeth was wearing the tight bodice of pale yellow silk that I had given her three years earlier, on the day of my wedding to her father. It clung becomingly to her long, lean torso, reminding me that she had developed into a woman—and a woman with more than a little of her mother's allure.

"Are you spying on me then?" She spoke defiantly, challengingly.

"I ask you again, where have you been?"

"On the river. With Uncle Tom." As soon as she said his name she blushed, her lips upturned in a girlish grin.

"Were there others with you?"

"A few others." Her words were neutral, factual. But her expression told me what I most feared to discover. They had been alone.

"We had the moon with us," Elizabeth blurted out, and then giggled. She's tipsy, I thought. He's given her wine to drink, and she's tipsy.

"Go to bed, Elizabeth. We will talk further in the morning."

"Why don't you go to bed? You look tired—and old. Fatigue does not become you. Staying up all night is only for the young." With that she left me, her challenging words festering in the air between us.

The incident left me deeply troubled. What was Tom doing? The old gossip about Elizabeth having borne Tom's child no longer seemed so absurd. What if he had seduced her? What if, because of the consequences of that seduction, they were compelled to marry? Where would that leave me, betrayed and brokenhearted?

I wept for a day. But then, gathering my courage, I began to seek answers.

I summoned Mistress Ashley and berated her for allowing Elizabeth to go out with Tom on the barge at night.

She collapsed in tears. "But she pressed me so!" she said when she had stopped sobbing. "She would not leave me be!"

"The next time she presses you to let her do something you know is not right, not seemly, you take her by the ear and bring her to me."

"She defies me."

"Punish her then."

Ashley shook her head, and made a vain effort to wipe the tears from her cheeks. "Punishing her only makes her more defiant."

"Ashley, I once saw King Henry force her to crawl the entire length of a great chamber on her hands and knees. I thought then that he was being cruel. I think now that he may have been right in what he did."

I became more gravely concerned when I talked with Thomas Parry, a sober, gray-haired man of business who oversaw Elizabeth's financial affairs and held the title of cofferer. I went to see him about her household accounts, which had recently shown a great increase in costs for dressmakers' fees and expensive stuffs.

"Aye, she's been spending a good deal," he told me. "She said she had her brother's permission, so I didn't question it. Now that her brother is king, he favors her in many things. I paid the bills. Besides, ever since she had her rights restored she's been much better off, in terms of her income, as I'm sure you know. King Edward has given her lands in the West Country and some patents on spices and the treasure trove from Fowey to the Hamoaze."

Lands in the West Country, I thought. Where Tom is recruiting his army of loyal tenants.

"Has Lord Thomas Seymour borrowed any money from the princess?" I asked.

"Odd that you should mention him, milady. He has been making inquiries like yourself, into her household accounts and the like. He asked me to show him what lands she held, and what her yearly rents were from her estates and patents. And he asked me something else too. What would you say to letting me have Wandelsford and Reddingfield in exchange for my Clapwell and Agensborough estates, he said. That way the princess's lands and mine would be next to one another, and both could be administered together.

"Well, I said to him, I don't know about that, sir. You'd have to speak to the Protector about that. And then he swore, not liking me to mention his brother the Protector, and he's never said anything more about it since."

"And have there been any loans?"

"Not so far as I know of, milady. I hope the princess has got more sense than to lend Lord Thomas any money, what with his reputation for spending it faster than he gets it."

"Thank you, Parry," I said. "You have been a great help."

"Do you think they'll marry, milady?" the cofferer asked me, unwilling to end our talk. "Is that why he was asking all those questions about her lands and income?"

"I don't know, Parry," I managed to say, my spirits plunging. "It will be up to the king to decide whom the princess marries."

"And the council, don't forget. Which means the Protector. I heard Milord Seymour and his brother quarreled over that, with Milord Seymour saying he could marry any woman he liked, even Princess Mary or Princess Elizabeth, if only he had the king's blessing, as it were, and the Protector saying no he couldn't, that the council had to approve."

I managed to end our interview without showing my dismay over what I had learned, but I could not sleep that night, and the next day I went in search of Tom.

I made the journey to Whitehall and found him engaged in a loud argument with a Roman moneylender, Signor DiGiornatta, a familiar figure at court as he lent funds—at usurious rates of interest—to officials and nobles who often overspent. They were in the Watching Chamber, adjacent to the room where the royal council customarily met, and Tom was shouting, the Italian responding in a lower, more controlled tone.

"I tell you I must have it, all twenty thousand of it, within a week. I have already promised ten to—to a business colleague, and the other ten I owe to others of your wretched band of moneylending scoundrels as interest on loans."

"Nothing would give me greater pleasure, *il mio barone,* but you see, you must first return the sum I lent you only last month. That was our agreement, as I remind you."

"Yes, yes, I know. But things have changed. My plans have changed. By God's precious blood, nothing is as it was under the late King Henry. Nothing whatever! Can't you see that?"

Tom's exasperation seemed to reach a peak, and he ran out of words.

"Perhaps if milord *barone* could ask his distinguished brother, *Il Protettore,* for some money—"

"If I hear that name again I'll—" Tom began, but a deeper, more commanding voice cut him off.

"You'll what, little brother?"

Edward Seymour, Lord Protector of the realm, entered the Watching Chamber with half a dozen men close behind him, and at once the guardsmen who stood by the door dropped to their knees. Ignoring me, the Protector walked briskly toward Tom, his black velvet cloak swaying behind him.

"This is a private matter between me and Signor DiGiornatta. It doesn't concern you," Tom snapped.

"On the contrary, everything that goes on at this court concerns me. Why are you attempting to borrow more money, when you are so deeply in debt already?" Edward Seymour stepped between his brother and the Italian, his eyes fixed on Tom. Tom glared back, saying nothing.

"Signor DiGiornatta," Edward said, his intense gaze still locked on Tom, "we have done with you here, for the time being."

"As you like, *Prottettore*." The Roman bowed to Edward's broad back and left the room.

"And I have done with you!" Tom hissed, and turned to follow the moneylender. But before he had gone a step Edward reached out and roughly grasped his arm.

"No, little brother. You are not dismissed. I want an answer to my question and I shall have it."

Tom wrenched his arm free and straightened his green damask doublet, its gold threads shining.

"If you must know," he said in a lower tone of voice, "I have incurred much expense since taking on the barony. As Lord Thomas Seymour I could live on the income from my estates. As Baron Seymour of Sudeley I cannot."

"We both know the true cause of your debt. The men, the arms you are buying. You are not discreet, little brother. Much is known."

I stood where I was, near the great double doors that led into the Watching Chamber, with the guardsmen, who had resumed their posts, standing nearby. Others had come into the chamber, no doubt seeking the Protector, for he was constantly besieged by clerks with papers that needed signing, messengers with news, petitioners hoping to win his favor. We all waited in silence for the tense confrontation between Tom and his brother to run its course.

"Uncle Tom! Uncle Tom!"

The high, thin child's voice rang through the vast room as the king, a diminutive figure in a doublet and hose of white satin, ran in and approached Tom and his brother. Edward was flushed and out of breath. He ignored those of us who knelt to him and, seeking Tom's side, reached up and took his hand.

"Uncle Tom, you promised to take me to see where the cannons are made. Did you forget?" Crestfallen, the king looked up pleadingly into his uncle's face.

"No, your majesty, I didn't forget. Other people delayed me." He glared at the Protector, who was looking down at the king, his former ferocity replaced by a mask of feigned welcome.

King Edward looked from one to the other. "You've been fighting again, haven't you? I can tell. I don't like it when you fight."

"The important thing is, your majesty, we both want what is best for you." The Protector's tone was unctuous, his smile ingratiating. Edward ignored him and turned back to Tom.

"Will you take me now?"

Instead of answering Tom reached out for the slim small boy-king and swung him up on his shoulders. "I'm ready at your command, sire," Tom said.

"I command you then, take me to see the cannons."

Trusting that his brother would not dare to countermand a royal order, Tom made his way toward the doors, with a beaming Edward riding on his shoulders. Catching sight of me as he passed, Tom called out casually, "Come along, Cat. I'll take you to see the guns."

"Yes, stepmother. Come with us."

And without a backward glance I followed where Tom led, alarmed by the scene I had just witnessed, nervous about what had happened between Tom and Elizabeth, determined to find out just what my volatile, forceful, exasperating lover was really up to.

46

I SENT THE PORTERESS OUT TO WAIT FOR TOM AT THE SMALL LODGE GATE of my gardens at Chelsea, the gate that no one used, and that was half hidden under an overgrown clump of lilac. It was barely dawn, the first faint pink light was reflected in the steel-gray river and I had been up for an hour, fretting over what we would say to one another when he arrived.

We had agreed to meet in secret, at my manor house, and we had made a pact that he would stay no longer than an hour or two. This would be the first time in a week that we would be entirely alone, and able to talk candidly. When Tom took Edward and me to the foundry, a huge hot room where muscular men, their faces blackened from ash and soot, tended blazing fires and steaming ovens, there had been no chance for conversation. The pounding of heavy mallets and the scraping of metal against metal had made talk impossible, and in any case we could not speak openly of personal things in front of the boy.

Now, however, we were sure to be alone and undisturbed.

I stood at the open window, watching the fields beyond the garden grow visible in the pinkish light. A fine mist hung over everything, veiling the garden, but as the sky lightened the mist dissolved, leaving the air fresh and sweet with the scent of new-mown grass and the fragrance of the herb garden I had planted along the south-facing wall.

I heard the faint click of the latch and knew that the porteress was letting Tom in.

I watched him coming along the path, between the dark yews and the paler hedges newly in leaf, his long loping stride full of vigor. He held a bunch of blue cornflowers, no doubt gathered in the course of his progress through the fields. He handed the flowers to me once he was in the house.

I took them and he hugged me, nearly crushing the flowers, and kissed me on the cheek. Releasing me he tore off his coat and flung it carelessly down as he always did. His linen shirt, open at the neck, was sweat-stained and his boots were muddy from his tramp through the fields. He lounged against a table, a half-grin on his handsome face.

"Tom," I began, but he interrupted me.

"Have you any ale, Cat? I've had a thirsty walk."

I went to the door and called one of the servants, telling her to bring ale and a manchet loaf.

"Tom," I began again, "tell me what happened the night you and Elizabeth went out on the barge."

"Elizabeth and I and that clucking hen Mistress Ashley and about fifty other people, you mean."

"What other people?"

Tom looked at me, a little sullenly as I thought. "Do you know how many people it takes to row a barge? But of course you do, you have one of your own."

"Were you alone with her?"

Tom shrugged. "Hardly at all. You know how Ashley hovers. Besides, Edward was supposed to be there. It was all his idea. A secret escape on the river. An adventure. Only at the last minute he got sick and couldn't come."

"You were out all night."

He chuckled. "We were stranded for a long time on a sandbar. We had to wait for the tide to come in to free us. The pilot was very chagrined."

"When she came home Elizabeth was half drunk."

"Ashley gave her a strong posset. She got cold. The posset warmed her, so Ashley gave her another one."

"Tom, why was it all so secret? I would never have found out if one of her bedchamber women hadn't confessed where the princess had gone."

Tom stood up and went to the window. After a moment he spoke.

"I didn't want you to know. I didn't want to worry you. So I didn't tell you."

"You have worried me far more by saying nothing."

"I'm sorry."

A jug of ale was brought, and mugs and a loaf with a knife to cut it. Tom ate and drank with a good appetite. I didn't feel hungry. I watched him eat, holding back from saying any more until he had finished. All that he said made perfect sense, I told myself. I had no reason to distrust him. And yet . . .

"Tom, I think Elizabeth is infatuated with you."

He wiped his mouth on a linen napkin before answering. "Of course she is. How old is she? Thirteen? Fourteen? Girls are always in love at that age—unless they are excessively pious."

"It worries me."

"Why?" The look he gave me was one of genuine innocence.

"You can easily imagine why."

"No Cat, I can't. I belong to you, and you alone. No silly girl and her passing whim is likely to sway me, or tempt me."

"Not even when she is a royal heiress? With much wealth in lands and estates adjoining yours?"

He had not been expecting that. For a brief moment he blanched, then recovered. He poured himself another mug of ale from the jug and drank deeply, wiping his mouth on the back of his hand.

"You've been talking to Parry." There was silence for the space of a heartbeat or two. Then, "And thinking the worst of me." He looked at me reproachfully. He reached for my hand and led me to the window-seat. We sat down there side by side, my hand still in his.

"Cat, I want you to listen to me. This is important. Edward wants Elizabeth to marry. I was his first choice to be her husband, but I told him very firmly that my heart belonged to someone else. Then he wanted her to marry the King of Denmark's brother, who agreed to come and live in England once they were wed. Before the marriage could be discussed, the king demanded to know what lands Elizabeth held and how much wealth she had in coin and jewels and income from her tenants and her patents.

I was given the task of writing up an inventory of all her possessions and income to be sent to the Danish court.

"Naturally I went to Parry, who told me what I needed to know. But I couldn't tell him the real reason for my queries. It had to be kept secret until the betrothal was announced."

He patted my hand reassuringly, and I admit that, listening to him, I felt much better.

"When will the betrothal be announced?"

"Ah! Alas, it is not to be."

"Why not?"

"Because the King of Denmark's brother died."

"Truly?"

Tom nodded solemnly.

"His ship went down in a storm in the Kattegat, and all his serving men and sailors were drowned with him."

There was nothing to be said to this. I crossed myself and silently prayed for the souls of the dead.

Tom moved closer to me and looked down at the floor. "The worst of it is, Cat, that Edward will probably order me to marry Elizabeth now. Or my brother will force me into a marriage I don't want, just to get rid of me. Let's put an end to all these threats to our happiness, once and for all. Will you marry me, Cat? Now, quickly, before anyone can stop us?"

I kissed him then, and he kissed me back, strongly and sweetly, and all my doubts fled like the shadows at daybreak.

"I will," I said.

We smiled at one another, a delightfully conspiratorial smile.

"Let's have the wedding here, in this garden. Just the two of us, and the priest, and a notary."

"And Margaret can be my matron of honor."

"Soon."

"As soon as it can be arranged."

Tom stood up, pulled me to my feet, and hugged me. When he released me his face shone.

"Oh, Cat, won't my brother be furious! But that only makes the thought all the sweeter!"

47

ALL THE BIRDS IN THE GARDEN WERE SINGING ON THE MORNING TOM and I were married, and I felt that my heart would burst from happiness.

I had waited so long for this day, hoped and prayed for so long that one day we would say our vows and from then on be husband and wife forever. The joy I felt was so great I could never find words to contain it, but anyone who has longed and yearned for years for some precious thing, and finally finds that precious thing within their grasp, will read these words and understand.

When I felt Tom put the gold wedding band on my finger, I knew it was real at last. He was mine and I was his. Only death could separate us.

At first only a few people knew that we were married, for I kept on living in my Chelsea house and Tom kept his household at Sudeley and in his London mansion. But after a few weeks Tom told the world—by which I mean, of course, the court—that I was his wife and then our troubles began.

Tom and I were blissfully happy when alone, but when we appeared together heads turned and there were whispers of condemnation and disapproval. I was the king's widow, it was said. I ought to wear mourning for at least a year, and ought not to even think of remarrying

for at least two years, if not longer. There were those who said that a
dowager queen should never remarry at all, especially a dowager queen
who had had three husbands already! Behind my back and sometimes,
quite brazenly, to my face I was called a wanton woman, a schemer, even
an adulteress, dishonoring my royal husband's memory.

In the beginning Tom and I laughed over these carping complaints,
and I dealt with the hissing rudeness and insults by picking up my skirts
and moving away from the offenders. But when Tom's brother the
Protector and the Protector's poisonous wife became my chief critics,
the assaults on my dignity grew harder to bear.

One afternoon I discovered a group of men in my bedchamber,
going through my chests and wardrobes, while my bedchamber women
wept and wrung their hands and my ladies-in-waiting protested loudly
and demanded that the pillaging stop.

"What is going on here? Stop what you are doing at once and
answer me," I said when I entered the room.

"We are here on orders from the Protector. We are to take back the
jewels you received from our late sovereign King Henry," said one of
the men, who continued to rummage through one of my large chests as
he spoke.

"Kneel when you speak to me, and address me as your highness."

"We have orders not to address you in that way any longer. You are
to be known as Baroness Seymour."

"Your insolence will be punished. As for my rank and style, I am the
queen dowager and will be during my lifetime. And my jewels, which
you will not find in this house, are my own possession."

"The Protector says they belong to the crown."

"He is wrong. Leave my house or I will call my husband's guard."

At the mention of Tom's guardsmen the men who were going
through my things paused. Tom's retainers were strong, tough soldiers,
and none of the Protector's men were eager to confront them.

"Do you give us your word that none of the jewels you were given
by our late master King Henry are in this house?"

"I give you my word as queen dowager."

The men left, but my lovely bedchamber, with my mother's great bed
with purple hangings, was in complete disarray. The Protector continued
to demand the return of all my jewels, and I continued to resist his
demands. I also continued to insist that when I dined, either in my own

home or at court, the servants knelt when presenting me with the platters of food and all others (except the king, of course) be served later.

All this was galling to the Protector's haughty wife Anne, who seemed to think of herself as a queen and not just as a stout, sharp-featured noblewoman with a tart tongue whom nobody liked.

When Tom and I attended a ceremony at which King Edward was creating several new peers, the Protector's wife and I approached the doorway to the Presence Chamber at the same moment. We collided, our wide skirts with their stiff metallic threads contesting for the available space.

"Make way for the queen dowager," Tom called out, and I pressed on through the doorway, despite the undignified shoving of my would-be rival.

"She's not the queen any more," shouted the red-faced Anne, puffing from her exertion. "She's only Baroness Seymour. I'm the highest ranking lady of this court!"

"You are certainly the most ill-mannered," I called out to her over my shoulder as I passed through the doorway. "And not of royal blood."

She had no answer to that. As everyone at court knew, I was descended through my grandmother Fitzhugh from John of Gaunt, and the blood of the Plantagenets flowed through my veins.

Haughty Anne fought for pride of place at every ceremony, attempting to grasp for herself the seat of honor at every banquet, generally striving against me at every opportunity. I ignored her insults and placed myself where I rightfully belonged, but her constant contentiousness wore me down and irritated me and Tom and I joked that one day I would lose my temper and bite her. When we were alone we referred to her as "the Pestilence."

"Here comes the Protector and the Pestilence," Tom would whisper to me, making me laugh, or "The Pestilence is about to strike again."

Nothing, it seemed, could dampen our spirits or quench our soaring happiness that first summer of our marriage, not the nuisance of my new sister-in-law or the nagging demands of the Protector (who never did find my jewels, or force me to return them) or the intrigues that swirled around the little king. Tom was more content than I had seen him in a long time. He was still very much at odds with his brother, but he had succeeded in acting against the Protector's wishes in the very important matter of his marriage, and foresaw more independence to come. His loyal army was large and growing larger, and his cannon foundry, though extremely expensive, was producing heavy guns which were being stored at Sudeley. Tom was his adoring royal nephew's favorite, as ever. The young king forgave Tom and me for marrying, as he was fond of us both, and he even sent us a wedding present of a pair of fine Scottish gerfalcons.

I saw all through the lens of my own happiness, of course; I did not realize in what real peril Tom stood from the Protector's growing power, or how vulnerable my own position was, as Tom's wife. I did not know, for Tom did not tell me, that he was using my credit to take new and much larger loans than he ever had before. I dismissed the sly looks and playful slaps Tom gave Elizabeth as harmless teasing. And I did not allow myself to calculate, in any serious way, what would happen to Tom and me on the day the frail king died.

Instead I reveled in my joy as Tom's loving wife. In our happy hours loving and joking in the great bed with purple hangings. In the warm sunlight of summer and the rich pleasures of autumn and the dream of many more joyful seasons to come.

And when winter arrived, I attained my greatest joy. I was sure that I was carrying Tom's child.

48

I WAS SO VERY, VERY SICK. EVERY MORNING AND EVERY NIGHT I WAS violently ill and threw up all the food I had tried to eat that day. In the afternoons I was sleepy and lethargic, hardly able to force myself to meet with my household officers or servants and make decisions on practical matters.

I missed Anne very much in these difficult days. She would have been such a help to me, had she lived. I needed someone with Anne's capable, practical shrewdness, but there was no one I could turn to. My servants were loyal, and I paid them well, which ensured their loyalty even more. But there was no one among them able to take my place on days when I was at my worst. As a result my usually well run establishment at Chelsea became somewhat slipshod, the kitchens not as well stocked as they should have been, the horses not exercised, the garden neglected and the rooms not aired or kept polished as scrupulously as I would have liked.

I was ill, and I was fretful. The holidays came and I lay on my bed, wishing I could join in the celebrating and merrymaking. Instead I met with Dr. Van Huick, a very skilled physician who had attended King Henry when he was alive and who Philip von Lederer urged me to consult.

Dr. Van Huick was a Dutchman, brisk and efficient in his manner, a square, strong man in his prime with a stiff brush of reddish-gray hair standing up from his forehead. I confided to him that I had had a miscarriage many years before, and that since then I had never conceived a child—until now.

"You have a sour womb," he said curtly. "You are lucky to have made a child at all. You are old now to be a mother, and with this sour womb you may not be able to grow the child until it is fully ready to be born. You must prepare yourself for that. I'm sorry.

"Lord willing, the child will come in August. July will be critical. Until then you must be very, very careful. You are getting thin."

"I can't eat. My stomach rejects everything."

"That should stop soon. When it does, you must eat eat eat. Stuff yourself like a goose. Make the baby fat and strong inside of you.

"I think you can give birth," he added, "if you are very careful. I will look after you."

The doctor's words made me as anxious as I was ill and I reached out to other mothers for comfort. My sister Nan had had a healthy son and I had gone to attend his christening. Her boy was three years old now and I had watched him grow and thrive. Several of my ladies-in-waiting had given birth when I was queen, and I had become godmother to their children. Even the Pestilence was brought to bed at regular intervals and all her children had lived.

I was given a charm written out in the old Saxon tongue to put under my pillow and a relic from Saint Gudrun to hang from the bedstead. My former mistress Anne of Cleves sent me a large packet of camomile tea to settle my stomach. Special prayers were said for me and my child in the chapels of Chelsea and Sudeley each day. I searched my Bible for stories of women blessed with healthy sons, and even, as I lay in bed, began to write a new collection of prayers of my own, thinking that I might have it made into a book after my baby was born.

Tom spent as much time with me as he could, but he was often away, looking after the affairs of the fleet and protecting himself at court from his brother's attempts to take away his authority and the Pestilence's spiteful encroachments on my prerogatives as queen dowager. When Tom was with me he was very sympathetic and regretted all my discomfort.

One very cold winter night he arrived at Chelsea bringing with him four heaping baskets of food.

"I wish you could have been at the banquet with me, Cat," he said as servants laid a table in my bedchamber. "My brother gave a feast for the Garter Knights and there was no end to the courses. I've brought you some of the tastiest dishes to sample for yourself."

I smiled weakly and tried not to gag at the sight of the plate of baked stag, cold lamb and capons with prunes and currants that was set in front of me. But the smell of the food made my gorge rise, and I was unable to force myself to eat more than a few bites.

"Cat! You must eat! You've become so thin and pale. You must eat for our child's sake."

I continued to make an effort but soon gave up and called for some camomile tea. I hoped I wouldn't be sick while Tom was with me. I shut my eyes and tried to concentrate on preventing my food from coming up.

"You know, Cat, our boy will be a very important person at court, right from his birth. He'll be the king's first cousin, and the son of a queen."

"A dowager queen."

"And he'll be rich, and Edward will give him many titles and lands." Which you will administer for him, I thought, making you much better off.

"Edward counts on me more and more, you know, Cat. He distrusts my brother and turns to me. He wants Parliament to make me his governor."

"And will they?"

"I expect so."

"But that will mean we'll be apart all the time."

"Not if you and the baby come to live at the palace."

I sighed, and felt my stomach lurch. To live at court again, to be at the center of that hornet's nest of intrigue. It was not something I looked forward to.

"You must find your strength again, Cat. Go for long walks, eat good healthy meals."

"I'll do my best," I said, as brightly as I could. But after Tom left my stomach rebelled, as it usually did, and the few bites of fine food I had managed to eat went into the silver basin I kept nearby for such emergencies. I was sick, I was miserable, and above all, I was worried. Would my sour womb reject the baby, as it had the baby Ned and I had made together so many years ago? Or if I did manage to give birth, would my baby be defective in some way, with a crooked back or weak legs? Or would it be a simpleton, like the boy Queen Anne's sister Mary had with King Henry, a poor wretched creature without wits who could hardly speak and who had to be kept out of sight lest he bring shame on his parents?

I was rescued from these morbid thoughts by Will, whose visits had become more frequent since I told him what a very hard time I was having. Will had always shown strong family feelings, and I knew I could count on him. When I married Tom, Will had taken Anne Daintry's children, all four of whom had been living with me, to live with him, and was raising them as his own. This eased my burden of responsibility considerably, and I was grateful to my brother. Not many men I knew would have devoted themselves to being a father to their wayward wife's four bastards—for that is what the children were, in plain terms. I was very fond of them, but Tom had objected to their living with us, and now that they were with Will I could continue to be their fond Aunt Cat while not having to deal with the day-to-day oversight of their care.

Whenever Will came to see me he always brought me something amusing, slippers shaped like ripe figs, green on the outside and red within, or a handful of beans that rocked back and forth and jumped like live things, or—my favorite—a mechanical box from which popped a toy figure that resembled the Pestilence.

"It is very like her, don't you think?" Will asked, picking up the box and studying the frowning, dark-haired doll that emerged from it. "You should have seen her, overdressed and heaped with jewels, the day the king of Denmark's brother came to court to pay his respects."

I felt a prickle of unease.

"The king of Denmark's brother? But I thought he drowned."

"He seemed quite fit. Not even wet."

"Is it possible the king has more than one brother?"

"As it happens, no. This brother is the king's only living sibling, and since the king has no children, his brother may inherit the throne—if he lives long enough."

So Tom lied about the shipwreck, I thought, and most likely about the reason he was making inquiries about Elizabeth's lands. Why? In the past he had said that he hid the truth from me in order to spare me anxiety. Was he doing the same thing now? What did I have to be anxious about, exactly?

Will sensed my unease, but he misinterpreted its cause.

"Something is bothering you, Cat. I can tell. Something beyond your upset stomach and your worries about the baby. Have you been hearing about what Tom is doing?" Will's ordinarily smiling face was so grave as he spoke that I was alarmed.

"He tells me some things, of course. Mostly about his brother."

Will took my hand. "I think you should know, Cat, that Tom is overstepping his bounds. He's putting himself in more danger than he knows. I am no intriguer or insider, and I keep to the margins of things at court as much as I can. But even I can see that what Tom is trying to do could lead to his downfall. He could be attainted. If he carries out the threats he is making, he could be convicted of treason."

I put the box Will had brought me aside and tried to sit up. "Tell me more," I said.

"A few days ago, when the council was debating the question of whom the Princess Elizabeth should marry, Tom took Edward away overnight, on his barge."

Just as he did with Elizabeth, I thought, and bit my lip nervously.

"No one knew where Edward was. The Protector was beside himself with fear, and lashed out at everyone in the prince's household. The palace was searched from attic to dungeons but there was no sign of the king. The Protector even sent men down into the moat—that evil-smelling sewer—to look for his body, in case he had fallen in.

"When Edward returned the next morning Tom was with him—and in a foul mood. It turned out that Tom had been trying to convince Edward to sign a document asking Parliament to appoint him Governor of the King's Person. Edward would not sign it.

"You can imagine the scene between Tom and his brother. Furious anger, harsh words. I tried to intervene, to restrain Tom and make him leave the palace. I did it for your sake, Cat. I was afraid of what Tom might say in his anger, and of what he might try to do.

"I managed to take his arm and lead him away, but not before he had threatened Parliament. He said that unless he was appointed Edward's governor he would kidnap him and this time no one would be able to find out where he was.

"It was all I could do to make Tom come with me, out of the

council room and into my coach. He fought me and swore at me. All I could think of, Cat, was you. Because of you and the baby I had to prevent Tom from bringing disaster upon himself."

It was the longest speech I had ever heard Will make, and by far the most serious.

"He is rash," I said with a sigh. "And very unwise. Yet he says there are many at court who admire his boldness."

Will shrugged. "They will cease to admire it if he finds himself in prison. And Cat," he added, "be sure you do not involve yourself in anything he is doing. Don't give him any more money. Don't help him or encourage him. It can only lead to your harm as well as his."

After Will left me I felt so disheartened that I began to rock back and forth on my bed like a child, seeking some shred of comfort from the soothing repetitive movement. Presently I sent for my fool, hoping to divert myself watching her silliness and antics.

She came bounding into my bedchamber, laughing and full of energy as she always was, twirling her wide red and blue skirts in a wild dance. I stopped rocking and watched her, laughing when she pretended to injure herself bumping into benches and walls, enjoying her parody of the formal dances we did at court.

I wondered, not for the first time, what went on in her mind. Ippolyta had been a fixture of my household for years, in and out of my bedchamber and antechambers many times a day, familiar with all that went on around me. Yet she seemed never to react to anything that was happening, and the fact that she was a Tartar from the Russian steppes—a place that, to me, was impossibly remote—barred her from mingling with the other servants. When not entertaining me she kept to her small, snug room at Chelsea, with its modest bed and wardrobe and her icon of a Russian saint hanging on the wall with a burning candle beneath it.

Now, watching Ippolyta's twirling skirts, my own disturbing thoughts whirling uneasily, I was surprised when she moved closer to my bed and whispered, in her heavy accent, a few chilling words.

"Beware, my good lady, beware!"

Startled, I put my hand to my throat, as if to stifle my involuntary reply.

"Oh Ippolyta," I cried out, "what will happen to us?"

But before the words were out of my mouth she was off in a blur of red and blue, stamping her feet and humming to herself as she crossed the room, leaving me alone to weep into my pillow.

49

ALONG WITH ALL THAT WAS WORRYING ME THAT SPRING I WAS constantly plagued by the defiance and animosity of Elizabeth. Ever since I reprimanded her for going on the river with Tom she had been a thorn in my side. All the earlier trust and friendship I had tried so hard to build between us was gone, and Elizabeth seemed to seize on any excuse to rebel against my authority and cause acrimony.

In her high-necked black gowns and plain black billiments she hovered like a harpy on the fringes of my life, always ready to challenge me or show me disrespect. Her very gowns—mourning gowns, worn to honor her late father—were a rebuke to me, as I had worn mourning for only a few months after my late royal husband's death and was criticized for my failure to show him proper respect by wearing black for a full two years. Her gowns were severe, but her youthful looks were ripe and alluring. With her long curling flame-red hair and fresh white skin, her tapered limbs and developing figure, she was as bewitching as a water sprite, and the slyness in her eyes would have provoked any man, I thought, even my Tom.

"I have hired a new tutor, a Cambridge man. Roger Ascham," she announced to me one morning when I went to observe her schoolroom. "My old one has been dead for months. It was time to find another."

"All the appointments in my household are made by me, Elizabeth," I said.

"Not this one. Ascham is a scholar, learned in Greek as well as Latin. I need help translating Isocrates and the Greek Testament. I am a better judge of Greek learning than you are, wouldn't you agree? Since your own knowledge of Greek is limited. So I appointed Ascham."

"He will have to earn my approval."

"I'll be sure to tell him so." Her smile told me that neither she nor Master Ascham considered me to be a good judge of scholarship. And on that point she was correct, of course; my Latin was adequate, so far as it went, but I knew very little Greek and in fact I had heard Roger Ascham's name mentioned in respectful tones by men whose judgment I trusted. He would be a good choice as her tutor—provided his character was sound.

Still, the girl's willfulness and constant provocations galled me, especially after I learned from Margaret that Elizabeth had begun to entertain my servants by mimicking me.

"She is very insolent, Mother Catherine," Margaret confided to me, clearly uncomfortable with what she was telling me. "She decks herself out in elaborate red gowns—the kind you like to wear, with all the pleats and lace and frills—and carries a big black Bible and a pen and inkwell, and talks about duty and sinfulness and how every woman ought to write books and have at least four husbands before she's too old to enjoy them."

"Is she as funny as Will?"

"Sometimes. But sometimes she is just spiteful. I don't know why she dislikes you so. Especially since you've always been kind to her."

"Thank you for your loyalty, Margaret."

"I'm sorry to have to tell you this, Mother Catherine. But I thought you ought to know."

"You were right to tell me."

I was angry. Henry had always called Elizabeth "the Witch's Brat." Now I saw why. But there was worse to come.

Tom had begun spending more time with me and less time at court. Ever since his violent quarrel with his brother the Protector he had avoided going to Whitehall unless absolutely necessary. It was a welcome change in our routine. I found it comforting to have him near me, especially at night, sleeping beside me and cradling me in his strong arms.

I loved waking up and seeing his dear beautiful face on the pillow next to mine. Sometimes I woke up early and raised myself up on my elbow the better to gaze down at him, sleeping there, his hands folded behind his head, his face in repose relaxed, free of the creases around his mouth and across his forehead that marred his features when he was awake.

This was my Tom, mine at last. Every beloved bit of him, from his delicious curling lips to the curves of his tan cheeks with their stubble of beard to his broad chest and muscular arms. All of him, his smell, his feel, the warmth of his skin, his very breath: all of him mine, and mine forever.

I reveled in those early waking moments, and looked forward to them.

But then something changed. I can't remember exactly when it was, only that the scents in the garden were at their most spicy and pungent and I was beginning to feel a little better. All at once I began waking early and finding that Tom was already up and gone.

The first few times it happened I thought nothing of it. Summer was coming on, the weather had been fine and Tom was an active man who liked to roam the fields and riverbank for exercise. But then, when it seemed he was up before me every morning, I asked him where he went so early. He answered nonchalantly that he was in the garden, or out walking, or that he liked to get up early and go out alone because it gave him a chance to think.

He was so evasive that I began to be curious. I decided to follow him, to see where he went.

I deliberately stayed awake all night and, before dawn, I felt him stir. He crept out of bed, and I could see by the light of the bedside candle that he slipped on a skimpy nightshirt (it was his habit to sleep naked) and put his big felt slippers over his feet. Running his fingers through his tousled hair he quietly left the room, and just as quietly I got up and, wrapping myself in my silk dressing gown, went out into the corridor after him.

It was not yet light, the birds had not yet begun to chirp and twitter and the servants were drowsing at their posts. I could hear a distant clatter from the kitchens and scullery but no other sound—except the soft scraping of Tom's slippers across the stone floor.

The corridor was dim, but I could see the shine of his white nightshirt ahead of me. I held my breath, hoping he would not become aware of my presence. I followed him up one corridor and down another, along seldom used passageways in the old house, until he came to the rooms used by Elizabeth and her servants.

He came to the door that led through an anteroom to her bedchamber. He hesitated—but only for a moment. Then, quietly, he let himself in.

My heart was beating so rapidly I thought my chest would burst. What was he doing there, at that hour? Was this his first visit, or had he been coming there every morning, deserting me for her?

I took a deep breath and crept nearer to the door, then pushed it open, entering the dark antechamber. A groom was there, seated on a bench, leaning against the wall, snoring. I hurried past him and saw that Tom had entered Elizabeth's bedchamber, which was dominated by a high carved bed whose thick velvet curtains were drawn. The door was ajar. I reached it just as Tom opened the curtains and looked down at the sleeping Elizabeth. Slowly he pulled down the light blanket that covered her, and I could see that she was wearing the tight bodice of pale yellow silk that had been my gift to her and that she had worn the night she went out on the barge with Tom.

Sick at the sight, and wanting with all my might to scream at Tom and slap and scratch Elizabeth, I forced myself to watch as he bent down, took the girl in his arms and kissed her.

I gasped, then quickly fled, past the snoring groom and back out into the corridor. As I fled I could hear a commotion behind me. The groom, awakened by my passing, was alarmed and shouted out for help. I could hear women's voices—Elizabeth's waiting women, no doubt, rushing into the bedchamber to help her. I thought I could even hear Tom's loud voice booming out. But by then I was running along the cold stones, aware chiefly of the sounds of doors opening and closing and the murmuring of many voices, intent only on reaching my own bedchamber and taking refuge there.

50

WE MOVED TO HANWORTH THEN, AND ALL WAS CONFUSION FOR A week. I kept to my bed, sick to my stomach and all but in despair, wanting to confide in Will (who I felt I could trust with my awful secret) yet holding back, reluctant to admit what I had seen to anyone, even my brother.

Tom was annoyed with me for I had told him, shortly after the incident in Elizabeth's bedchamber, that I would not give him any more money and had instructed my comptroller to put new locks on all the chests of coins and all my jewelry boxes and had sent letters out to the bankers I dealt with informing them that from now on they were to extend credit to no one, not even my husband, in my name.

The incident in Elizabeth's bedroom had caused a considerable stir in my household and among the waiting women and other servants. They had seen Tom entering Elizabeth's bedchamber before, and had witnessed him tickling the princess in her bed. They had heard her shrieks of laughter and had been embarrassed. Nothing sexual had happened—or so I was assured. Only impropriety—extreme impropriety—and, of course, humiliation for me, as the gossip quickly spread and I was put to shame.

"Can't you see, Cat, we've got to jolly the princess out of her sullen mood," Tom said when I confronted him after we had settled in at Hanworth. "We need her on our side in the struggle against my brother. I was merely trying to joke with her. I admit I played on her infatuation, but that was all part of the plan to win her over. She wants to act the part of a woman but she's still a child underneath her pose of being all grown up and haughty."

I dismissed his words with a wave of my hand. "Henry was right about her. She's the Witch's Brat all right. A temptress. I'm not having her in my house a day longer."

"Please, Cat, just give me one more chance before you give up on her. Let's go and see her together, you and I. Talk with her. Find out why she has been acting in such an unfriendly way toward you—and an overly friendly way toward me. If she sees us together, sees how much we love each other and that we both want what is best for her, I know things will change."

At first I refused, but gradually Tom wore me down by his insistence. All we had to do, he said, was go together to find Elizabeth and talk to her. Then everything would be well again.

We came upon her in the garden of Hanworth on a warm afternoon. Despite the heat of the sun she was dressed as always in her high-necked black mourning gown, a wide-brimmed hat protecting her delicate complexion.

She frowned as we approached.

"Hey-ho, milady," Tom said in a light tone as we came up to her. "Such a dark face! It's me! It's your uncle Tom!"

"And his clinging wife." I cringed at the ugliness of her words. Tom put his arm around me.

"Surely you can find a kinder welcome for my beloved Catherine, who as you know has been ill." When she said nothing he reached for Elizabeth's hand, seized it and attempted to press her unwilling palm to my bulging belly.

"Feel it, Elizabeth. Feel our baby kicking."

Wrenching her hand away, she attempted to slap Tom, but he was too quick for her. He caught her hand again in midair and glared at her.

"You will obey me this instant. You will put your hand on the queen's belly, and feel our child kick." He released her hand.

Very slowly, and without looking at me, Elizabeth began to reach toward me. She let her hand rest against my gown for the merest instant, then pulled it away.

"I feel nothing," she shouted. "The baby is dead!"

His face reddening with fury, Tom drew a knife from his belt and raised it over Elizabeth's head.

"You would not kill me," she murmured. "You like me too much."

Her words unleashed a fresh burst of anger. With a savagery I had not known he possessed Tom began slashing at Elizabeth's black gown with his long-bladed knife, cutting great tears in her skirt, ripping away at the yielding cloth until it lay in ribbonlike shards on the grass. The princess stood where she was, her eyes tightly shut, her arms held straight down at her sides, unable to move. Tom began circling her, slicing at the wide sleeves of the gown, cutting it until it split at the back and even ripping at the high neck of black silk so that it fell open and gaped wide over the helpless girl's heaving chest.

Something came over me then, a horrible feeling, a feeling I had never known before. In that moment I hated Elizabeth as I had never hated anyone, not Bishop Gardiner, not King Henry, not Thomas Burgh or any of the others who had used me cruelly. I hated Elizabeth with the pure, fiery hatred of jealousy.

I grabbed her arms from behind and restrained her so that she could not escape while Tom cut away the rest of her gown and most of her underskirts and even her stiff undergarments. His face, as he cut and slashed, was not the face of the man I loved, but someone quite different, someone quite alien to me. There came into my mind the horrible story I had once heard from Catherine Howard, of Tom's rape of a woman and murder of her husband.

Elizabeth had begun to sob, but I felt no pity for her, only an overpowering desire to join Tom in his frenzy of destruction. I slashed at what remained of the princess's clothing with my fingernails, tearing and ripping until the blood came. Was it my blood or hers? I wondered, beyond caring, merely curious. My nails were all but gone, yet I clawed on, baring the girl's thighs and belly, leaving only the scantiest of covering for her modesty.

"Stop, I beg of you, stop!" she yelled. "I'll be good! I promise! I'm sorry Uncle Tom!" Suddenly finding her strength, Elizabeth freed herself from my grasp and ran, calling out Mistress Ashley's name as she went and leaving behind her a heap of black scraps, fluttering gently in the warm air, stretching out like long snakelike fingers across the immaculate green lawn.

51

I SENT ELIZABETH AWAY, OF COURSE. I HAD TO. I KNEW THAT SHE WOULD be well looked after at Cheshunt, and in the meantime I would be unburdened of her and able to bear my child in peace.

Dr. Van Huick said the baby would be born in August, and time was growing short. Tom wanted him to be born at Sudeley. So we left Hanworth for Sudeley, and once there I busied myself overseeing the preparation of the nursery, while Tom drilled his soldiers and inspected the store of arms and provisions he was amassing in the basement of the castle.

"Our boy will come into the world in a season of war, Cat. In a fortress, surrounded by men at arms. He will be a warrior, tough and strong."

He put his hand on my belly and waited until he felt the baby kick. Then he smiled at me. "Ah yes, Cat. You've made a warrior there."

Tom's talk of warfare alarmed me. Will had warned me that Tom was becoming more and more rash in his ambitious plans to become Edward's guardian and replace his brother as the most powerful man in the realm. Now I saw that he intended to gather his forces and strike— and soon. But when I asked him about what he was doing, he was evasive.

"It's better for you to know as little as possible of my designs, Cat," he said. "I would not have you put at risk." It irked him, I knew, that

I had decided not to give him any more money. But I sensed no resentment in his attitude toward me. Indeed he seemed cheerful, even lighthearted, as he busied himself overseeing the building of carts and the buying of horses to pull them, the storing of extra hay in our barns and the work of the dozen German armorers he had installed in one of the outbuildings, their hammering and clanking a constant background sound as the summer wore on.

At Dr. Van Huick's insistence I rested for several hours each day, conserving my strength for my delivery to come, and when not resting I sewed blankets and gowns and caps for the baby and visited the nursery, doing my best to ignore the increasing commotion around me.

It was, as Tom remarked, a nursery fit for a prince. I spared no expense in buying a cradle of polished wood, carved with figures of mythical beasts, lions and unicorns and winged horses, and I had an Italian craftsman make a small thronelike chair of estate for our child with cushions of cloth of gold that gleamed in the candlelight. There were chests and wardrobes for the baby's bedding and tiny garments, a gold basin for his bath, rocking chairs for his nursemaids and pieces of coral for him to chew on when he cut his first teeth. I hung a gold cross over his cradle and hung miniatures of his grandparents on the wall, suspended from velvet ribbons. Beautiful large tapestries depicting the twelve months of the year adorned the room, along with a terracotta bust of an angel, serene and smiling, one graceful hand outstretched in blessing, her wide wings unfurled.

As a final enhancement to the room I blended an aromatic oil from jasmine and lily and orange blossoms and had my servants pour a few drops onto a large pomander each day, so that the air was always fresh with the delicious scent.

Only a few more weeks, I told myself. Only a few more weeks and then this lively little kicking child inside of me will be born and resting here in this room, warm and content and in my arms.

I let this lovely thought take possession of me, as much as I could, while outside in the courtyard and outbuildings of the castle the noise and activity continued to build. By day there was the sound of tramping feet and whinnying horses, the clopping of hooves and the creak and scrape of carts coming and going. By night the torchlit castle was heavily guarded, with soldiers wearing Tom's new livery of yellow and green standing, pikes held across their chests, keeping watch during the hours of darkness. There were cannon being brought up from the south, from the two foundries Tom now owned, and placed on the ramparts. New stables were being built in haste for the horses that arrived each day, with quarters for the grooms and, in the distance, an exercise yard that stretched on and on.

I could not even guess how many soldiers there were at Sudeley—certainly hundreds, perhaps even thousands. I told myself that this was surely not possible, yet when I looked out over the castle ramparts and saw the men standing together in clusters, or waiting in long lines for their food or marching in groups along the cliffs that overlooked the riverbank, their numbers seemed to me very large indeed. And always Tom was in the midst of them, shouting orders, directing servants and carters, waving on newcomers arriving along the dusty road.

Will came, fresh from court, and brought us news that the king was very ill.

"All is in confusion once again," he told Tom and me. "There are rumors of poison."

"There are always rumors of poison when a king is ill," Tom said dismissively. "But everyone knows Edward has been sickly since he was a child. There is nothing any poisoner could do to him that his own body won't do to itself before long."

"You are cold," I said to my husband. "I thought you loved Edward."

"Of course I am fond of him. But this is a time for action, not for putting on long faces because the king is weak and likely to die. The question is, who will save the realm from collapse?"

With the news of Edward's worsening condition, the activity at Sudeley became heightened. Water from the river was collected and stored in barrels. Chests of candles and lanterns were brought to a central storeroom where they could be given out in case of need. The sound of musket fire seemed never to cease—the men were practicing their shooting on a hastily improvised range on the hill behind the castle. Stores of corn, flour and salted fish, casks of wine and freshly brewed beer were hauled from place to place and, as it was harvest-time and our fields were ripe, laborers were brought in from the surrounding villages to help our tenants in bringing in the crops.

Meanwhile I counted the days until my baby was due to be born, and Dr. Van Huick came to see me each day and feel my belly.

"This is no place for you," the doctor said one day toward the end of August. "You should be in a quiet country house, not in the middle of an armed camp."

I passed on the doctor's remark to Tom at the end of a long hot day. He was in my bedchamber, stretched out on a pile of cushions, a tankard of beer at his elbow. He took a long draught from the tankard and looked at me.

"You will soon have all the quiet you need. We march south in two days' time." He looked at me steadily. "We cannot wait any longer."

"But Tom, can you not wait until after the baby is born? Must it be so soon?"

"The child is vital to my plans. He will be born when I and my men have seized the capital. I intend for him to be the next king."

"But how—but surely—" I shook my head in disbelief. No words would come.

"Edward is clearly too weak to rule any longer. If he dies so much the better. I intend to force Parliament to heed my authority and declare our son to be Edward's successor."

"But what of Princess Mary, and Elizabeth?"

"Mary would never be accepted as queen. The realm is no longer in thrall to the pope, and would not accept a Catholic queen. As for Elizabeth—" He shrugged dismissively. "She is only a girl still. She has no army, and no time to build one. Besides, she will support me when I command Parliament. She is too attached to me to do otherwise." The cynical smile that spread across his face was chilling. "No one will dare oppose me, Cat. Not even my hateful brother. Now, at last, we will see who is the stronger. Once and for all, we will see."

I wanted to urge Tom not to carry out his rash scheme, to think of all that could go wrong. I wanted to say, "Spare me, spare our child." But I knew he would not listen. And my heart was pounding and the baby had begun fluttering in my belly. My limbs felt heavy. It was all I could do to get into bed and lie there, full of anxiety over what Tom had told me yet unable to do anything to prevent what was to come.

The fate of the realm was in other hands than mine, I told myself. I was powerless. My task was to deliver my son. I prayed for strength to do what I could, and for the king, and that God in his mercy would guide Tom and those who followed him.

Exhausted and sick at heart, I went to sleep.

52

WHEN I AWOKE THE MOON WAS RISING BRIGHT AND FULL OVER THE hills behind the castle, a yellow harvest moon that illuminated everything in its path. Watchfires had been lit and a cordon of guardsmen was, as usual, in place around the castle walls which glowed golden in the moonlight. The air was still. Other than the occasional whicker of a horse and the calls of the watchmen to one another, I heard no sound.

Then, in the distance, came the muffled noise of hoofbeats on the road. A rider was galloping toward us, his swift pace a clear signal of alarm.

I heard shouting as the rider came closer, and urged his gasping, panting horse up the last steep incline of the road. From the courtyard came the sound of running feet and a clamor of voices. I could not tell what they were saying. I sent one of the bedchamber servants to find out what was happening. Shortly afterwards the girl returned, red-faced and out of breath.

"Oh milady! They say the men are coming from London! The Protector's men! Oh I'm sorry milady but I can't stay here. It's not safe!" And turning swiftly in the doorway she was gone.

I had a sudden urge to follow her—but knew that in my condition I could barely waddle across the room, much less run to safety somewhere outside the castle. I called for the guardsmen who normally kept watch in the corridor outside my bedchamber but there was no sign of them. Was everyone deserting me? Where were the rest of my women? Where were my grooms? Where was Tom?

Then I heard Tom's voice, clear and masterful, in the courtyard below, mustering the men and sending them here and there. I felt reassured. Tom was in command. All would be well.

I sat in the window embrasure, watching the going and coming of men in the courtyard, glad to see that, although many servants were leaving the castle, scrambling down the hillside dragging sacks full of their possessions, the soldiers stayed where they were and did as they were told.

After half an hour or so there came a lull, and then, all of a sudden, a renewed outburst of shouting, and the boom of a cannon from our ramparts—a boom so loud and powerful that it shook the walls.

I looked out the window and saw, along the road, a line of men, their armor gleaming in the bright moonlight. They were coming toward the castle, in their hundreds, many of them, so many! I heard their guncarts rattling, the tramping of their boots. I could make out the royal banners of the house of Tudor waving at their head. On and on they came, rank on rank in seemingly endless array. I heard the boom of cannon once again from our ramparts and felt the floor shake under me.

Where could I go to be safe?

At the sound of the cannon the oncoming men scattered, running to the edges of the road and off onto the verges. The firing cannon seemed to quicken them into greater haste, and they loped closer, tramping across the fields, crushing the new-mown hay, the closest of them beginning to climb our hill.

Musketfire came from the courtyard and I had to put my hands over my ears.

I heard a shouted voice behind me.

"Come away from the window, Cat. Put out those candles. Quick, come with me." I felt two warm hands close over my cold ones.

"Will! Oh, Will, I'm so glad to see you! Where is Tom? I heard him down in the courtyard with the men, but that was long ago. Why isn't he here?"

"If we are to survive the night, Tom had better be where he is, up by the drawbridge, defending the castle. I hope to God he's as good at fighting as he is at boasting about it."

Seizing a lantern, Will led me along a dark corridor to a narrow spiral staircase. I started to climb it, hampered by my large ungainly body. I was very awkward and very slow.

"I can't. I'm stuck."

"You must. I'll push you."

Clinging to the iron railing and losing my footing often, my fear increasing as I rose higher into the darkness, with Will shoving me quite indecently from behind I managed to ascend into a very small room at the top of the tower. Will soon joined me, the light from his lantern revealing a space hardly big enough for a cot and a bench. Tiny barred windows high up in the old stone walls let in cold air.

It had taken all my strength to haul myself up the staircase. I sank down onto the cot, panting and gasping. A sudden loud boom shook the room and brought dust down from the ceiling onto me, making me cough. Then there was a terrific crash.

"What was that?"

Will moved the bench under one of the windows and climbed on it in order to look out. I heard him swear.

"It's the drawbridge. They've forced the drawbridge down."

I had a horrifying vision of the invaders from London, rushing across the bridge and into the courtyard, weapons raised, and of Tom falling before them.

"Tom! Is Tom all right?"

"I can't see him. He's not there."

I was having trouble breathing. I could not stop the fearsome images from crowding into my mind, images of brutish men, striking with their sharp pikes and spears and knives, their faces savagely distorted as they rushed into the castle. Images of mayhem. Destruction. Blood lust. I heard the clank of metal on metal and the screams of men and horses.

Where was Tom? Why hadn't he come for me? Why couldn't he make it stop?

I felt myself writhing on the cot, fighting for breath. As if from a distance I heard Will's voice calling my name. But I could not answer. I was choking. My mouth was full of dust.

"No!" I called out weakly. "No! Don't let them! Don't let them come!"

Then there was a thunderous smashing sound and I heard stones falling amid renewed cries.

"They've breached the inner wall. Lord defend us."

All was a blur of noise and fear. I felt myself sinking, falling, unable to help myself, unable even to scream.

The world is ending, I thought. Right here, right now.

Half in dream, half struggling to wake, I felt a strong, sharp, gripping pain in my belly, a pain that wrapped itself around me like a tight girdle and squeezed me until I could not help but cry out.

"Will! Will! Help me! It's coming! The baby is coming!"

I grabbed the edges of the cot and gripped them as tightly as I could, squeezing my eyes shut against the pain. But it was too strong for me. I could not resist it. It rolled up and over me in a great wave of agony until I was lost, dissolving into a black mist, my strength gone and my mind awash in darkness.

53

IT WAS THE THIN, HIGH, FEEBLE WAILING OF MY CHILD THAT BROUGHT ME back to awareness. A wailing sound, a sobbing cry. I opened my eyes and saw the little face of the baby in my arms, the pink mouth open, the tiny eyes shut.

It was daylight. The shouting and booming had ceased.

"You have a daughter, Cat. What shall you name her?" Will smiled down at me, looking very weary.

I became aware of others in the small room, Dr. Van Huick and Margaret and a soldier. A soldier in the Tudor livery, standing guard next to the door.

The baby was still crying. I put her to my breast and she began to nurse greedily.

"Mary," I said. "I'll call her Mary."

We had never thought of what we would name a daughter. We had always assumed our baby would be a boy. But I had always loved the simple old-fashioned name Mary.

Margaret came and kissed me and touched the baby's soft pink cheek. "Philip and I will take you to live with us when this is all over," she said. "Both of you."

"But surely we will live here, with Tom—"

"Cat, Tom has gone."

As soon as I heard Will's words I knew, in my heart, that he was indeed gone. That he would not come back. I would never see him again.

And as soon as I knew this, I felt all joy, all force, all spirit go out of me.

Dr. Van Huick, who had been watching me with his keen blue eyes, stepped to the cot. "You have done well, milady. For a lady with a sour womb to bear such a fine child is no small thing. You are strong. You must stay strong—for your child's sake." He searched my face.

I did my best to smile. "Thank you, doctor." He frowned, then left the room abruptly, saying he had to attend to wounded men.

I must have slept then, for when I awoke the room was dim and only Margaret sat on the bench near me, dozing. Mary was no longer in my arms but lying on a cushion beside me, sound asleep.

Later, I ate some of the soup Margaret brought me and with her help, washed myself and the baby.

"Everything is so still," I said to her.

"They've all gone. Tom and his men ran as soon as the walls started to come down."

"So it was all in vain." I thought for a moment. "All that effort and expense. All Tom's hopes."

"They are saying he was a traitor. That he will be hanged—when he is caught."

"Where has he gone?"

Margaret shook her head. "Here, let me give you some more soup."

I began to feel better the next day, and was able to sit up when Will came in to see me.

"Now then, Cat. Tell me, how many soldiers does it take to guard the Pestilence?"

I shook my head, smiling.

"None. No one wants to come near her, so she needs no guarding." I laughed. "I can see you are better." He put his hand on my forehead. "But you are still hot. I'll see if I can find some willow bark to make you some tea."

"Have all the servants gone?"

"A few have come back. I saw a girl in the scullery."

"Tell me what happened, the night Mary was born."

"What do you remember?"

I shook my head. "Shouting. The room shaking. Loud noise." I winced at the effort to bring back that fearsome night. "I was frightened, so frightened. And I hurt so much."

Will got up and paced the few steps between the window and the door, then turned and paced again. "Ah, Cat. What a night! I kept thinking they would destroy us all, that the tower would be knocked down. I was so afraid for you. At first I thought you had died. But you were still breathing, so I went to try to find Dr. Van Huick. It took me an hour, maybe longer. I finally found him in the dungeon, with some of the Germans, setting a soldier's broken leg. I got him to come with me. We met some of the Protector's men who were roaming through the castle. They had broken into the wine casks and were drunken. They tried to tie us up but we pleaded with them. Finally they let us go.

"It was a miracle you were still alive when we got back. You were lying in a pool of water and there was some blood too. Somehow Dr. Van Huick managed to get the baby out. You put up such a struggle—it was horrible. I hope I never have to go through anything like that again."

"Dearest Will, what would I have done without you?"

My fever grew worse during the night. I awoke coughing, my vision blurry. Margaret put a cold cloth on my head and fanned me. I drank great quantities of willow bark tea and water, yet I was still thirsty.

"Cat," Margaret said as I lay back against my cushions, "there is a message for you. From Tom. Will thought I shouldn't show it to you, but I think you ought to read it."

"Will you read it to me?"

She unfolded the single sheet and, carrying it over to where the lantern hung on the wall, read Tom's words:

"My darling Cat, we are betrayed and I must flee. We are not strong enough to stand against my brother's men. I wish I could take you with me, but there is no time. I am going to the place I once told you of, my safe place. Come there to join me if you can, you and our son. I love you, and only you my darling. Tom."

I cried then, until I had no tears left. At least I knew that he loved me. And I knew where he was—if he had made it there safely. He told me once of an island off the coast of Cornwall where there was a village of smugglers and a ruined abbey. He said that if he was ever in danger he could go there, and the smugglers would protect him, as he had often done favors for them in the past.

It was a beautiful place, he said, warm and mild, where flowers and crops grew well and there were always plenty of fish. One could spend a lifetime there and be safe.

I shut my eyes and imagined myself there on Tom's island, with Mary in my arms, until I fell asleep.

54

I DOUBT WHETHER I WILL LIVE UNTIL MORNING.

I have the fever, the burning fever that comes to so many women soon after they give birth. It has been five days now that I have fought to overcome it, this all-consuming fiery heat, but I know I cannot fight it much longer.

My forehead is wet and my hands are clammy with sweat. I imagine things. I imagine that Tom is lying beside me on my cot, saying "You will be well soon, sweetheart," in his low reassuring voice. I struggle to believe that voice, but I know it is not real.

"Here, Mother Catherine, drink this and it will make you stronger." I try to drink the willow bark tea Margaret offers me but I can hardly swallow any of it, my throat is so swollen and sore.

The cushion under my head is damp with sweat and I long to throw off my blankets and feel the cool breeze on my overheated body. Dr. Van Huick says I must keep the layers of thick flannel covering me, otherwise I will catch a chill. I am obedient. I do what he tells me. I have no will left.

I feel as though I am being drawn closer and closer to the edge of a vast abyss, and though I hold back from falling into its depths, the pull of those fathomless depths is becoming stronger and stronger. Especially now, tonight, when the rain is driving in through the high barred window above me and dripping down the stones of the wall beside my cot. I know I should call out for someone to stop the rain from coming in, but I cannot.

I have not the will to go on.

Why is this happening to me now? Just when I have been given a child of my own. A sweet, perfect child with blue eyes and a tuft of reddish hair like her father's. A daughter of my own. Mary. My dear Mary.

I suppose they will bury me at St. Anthony's church, here at Sudeley, but I want to be buried beside Ned, my beloved Ned, in Gainesborough church. Ned, the only man who ever loved me just for myself, and who loved me so truly and so deeply. My wishes will be ignored, I suppose, even though I was once queen of this realm of England. Yes, queen!

It all seems so meaningless now, as I look back over my thirty-six years of life and count as most precious the days when I knew love, not the days when I held power or possessed riches.

Besides, even a queen can be the victim of her own illusions. She can marry a man she trusts, loves, believes in—and then discover that he has betrayed her and abandoned her.

I am so thirsty. My lips are dry and my tongue feels as if it is covered in fur. I drink more water, but the thirst does not go away. My skin is hot to the touch. I am made of fire.

Oh, if only the cool rain that is coming through the window would fall on my face, on my arms and legs. A cascade of cool rain. A waterfall. A cloudburst. Are there waterfalls where Tom is, on his faraway island? Is he thinking of me?

My dear Mary is crying but I am too weak to try to nurse her and my milk has all but dried up. I fight to stay awake, but it is useless. I am slipping back into the dark abyss of oblivion again. As if in a dream I see my mother, and my father, looking just as he did when I was a little girl, wearing his great gold chain of office, and my dear old dog Jenny, the sweet spaniel I loved so much, and Grandmother Fitzhugh in her black gown. And beyond them, growing ever clearer amid the gathering darkness, is Ned, my own dear Ned, his eyes soft and loving, holding out his hand to me.

I lift my hand to grasp his, eager to follow him, eager to go wherever he leads, down the bright corridor I glimpse behind him, where all is peace and light. . . .

Enhance Your Reading Group Discussion of

The
Last Wife *of*
Henry VIII

Visit **www.readinggroupgold.com**
for an extensive guide to this breathtaking novel.

Boost your reading group discussion
of The Last Wife of Henry VIII with:

- ❧ Questions and answers with the author
- ❧ Behind-the-book information
- ❧ A discussion guide for your reading group
- ❧ Much, much more.

If you haven't already, visit **www.readinggroupgold.com**
to check out the comprehensive listing of available
reading group guides, original essays by the authors,
recommended reading lists, historical timelines,
and so much more.

Reading
Group
Gold

www.readinggroupgold.com

 St. Martin's Griffin

A PASSIONATE, PROVOCATIVE PORTRAIT
OF FRANCE'S ILL–FATED QUEEN.

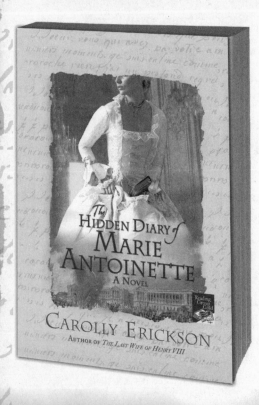

"I read *The Hidden Diary of Marie Antoinette* in two days and when I finished it, I reread the final pages, as hungry for more as a child scraping the last crumbs of chocolate cake off her plate with her fingers."

—Judith Warner, *The New York Times Book Review*

From naive princess to glamorous queen, from joyles wife to doomed mother, Carolly Erickson gives heart to one of history's most controversial figures.